THE BODY ROCK

K. T. MCCAFFREY

For Mary and Barry

1

His mind was made up. This would be the day: the second day of May, his birthday. Eighteen years of existence on Planet Earth, time to take charge of his own destiny. Even though the afternoon was decidedly cool, a fine film of sweat covered Jamie Wilson's brow. Perhaps I ought to let a little air into the room, he thought. Yes, good idea. Putting the ladder to one side, he took a break from the arduous work, moved to the window and opened the top fly section. Better, much better. Inhaling the fresh air, he closed his eyes, tilted back his head and filled his lungs. For once, the allergies that had plagued him since childhood were not acting up. It felt good. Opening his eyes again, he stood still for a moment and absorbed the view his upstairs window presented of the world, the same view he had looked on for as long as he could remember: The garden, a horticultural masterpiece, cultivated over a period of years by Ethel Cassidy, an inspired woman whose use of colour, form and textures turned an acre of dull earth into a priceless living canvas.

This afternoon, soft drizzle fell noiselessly from a grey sky. In the distance he could see sail boats bobbing up and down on a darkened sea as they passed by the small island known as Ireland's Eye. Gulls swooped and played as they traced the churning wake of a fishing boat making its way towards Howth harbour. A world of sound filled the air outside his window: children's laughter floating on the breeze, a puppy's forlorn yelps demanding attention, a distant bus struggling to climb a familiar hill once too often, its diesel engine protesting loudly in the effort. Worldly sounds. Familiar sounds. Sounds augmented by echoes from earliest childhood; the squeak-squawk of a tree swing, his own childish entreaties to be pushed higher; a flowing melody played by his mother on the violin . . . a story about Orpheus enticing the animals out of the forest and inspiring the birds to dip and soar.

Enough. He had work to do, a mission to accomplish.

Taking hold of the string hanging from the window blind, he pulled it down and blinkered the outside world. Better. He returned to the centre of the room where chips and chunks of plasterboard lay scattered on the mass of newspapers he had spread across the carpet. It looked a mess. His earlier endeavours with chisel, hammer and saw had left a trail of dust and debris scattered in all directions. Bit by bit, he set about gathering up the chalky remains and emptied them into a refuse sack he had earlier brought to his room. If today had been a normal day, he would have got the vacuum cleaner and run it across the carpet but today was anything but normal, today was by any standards a most extraordinary day. He scanned the room and satisfied himself that it was as good as could be expected, under the circumstances.

Leaning his body forward, he placed his hands palms down on his bedside table and stared at the objects lying there. A birthday card from Angela Devine lay open to his view. A subtle message in rhyme, written in neat script, told him that she still cared deeply for him. He frowned. A mental image of Angela slid its way into his consciousness. How beautiful she looked. Angela, like himself, a first year Arts student in the City of Dublin University, shared his interest in classical literature. Their love of books had, in a roundabout sort of way, led to romance. It was a situation he found difficult to handle. When Angela intimated that they should become lovers, he had concocted excuses to put off such a development. His behaviour had been inexplicable but he felt confident that she would understand his motives when she received the letter he had posted to her earlier that morning.

A second greeting card, large and expensive, embossed with the legend 'Happy Birthday, Son' dwarfed Angela's offering. The keys of a brand new BMW lay beside his father's card. The surprise gift gave him the added encouragement to proceed with the elaborate plan he had embarked on to mark his eighteenth birthday.

And then of course there was his mother's gift.

He shuddered but forced himself to look at her offering once more. She had gone to a lot of trouble – he had to give her that – but knowing how she operated, he suspected she had got some secretary to put the package together. The gift, which came in a blue folder, was tied with a wide silk ribbon in blue and finished off with an elaborate multi-looped bow. The contents amounted to a virtual charter to explore the city of Paris for a long weekend: two airline tickets, destination Charles de Gaulle Airport and a wallet stuffed with French francs in all denominations. Accommodation had been booked for five days in the Elysées Regenia, a four-star hotel which, according to the accompanying brochure, was located on the prestigious Avenue Marceau, between the Champs Elysées and the Seine. His mother, never one to do things by half, had included pre-paid tickets for trips to the Pompidou centre, the Louvre and the theatres of Pigalle. And just in case he found extra time on his hands, there was an array of colourful literature for him to consider, leaflets extolling the merits of Montmartre's Place du Tertre, Notre Dame Cathedral, the Pont Neuf and Bohemian restaurants in the Latin Quarter.

Ordinarily, he would have been thrilled with such a present. He had been to Paris a few times with his mother when he was younger and had enjoyed the great city, though her main interest at the time centred around the boutiques on the rue Etienne Marcel and around Place de Victories. Even so, he retained fond memories of walking through the narrow streets of Le Marais with its art galleries, cafes, beautifully carved doorways and turrets. On one occasion he had persuaded her to allow him spend a whole morning in the dusty bookstalls along the Left Bank. Good memories. Better times. But today, his mother's birthday package, failed to elicit a glimmer of interest in him.

Back to work. Smoothing a cutting from the morning's *Post* with his fingers, he applied adhesive paste to its other side and carefully slotted the L-shaped article into position on a collage of newsprint already fixed to the wall. He made sure that the dateline, 2nd May remained attached to the cutting.

Almost ready. Just one last task to accomplish.

Trying hard to remember his time as a boy scout, he practised what he had learned about tying knots. It was a bit like riding a bicycle – once you accomplished it, you never lost the knack. And so it was with knots. His fingers proved as nimble as ever, adept at reef knots, slip knots, bends and half hitches. Finding the right knot was the trick. After a little trial and error, he managed to achieve exactly what he wanted.

Pleased with his skills, he tried to visualise his parent's reaction when they saw the results of their son's handiwork. A brief smile of satisfaction lit up his face.

Looking out the boardroom window, two floors above the hotel's storage area, Todd Wilson watched a barman toss an empty beer crate on top of an already untidy pile of similar crates. The barman's carelessness reflected perfectly the overall air of neglect about the place. It was not a pretty sight: unattended flower beds, rusted flag poles, wild shrubbery, overflowing dustbins, damaged laundry baskets and broken signs, all indicative of abject slovenliness. But the ugliness did not bother him. A smile, partially concealed by a well-cultivated moustache, played on his lips as his appraisal of the hotel's environs continued. He loosened his tie, unbuttoned the top of his shirt collar, put his hands in his trousers' pockets, gave free vent to his belly, and allowed his stocky body to rock back and forth on his heels. He had never felt happier in his life.

For him, 2 May represented a major milestone, the completion of a deal to purchase his first hotel in Britain. It was an ambition he had nourished for several years and now at last that aspiration had become a reality.

Turning away from the window, he returned to the boardroom table and sat down opposite the two men who had spent the last three days in Edinburgh with him, 'Time, gentlemen, to drink a toast,' he said to them as he broke the seal on a bottle of Jameson ten-year old Irish whiskey. 'To The Thistle and Rose.'

Niall Moore, chief accountant with Wilson Enterprises took his glass and clinked it against Wilson's. 'To The Thistle and Rose,' he said before swallowing most of the contents in one go, 'to the first of the Wilson Group hotels in Britain.'

Fred Kitt, legal advisor to Wilson and lifelong teetotaller, poured a glass of orange from the pitcher in the centre of the table and joined in the toast. 'To a good deal.'

Business completed, Kitt and Moore left the

boardroom, eager to change out of their business suits and into something casual, before joining their boss to sample to Edinburgh's night life.

Waiting behind, Wilson lifted the telephone, dialled the international code for Ireland and pressed the numbers that would connect him with his Dublin home on the Hill of Howth.

It was ringing.

Eagerly, he waited to hear his son, Jamie's voice. It bothered him that he couldn't be there for the boy's eighteenth birthday but he felt sure that the new BMW would more than compensate for his absence. One day The Thistle and Rose would belong to Jamie but he hoped to have a long list of properties added to the Wilson chain before that day came.

The phone continued to ring.

He would surprise his son by singing the words of 'Happy Birthday' when the phone was picked up.

Still no response.

It occurred to him that his son might be out in the car, putting the powerful engine through its paces. He let the phone ring on, imagining Jamie behind the wheel of the BMW. It was a pleasant thought. Replacing the unanswered phone in its cradle, he decided he would try again after he returned from his liquid tour of Edinburgh.

'If you would sign there for me, please,' the shop assistant said to Ethel, handing her a pen and indicating the blank space on the Visa docket.

'Yes, of course,' Ethel replied, taking the ballpoint from him. In a distinctive hand she wrote the name Ethel Cassidy. The assistant, a young man of nineteen, maybe twenty, passed the docket through the Visa machine and returned the top copy. 'Would you like me to gift-wrap the book, Ms Cassidy?' he asked, reading the name from her receipt copy.

'Yes please, that would be nice, thanks,' Ethel said, giving him the benefit of her best smile.

Wrapping the book in art nouveau decorated paper, the young man glanced awkwardly at his customer. She was, he could see, a shapely woman in her early forties, wearing stylish, well-fitted clothes. The smile in her soft brown eyes, which he mistakenly took to be flirtatious, caused him to blush. For an older woman – anything past thirty-five, he considered ancient – she struck him as damned attractive. With high pronounced cheek-bones, straight nose, generous mouth, and short-cropped ash-blond hair, he lamented the fact that his mother, who he thought might be roughly the same age, looked dowdy and mumsy by comparison.

Once outside the shop, Ethel looked approvingly at the neatly wrapped parcel, careful not to let any of the falling rain get on to it, and extracted the birthday card that she had bought earlier in the day from her handbag. She did not doubt that Jamie would get more expensive presents from his parents and friends but she felt confident that he would appreciate the thought she had put into her gift: a rare clothbound edition of the complete stories and poems of Edgar Allan Poe with fine reproductions of the original illustrations. Jamie had, she remembered, a particular liking for Poe's dark literary world of mystery and imagination.

Her thoughts wandered back to fond memories of Jamie with his head stuck in a book, oblivious to all but the characters contained within the printed page in front of him. Although she no longer worked as housekeeper for the Wilsons, she had acted as nanny to Jamie in his earlier years and still felt as close to him as any mother would feel towards a son. Knowing that Jamie, in turn, had held her in similar high regard meant everything to her. But this bond between them had been dramatically shattered three weeks earlier. It was not something she wished to dwell on now, no, not on the day of his eighteenth birthday. She purged her mind from all thoughts of the recent unpleasantness, blotted out the angry accusations Jamie had hurled at her and forced herself to concentrate on happier times instead.

From the beginning she had fallen in love with the boy. She had read stories to him before bedtime when his parents were away. Roald Dahl, she remembered, was a particular favourite of his. He would struggle to stay awake in order to hear her read to the story's end. Right from his primary school days, through to his secondary education and more recently university, he had never lost his love of the written word. The more Ethel thought about it, the more convinced she became that he would appreciate the book she had bought for him.

On the east side of St Stephen's Green, amid a sea of umbrellas, she climbed aboard a bus that took her all the way to Howth Head. She got off at a bus stop that was less than a hundred yards distance from Wilson's home. Thankful that the rain had eased off, she closed her umbrella and approached the ornate pillars and wrought-iron gates that graced the house's winding driveway. Seeing the garden always had the effect of lifting her spirits. May was the time to prune the *Kerria japonica* and *Prunus triloba*, spray the roses, hoe between the plants and water the newly planted beds. It was a time when the sweet scent of cherry blossom filled the air, when berberis, primula, sweet rockets and forget-me-nots ran riot with colour. Year in, year out, the garden and its cycles had been a source of unending pleasure for her. In recent times, changes had taken place, changes she strongly disapproved of. Missing was the old horse chestnut, on whose boughs Jamie's swing had hung for so many years. A small fountain with a gilded statue of a Mannequin Pis now usurped the spot where the venerable tree once stood.

Ethel walked the brick-laid drive to the front door of the house, an elegant two-storey red brick with balustrades around the roof, long windows with cut-stone architraves, and porchless entrance. The original house, built over a hundred and fifty years ago on the slopes of Howth Hill at a time when there were few houses nearby, had been seamlessly assimilated into a series of embellishments added down through the decades but it still enjoyed a commanding view of

Dublin Bay.

She pressed the bell and heard the muted response of chimes ringing in the hallway. It was not yet five o'clock and she hoped that neither of the senior Wilsons would be at home. Todd's Volvo was missing from the driveway but there was a black BMW parked beside the garage. Observing its unsoiled tyres and plastic covered seats, she could tell it was a brand new car. Evidence of the recent shower remained on the car's exterior as raindrops ran like mercury rivulets along its roof and bonnet. In a flash of inspiration, a thought hit her – it's Todd's birthday present to Jamie. An audible sigh escaped her lips as she thought about the relationship that existed between father and son. Nothing has changed. He still thinks he can buy anything with money . . . dear, dear God. She cast a sad glance at her neatly wrapped book, finding it difficult to hold back the tears welling up in her eyes.

She pressed the bellpush again, allowing her finger to dwell a little longer this time. Still no response. She waited long enough to realise that there was no one at home. The letterbox, she could plainly see, was too small to accept the gift and she felt uneasy about leaving it on the doorstep. It would be such a pity if the rain came pelting down again and ruined it. Visualising Jamie unwrapping a wet soaked present, she came up with a solution; she would let herself into the house.

Rummaging through her handbag she found her old set of keys to the house. It made no sense that she should have held on to them but on the many occasions over the past few weeks when she considered handing them back to the Wilson's, some sort of unexorcised ghost forced her to hold on to them. For whatever reason, irrational or not, she was glad now she had. No longer an employee, she had no right to enter the household but the sudden compulsion she felt was irresistible. She inserted the key into the lock, pushed open the door and stepped into the hallway.

The house was silent except for the sound of an antique grandfather clock, unhurriedly tick-tocking in the hallway. She went straight to Jamie's room. Out of habit she knocked on the door first. 'Jamie, it's me, Ethel; you in there?'

No answer. A thought struck her: could he still be cool with her since their recent row? No, she didn't think so; Jamie was not the sort to hold a grudge. She knocked again, called out his name, gingerly turned the handle and then hesitated. It didn't do to go rushing into an eighteen-year-old boy's room, she knew that much, so announcing herself again, she eased the door inwards.

It was a full second before her scream began.

In that awful moment of horror, she saw the spectacle of Jamie hanging by a rope from the ceiling. Refusing to believe what her eyes were telling her, she ran to the centre of the room, reached for his feet and tried to lift his body upwards. It was no good. She could see the two jagged holes cut through the plasterwork in the ceiling above him and the rope strung around the overhead rafter. Frantically, she righted the small overturned table and chair that lay on the floor beneath him. She climbed up to relieve the pressure of the rope on his neck. Her actions were futile. The truth had, by now, dawned on her; Jamie was dead.

2

Midday sun beat down with a vengeance. 110 degrees, flies everywhere, people watching her, listening to her every word, a cameraman and sound engineer recording her visit for posterity. Sweat trickled down Maeve's back and between her breasts, and gathered in the dimple at the base of her spine. Maeve Wilson stood in front of the clinic building on a small makeshift wooden platform especially prepared for the occasion. Ignoring the insects crawling around her feet, she tried not to show her discomfort. Her scripted address, large type on double spaced lines on the pages before her, began with an outline of projects undertaken by her organisation, SUCCOUR, and then shifted focus to what she perceived as the fundamental problems bedevilling Africa.

'. . . And so, we must do something about the causes of poverty rather than simply concentrating on the symptoms alone. It is time to stop clapping ourselves on the back for the aid we have brought here and focus instead on the causes for all this misery.'

Fergus Massey, her fellow director and project manager, watching the faces of the invited dignitaries gathered in front of the clinic, could tell they liked what she was saying. Over the years, Maeve Wilson had gained a reputation for talking tough, for ignoring some of the 'given' political considerations and for apportioning blame where it rightly belonged – especially when it came to Africa's ills. Massey wiped the sweat from his brow as he returned his gaze to Maeve, caught her attention for a brief second and nodded approvingly. With just the merest flick of an eyelid, she acknowledged his encouragement. Their subliminal exchange was missed by the assembled group who continued to hang on to her every word. With alacrity, she rounded on the external institutions, pointing the finger of blame in their direction, one after the other. Banks were, as usual, top of her hit list. 'Crippling debts imposed by the International Bank are a big part of the problem,' she told them. 'For every single pound or dollar of aid we give, four pounds or four dollars in debt repayments are taken out. Put bluntly, the western world is raping the Third World.' A ripple of applause greeted this pronouncement.

Getting into her stride, Maeve disregarded her script. 'And what about the wars?' she asked rhetorically. 'Same story: money, power, corruption, greed. In every conflict that erupts, agents from the West back one side or the other while, at the same time, selling arms to both parties. And who suffers? Who always suffers? Not the arms dealers, not the government ministers who oversee the madness, no, it's the ordinary people who suffer: mothers, fathers, sons and daughters, decent people who have nothing to do with these conflicts.'

Maeve stopped to take a sip of water before continuing. The film of sweat covering her body had begun to run in rivulets. She hoped her white, lightweight linen suit would hide the dark patches that were multiplying by the minute. It wasn't that the people watching and listening to her would mind, or even notice for that matter – most of them looked as though they had sprung leaks themselves – what bothered her was the thought of unsightly damp areas being picked up by the camera and shown at a later stage on television back in Britain and Ireland.

The print and broadcasting media had helped document Maeve's efforts in Africa, a factor she never ignored. For five years on the trot Maeve Wilson had made an average of four annual visits to the SUCCOUR centres in Ethiopia, each visit faithfully recorded by the press. On most occasions she accompanied either one or two of her organisation's supply trucks. Because of Ethiopia's ongoing border wars with Eritrea, entry had been restricted from the ports on the Gulf of Aden. It meant that instead of using airlifts to bring in their goods they were forced to take the more arduous overland route.

Today, she was visiting Kalu in the northern region of the country, an area suffering its third consecutive year of appalling drought. Here, midday temperatures passed 40 degrees on a regular basis. As chairperson of SUCCOUR, she took what little comfort she could from what her agency, assisted by local government and local communities, had achieved in alleviating some of the suffering. But she was quick to acknowledge, it wasn't enough.

No matter how much Maeve Wilson might like to attribute blame to the western world for Ethiopia's woes, the country's inhospitable climate remained the main culprit. The area would always remain vulnerable to unpredictable rainfall and long periods of drought; the quality of land would, as a result, always remain poor. Without aid from world agencies the country was in danger of another famine similar in scale to the one experienced in 1984. Back then a million people were allowed to die. It was also the year that Maeve Wilson first became aware of the problem of poverty in the Third World.

As she continued to talk, outlining what her agency intended to do over the coming months, Fergus Massey was handed a printed message by the clinic manager, an English woman named Cheryl Oakley. 'This has come through the e-mail for Maeve,' she said, her face beaded with sweat, a note of concern in her voice. 'It's marked "most urgent" and sounds like trouble back home.'

'Thanks, Cheryl, I'll give it to her straight away. She's about finished anyway.' Massey read the message as he made his way to Maeve and frowned. According to the note there had been an accident involving Maeve's son Jamie. A telephone number was attached to the message with an instruction to make contact immediately.

A uniformed Garda officer standing rigid with his back to the front door prevented Todd Wilson from entering the house. 'I'm very sorry, sir,' the policeman said with a rich Kerry accent, 'but I cannot allow you to go in there. 'Tis a crime scene . . . restricted area you see, so, I'm afraid you are prohibited from entering the property.'

'That's where you are wrong, my young friend,' Wilson said, speaking quietly but making no attempt to hide his annoyance, 'I am Todd Wilson and this is my house, so if you don't mind, kindly move aside and allow me to go inside.'

'I'm sorry, sir . . . I'd no idea in the world . . . '

Wilson pushed the front door open and stepped into the hallway. Two detectives, deep in conversation at the foot of the staircase, stopped in mid-sentence and turned their heads to look as he entered. Although both men knew Wilson, they seemed unprepared for his sudden arrival at the house. For an awkward moment no one spoke. Wilson stared past the two men, his eyes travelling up the length of the stairs. Detective-Inspector Jim Connolly, the more senior of the two officers was first to speak. 'Mr Wilson, I'm truly sorry about your son . . . terrible, terrible tragedy, awful thing to happen. We're almost through examining the scene and . . . '

His words were cut short as Wilson, in a sudden move pushed towards them, making his way to the stairs. Connolly, a big man in his late forties, over six feet tall with a build to match, hindered Wilson's progress by placing a hand on his shoulder. 'I think, sir, it might be best if you didn't go up to your son's bedroom just yet . . . like I was saying, our people are still there and . . . '

'Take your hands off me, Detective, this is my house and I'll go exactly where I please, OK? Now, if you don't mind I'd like to see where . . . where my son . . . '

'Look, this is hard for all of us, and believe me I understand how you must feel, but just the same . . . '

Ignoring the detective's protestations, Wilson continued on his way up the carpeted steps until he reached the landing. A flash of light, coming from the slightly ajar door of his son's room startled him. 'What the hell?' he muttered as he barged into the room. What he saw there stopped him in his tracks. A white-clad forensic photographer, using a camera mounted on a tripod, and surrounded by white umbrella-like re-flectors, was taking shots of the newspaper cuttings pasted on to one of the room's walls. Like a rabbit stunned in the glare of oncoming car lights, Wilson's eyes stared at the scene for a moment without appearing capable of taking it all in. A rope hung from exposed rafters, visible through the ceiling's broken plasterwork and a table and chair remained in position at the centre of the room. A detective, wearing white overalls that looked three sizes too big for him, continued without interruption to dust the furniture for fingerprints.

'I want you all out of here immediately,' Wilson said, his voice low, straining to remain under control, his eyes by now scanning the newsprint display on the wall. 'I want every last one of you out of here this very instant. Do you hear me?'

'I'm sorry, Mr Wilson,' Connolly said, making his way into the room from the landing, 'I realise how distressing this must be for you, but we have a job to do here; we still have procedures to follow, reports to fill out and ...'

'And I said I want you out of here immediately,' Wilson repeated, his voice taking on an ugly tone. Silence prevailed for a moment. Connolly opened his mouth to reason with him but before a word was spoken, Wilson's self-restraint snapped. In a move that took everyone by surprise, he lunged at the photo–grapher and knocked the man sideways with a fist to the side of the head. He then yanked the camera off its tripod and attempted to expose the film. Connolly moved immediately to restrain him and retrieve the camera but only succeeded in getting a knee in the crotch for his efforts. As the detective-inspector doubled in two and groaned with pain, his partner, with the help of the fingerprint expert, succeeded in bringing Wilson under control.

Within seconds all the fight had gone out of Wilson and he began to tremble all over, his eyes gazing into the middle distance. Connolly, recovering quickly from the sudden impact, straightened up and faced Wilson. It was immediately apparent that his attacker was no longer a danger to him or his men. 'Please, Mr Wilson,' he said, his voice attempting to show compassion, 'I think it might be best if you were to come with me now.'

'Where is Jamie? Where have you taken my boy?'

'Jamie is down at the coroner's building in Store Street. Come on, sir, I'll take you there. We'll use my car.'

Without a word, Wilson followed the detective out of the room and headed down the stairs.

A quick glance in the rear-view mirror allowed Connolly to view the passenger in the back seat. The normally debonair businessman looked dishevelled and bewildered. Connolly had known Wilson for a number of years, their paths having crossed on several occasions in the course of various investigations. Todd Wilson was a man of influence who appeared to enjoy his elevated place in society and the privileges such prominence brought him. However, Connolly knew there were people who asked questions concerning Wilson's wealth, and where exactly that wealth had come from.

In a roundabout sort of way Connolly himself had benefited from Wilson's acumen. To supplement his policeman's salary he liked to dabble in the stock exchange from time to time. On the advice of a friend he had invested more heavily than usual in one of Wilson's companies and was pleased when those shares out performed most of his other more modest investments. In recent newspaper articles, Emma Boylan, an investigative journalist with the *Post* had hinted that Wilson's business ethics were, at best, questionable. She insinuated that he had used his position and influence to get around certain planning restrictions. Shares in his companies had dipped a few points since the article appeared. More significantly, the same articles had appeared as part of the collage on Jamie's wall.

As Connolly pulled his car in towards the kerb outside the coroner's office, he wondered about the article. Was it possible that the investigative piece by Emma Boylan had caused young Jamie Wilson to take his life? Could that same article be responsible, at least in part, for the great distress now evident in Todd Wilson's demeanour? Could the current insidious whispering campaign against Wilson have a bearing on the boy's death and the father's distress?

In recent months, a rumour had been doing the rounds that Wilson had picked up a young male hitch-hiker and had made improper advances towards him. There was nothing to substantiate the rumour but the story refused to go away. To his knowledge no one had come forward to make an official complaint about the incident – if the incident ever happened in the first place – but stranger things had happened and he knew it wouldn't be the first time a prominent citizen did something really stupid like this. On top of that, there was the well-documented rift between Todd and his wife, Maeve. In recent years the two of them were rarely seen together and when they did appear, the animosity between them was evident for all to see. Connolly wondered about the Wilsons' volatile relationship and how the effect of being constantly in the public eye must make life difficult for them, and for their son. But even allowing for the strained relationship in the marriage, would Todd Wilson really allow himself to get mixed up in a sordid homosexual situation?

Connolly did not think so.

Ethel Cassidy stood towards the back of the crowd as a mid-morning downpour added its gloom to St Aidan's churchyard. Through tears, she watched mourners pay their last respects to Jamie Wilson. She participated in the graveside recital of the Rosary decade as it droned to its weary conclusion, her mind not on the repetitive prayers but turning instead to a series of events in Jamie's short life, events where she had stood in for his absent parents, events she would remember and cherish for the rest of her life. Wasn't it ironic, she thought, that this occasion should be the first time in many years that Maeve and Todd stood shoulder to shoulder at an event that concerned Jamie? That it should be the boy's funeral made it all the more unbearable for her.

With the prayers over, she watched as the chief celebrant shook hands and sympathised with Todd Wilson. Under the protection of a large black umbrella, held in position by a freckle-faced altar boy, the priest turned to Maeve and offered her his well practised words of formal condolences.

Ethel Cassidy watched and wept, knowing it was all part of a ritual that had to be observed. She felt at though she had been transported outside her own body, observing the macabre scene from some invisible viewpoint. Incredibly, she could see herself plain as day, raindrops falling on her face, as she stood with the other mourners by the graveside. She could see Todd and Maeve being embraced by friends, a touching tableau of shared grief. Even allowing for the bleakness of the occasion and the tragic circumstances of Jamie's death, it surprised her to see tears in Todd's eyes: his was not the sort of face that accommodated bereavement with any degree of grace. With thinning hair plastered to his skull by the unrelenting rain, puffed eyes, full moustache, weighty jowls and pug neck, the man had for once shed his aura of power and assumed instead the image of grieving parent. By his side, Maeve stood, her head bowed, statue-like, her fingers interlinked with his, her face pale, her eyes lost, looking for once every day of her forty-two years of age.

Ethel was not surprised by the array of dignitaries taking their turns to offer condolences to Todd and Maeve: they were all there, the elected representatives and state officials, the city's lord mayor, several high-profile business chiefs, a television chat-show personality and a small group of university students. The students, she knew were from the university that Jamie had attended. One of them, a tall girl with glasses, pressed her head on a friend's shoulder and wept openly. Ethel knew this girl. Her name was Angela Devine. She lived in Sutton, a village just down the road from Howth, and had been a frequent visitor to the

Wilson household in the past year. Like Jamie, Angela attended the City of Dublin University but Ethel suspected that the two students shared more together than their love of learning. Looking at the tears streaming down the girl's face, Ethel noticed an envelope clutched tightly in her hand, the handwriting on it smudging as raindrops merged with the ink. Probably a Mass card, Ethel thought, feeling sorry for the girl, knowing full well the depth of sorrow she must be experiencing.

As the crowd began to disperse and prepared to leave the cemetery, Ethel moved around towards the edge of the grave and approached the grieving parents. She hesitated for a moment while Maeve was being comforted by Fergus Massey, the project manager of SUCCOUR, well-known friend and confidant of both the Wilsons. Indeed, Massey had loomed large in her own life for longer than she cared to remember but she banished all such thoughts from her mind; today was not the time to dwell on dark events from the past. Massey, seeing her approach, held out his hand in readiness for her to shake. 'I'm so terribly sorry about what's happened,' he said, aware that his proffered hand had been ignored. 'Poor Maeve . . . and Todd of course . . . they are taking this very badly . . . both of them gutted . . . as you must be. It's a bad situation all round. My deepest sympathies.'

Ethel stared at him with hostile eyes for several seconds, not saying a word, before averting her gaze to Maeve and Todd. Maeve, seeing her approach, lifted her arms in a display of grief, a gesture that invited embrace. Ethel refused to accept the offered arms. For a moment the two of them stood there, face to face, neither speaking, as hurtling sheets of rain plunged out of the dark sky, its noise seeming to heighten the tension between them. When Ethel spoke, she addressed both Wilsons and Massey.

Chatter in the cemetery came to a stop.

Her voice was passionate but firm. 'I'll say this for you lot, you did a better job on poor Jamie than you did on me – at least you buried him under the ground.'

3

'It really is beautiful, isn't it?' said Emma.

'Yes,' Vinny agreed, looking at the scene in front of them through the viewfinder of his camera. In the oppressive afternoon heat, the newly-weds stopped to get their breaths back while admiring the Real Maestranza bullring. Emma Boylan and Vinny Bailey, on their third week in Andalucia, felt that they would never get used to the sun's unrelenting heat. Today they had taken a tour bus – thankfully, air conditioned – to the town of Ronda. Standing now, inside the empty bullring, with its encompassing symmetrical arches, Emma was duly impressed.

'When you consider its use,' Vinny said, 'it is most graceful.'

'Its use? Oh, you mean the bullfighting?'

'Yes, pity there's none today – I'd like to get a few shots of that.'

Emma grimaced. 'Well, I'm glad there's no fighting today. I'd hate to see them sticking their swords – or whatever it is they use to torture the unfortunate animal . . . all that blood, so cruel, ugggh.'

'Oh, my, my, Emma, you're being very politically correct. But, you see, the Spanish people don't see it as cruel at all . . . it's their national sport.'

'Sport? Ha!' Emma said, dismissing his suggestion. She smiled to herself and wiped the sweat from her brow, preparing for yet another photograph. She wondered if perhaps it was time to get even and turn the camera on her husband; photograph him in his shorts, multicoloured shirt and straw hat. She had to admit he had taken a tan well and looked great in his minimalist summer gear. What a change it made! His more familiar attire, the clothes he wore at home were, in stark contrast, unfettered by any serious consider-ation for current fashion fads. A few inches short of six feet, he was handsome, had a well-defined body, good legs, a 'lived-in' face and longish, dark brown hair. The hint of silver at the temples set against the bronze tan conferred distinction on his face. Yes, Emma thought, she would definitely like to capture that look for posterity.

It was late in the evening when Emma and Vinny made their way back from Ronda to Los Boliches, their base for the duration of their honeymoon. Los Boliches, or indeed, Spain for that matter, would not have been on top of either of their lists as favourite destinations for their nuptial sojourn: Emma had Moscow or Rome in her sights; Vinny favoured Provence or Brittany. In the end it was Emma's father who made the decision for them. He had owned a luxurious apartment in Los Boliches for the past twenty years and insisted they should use it for their honeymoon.

They convinced themselves that it was a great idea. After all, Emma had been to Spain as a teenager – with her father and mother – and had thoroughly enjoyed the experience at the time. A lot had happened to her in the twenty intervening years to change her rose-tinted view of the country but, thankfully, not all of it.

Spain, or at least Los Boliches, the part of the country she remembered best, had not fared too well over the same period. What had once been a quaint little fishing village had been raped and lobotomised by greedy developers and merciless speculators. Except for chirping crickets, siesta time, mosquitoes, boisterous banter, the smell of burnt earth and the ever-dependable sunshine, all had changed. The din of cement mixers, pneumatic drills, ghettoblasters, late-night disco bars and firecrackers were all part of the new order.

'Jeez, I'm whacked ... completely knackered,' Vinny admitted. 'It's been a long day.'

'What's this – forty and fading? It sounds to me a bit like the build up to the old "I've-got-a-headache" ploy to me,' Emma said, trying to hold back the laughter.

'I'm never that knackered.'

They strolled arm in arm along Avenida Acapulco towards their apartment, grinning at each other like a pair of frisky Cheshire cats. On the footpath outside a small newsagent, less than a hundred yards from their apartment, papers from all corners of the globe were displayed on revolving racks. From the start, when Emma discovered that they stocked the *Post*, the newspaper she worked for as a journalist, she made a point of not stopping to glance at the headlines.

With only a day and a half of the honeymoon remaining, she had been as good as her word. Had it not been for a group of tourists blocking the footpath at the newsagents, she might have stuck to her promise. While endeavouring to get past the obstruction, the front-page headline on the *Post* caught her eye: *Todd and Maeve Wilson's Son Commits Suicide.* In an instant she had the newspaper in her hands. 'Good God, Vinny, will you look at this!' she said, showing him the headline. 'Can you believe this? That last article I wrote was on the subject of Todd Wilson. I questioned the man's integrity, made suggestions that his business ventures might not stand up to scrutiny. Christ!'

Vinny shook his head. His reaction had less to do with the story on the newspaper than with the look on his wife's face. Over the past few weeks he had got used to her relaxed attitude to life and the contented, dreamlike look in her eyes. Making love each night in the balmy heat, she had repeatedly whispered 'I never want this to end.' His reassurance that it would always be so never failed to bring a baby-like cry of joy from her. He knew of course, as she did, that eventually the real world would impinge on their idyllic holiday. His only surprise was that it should happen so soon. Watching Emma pass a handful of pesetas to the newsvendor, there could be no doubting the change of mode: her expression was that of the consummate professional, the investigative journalist with a mission to accomplish.

Ethel Cassidy woke from her sleep. Her left arm, where she had lain on it, was a mass of pins and needles, the sensation adding to her momentary sense of dislocation. Relief flooded through her as it dawned on her that she was in her own bed, in her own house, her own safe cocoon. This small compact, tidy abode represented all she needed. Her violin and bow hung from a hook on the wall, a reminder of her days as a musician. With her sister Marina and her best friend, Maeve Wilson, she had, for a while, shared in the wonderful world of music. They had studied together, played together, laughed together, cried together, until . . . On either side of the instrument, a series of neatly framed music certificates and portraits of classical composers adorned the wall. The absence of a television set was offset by the presence of her one great indulgence: a hi-fi player and a large collection of vinyl LPs.

The clock on her table said 1.45 am; that meant she had been asleep for less than two hours.

After Jamie's funeral she had lost count of time, her mind going over and over the scene at the graveside. She still could not believe she had found the courage to utter the cruel words she had used at the graveside but glad at the same time she had. Since the dreadful evening three days earlier when she had discovered Jamie's body, her whole world had gone out of kilter. Things should have been so different. This was the time of year when, under normal circumstances, she would be getting the window boxes ready for the summer season. The continuance of the plant cycle never failed to give her a quiet satisfaction, providing her with a link, albeit a tenuous one, to the garden she had tended so lovingly in Howth for so long. As her fingers worked their way into the compost and gently uprooted bulbs from the pots she kept in the hallway during the winter months, she made herself believe she was still in the Wilson's garden.

She had gone to bed around midnight. Her thoughts were, as they had been since the funeral, with Jamie. She had lost the capacity to shed any more tears. For the first time in her life she appreciated the words in Seamus Heaney's poem, 'Mid-Term Break'. In the poem, a particular favourite of hers, a mother whose son is killed in a car accident does not exactly weep but 'coughed out angry tearless sighs'. Ethel could now identify with Heaney's sentiments. Sleep, brought on by fatigue, came quickly but it had been a troubled sleep. She had been dreaming about Jamie. The scenes were all jumbled up, happy scenes that developed into sad scenes and moments of tenderness that turned into screaming matches.

'Higher, Nanny, push me higher,' Jamie yelled.

'All right, but hold on to the ropes.'

'Go on, Nanny, push me higher; I want to go all the way up to the sky.'

It was a glorious summer's day. The six-year-old boy yelled with delight as he strove to gain extra height with every forward swing.

'Look, Nanny, look,' Jamie yelled, letting go of the

rope with one hand and pointing to the sky, 'look at the big jet plane up over our house.'

'Jamie, be careful, don't let go of the rope.' But the warning was too late to save the boy from tumbling to the ground. Luckily, he had not hurt himself but the fright had caused him to cry loudly.

Todd Wilson, hearing the commotion, dashed out from the house, saw Jamie on the ground and scooped him up in his arms. He turned to her with a look of rage in his face. 'You stupid, silly cow,' he roared, 'I can't even rely on you to look after the boy. How many times have I told you that the swing is dangerous and that tree . . . that tree is nothing but an eyesore. I'll have it cut down one of these days . . . that'll solve the problem.'

'Jamie stopped his crying and turned his face away from his father. 'Don't let him cut the tree down, Nanny,' he said, grabbing at her skirt. 'Please don't let him cut my tree down.'

Ethel had almost dozed into sleep again when she heard a noise. It sounded as if it was coming from outside her door. With eyes wide open and ears on full alert, she jerked her body upright in the bed. She held her breath. Except for the sound of the clock there was silence. She tried to convince herself that the noise had been a figment of her imagination when she heard another sound. Living on her own in the little two-storey terrace house, she had got used to all the noises that go with such an old building. But this was not one of those familiar noises. Something was moving on the stairs. Something heavy. The creaking came from two different parts of the stairs. Two people? Sitting bolt upright, she wanted to scream but could not. Eyes glued to the sliver of light beneath her door, she detected movement. A break-in. Oh, Christ. Her instincts were to bury her head beneath the blankets and pray that everything went away, but she knew that would get her nowhere. Terrified, shaking with fright, she got out of the bed and moved barefooted to the door. The noise was clearer now. There was absolutely no doubt in her mind any longer; two people were moving about on the stairs.

Pressing her ear against the door, she became aware of another more subtle sound. Over the thumping of her heartbeats she thought it sounded like water dripping down the steps of the stairs. *Holy Jesus Christ, Blessed Mary ever Virgin help and protect me. What is going on?*

She placed her hand on the door handle, trying to summon up enough courage to open it and peep into the landing. She couldn't do it; she was too scared. A male voice shouted: 'OK, Mick, let's get to hell out of here.' A noise of feet pounding down the stairs followed. The front door closed with a bang. Silence. Now, a new sound. Noise from the spring-flap on the letterbox followed by a loud rumbling sound.

Wooouuuph. A thunderous noise roared through the house. Bright light shone beneath her door. She could smell petrol. *Fire: the place was on fire. Oh, Sweet Jesus.* She opened the door and gasped. A vision of hell confronted her. Balls of flame roared through the hallway, funnelling their way up the stairwell to the landing. A wall of heat hit her face, hot enough to singe her hair. Immediately she slammed her door shut. She screamed. Smoke poured in through the sliver beneath her door and began to choke her. If she did not get out of here soon she would suffocate. She could hear the fire growing in its intensity, the crackle and roar outside her door growing to deafening proportions. Escape through there was impossible.

The window; yes she would have to try the window! In a demented fit, she pushed and pulled at the bottom of her window. It wouldn't budge. Then she remembered, in her confusion she had forgotten to release the latch on the middle section. Coughing and gasping for breath, she pulled the small latch free. Behind her, a rim of fire licked the doorjamb causing the bubbling paintwork to flash into multicoloured flame. With a supreme effort, she yanked the bottom half of the window open and bellowed for help – fire, fire, fire! She swung her legs out through the open window, knocking the empty flower box to the street below, and allowing her legs to dangle down on the outside. The drop to the footpath was about ten feet and there was a spiked railing situated three feet from the wall. She was afraid to jump.

The open window, feeding fresh oxygen to the flames, quickly turned the room into a seething inferno. Feeling the hot breath of flames on her back, she glanced behind and screamed again. In disbelief, she watched as the blazing skeletal frame of her beloved violin fell from the wall. As the instrument hit the floor a great rolling ball of flame engulfed her, turning her into a human torch. Its thunderous force propelled her bodily from the windowsill.

Neighbours, dressed in their night attire, rushed into the street. The sight they saw would remain with them for the rest of their lives. Ethel Cassidy, her nightdress and hair burning fiercely had been impaled on the railings outside her house. Above her, angry flames shot from the bedroom window, sending huge billowing clouds of smoke into the night sky.

4

Monday morning, 8.15 pm, the start of another week but already Bob Crosby felt tired. The late May weather, dry for a change, did little to lift his spirits. His workload as editor of the *Post* newspaper, seemed to be getting bigger and bigger. Pressures mounted on a daily basis. I'm getting too frigging old for this game, he told himself; it was something he told himself on a regular basis since his last birthday. It had been two months now since he celebrated his fifty-fifth birthday, though he considered the word 'celebrate' something of a misnomer. It was an occasion he would rather forget but as with all good misadventures, he could not. Annette, his wife, had dragged him along to Bannon's, an upmarket restaurant off Baggot Street, to mark the event. In all honesty, it had taken little persuasion from Annette to get his compliance on the matter; he was never one to turn down an offer of what promised to be a good meal.

During the gastronomic extravaganza he had complained of not feeling well and, just as the waiter placed the dessert in front of him, he felt dizzy and had to hold on to the edge of the table to steady himself. The cause turned out to be straightforward enough: he forgot to take his blood pressure tablets that day. The rich food, washed down with generous helpings of wine was more than his system could cope with.

The last time he stepped on the bathroom scales, his weight had read an alarming eighteen stone; alarming because it was a full stone heavier than it had been when he last visited his GP for a check-up. At the time, the doctor warned him of the serious risk to his health if he did not shed some of his bulk.

But his battle with the bulge and his real and imagined health difficulties were not the most pressing problems bothering him this morning. The suicide of Todd and Maeve Wilson's son, followed three days later by the horrific death of the Wilson's housekeeper, had caught the imagination of the country at large. There had to be a story behind the two deaths but so far no one had come up with any plausible theories. The *Post* had carried a story by Emma Boylan some weeks earlier in which Todd Wilson's business ethics had been held up to scrutiny. The article had now become the focus of wild speculation. Emma had been on her honeymoon when her piece appeared and unaware of the storm her story was causing. This was unfortunate as far as he was concerned. It robbed the paper of a golden opportunity to expand and develop the more sensational aspects of her piece at a time when the readers were hungry for more background information on the Wilsons.

But help was at hand. Emma Boylan's return to work promised to resolve some of his problems. He had seen her enter her office a few minutes earlier and knew it wouldn't be long before she called in to see him. Even from the brief glimpse he had of her, he could see she was in high spirits. The holiday sunshine had added new highlights to her ringlets of golden brown hair and the delicate freckles across her nose had merged into an even tan that accentuated the classical features of her face.

As he extracted two files from his desk, one concerning Maeve Wilson, the other concerning her husband, Todd, a familiar-sounding knock on his door heralded Emma's arrival in his office.

'Well hello there Emma,' he beamed, 'what a lovely tan, you look the very picture of health and happiness. I don't suppose you brought any of that Spanish sunshine back home with you?'

'Not much hope on that score, I'm afraid; I think I lost half the tan while waiting at the arrivals terminal for my luggage.'

'Nothing changes, still you look pretty good to me.'

'Thanks, Bob, you're not looking so bad yourself,' she lied, 'a little flushed, but nothing a good holiday wouldn't cure.'

After a little more innocuous chit-chat, conversation turned to work. It became immediately apparent to Emma that something was troubling Crosby.

'Bob, I know that look on your face. It's the one that spells trouble; so tell me, what's wrong?'

'I hate to be the one to lay this on you, Emma, first day back and all that, but you're right; there is something wrong, something we have to deal with straight away.'

'You're talking about the piece I wrote casting aspersions on Todd Wilson's business ethics, right?'

'Right.'

'I knew as soon as I read about Jamie Wilson's suicide that my article would take on a new life.'

'You can say that again. But there's been another development in the past twenty-four hours that you won't have heard about yet. Last night, the house where Ethel Cassidy lived was burned to the ground.'

'Ethel Cassidy? Who's she?'

'Your question should be: Who was she? The woman is dead; she burned to death in the fire. As to her identity, well that's where things start to get interesting. Ethel Cassidy worked as housekeeper for the Wilsons until recently. I've done some checking, talked to the usual reliable sources but all I've been able to find out is that she was a long time friend of Maeve Wilson. Apparently the two women have been friends since the days when they played with the Dublin City Orchestra.'

'And this woman, Ethel Cassidy has burned to death? Any suspicions of foul play?'

'Too early to say. But you have to admit it's a hell of a coincidence; first Maeve Wilson's son hangs himself and then, less than a week later, her longtime friend, Ethel Cassidy burns to death. Strange, is it not?'

'Strange . . . and more than a bit creepy. There has to be a connection.' Emma thought for a second before continuing. 'The common factor is staring us in the face: Todd Wilson.'

'Yes, indeed, my thoughts exactly. Your article pointed the finger at Wilson, so it'll come as no surprise to you to know we have had a stinging letter from his solicitors.'

'When? I heard nothing about this.'

'You were already on your honeymoon when it arrived.'

'Before Jamie Wilson's death you mean? Are you telling me that Todd Wilson got his solicitors to contact the *Post* before his son's suicide?'

'Yes, Emma, we heard from his solicitors three days before Jamie took his life.'

'Now, that is creepy.'

'That's one way of putting it,' Crosby said uneasily, 'but because of what's happened you're going to have to back up your allegations; get hard facts, do an in-depth job on the issue.'

'That's exactly what I intend to do. And I'm going to broaden the scope of my investigation: look at how his wife Maeve fits into the picture, see if her relationship with this other unfortunate woman has a bearing on what's happened.'

'You'll have to be very careful on that one, Emma. It's one thing to dig the dirt on Todd Wilson but his wife Maeve is a different proposition altogether. She represents the nearest thing we have in this country to a Mother Teresa. Be very careful. The people love her and there's no doubt that she's doing wonderful work for the Third World.'

'I agree with you, Bob; I accept all that, but it can't

do any harm to find out what her views are on her husband's various enterprises. Rumours have it that their marriage is not in the best of shape.'

'Rumours also have it that the Wilson picked up a male hitch-hiker and made sexual advances towards him.'

'Yes, Bob, I've heard that one too but I'm not inclined to believe it. I've met and interviewed Todd Wilson on a number of occasions and I'd say there's no truth to that story.'

'I'm with you on that one, Emma. I think it's nothing more than a malicious whispering campaign. Let's forget it for the moment; concentrate on his business interests and – a word of warning – tread softly where Maeve Wilson is concerned. Oh, yes, another thing, Ethel Cassidy's funeral takes place in the morning; it might be a good idea to pay your respects; you'd never know who you might meet there.'

Emma hated funerals. She had always hated them. It was an irrational hatred and probably stemmed from an incident that happened in a graveyard back in Slane, the village where she lived as a child. It happened when her best friend, Rose O'Loughlin, died at the age of seven from a rare blood disease. Like most children of that age, Emma had little understanding of the notion of death. In answer to her questions on the subject, her mother tried to explain the concept by telling her that Rose was going straight to Heaven and that one day they would meet again and be united. The picture of Heaven, as described by her mother, had all the attractions of her favourite fairy tale stories. But all that changed when she accompanied her parents and Rose's parents to the burial. If Heaven was such a wonderful place, she wanted to know, why was everyone crying. And the white coffin frightened her – why should Rose be hidden away in such a small box; that couldn't be pleasant.

As the coffin was lowered into the ground she watched as her friend disappeared into darkness at the bottom of the hole. 'Mummy,' she asked, pointing into the hole, 'is that Heaven? It's not like what you said at all. You said Rose was going to Heaven but all I see is an ugly, ugly hole.' She had been traumatised by the event and had difficulty in sleeping for weeks after-wards. In time, the frightening memory faded but she would always have a dislike of graveyards.

Standing among the mourners now, she spotted Todd Wilson beside Fergus Massey, both men standing towards the back of the crowd. There was no sign of Maeve Wilson among the mourners but Emma could understand that. It couldn't be easy for the Wilsons, so soon after the funeral of their only son. The strain showed on Todd's face as his head remained bowed, his eyes little more than slits. The man beside him, Fergus Massey, was known to Emma because of his work with Maeve Wilson in connection with Third World charities. Emma had also come across his name while researching Todd Wilson's list of companies. Both men, she had discovered, had shares in a number of business enterprises. Emma considered approaching Todd Wilson to sympathise with him on the death of his son but rejected the notion. Wilson would in all probability take offence and consider her presence no more than harassment.

It was while these thoughts occupied her mind that a familiar figure moved up beside her. Detective Inspector Jim Connolly, a man she had got to know because of his friendship with her boss, Bob Crosby, spoke in little more than hushed tones. 'Thought I might see you here,' he said, 'though I'm not so sure Todd Wilson will be too happy if he catches sight of you.'

'You think so?'

'I know so. After the hatchet job you did on him he'd probably throw you in on top of the poor woman's coffin.'

Their conversation stopped when a loud wail came from a woman beside the graveside. Emma watched as a slim woman dressed in a neat black suit stretched her hands to the heavens and tilted her head upwards. Her cry of anguish, loud and shrill like a wounded animal stunned the mourners. Looking at the woman's face, even in its moment of torment, Emma could see she had a remarkable presence. As she moved, sunlight caught the coiled chignon of her ash-blonde hair, giving it an almost unnatural glow against the sombre setting. As the rosary prayers began the woman turned her back on the ceremony and strode quickly away from the graveside, a look of defiance etched on her face.

Mourners continued to mumble their Hail Marys but it was obvious their thoughts were with the striking woman who had just left them.

Connolly nudged Emma on the arm. 'That was Ethel Cassidy's twin sister Marina. She lives in Liverpool . . . came over for the funeral.'

'How do you know that?'

'She came into the station last night, wanted to talk to someone in authority about her sister's death. I was the one who pulled the short straw.'

'You mean you were the one to talk to her? What did she want?'

'What didn't she want, more like. Kicked up holy murder, said she knew her sister had been murdered, wanted to know why we were – to use her words – sitting on our arses instead of arresting the killer.'

'I don't suppose she told you who the killer was?'

'As a matter of fact she did. She claimed Todd Wilson killed her twin sister.'

5

Five days after her son's funeral, Maeve Wilson was back behind her desk at Dublin branch office of SUCCOUR. Getting back to a normal routine had never seemed more important to her before. Since Jamie's death she had avoided mixing with people as much as possible, wanting to be alone with her grief. It was for that reason she had not gone to Ethel Cassidy's removal. That and the fact that her husband Todd would be in attendance seemed good enough reason to stay away. Given these circumstances, she felt sure that her one-time friend, Ethel, would have understood.

In keeping with this need to avoid meeting people, she declined to give interviews to the media. All efforts by the press to contact her were met by a polite but firm refusal from Sean Beggs, the aid agency's press-officer. Maeve hoped they would understand. She considered it important to maintain a positive relationship with the press and TV people; without their goodwill she would have great difficulty getting her appeals for Third World contributions across to the public.

Her fellow director, Fergus Massey, encouraged her to take more compassionate leave. It was a kind gesture by Massey, a friend long before SUCCOUR ever came into being, but the five days she had already taken would suffice. There were only so many tears one could cry and besides, she hoped the work would help to occupy her mind with less morbid thoughts.

Massey had been in the office when she arrived. One glance at his flawless good looks and athletic figure made her feel positively dowdy by comparison. He had insisted on making her a cup of tea. He sat by her desk now, cup of tea in hand, making comforting sounds designed to help ease the pain he knew she must be experiencing. Inevitably, the conversation changed to more serious topics. For two days the newspapers had carried articles on the Ethel Cassidy tragedy and had featured photographs of the burnt-out house. They both found it difficult to believe such a thing could happen. But always the conversation returned to Jamie, each time accompanied by tears from Maeve. Fergus Massey was a good listener, always finding the right words and gestures of comfort to ease the torment she was going through.

Although Massey acted as the projects manager with SUCCOUR, he seldom visited the Dublin office, preferring instead to conduct business from his palatial home in Abbeyleix, County Laois. With the installation of a website and ISDN lines, the computer in his house offered total online access to the Dublin office. Maeve suspected that his presence in the Dublin office today had as much to do with his concern for her recent bereavement as it had to do with the organisation's current difficulties.

Three weeks before Jamie ended his life, on the eve of her trip to Ethiopia, Maeve had sat in the same chair where she sat now and received a telephone call from her field operator in Addis Ababa. Long distance bad news. He informed her that £85,000 had been taken in an armed robbery from their headquarters there. On the day in question, Maeve contacted Massey and asked him to deal with the situation. Now, almost four weeks later, a fax message coming through on her desk showed that the problem had not gone away.

She showed the message to Massey and asked why the situation remained unresolved. He read the message, frowned but told her there was nothing to worry about. 'I'm dealing with the problem,' he informed her, attempting to sound light-hearted, 'so there's no need to concern yourself with that matter right now.' Maeve could see he was stalling. She hated it when he did that but on this occasion she suspected his motives were for the best. Pushing her personal feelings to one side, she insisted he bring her up to speed on the situation.

As Massey went into detail on the organisation's on-going problems, Maeve looked at his face; even the obvious stress of business did little to alter the man's flawless features. She found her mind travelling back to an evening in a Dublin hotel, to the time she first met Massey and his best friend – Todd Wilson.

Although she was a member of the Dublin City Orchestra at the time, she also played part-time with a musical quartet. She was twenty-two years of age then,

... ters in the restaurant of the ... with drive ... of the day. Then ... and some of the more ... nights a week, from 9.30 pm until midnight (with two ten-minute breaks) did not interfere with her work in the orchestra and brought in much needed extra cash.

On a number of occasions she noticed four young people enjoying themselves, ordering the finest foods and drinking the best wine the house had to offer. She suspected that they were closer to her own age group than to the more 'settled' regulars who frequented the restaurant. Unlike those diners around them, they paid scant attention to the music, preferring the sounds of their own high-spirited banter. Like her fellow musicians, Maeve felt a little irritated by their behaviour.

'Who are the motormouths?' she asked Tom Foxe, the cellist in her group, during one of her breaks. Tom, a fount of knowledge when it came to knowing who was who in Dublin, had by his own admission enough useless information stored in his head to put the Trivial Pursuit people out of business. 'They're part of Dublin's brat pack,' he informed her, 'all money, mouth and loose morals. The good-looking fellow, the one guaranteed to get all the girls' ovaries churning, the

entertain d...
melodious pop tun...
she performed light classics an...
Foxe, accounted for the rest of the quarte...
Twin sisters, Ethel and Marina Cassidy, als...
Meath, a talented violinist with... rings and...

his e... beefy t... nose; do y... because she... to find out if Te...

'He is one of th... son – spitting image... build, same swagger. ... not quite in the same league a... the two lads have been friends si... Wilson senior owns a couple of pubs, ... offices and a stall at the big race meetings. Not much class there I'd say – just loads of dosh. The women with them are airheads. They represent the real dessert for the two boyos.'

For two weeks, after Foxe's less-than-kind assess–ment, the foursome failed to make an appearance in the restaurant, but just when Maeve thought she had seen the last of them, they returned; well at least, three of them returned. The handsome one called Fergus Massey still had the blonde by his side, but Wilson, the one with the moustache, had no companion. Something else was different: they were less vocal than before.

Maeve found herself being drawn to Massey's good looks. His toffee coloured hair, beautifully groomed, swept over his ears and covered his collar at the back. He had extravagantly sculpted features, not unlike Michelangelo's David. Maeve was no less susceptible to his attractiveness than the blonde girl holding his hand, nor could she help noticing the sparkling engagement ring on the young woman's finger. One day, she thought wistfully, a man would look into her eyes the way Massey looked at his girlfriend.

Glancing at the table once too often, she noticed that the man with the moustache was staring at her. She blushed at having been caught and looked away immediately. Later that evening, in spite of what happened, she stole another quick glance in their direction, and again made contact with Wilson's eyes. He smiled back at her. Instinctively, she knew he wanted to meet her.

She was right. During the break he made his way over to her and introduced himself. He complimented her ability as a musician and claimed to be a lover of light classical music. She found him to be a pleasant young man and chatted amiably enough with him. He was nowhere near as handsome as his friend Massey but he did have a pleasant personality and dressed well, and the moustache gave him a dashing, debonair look.

In the two weeks that followed, he visited the restaurant on a number of occasions and made it his business to chat to her each time. He introduced her to his friend Fergus Massey and Fergus's fiancée. Her name was Jillian Harrington and she was nothing like the 'blonde bimbo' Tom Foxe had perceived her to be. She was a final year law student in Trinity College and Maeve found her to be most charming. Maeve, in turn, introduced her fellow musicians, Tom Foxe, Ethel and Marina Cassidy to her new-found acquaintances. They had a drink after the music session had finished and passed some pleasant times together. Like Maeve, the Cassidy twins were smitten by Massey's looks but, seeing the way he looked at Jillian, reluctantly accepted that he was not available.

Three weeks after their first verbal exchange, Wilson asked Maeve for a date. She accepted. A whirlwind courtship followed. They were married within the year. Fergus Massey was their best man.

The gentle pressure of Massey's hands on hers wrenched her mind back to the present.

'So what do you say, Maeve, will you meet him?' she heard him say.

'I'm sorry, Fergus, I lost concentration there for a few moments. What was it you were saying?'

'I was asking if you'd like to come down to my house some evening – stay overnight – have dinner with the two of us.'

'With you and Todd?'

'Yes, Maeve, he talked of little else at Ethel Cassidy's funeral. He wants to meet you, talk to you about Jamie. He feels gutted, devastated . . . Christ, we all do! You haven't been to the house since the funeral. That's hard on him. I think what he needs most of all is a chance to talk – to talk to you.'

'The time for talking is long past . . . what would be the point?'

'Look, I think you owe it to one another, husband and wife, father and mother – for Jamie's sake.'

'I'm sorry, Fergus, I realise that Todd is your best friend and that you are in an awkward position because of our relationship here, but you're wrong. I owe him nothing; I blame him for everything that's happened. If I never see Todd Wilson again, it'll be too soon.'

'You don't mean that, Maeve. You're being too hard on him; it's not like you. You haven't got a vicious bone in your body. You'll change your mind in a few days when you think about what I've said.'

'No, that's where you're wrong, Fergus, I tell you I will never, never, never talk to that man again! Do you understand?'

'H'm, we'll see.'

6

It had been a good day for Vinny Bailey.

After an early breakfast, he left the apartment and headed for Durrow, a picturesque village in the Midlands. Before slipping out of the house he tiptoed into the bedroom, placed a featherlight kiss on Emma's lips and whispered, 'Good morning.' Thinking she was still asleep, he was surprised when her arms reached up and pulled his head down to hers.

'Tell me it's not Monday morning,' she pleaded in a sleepy voice. 'Tell me I don't have to go back to work today.'

'I'm sorry, darling, but it *is* Monday morning. The honeymoon is over. We're back in Ireland and we both have a living to earn.'

'Spoilsport.'

'You'll love it as soon as you smell the newsprint.'

She replied by throwing a pillow at him.

An hour and a half later he parked his Citroën 2 CV6 directly outside the front door of Midland Antiques, a shop in Durrow. As an antique dealer, Vinny made a comfortable living specialising in the purchase and sale of fine art. Back in his student days at the National College of Art and Design, he had been fortunate to study under two of Ireland's most eminent painters, and from them he learned to appreciate aesthetic values in works of art. It was a source of great regret to him that his studies in the art college were disrupted before he could sit his final examination – his youthful exuberance had brought him into contact with the Republican movement – but he did succeed in rounding out his education in his father's studio. Working under Ciarán Bailey's guidance, he developed a love of paintings and fine antiques. However, it became apparent to him within a few years that he would never aspire to his father's level as a painter, so he decided to concentrate on antiques instead. It was a decision he never regretted.

A few days before taking off on his honeymoon he had heard through a tip-off that Midland Antiques had an item of special interest to him, a full scale cartoon design of a stained glass window by Harry Clarke. He had not been able to chase it up at the time and was delighted to discover the item was still on the market.

The proprietor, a wiry little man with the unlikely name of Paul Newman seemed eager to help.

'You know anything about Harry Clarke?' he asked.

'A little,' Vinny replied.

'A little, I see, In my experience a little usually means a lot. I'd say now, you're one of them clever connoisseur heads from Dublin. Am I right?'

The suggestion would have made Vinny laugh if it were not for the close scrutiny the dealer subjected him to. Vinny gave as good as he got, returning an all-encompassing once-over appraisal of the dealer.

Wearing a double-breasted suit – a shiny brown pinstripe affair with wide lapels – Newman looked only marginally less antiquated than the objects for sale in his shop.

'I'm no connoisseur,' Vinny answered finally. 'Far from it in fact, but I do like the works of Harry Clarke.'

Newman shrugged his shoulders and spread the drawing out in front of Vinny.

'This drawing depicts The Angel of Peace,' Newman announced in an all-knowing voice, 'and according to the notes on the back, the finished stained glass window was completed in 1918.'

'What sort of money are you looking for?'

'£5,000.'

'Far too much – it's only a drawing.'

'D'you want it or not?'

'Yes, I do, but at a price that makes sense.'

Newman pushed back the grey felt hat on his head and smiled. 'Right, well in that case maybe you'd like to make me an offer.'

After haggling for ten minutes Vinny parted with a cheque for £3,580 and shook hands on the deal. As Newman accompanied him to the door, Vinny noticed a stack of paintings, twenty or more in total, and asked if he could have a look at them. Newman seemed reluctant to show the collection to Vinny. 'No point in looking at them,' he said with a dismissive wave of his hand, 'they're already sold to one of my biggest customers.'

Vinny was impressed. 'I'd still love to have a gawk

at them if you don't mind,' he pushed.

'I suppose it's OK. All right. Go ahead. I'd like to hear what you think of them.'

Carefully, Vinny inspected each painting in turn, all of them large-scale oils on canvas, all framed in elaborate gilt and all with a consistency of style that distinguished British portraiture in the later eighteenth century. 'They all look as though Reynolds or Gains–borough could have painted them.'

'I wish,' Newman said wistfully, 'but you can see from the signed names they aren't. They're still masterpieces; all of them have the same sort of breadth and dignity you expect from that great age.'

'Where did you get them?'

Newman hesitated for a second before answering. 'You might well ask, my friend. It took me six months to assemble this lot; I had to travel the highways and byways of Britain to find them.'

'Did you get them for a gallery or what?' Vinny asked as he continued to examine the paintings. Again, Newman appeared to hesitate before answering. 'These works of art will grace the walls of the new Smithfield Court Hotel in Dublin.'

Vinny had heard about the Smithfield Court; it had been in the news in recent days because it was owned by Todd Wilson. 'Dreadful to hear about Wilson's son,' Vinny commented.

'A real tragedy,' Newman agreed. 'These paintings should have been picked up about a week ago but, well, with all that's happened . . . A terrible thing altogether.'

'Yes, I know,' Vinny said, remembering how he had first heard the news while walking with Emma up Avenue Acapulco in Los Boliches.

Vinny left Newman's antique shop with his Harry Clarke drawing carefully placed in a plastic tube, delighted with his purchase but unable to stop his thoughts returning to Todd Wilson's paintings. He tried to imagine how the death of a son would affect a man and how insignificant a collection of paintings, irrespective of their cost and importance, must be in comparison. Although he had never met Todd Wilson, he felt a pang of sorrow for him.

Dismissing such thoughts he placed his Harry Clarke in the car's boot and headed back towards Dublin. Making only one stop on his homeward journey – coffee and a biscuit in Naas – he arrived in Little Bray just after midday. Little Bray, as its name suggests, is an adjunct to the main town of Bray, twelve miles south of Dublin city, and is the place where Bailey's Fine Art and Antiques Store is located. Jointly run by Vinny and Ciarán Bailey, the shop specialises in original paintings and the restoration of damaged canvases.

Ciarán had not seen his son since the wedding and insisted they have a nip of whiskey to mark his return. 'To your future,' the old man said, tipping his glass against Vinny's, 'and to that charming lady you married. You know what son, you're a lucky lad there, Not only is she a looker but she's a bright lass as well.'

It pleased Vinny that his Dad should like Emma; to him it was a bit like getting a seal of approval. It had never occurred to him before just how much something like that mattered. Sipping his whiskey and chatting with his father, he could not help noticing how frail the old man had become in recent times. In spite of suffering from angina, Ciarán Bailey, at sixty-seven years of age, worked more hours than most men half his age.

After refusing a second glass of whiskey, Vinny fetched his latest acquisition from the back of the Citröen and showed it to his father.

'What do you think?' he asked.

'Ciarán flattened the drawing on the table. 'H'm, let's have a look; what have we got here? A Harry Clarke, I declare. It's certainly in good condition. Not many original Clarkes around these days. Worth a few bob, that.'

'How much would you say?'

'H'm, let me think; I'd say it must be worth the guts of four or five grand . . . maybe more.'

'That's what I thought,' Vinny said, feeling relieved. A long discussion followed with both men evaluating Clarke's artistic skills until at length, with the subject exhausted, Ciarán invited his son to follow him into the studio. 'I've something to show you, son,' he said. 'It's my wedding present to yourself and your good woman.'

As always, pungent odours of turps, oil paint and varnish permeated the room, reminding Vinny of his lifelong addiction to the specific redolence of his father's studio. Nothing had changed. The place pulsated with colour and there were canvases piled everywhere, along with a huge array of pots and tubes of paint, brushes, palettes, linseed oil dippers, and several multi-daubed smocks. In the centre of the studio, a painting, covered with a loose white cloth, sat on an easel. Ciarán removed the covering with a flourish of hands that would do justice to a magician.

'I hope you and Emma like it,' he said.

Vinny's eyes opened wide as he stared at the picture in silence, slowly shaking his head from side to side.

'Well, come on, lad, do you like it or not?' Ciarán prompted.

'Like it, Dad? I'm speechless. It's the most beautiful thing I've ever seen, I'm . . . I'm gobsmacked . . . simply lost for words.'

His father had painted a full-scale copy of Renoir's painting, *Luncheon of the Boating Party*, but it was more than just a reproduction of a group of young friends sitting around a tavern table by the banks of the Seine: He had superimposed portraits of Emma and Vinny in the painting with a subtlety that did not, in any way, take from the original masterpiece.

'You've spotted the deliberate mistakes then,' Ciarán said with a chuckle of laughter.

'Yes, and I'm overwhelmed, completely bowled over. I don't know how you did it, but it really looks like myself and Emma are genuinely there, part of the scene.'

'Well, I'll tell you what gave me the idea,' Ciarán said, fetching a book and opening it at a page that showed a true reproduction of the original painting. 'You see the young woman on the left of the picture playing with a dog; well, she was Renoir's favourite model, Aline Charigot, and if you look at her face you'll see that she resembles Emma; similar golden brown whorls of hair bunched around the neck, the same bright happy eyes, full lips, slight turn-up on the nose, and look; an identical strong profile. It's uncanny when you consider that there is a hundred years span between their lives.'

'It's extraordinary,' Vinny agreed, 'but I see you had to do rather more extensive alterations to the fellow straddling the chair.'

'Ah, yes, our friend Gustave Caillebotte,' Ciarán said, pointing to the young man in the foreground of the composition wearing a straw hat on his head. 'A little extra creativity was needed all right but the basic shapes and features were not that different from your own. Do you think Emma will like it?'

'Dad, it's something we'll both treasure for the rest of our lives.'

After saying goodbye to his father, Vinny drove back to the city in time to avoid the evening rush-hour traffic, and parked the Citröen in the basement car park attached to the apartment block that Emma and he currently called home. Bright and spacious, their suite on the third floor of Hubband Bridge House overlooked Herbert Place and was adjacent to a clean section of the Grand Canal.

Inside the apartment, he propped his father's

painting up against the wall and sat, totally absorbed, in front of it. He couldn't wait to see the reaction on Emma's face when she saw it.

Thinking back to how dreamily she had looked that morning, half asleep, pulling his head down to kiss her, he felt a warm glow of delight. Later, this evening, when she returned from her first day back at the office he would surprise her by dishing up a meal with a Spanish flavour. To add to the occasion he would serve a bottle of Rioja and organise suitable background music. He might not succeed in capturing the ambience of Spain but he felt sure their lovemaking afterwards would be just as hot.

7

Emma noticed that Connolly's hair had been shorn since she talked to him at Ethel Cassidy's funeral. A mistake; that was Emma's verdict. Not that it bothered her one way or another how the detective-inspector chose to style his hair but she had to admit it looked rather debonair before the trim, with the silver-white strands swept back from the temples to blend into the grey hair. She suspected that the detective had opted for a closer cut in order to lessen the effect of his thinning crown. Watching him and the *Post*'s news editor, Bob Crosby, congratulate each other on the performance of some stock exchange shares, they had recently invested in, put her in mind of punters backing a favourite filly on Derby day. Their conversation turned to the goings-on of some of their mutual acquaintances in the Fitzwilton Lawn Tennis Club – a place where neither of them had hit a ball in years – Emma could not help pondering on the similarities of the two men. Both were products of the Jesuits Clongowes Wood College and both of them retained an 'old-boys' network with their former classmates; those like themselves who had all risen to the top of their chosen professions.

Having got off a few well worn bon mots, Connolly moved on to the reason for his visit, his dark intelligent eyes glancing quickly from Emma to Bob and back to Emma again. 'I assume you know why I'm here?' he said, a thin smile flickering on his lips. 'Because of the *Post*'s recent article on Wilson, and because of his son's subsequent death – and the death of Ethel Cassidy, I think it might benefit us all to have a little chat?' Connolly turned his focus on Emma and spoke with studied casualness. 'It surprised me to see you at Ethel Cassidy's funeral knowing, as you did, that Todd Wilson would be there.'

'Of course I knew; he was the real reason I attended the burial if you must know.'

'Well then, in that case I admire your nerve. After what you wrote about the man, don't you think your timing might be considered just a tad insensitive? You must be aware that quite a few people are blaming your article for Jamie Wilson's suicide.'

'And I suppose I'm to blame for the fire in Ethel Cassidy's house too,'

Connolly ignored Emma's sarcasm. 'No, Emma, nobody has blamed you for that, not yet at any rate, but I can tell you this: Ethel Cassidy's sister Marina was right about one thing; her twin sister was murdered, the fire that took her life was started deliberately.'

'You're sure – absolutely sure of that?' Crosby asked.

'Oh, I'm sure all right, there's no doubt. We have witnesses who saw two men leaving the house and we found an empty petrol container at the scene. The callous buggers who perpetrated this crime didn't even bother to make it look like an accidental fire.'

'Well, in that case,' Emma offered, 'Ethel's sister is correct about its being murder. Could it be possible that she's also right about the perpetrator's identity? What do you think? Have you talked to the woman since?'

'The damn woman has gone and disappeared. I've no idea where the hell she's staying – that's if she hasn't already popped back to Liverpool. We're trying all the hotels and guest houses, ringing friends from the days when she played with the Dublin City Orchestra but I'm not holding my breath.'

'It's all a bit mysterious,' Emma said. 'First Todd's son; then this woman turns up out of nowhere and accuses Todd of killing her sister. All very odd, I'd say. Have you any theories, Detective-Inspector?

'Theories, Emma? Huh, we've enough theories to beat the band; we have theories coming out our . . . ' He stopped, deciding not to use the crude expression on the tip of his tongue. 'The truth is,' he admitted after a pause, 'we have no real leads.' For a brief moment, Connolly shed the air of composure he usually managed to maintain as he smashed his fist into the open palm of his other hand. 'I want to catch the bastards who did this.' He was practically shouting. 'I was present when we scraped Ethel Cassidy's charred body off the railing; it was the most horrible sight you could ever imagine.'

Nobody spoke for a second. It was as though all three of them had been miraculously transported to Ethel Cassidy's house, forced to witness the terrible event.

Bob Crosby was first to break the silence. He looked Connolly directly in the eye as he spoke. 'Why? Why would someone want to do such a thing,' he asked. 'Surely to God there can't be a connection between Todd Wilson and what happened to her.'

'Somebody wanted her out of the way, that's for sure,' Connolly said, 'and we have to assume it has something to do with recent events involving the Wilsons.'

Emma looked at him shrewdly, understanding immediately what the detective was referring to. 'You think my exposé on Todd Wilson's business affairs is at the root of this, don't you?'

'I certainly think it might have a bearing on all that's happened. I've re-read the article myself this very morning and to be honest, I couldn't find anything that stood out as significant enough to lead to murder. But that's not to say there isn't something in there that I've missed.'

'Well, that's because I had to be careful how I wrote the article,' Emma said defensively, 'I can't leave the paper open to prosecution so I've got to trip carefully around the subject.'

Connolly clasped his hands in front of his stomach and rotated his thumbs. 'It's what's behind your article that concerns me – the bits you haven't allowed into print.'

'What exactly are you getting at, Detective?'

'I don't wish to be rude, Emma, but in your effort to avoid being sued for libel you and other top journalists have developed a subculture in the way you report matters. Innuendo appears to be your stock-in-trade. You rely on gossip, tip-offs, suspicions and anecdotal evidence. That's how you present your stories.'

Emma was about to protest but could not get a word in before Connolly continued. 'You see, Emma, in spite of what I've just said I do believe there might be something to your story and I would welcome your help on the matter. You see, there's a huge difference between suspecting wrongdoings and proving that the wrongdoings really exist; there's a huge gap between suspecting Todd Wilson of shady business deals, on the one hand, and suspecting him of murder on the other. I'm hoping that with your help, we can make that leap.'

Emma glared at Connolly, not bothering to mask the expression of exasperation on her face. 'Look, Detective Connolly, I'm not sure whether I'm being patronised or insulted by you – or both at the same time, but I think it would help enormously if you could tell me exactly what it is you want from me.'

'No offence intended, I assure you, Emma, but what I need from you is a little cooperation on my investigations.'

'Like what?' Emma asked.

'Like sharing the notes of the interviews you did while researching your piece on Todd Wilson and giving me whatever background information you can on his various business enterprises.'

'You're joking,' Emma stormed. 'First you make little

of my work and then you've the nerve to ask me to share it with you.'

Connolly's response cut like a whiplash. 'You would like to see the perpetrators of Ethel Cassidy's murder brought to justice?'

'Yes, of course I would, but I am an investigative journalist. The day I hand over my research and interview notes to the law, I might as well throw my hat at being a journalist. You know I can't do that.'

Emma was relieved when she saw Crosby clear his throat to indicate that he wished to make a comment. He had always backed her on such points of principle. She had no reason to suspect that his views would differ on this occasion.

She was wrong.

'I think in this case,' he said to her, 'circumstances are different. Both you and Jim want the same thing. It could well be that you'd both benefit from getting your heads together. Besides, Emma, it could benefit the *Post* to have the law on our side if things get very ugly. If you go around accusing Todd Wilson, you'd better be sure of your facts. Wilson is, to all intents and purposes, a respectable businessman. He is well liked by the public; the financial journalists heap praise on him; his wife is only short of being made a saint for her work with charities.'

'That means shag all,' Emma said in a strangled sarcastic voice, 'that just means ...'

Crosby stood up and approached Emma, his substantial stomach undulating before him, his hands raised in a gesture that she knew meant stop. 'Enough, Emma, enough, all right?' he said, his tone firm and dissuasive, 'I think it's best that you work with Jim on this one. Think of it as being for the better good.'

Emma opened her mouth to protest but not finding strong enough words to express the uncoiling fury she felt, said nothing. She pushed up from her chair, her face flushed red with anger, stormed out of the room and slammed the door behind her with enough force to challenge its hinges. The two men left sitting in her wake looked at each other, shrugged their shoulders and sighed. 'Women,' Connolly said, 'that's bloody women for you.'

8

Shelving the serving of the Spanish paella was one of Vinny's better ideas. His culinary experiences, mostly acquired during his years as a student back in the early eighties, were little better than elementary, though he did pride himself on having some degree of flair. Back in those college days, sharing a flat in Rathmines with two fellow art students, anything more adventurous than beans on toast was considered the height of cordon bleu. After much deliberation, he settled on a simple dish, chicken and asparagus sauce.

Before Emma arrived on the third floor landing, before turning the key in the apartment door, a rich aroma of food filtered through to her nostrils. Once inside, she saw Vinny through a haze of steam, so intent on his endeavours in the small kitchen that he failed to hear her above the sizzling and popping sounds of his pan.

'Um, smells pretty good – whatever it is,' she said, coming around the kitchen counter and pecking him on the cheek.

Forgetting the grease on his hands, Vinny hugged her tightly and kissed her on the lips for a full minute. 'Courting in the kitchen was never like this,' he said, breaking the embrace. 'And how was your day, then?

You look a bit – a bit under the weather. Rough, was it?'

'Yes, I'm whacked; it's been a long day but I'd rather not talk about it right now if you don't mind. First I want to hear what sort of a day you had yourself?'

'Better than yours it would appear,' he replied. 'I've had a good – and profitable – day.'

Steam billowed around Vinny's head. A loud sizzling sound filled the room as he added extra liquid and tomatoes to the browning chicken pieces. No amount of heat or steam, however, could impede his recital of the day's events. With the enthusiasm of a man who had just discovered the crock of gold at the rainbow's end, he told her about his acquisition of the Harry Clarke original drawing and his plans to turn a handsome profit on the deal.

The combination of food, wine, and music could not have been better and even though Emma tried to be cheerful and bright, she suspected that Vinny sensed her unease. Playing softly on the hi-fi, the sound of guitarist, Paco de Lucia performing his rendition of 'Concierto de Aranjuez' would, under normal circum-stances, have lifted her spirits but on this occasion the highly accomplished musician failed to create an impression. Several times during the meal she noticed Vinny looking at her with a questioning stare. That she was fatigued would be evident to him, she realised, a fact that made her appreciate all the more that he did not press for an explanation.

After serving dessert – *crèpes suzette*, with Cointreau flavoured orange butter – and coffee, Vinny took

Emma's two hands in his and pulled her gently up from her chair and away from the table. 'Close your eyes and follow me,' he bid her.

'What – what are you up to now?'

'Shh, don't ask. Just follow me and all shall be revealed.'

'You're mad, you know that, Vinny Bailey.'

'Of course I'm mad – I married you, didn't I.'

Vinny held on to her two hands as he walked backwards, playfully pulling her towards the living room. 'Now, you can open your eyes and see what my father has given us for a wedding present.'

She gasped when she saw the painting. 'It's the most beautiful gift I have ever seen; how on earth did your Dad ever get such an idea?'

Vinny related the story he had heard earlier in the day from his father and was surprised when he noticed tears in Emma's eyes. 'Whatever is the matter?' he asked.

Instead of an answer she threw her arms around him, hugged him tightly, and began to cry. 'Oh, Vinny, I love you – and I love Ciarán, that sweet, sweet man . . .'

'Emma, for God's sake, what's wrong with you; what brought all this on?'

'Why is it, Vinny, just when a person thinks everything is wonderful, when you think that maybe – just maybe – the world is not such a shitty place after all, something always happens to ruin everything?'

'Sorry, Emma, I don't follow . . .'

Emma told Vinny about her meeting in Crosby's

office with Connolly. She told him what the detective had said in regard to the murder of Ethel Cassidy and how he had requested her to hand over the investigative notes she had made while researching the article she had written on the business activities of Todd Wilson.'

'And what's so bad about that,' Vinny asked, 'I don't see what the big fuss is. If Todd Wilson has been up to no good, then it's in everybody's interest to expose him. If on the other hand he has nothing to answer for, what harm can it do? The way I see it, there's a sicko out there somewhere, a madman with no regard for human life or limb, right? So, it's in all our interest that he's stopped before someone else gets killed. That being the case, then surely anything that might possibly shed light on the woman's murder has to be a good thing.'

'I agree the killer has to be stopped – that goes without saying – but you don't understand my predicament, Vinny. What I'm talking about is a breach of journalistic ethics.' Using her finger tips for emphasis, Emma repeated the arguments she had put to Connolly and Crosby some hours earlier.

'I see what you mean,' Vinny said sympathetically. 'So, what are you going to do about it?'

'Jesus, I don't know Vinny. I think I'm going to have to hand in my notice. Tell Crosby to stick his job.'

'Would that be such a bad idea?'

'What?'

'Well, you could forget all about this murky world of crime. Give them the notes you made; leave it to the police; leave it to the experts.'

'I see,' Emma said, with more sarcasm than she had intended.

'No, I don't think you do see, I think – '

' – And I think you're forgetting something, Vinny. You're forgetting that investigative journalism is what I do for a living – and – and I'm bloody good at it.'

'Nobody said you weren't – Christ, you know I'm with you a hundred percent in everything you do – but now, well – it's different.'

'Different?'

'Yes, different, damn it. You're married now. You're - '

'I don't friggin' well believe I'm hearing this! Why not just lead me to the kitchen, handcuff me to the sink? That's what you'd like, eh?'

'No, Emma that's not what I want at all. Look, let's calm down, OK? All I'm saying is – '

' – that I should give up my job.'

'Will you let me get a word in edgeways, Emma? What I'm suggesting is that you move to something a little easier. You know, like the fashion pages, the social round-up. Damn it, I don't know, but something a bit less stressful.'

'OK, OK, OK, all right, enough. I've had enough. It's been one long godawful day and what I do not need right now is to have a fight with you.'

'Oh, shit, you're right. I'm really sorry. It's just that – '

'I know Vinny – it's OK – it's all right, no need to say – '

Silence.

'Was – was that our first argument?' Vinny asked.

Emma did not answer. She began to cry.

Vinny took her in his arms. 'I love you. I love you more than anything, you know that. I want to give you my absolute backing no matter what you decide to do.'

Emma looking into Vinny's eyes. What she saw was a mixture of confusion and love there. 'Why don't we sleep on it,' she suggested.

'Good idea!'

Each day seemed like an eternity since his son's burial. Todd Wilson was finding it difficult to come to terms with his grief. He should have travelled to Edinburgh to sort out problems that had arisen in connection with the planning authorities over his proposals to develop The Thistle and Rose but he cancelled the meeting; he just couldn't work up enough energy, or enthusiasm, to talk to anybody. All his business interests had been put on hold, something he had never done before, and the strange thing was he didn't care.

This evening as the low grey skies darkened, heralding nightfall, his thoughts were jumbled, sad, oppressive. Alone in his house, shadows lurking in the corners of the silent room, he sat down heavily in his favourite armchair and looked vacantly through the window that faced the harbour. The house, situated on the lower slopes of Howth's 576-foot summit had stood in its prime location since the year 1847, the same year that the railway had come to the peninsula, joining

Dublin city with its most picturesque promontory. Back then, it had been a modest pile.

Little remained today of the original construction built by Todd's great grandfather, Myles Wilson. A series of extensions and refurbishments had, over a period of many decades, all but obliterated the original walls. Each generation of Wilsons appeared to have accepted it as a duty to enlarge and beautify the settlement. Without interruption, through bad times and good times, it had remained in the family ever since. If old Myles ever decided to revisit his house, it is doubtful that he would recognise the place in its present palatial condition. And yet, in all probability, the founding father of the Wilson dynasty had once sat in the very same spot that Todd occupied, regarding the same panoramic view of Howth harbour.

Never in the house's long history, never until now, had the edifice lent itself to the scene of a suicide. No, nothing like that had ever happened before; but it had happened now; it had happened during Todd's watch and, as if to underscore the event, the victim had been his son. The room where the tragedy had occurred, situated on the floor above him, had been sealed shut. It would remain that way as far as he was concerned.

This evening, the scenic beauty of the fishing village with the tiny island, Ireland's Eye visible in the distance was wasted on him. He took hold of the whiskey decanter in front of him and helped himself to his sixth drink of the day. The glass in his hand, Waterford crystal, made its familiar pinging sound as the decanter touched the rim. 'Cheers,' he said aloud before taking a generous mouthful. Alcohol allowed him to ignore the exhaustion that had crept up on him; it helped diminish the heart wrenching emotions of the past week but it failed totally to anaesthetise the pain and it failed to provide any answers. So many questions hung in the air but no answers.

Why had Jamie done it?

Why? Why? Why? He had asked himself the same question a thousand times since the funeral. He apportioned some blame to himself and Maeve. He thought about his relationship with the boy and regretted all the times he should have been with him and had not made the effort, times when he had allowed business interest to occupy his time instead. On reflection, he readily accepted that he had not been the best father in the world but neither did he concede that he had been the worst father. He had always made sure that Jamie wanted for nothing but it was obvious to him now that his efforts had fallen short – woefully short.

In recent years, as Maeve became more and more involved in her Third World crusade, their marriage suffered proportionately. Rows became the norm. They hurled abuse at each other over the simplest of things until finally, they needed no excuse at all to fight. Always, in the background, there was young Jamie, listening to them bickering, quarrelling, throwing abuse at each other and occasionally, when things really got out of hand, throwing household objects at each other.

Helping himself to a mouthful of Jameson ten-year-old, he watched as refracted light from the golden liquid created honeycomb effects on the facets of the cut glass. Each facet, it seemed to him, reflected a distorted image of his face, all of them seeking answers, all of them combining to project a multiple display of his inner despair. It was difficult to understand how it had all gone wrong. Estimating the effect their warring must have had on Jamie was less difficult to measure.

But in spite of the unrelenting domestic strife and strain that bedevilled his household, Todd looked elsewhere to lay blame for what had happened. He thought about the rumours concerning the male hitch-hiker he had offered a lift to and cursed himself for ever having stopped for the young man. Each day, it seemed to him, the gossip and speculation grew more fanciful. There had to be somebody out there who hated him enough to orchestrate the campaign, to fan the winds of gossip into a storm; but who that somebody was, he had no idea. Yes, he had made enemies over the years, it was impossible to be successful in business without having to take hard decisions along the way. Hard decisions hurt people from time to time; it was an undeniable fact but that was life, damn it! There wasn't a lot he could do about it.

The thing that had really scared him though, was seeing some of his more controversial business interests, as reported in the press, cut out from newspapers and pasted on Jamie's wall. Until he saw the collage of cuttings, he had no idea his son took such an interest in what he did for a living. The article's headlines said it all: *Developer Under Investigation. Residents' objections stall Smithfield Court complex. Todd Wilson is quizzed by Dáil committee. Wilson named in hush-hush money probe.*

Other headlines told similar stories but it was the last article Jamie had pasted to the wall that caused him most annoyance. He knew it had been the last article because of the dateline: 2 May, Jamie's birthday, the day he took his life. The article had appeared in the *Post* and had been written by Emma Boylan. Its headline read:

Todd Wilson's Suspected Links to Organised Crime

The article featured a series of photographs that depicted properties connected with companies in which he had an interest. One picture showed a new shopping and leisure complex on the west side of the city with accompanying text outlining a list of planning regulations that had been flouted. An artist's impression showed front and side elevations of the new Smithfield Court Hotel, side by side with views of how Smithfield village looked before the recent development. The older scenes showed a cobblestone square with groups of happy smiling boys on horseback as they participated in the horse market that took place on the first Sunday of every month. Even though the centuries-old cobblestones had been salvaged and relayed, the article criticised the installation of twelve new ornamental lighting masts and took issue with the two-tiered glass enclosed platform perched 220 feet on top of a distillery chimney that had stood in the square since 1895. Emma Boylan's article had ended by questioning how a European capital city could tolerate the destruction of a unique amenity and in doing so, eliminate all traces of an ancient tradition.

None of this comment bothered Todd Wilson too much; he had heard it all a thousand times before. His response never varied: tradition will not put food on the tables of people on the dole queue. He could live with such criticism but he was forced to treat Emma Boylan's assertion that he was linked to organised crime more seriously. She had discovered that one particular member of the consortiums he was involved with had once been convicted on fraud charges and money laundering. Since reading the article, Todd had checked this out and found, to his dismay, that Emma Boylan's report was correct. But he did not accept her contention that is followed that he, Todd Wilson was, by association, connected to organised crime.

Sipping whiskey, its effects on him now noticeable, a vision of his wife invaded his mind. He spoke to her as though she were present beside him. 'Where are you hiding out?' he demanded of the imaginary image, 'I need to talk to you, d'you hear me, I need to talk to you.' He took another swallow of whiskey before continuing his one-sided conversation. 'Tell me, Maeve, what did you think of Ethel Cassidy's twisted words at the grave? Who exactly were they directed to? What could the ould bitch have meant? Damned if I know what got in to her. And her death – burned almost to a cinder – skewered on the railing spikes! Christ! You know I disliked the woman – had to sack her – no choice – but to end up like that, spiked. She always did have too much influence over Jamie – our fault I suppose.' He stopped for a second as though waiting for an answer, and then, apparently getting a reply, nodded his head in the affirmative. A long silence followed before he made his next move.

Involuntarily, he stood up, staring wildly into space, his head at an unsteady tilt and threw his whiskey glass against the wall, smashing it to smithereens. 'Goddamn you, Maeve! Where the hell are you?' he cried out loud. 'We need to talk; I need to discuss certain matters with you, d'you hear? I need some goddamn answers, so I do, and I need them now, d'you hear. D' you hear me you bloody old bitch?'

An eerie silence was all that greeted his drunken outburst.

9

Of all the world's capitals, London is about as huge, as cosmopolitan and as diverse as it is possible to find but it was the city's offer of anonymity that lured Maeve Wilson there. Looking out the bedroom window of her hotel, she watched the late-night taxis drive swiftly along Sloane Street, past Cadogan Place, as they ferried their passengers to and from the great city's inexhaustible range of destinations. Past midnight, it was probable that most of them were returning from theatres in the West End district or from some dining extravaganza shared with friends in some chic restaurant. Perhaps some were heading for all-night parties, while others, undoubtedly, were making their way to the arms of a lover in some hidden location, lost to the enquiring eye in the vastness of London's sprawling metropolis.

Turning her gaze from the window and the unending activity in the streets below, she pulled the drapes shut and sat in one of the comfortable armchairs provided for her comfort in the hotel's sixth-floor suite. This was the same place she had come to on a few previous occasions when pressure of work or the tedium of domesticity had got too much. To her, the Cadogan Hotel represented a refuge, an oasis, a place to get away from the troubles of the world, a place to escape from the many personal problems that beset her from time to time. Other people she knew went to shrinks, doctors, priests or took to drugs and drink in times of stress but she went to the Cadogan. Staff in the hotel had got to know her and always looked after her with courtesy and efficiency.

It was after her first visit to Africa, twelve years earlier, after her initial exposure to the squalor and misery of the aid-camps in Ethiopia, that she discovered the hotel. In the intervening years, she had learned how to deal with the situations that confronted her on her frequent visits to Africa but problems of a different kind, problems more to do with the domestic front, brought her to London in more recent times. Her present visit to the Victorian building – once the home of Lillie Langtry, the actress famously befriended by King Edward VII when he was Prince of Wales – represented an escape from all that had happened to her in the past few weeks. She had tried to ride out the storm, even going back to work for a few hours, but the unrelenting pressure had finally got to her. Three days in London, she knew, would help her to sort out the conflicts doing the rounds of her brain.

Since arriving at Heathrow Airport in the early afternoon, her efforts at unclogging her mind had been only partially successful. After checking into the Cadogan she had afternoon tea served to her in the hotel's drawing room, the same room where once Lillie Langtry and Oscar Wilde entertained their friends, before taking advantage of the fine weather outdoors. She had made her customary reconnoitring visit to Harrods – she had inspected each floor with a view to the next day's purchases – she strolled around Sloane Square, she sat on a bench in Hyde Park and finally returned to the hotel where she dined alone in the elegant Edwardian restaurant. During all this time, her thoughts refused to concentrate solely on the world around her, returning instead to Jamie, to Ethel Cassidy, to her husband Todd and to Fergus Massey and his attempts to resolve the persistent financial problems bedevilling her organisation, SUCCOUR.

Eating one of the complimentary chocolates left in her room, she thought about contacting Todd. She wondered if he, like her, wanted to talk about Jamie. She reached out to the telephone to make the call but stopped in mid-action. She was not yet ready to confront him, not yet ready to take onboard the recriminations that would follow – in both directions – from such an encounter.

Without wanting it to happen, her mind took flight, whirling back to the time when she had been infatuated by Todd Wilson and his ilk. She smiled to herself, a sad sort of smile. Extraordinary as it seemed to her now, she once believed she loved him. In his own way, she supposed, he probably thought he loved her too.

She was twenty-two years of age, working as a musician with the Dublin City Orchestra. The orchestra had finished performing the Brahms Violin Concerto and she had, for the first time, been chosen to play the solo. As leader of the first violins she normally played alongside her good friend Ethel Cassidy and Ethel's twin sister Marina but on this occasion the solo artist who should have been out front, the guest violinist, had cancelled at the last minute. It was the sort of break she had always hoped for and she made sure to take full advantage of the opportunity. The conductor, Heinz Schröder, took the trouble to compliment her after the performance. 'I was enthralled by your artistry,' he said enthusiastically. 'You have justified my faith in you; you have provided magical moments by capturing the composer's lyrical beauty and vitality so completely.'

After the performance, a midday recital in the National Concert Hall, she joined Ethel and Marina for a sandwich and coffee in Hourahan's pub on the corner of Leeson Street. 'You were great today,' Ethel enthused. Marina agreed. 'First time I ever heard old Schröder lavish so much praise on anybody.'

Maeve laughed. 'I wouldn't mind that old goat; all the time he was talking to me he was looking at my boobs. I could see his eyes popping out of their sockets trying to squint down the bit of cleavage I had showing.'

'Well, isn't he the dirty ould devil,' Marina said, a mischievous smile on her face.

Ethel agreed. 'And you a married woman and all.'

'Not only am I married, girls, I just found out this morning I'm in the pudding club – preggers. I'm pregnant.'

'Congratulations,' the twins said in unison. 'That's great news.' Ethel added, truly delighted.

'I bet Todd was over the moon when he heard,' Marina said, more a question than a statement.

'Actually, he doesn't know yet.'

'You haven't told him?' Ethel and Marina asked, echoing each other.

'No, I haven't had a chance yet. He went to Cork early this morning on some important business; he's staying at the Albert Hotel, no less. I didn't know the good news then. I'm going to surprise him by taking the Cork train to join him there; he'll get the surprise of his life.'

She managed to make the 4.35 pm train seconds before it pulled away from the platform in Heuston Station. It was the first week of August, the weather was glorious and she could never remember a time when she felt so content with life. The train was packed with holidaymakers; families with their children; young men with their young ladies, a symphony of happy banter, laughter and smiling faces everywhere.

A group of elderly passengers in her carriage, sitting stiffly and solidly in their seats before the train pulled out of the station, relaxed as soon as the journey got under way. Like her, they were lulled by the hypnotic rhythm of the wheel's clickity-clack contact with the rails and the constant clattering of the carriage. Sun-drenched fields flitted past as telephone wires, stretching from pole to pole, looped up and down like yo-yos. Distracted, occasionally, by the non-stop activity of her fellow passengers, she found herself smiling at total strangers who happened to look in her direction.

She had an almost uncontrollable compulsion to yell out to them – I'm pregnant. Of course she did no such thing but the joy of it all was making her giddy. It was such a change from the feelings of inadequacy she experienced during the first months of marriage. Todd had wanted to start a family straight away but she failed to conceive. After a year with no success she sought the help of Dr A. J. Pinkerton, a gynaecologist with a practice in Ailesbury Road, one of Dublin's better addresses. One couple in six, he informed her, encountered problems with fertility. Not only that, but in 35 per cent of couples, male-factor infertility is diagnosed. Accepting his advice, she underwent a series of tests that included, among others, the treatment of ovarian stimulation. Dr Pinkerton, unhappy with her progress, requesting that her husband supply a sample of his semen for analysis. Todd, being Todd, was furious. He felt the request cast doubt on his virility, a notion he could not even begin to contemplate. There was also the embarrassment of it all, a situation made more acute because it was his friend, Fergus Massey, who had recommended Dr Pinkerton in the first place. As it turned out there *was* a problem with Todd's semen; it had a low sperm count. Only after a series of intra-uterine inseminations and in vitro fertilisation tests had she eventually become pregnant.

But she could forget all that now, brush aside the concerns and fears that had for so long bothered her and frightened Todd; she would now give him the child he so looked forward to.

The three-hour journey passed pleasantly, her mind filled with dreamy cotton-wool plans for the future of her unborn baby.

A taxi took her from Cork's Kent railway station, crossed to the south side of the River Lee, drove into Anglesea Street and dropped her off in front of the impressive Albert Hotel.

'I'm Mrs Todd Wilson,' she informed the receptionist. 'My husband is staying here. Can you give me his room number, please.' The receptionist, a pretty woman with sparkling eyes who looked young enough to be still at school, smiled and looked up the number unhesitatingly. 'Yes, Madam, we have a Mr Wilson staying with us; he's in room 205, second floor. Would you like me to tell him you are on your way up?'

'No, no, not at all, thank you, no need; I want to surprise him – I have a bit of good news to tell him.'

The receptionist's smile was replaced by a frown. 'I had better check all the same,' she said. 'Hotel policy, and besides, he might not be there right now.' She dialled a number and waited for a response. There was none. 'I could page him for you if you'd like,' the smiling face said, 'or perhaps Madam would like to try the restaurant or the bar; he could be there.'

'No, don't page him, I'll have a look for myself.' After receiving directions, she made her way to the restaurant and spotted Todd almost immediately. With Fergus Massey by his side, he was leaving the bar and being directed by a waiter to a table in the dining area. She could see that both men were in high spirits as they carried drinks in their hands. Todd, smiling and joking with Fergus, was about to take his chair at the table when he noticed her walking towards him. The smile on his face froze and the glass dropped from his hand. 'What the – Maeve – but, but – God, Maeve, you've given me the fright of my life; what on earth are you doing here – I mean, how did you get here – what – ?'

'Well, I wanted to surprise you, Todd,' she said, kissing him on the cheek, 'but seeing the effect my presence has on you, I think I should do it a bit more often.'

Fergus Massey, who seemed equally stunned by her appearance gave her a perfunctory hug and a peck on the cheek. 'Maeve, goodness me, Maeve, what a surprise! Let me get you a drink, OK?'

'Thanks, Fergus. I'll have a mineral water.'

As soon as Fergus made his way towards the bar, she sat down beside Todd and reached out to hold his hand. 'Todd, I have the most wonderful news, the sort of news that just couldn't wait, so I hopped on a train in Heuston and – '

'What the hell do you think you're playing at, Maeve?' Todd said, his voice low and angry, the words hissing through clenched teeth, 'I'm down here with Massey trying to put the finishing touches to a big business proposal and the last thing I need right now is for my wife to come barging in – in the middle of – in the middle of – of getting it right.'

Stung by his words, she took her hand away from and stared at him in disbelief. The man she had married had suddenly turned into an alien creature, a complete stranger. Temporarily lost for words, she looked around and saw other diners happily enjoying their food, all of them oblivious to the state of panic overtaking her. A cacophony of sounds funnelled into her head; shrieks of laughter, boisterous talk, knives and forks scraping plates, spoons stirring tea, glasses clinking in the bar and the sound of canned music.

Fergus Massey, standing at the bar counter, situated to one side of the dining area caught her eye. He was engaged in an animated conversation with two young women and a waiter. One of the women, a glamorous redhead, stamped her foot on the ground, pushed her drink glass into the waiter's hand and stormed out of the bar. The second woman, dressed like her companion in stylish evening wear, slapped Massey across the face, emptied her drink down the front of his shirt, and ran from the bar. During this altercation, the waiter, a small, red-faced man wearing an ill-fitting hairpiece, raised his eyes upwards in a gesture that sought guidance from a higher power.

Maeve returned her gaze to her husband who, like her, had witnessed the scene. 'Just what in God's name is going on here?' she demanded. Todd's face had by this stage turned red. He groped for words but said nothing. It was then that she noticed the four settings on the table, complete with wine glasses and a bottle of sparkling white wine sitting in an ice bucket. There was no need to see any more. At that moment she knew precisely what was going on. She stood up, accidentally knocking her chair to the floor as she did so, and strode out of the restaurant with tears in her eyes.

All that had happened over eighteen years earlier but the hurt still remained. She tried to dismiss the memories of her first betrayal but, maddeningly, the images refused to go away. She found it difficult to believe she had ever been so naive and stupid. What she didn't know back then was that the incident was only the first brush with the ugly realities of life's cruel betrayals, a lesson that should have prepared her for what lay ahead but did not.

Two days after the Cork incident, Fergus Massey called to her home. He assured her that she had jumped to the wrong conclusions. The ladies in the hotel, he assured her, were marketing people. He had arranged the meeting himself, he told her. Their job was to promote Todd's first high-street turf accountant shop, it was as simple as that, the fact that they were female was purely coincidental. She had believed him at the time; she still believed him to this day but she had no doubts in her mind about Todd's role in the affair. She found out soon enough that the Cork incident was merely the first in a series of infidelities that would grow more frequent as the years passed.

Undressing for bed, she looked forward to a good night's sleep. As always, she would spend the first of her three nights stay in London alone. The following two nights, she fully expected, would turn out to be more exciting, a lot more exciting.

10

There was a palpable tension between them. Detective Inspector Jim Connolly placed his hands together, as though praying for divine intervention and watched Emma across his fingertips, waiting for a reaction. Slowly, carefully, Emma examined each of the large format photographs that the detective had placed in front of her, without saying a word. He had given her two separate batches of black-and-white prints. The first lot showed aspects of Ethel Cassidy's burned-out house and several gruesome studies of the woman's body as it had ended up, spiked and badly burned, on the railings outside the building's gutted shell. It was difficult not to be affected by the graphic violence depicted in the photographs but Emma tried to remain detached and objective. After all, that was why she had agreed to Bob Crosby's entreaty to work, and cooperate, with the detective.

It wasn't what she had wanted to do but after an early morning meeting with her editor, he had persuaded her as to the merit of his scheme. It felt all wrong to Emma, a factor that contributed to the sick feeling in her stomach on her way into work earlier that morning. At the time she had blamed the fumes from the congested traffic for the nauseous feeling but now, sitting in her office, the feeling of discomfort persisted. What she did not need was a confrontation with her boss but she had made up her mind to tell him what her intentions were. Crosby's reaction to her notice to quit her job had been typical of the man. 'What nonsense, Emma, what utter nonsense; why on earth would you want to go and do a foolhardy thing like that?'

Her answer came out sounding rehearsed, which of course it was. 'I refuse to share my investigative notes with Connolly; it goes against everything I stand for – a matter of principle.'

'Ah, come on Emma,' he said owlishly, 'we're all adults here. This is the real world we're living in. Don't tell me you were taken in by my little charade in front of Connolly? All I was trying to do was give the appearance of fully cooperating with the boys in blue.'

'What do you mean – appearance?'

'Look, Emma, I agree with the stand you took yesterday against Connolly. I was proud of you – never seen you so mad at anybody – all fired up, a regular spitfire – and your defence of journalistic ethics – most admirable, nothing short of heroic.'

'Bob, are you taking the piss out of me or what? You sided with Connolly against me, remember? You ordered me to hand over my notes.'

'Play-acting, my dear, I was simply play-acting. I knew you would react the way you did – I was counting on it. In fact that's what I wanted Connolly to see. You were great. Now that he believes I have overruled you, he will fall over himself to give us what he's got.'

'Well, I don't know about you, Bob, but I sure as hell wasn't play-acting; I still see this as a matter of integrity.'

'Of course you do, and you're right. All I want you to do is give the appearance of cooperating with him. You don't have to hand over everything. Just let him see your notes on what's already in the public domain; stuff you've gone into print with already. Show him a few other bits and pieces that are of no great consequence; that way everyone's happy. He'll believe he's got what you have and in return, you will be privy to his stuff.'

'Won't he do exactly the same to me?'

'Of course he will. It's all part of the game but – and here's the bit that's important – it's probable that you'll benefit more from the exercise than he will. It means he won't hinder you from poking your nose into matters that, under different circumstances, he could prevent you from investigating. Just play along with him, Emma; that's all I ask.'

And that was precisely what Emma was doing now, sitting across the desk from Detective Inspector Connolly, poring over forensic photographs. In return she had handed a select number of pages from her notebook and a wad of photocopies she had secured from the companies' office. Most of the notes and documents concerned businesses in which Todd Wilson had an interest. Emma had interviewed people who had, in the past, worked in some of these companies. Mostly, what they had to say consisted of innocuous anecdotal accounts of how the various enterprises were run but some of the comments were more serious. Emma held on to a few bits and pieces she intended to follow up herself at a further date but passed the rest to Connolly. He appeared pleased with what he had got. Bob Crosby was right; it was a game and in time she might even become good at playing it.

The second batch of prints in front of Emma was shot at the scene of Jamie Wilson's suicide. Although not as dramatic as the Ethel Cassidy shots, they were, in many ways more terrifying. In one print, a rope with a noose at its end hung from an exposed beam in the ceiling. Emma didn't need to see the boy's body to imagine his last gasps for breath as he died. What would drive someone to take such action? It was the question uppermost in her mind as she examined the other photographs. Several prints showed the black marks on Jamie Wilson's neck but it was the close-up shots of the newspaper cuttings on the wall of his bedroom that caused her most interest. Several of the articles, she could see, were pieces she had written herself; mostly to do with Todd Wilson. She could not help but notice her article dated 2 May, the day Jamie had committed suicide. It chilled her to think that one of Jamie's last acts before taking his life had been to paste the most critical article on his father she had written. Other items had been culled from the financial pages of the main newspapers; again, the subject matter in each piece concerned Wilson.

In contrast to this media exposition of Wilson's business activities were several cuttings concerning the charitable works of Maeve Wilson. All articles in this selection contained photographs of Jamie's mother. Many of the pictures had been taken in Ethiopia and most showed her surrounded by aid workers, meeting patients in field hospitals, unloading medical supplies from SUCCOUR trucks, or shaking hands with important legislators and world leaders. In all of the pictures Maeve Wilson looked heroic and always, it seemed to Emma, aware of the camera.

Looking at how Jamie had arranged the newspaper cuttings, each piece selected so that it slotted neatly beside the next, it was obvious that he had taken great care with the display. It was because of this attempt to harmonise all the shapes into an aesthetic composition, that Emma noticed two blank spaces where cuttings had been removed. 'What happened to the missing pieces? Emma asked.

'Wish I knew,' Connolly answered. 'According to my experts, the ones who examined the wall, two pieces were removed shortly before, or immediately after, the suicide.'

'Interesting. That should narrow down the question of who removed them.'

You're right, Emma, but it doesn't help much. You see, with the exception of Jamie himself, the only other person to visit the room before the law arrived was Ethel Cassidy.'

'And she's dead.'

'Exactly. So, you see, the only two people who might be able to tell us what happened to the missing articles are dead.'

Emma examined a 'blow-up' photograph showing the exposed portion of wall where the missing newspaper cuttings had once been. Small fragments of the newsprint, showing traces of letters, had remained glued to the paste.

'Looks like whoever did this was in a hurry,' Emma remarked.

'Why do you say that?'

'Well, it seems to me that Jamie was very careful in how he assembled this lot – look at how neat the whole display is. If he'd been the one to do the removing, it would have been a far neater job, don't you think?'

'You could have a point there,' Connolly conceded.

'So, by a process of elimination, that must point to Ethel Cassidy.'

'Which leaves us with the intriguing question: why Ethel Cassidy? Why would Ethel Cassidy go to such trouble?'

Emma considered the question for a moment before giving the detective the benefits of her thoughts. 'I'd say it's most improbable that a woman under such dreadful stress – what with Jamie hanging from a rope and the police on their way – would have the presence of mind to do such a thing.'

'Connolly pouted his lips in contemplation. 'I don't know, Emma, I've known people to do the damnedest things – especially when they're under pressure.'

'Have you been able to make out any of the words?' Emma asked.

'Very little I'm afraid. You can see for yourself some of the headline. The letters – E-L-A-N-D-S-E-Y – on one line and - R-A-G-E - on the line beneath. Our experts have tried to estimate the column's width in order to establish how many letters are missing. Their best guess it that the headline probably read: 'Ireland's Eye Tragedy.'

'Ireland's Eye,' Emma said, trying to make sense of this new information. 'That's the little island just off Howth Head, isn't it?'

'Yes, Emma, Ireland's Eye is about a mile or a mile and a half away from the pier in Howth. You can actually see it from the window of Jamie Wilson's bedroom. We've searched through all the newspapers looking for such a report and have come up with nothing. We're still going through microfilm records of old newspapers but so far we've drawn a blank.'

'There must be a connection,' Emma said. 'There has to be a reason why a woman – seeing what had happened to Jamie – would find it so important to remove the cuttings.' She paused for a second and looked Connolly in the eye before continuing. 'It also poses the question: was she murdered because of what was printed on the missing pieces? Did someone know she had them – and fearing what she might do with them, kill her?'

Connolly nodded, giving credence to her line of thought but made no comment.

'Can I have copies of the photographs?' Emma asked, 'I'd like to talk to one or two old newspaper hounds that I know, see if they can help me turn up something.'

'Good idea, Emma. I'll get a set of duplicate prints made for you,' Connolly said, far too readily for Emma's liking but then followed up with a request: 'I'll expect you to let me know if you dig up anything of interest.'

'But of course,' Emma replied.

11

PRESS RECEPTION
VENUE: Paramount Hotel, Temple Bar, Dublin.
TIME: 11.00 a.m.

Nobody could have anticipated the far-reaching effects of the press reception held in the Paramount Hotel on Wednesday morning. Notice for the briefing had been a last-minute affair. Late, the previous evening, a fax message had been sent to the national media advising them that charges would be brought against Mr Todd Wilson. The one page fax, sent from the office of Ormsby & Neville, Solicitors, claimed they represented a young man who had been molested by Mr Wilson. Further details would be given at the press reception where, according to the message, the media would have an opportunity to hear the accusations, first-hand, from the victim.

Like other media personnel, Emma Boylan responded to the call. Instead of following up on the inform-ation she had gleaned from the photographs Connolly had given her, she found herself doing battle with Dublin's notorious traffic as she made her way to the Paramount Hotel. Snarled cars, buses, lorries and scurrying pedestrians, a daily feature along Aston Quay, slowed Emma's progress down to a crawl as she drove alongside the River Liffey towards the Grattan Bridge junction with Parliament Street. She couldn't be sure whether to blame the smell coming from the Liffey's dark, murky water or the traffic fumes for the sick feeling she was experiencing. Whatever the reason, it was important that she get out of her car soon, otherwise she felt sure she could not hold back the urge she felt to retch.

Parking her car – illegally – in Exchange Street, she saw several journalists of her acquaintance make their way into the lobby of the Paramount Hotel. There was an undoubted buzz of excitement in the air. The same question appeared to be on every one's lips: Could what had been, up to now, a whispering campaign be brought into the open, given the oxygen of publicity?

Proceedings were running ten minutes behind schedule. Taking a seat towards the back of the small conference room, she watched as rival media representatives jostled for prime positions. Television reporters along with their cameramen, believing themselves to be a cut above the rest, attempted to sideline radio and newspaper journalists. Emma preferred to remain aloof from the pack. That way, she had discovered through hard-won experience, gave her a better overall picture of proceedings.

An uneasy calm descended on the assembly as she watched three men take their seats behind a baize-covered table. The man sitting on the chair in the centre glanced at his watch before addressing the gathering.

'Good morning ladies and gentlemen of the media, my name is Edward Doyle-O'Brien, public relations officer acting on behalf of solicitors, Ormsby & Neville. I would like, first of all, to apologise for running a little late and to thank you for coming here in such strong numbers.'

Emma detected a smugness about the speaker that prompted her to bestow her full-of-shit accolade on him. A slim, athletic looking man in his early forties with too much gel in his hair, dressed in a well-cut, blue pinstripe suit, he paused for effect and flashed his best PR smile before introducing the two men accompanying him. 'To my right,' he said, indicating a formally dressed middle-aged man with a shiny bald head and dark horn-rimmed glasses, 'is the senior partner with Ormsby & Neville, Mr. James Norton.' Mr. Norton acknowledged the introduction, oblivious to the palpable wave of apathy coming from the floor, by contorting his face into what he must have imagined was a smile. It was obvious to Emma that Mr. Norton had not gone to the same school of charm as his hired PR man.

Edward Doyle-O'Brien then turned to his left, where a young man, dressed in denims, open neck shirt, and shaven head, sat with an insolent look on his face. Emma could see that he was quite good looking but the expression of contempt struck her as being more studied than real. It was as though someone had asked him to strike a particular pose. The PR man introduced him with an expansive wave of his hand. 'This is Johnny

Griffin,' he said, as though introducing some celebrity, 'he is an eighteen-year-old student and is the subject of this press conference. In a moment I will allow Johnny to read a statement to you, let you hear first hand his account of what happened to him.'

The PR man returned to his script before continuing. Emma could not help but notice how his voice had taken on a more sombre tone than before. 'The firm of Ormsby & Neville are conscious of Mr Wilson's recent sad bereavement and would not, ordinarily, want to inflict further grief at such a time.' He paused and nodded his head grimly, his face assuming the characteristics of a concerned clergyman, before continuing. 'However, circumstances have dictated that we must act now. I have no doubt that all of you gathered here today have heard the rumours circulating in recent weeks concerning Mr Wilson's conduct in this matter. For young Mr. Griffin, for his family, for his fellow students and for his girlfriend the situation has become intolerable. His privacy and that of his family and friends have been shattered. They have been subjected to phone calls all hours of the day and night; reporters have camped outside his doorstep and pestered members of his family; but worst of all, Johnny Griffin has had to endure catcalls in the street, hear himself being called abusive names.

'It was with the greatest of reluctance, and only when the situation had got completely out of hand, that he has decided to do something about it. In effect, he has been left with no other choice.'

The PR man paused for a moment, gauging the effect his words were having on his audience, before turning to face Johnny Griffin. 'Johnny will now read a statement but for legal reasons I must ask you all in advance not to put questions to the boy when he has finished. Mr Norton, in his capacity as the boy's solicitor, will however try to answer questions of a technical, or procedural, nature, should you require additional information.'

Johnny Griffin put his hands to his mouth, cleared his throat and began reading from his statement. His voice, when he spoke, sounded nervous, but after a few sentences he became more assured. 'Two months ago, on 17 March, I set out from my home town of Castlepollard – that's in the County Westmeath – around 2 o'clock in the afternoon, to hitch a lift to Delvin. My girlfriend lives in Delvin and she had asked me to attend the local St Patrick's Day parade with her. Within a few minutes I got a lift as far as Collinstown. I had to hang around the cross in Collinstown for about ten minutes before getting my next lift. A few drivers saw me but didn't bother to stop. I was delighted when Mr Wilson's Jaguar pulled to a stop. He owns the new hotel outside Castlepollard, so I knew who he was. He told me he was on his way to Athboy and would be delighted to drop me off in Delvin. We chatted about this and that for a while and then he asked me did I have someone special in Delvin. I told him I had a girlfriend there and that I was going to meet her. He made suggestive remarks about what myself and my girlfriend might get up to when we were alone. I went along with this conversation for a while, giving as good as I got, trying to be polite on account of him giving me the lift but I began to feel uneasy when his remarks became more and more personal.

'He began to ask me questions like: Was I well hung? Was I able to satisfy my girlfriend? Did she go down on me, and other questions of a similar nature. I became flustered and didn't know what to say. It was then that he put his hand on my thigh. For a moment I thought it was just a friendship thing but knew I was wrong as soon as his hand moved up to my crotch. I was so shocked that I didn't know how to react. I asked him to take his hand away. But he took no notice of what I said. He pulled the car to the side of the road and parked it in a gateway to a field. I was in a state of fright by this stage. I wanted to get out of the car and run but before I could open the passenger door he pressed me back into the seat, pushed a lever to make the seat recline, started to unzip my fly and force my pants down over my hips. I struggled like mad but I was no match for the weight and strength of Mr Wilson. I lay there, pinned down to the seat, unable to break free while he groped my private parts and engaged in an act of sexual stimulation. I remember crying.

'When he had finished, he helped pull my pants back up and drove on towards the village of Delvin. He acted as though nothing out of the ordinary had happened. I was by this stage in a state of shock and unable to speak. He stopped at Doran's pub, on the outskirts of

Delvin and asked if he could buy me a drink. In a confused state, I agreed. I can remember sitting at the counter in Doran's Lounge and having a whiskey and water. The pub was busy with drinkers and they all seemed to know Mr Wilson. He shook hands with most of them and bought a round of drinks for the 'house' before leaving with me.

'Outside the pub, I refused to get back into the car. I told him I would prefer to walk the rest of the way. It was less than a half mile so it didn't bother me; I just wanted to get away from him. He seemed a bit put out by this. But before he drove away he produced his wallet and peeled off five twenty pound notes and gave them to me. Along with the money, he gave me his business card and told me to call him anytime I felt in need of some action.

'I have tried to live with what happened that day but find I cannot. I wake up in the middle of the night and cry. I can't eat, I can't sleep, I can't touch my girlfriend and I fear I am on the edge of a nervous breakdown. I have contemplated suicide on more than one occasion. I have talked to my local priest about what happened and he told me that the only way to deal with my distress was to confront the issue. That way, and only that way, he assured me, would I be able to lay the ghost of what had happened to rest and begin to put my life back together again. I have taken his advice. That is why I am talking to you today. Thank you for hearing what I had to say.'

Johnny Griffin sat down to startled silence.

It was a full ten seconds before the press corps found its voice but when it did, the raucous roar that erupted was not a pretty sound. It was as though the hound pack, having smelt its prey, began howling for blood. For a time it looked to Emma as though Edward Doyle-O'Brien was about to lose control, but he surprised her by regaining the upper hand. Obviously, his skill in the art of PR handling was better than she had first suspected. Emma listened to the questions coming from the floor but decided not to participate. She would wait until this free-for-all concluded and then, in her own time, make plans to unearth whatever lay behind this press conference. Most of all, she wanted an opportunity to talk, eyeball-to-eyeball, with Johnny Griffin. His remark that he had thought about suicide caused her most concern. Griffin, who was obviously aware that Todd Wilson's son had committed suicide, must have calculated the inference his remark would have. It was certainly an inference that occurred to Emma.

She was not satisfied with Johnny Griffin's story.

She had nothing to back up her instincts except a gut feeling, and that gut feeling was telling her to question the motives behind Johnny Griffin's press conference. Why a press conference at all? Why hadn't he gone straight to the Gardaí and made a formal complaint to them. That would have been the logical course of action. He hadn't done that; instead he chose to turn the whole thing into a media circus. Why?

Like most of the media people, Emma left the hotel

as soon as the briefing concluded, determined to avoid getting caught up with the few die hard reporters who would try to persuade her to join them for a drink in the bar.

Moving outside the hotel, Emma discovered to her annoyance that her car had been clamped. Furious with herself for not taking care to park properly, she kicked out at the yellow metal clamp locked to the wheel. This was the first time she had been caught flaunting the law in this regard. 'Do not remove this car', the notice pasted to her windscreen said in large block letters. 'No fear of that,' Emma cursed, examining the notice to find the telephone number that would put her in touch with the proper authorities. Trying to hold her temper in check, she used her mobile phone to contact them. It wasn't so much the £75 fine that bothered her most but the fact that she would have to wait around for half an hour before the de-clampers arrived. It meant her whole day's schedule was now running late.

While waiting, she returned to the hotel's lobby and began contacting people on her mobile phone. She gave Bob Crosby a brief up-date on what had transpired at the press conference and discussed the implications Griffin's revelations would pose for Wilson. When Crosby asked why she wasn't on her way back to the office, she told him, using colourful language, about her car being clamped. Crosby managed to infuriate her still further by appearing to derive an almost boyish delight from her predicament. 'I'm glad to discover that there's someone who can get the better of you,' he said good-humouredly.

It was while looking in her notebook for the telephone numbers of other contacts that she saw Marina Cassidy. This was the woman that Detective Inspector Connolly had said he couldn't locate. Emma watched as Ethel Cassidy's twin sister walked through the lobby and pushed through the revolving door that led to the street outside. Emma, who had seen her briefly at Ethel's funeral, had not realised just how striking the woman looked. Tall and sophisticated looking, Marina Cassidy carried herself with the confidence of a top model. High, pronounced cheek-bones and wide-set eyes gave her face an elegant quality that lessened the effect of ageing.

Emma was about to follow her, intending to tackle her on the subject of Todd Wilson, when the Dublin Corporation people arrived to release her car. For the second time in less than half an hour she cursed them.

As soon as she got her car back to the *Post*'s car park, she intended to set about arranging a meeting with Marina Cassidy. Her visit to the Paramount Hotel and her subsequent trouble with the clampers might not, after all, turn out to be such a waste of time; she now knew that Marina had not gone back to Liverpool.

12

It had been a pleasant experience. Different. Being able to shop without worrying about who might be watching what she bought made a change. That was one of the great things about London as far as Maeve was concerned – no one knew her there. At home in Ireland, the situation was so different. In Dublin, or any other Irish city or town for that matter, people recognised her on account of her involvement with the Third World relief agency work. It meant that her every move, her every purchase, was open to scrutiny, analysed and commented upon. From time to time this intrusion reached ridiculous proportions with gossip columnists deciding to get in on the act, reporting the most trivial incidents in her life. It was most irritating. She could never fully understand why people felt she should go around in rags just because the people she collected money for had nothing. In London, thankfully, she could get away from all that petty parochialism.

Apart from the older, long-established stores like Harrods, Liberty and Harvey Nichols, she had managed to get to some of the more trendy boutiques. But the usual buzz she got from such shopping expeditions failed to emerge on this occasion. Thoughts of her son Jamie were never far from her mind. At one stage she found herself wiping tears from her eyes. Despite a conscious effort to exclude recent sorrows, images from the past continued to invade her spirits, images of a smiling Jamie looking into her face with the sort of love and trust that only children possess. At one point during the day she had sat, sipping coffee, in a small cafe in Knightsbridge and allowed her mind to revisit the past, to relive again moments shared with her son.

Jamie clung to her as she stepped from the small boat on to the railway sleeper that jutted out from the rocks and served as a jetty. Nothing excited the six-year old more than being brought for a trip to Ireland's Eye. To Jamie, the small island off the coast of County Dublin represented a world of fantasy which never failed to engage his mind in the most colourful flights of imagination.

This trip to Ireland's Eye had been organised by Fergus Massey. Todd's old boat, the one they had used until recently on such trips, was no longer seaworthy and lay abandoned in dry dock. With no great inclin-ation to repair the small vessel, he quite happily let Massey take over the operation. Fergus's enthusiasm for the task bordered on the obsessive. For someone who hailed from the midlands and hadn't learned to swim until his twenties, he loved all things nautical. Apart from the small pleasure boat he used to take them to the island, he owned a Dublin Bay seventeen-footer, one of the world's oldest surviving one-design keel boats, dating back to 1895. He raced it with a crew of three but he could sail it single-handed when he had a mind to. Along with Todd, Jamie and Ethel Cassidy, she had, on occasions, gone to watch Fergus and his picturesque rig competing in regattas.

On the crossing, she noticed a coolness between Fergus and Jillian. On the two previous trips to the island Jillian had not accompanied her husband. At the time, Fergus passed it off by saying that Jillian had relations coming to the house. But it was plain for all to see that the Masseys' marriage, unlike their boat, had hit choppy waters. After seven years, they had not succeeded in starting a family, something both of them desired and a factor that led to arguments and personal recriminations. In recent weeks, the stress in their relationship had reached breaking point. Not having them speak to each other, as today, was, in her opinion, almost preferable to the constant bickering they usually indulged in.

Never had the island seemed more like paradise to her, never had the weather been more idyllic. The sun beamed down from a cloudless sky as a soft westerly breeze fanned the heat gently around her body. It was Wednesday, which meant that unlike the weekends, they were the sole occupants on the island, except for the wildlife. Jamie, holding on to his father's hand was adamant that he didn't want to visit the derelict Martello tower, insisting instead that they take him to the inlet known as the Long Hole, a spot he called the Pirate's Cove. Fergus joined Todd and the boy on the trek. Holding Jamie between them, occasionally swinging him in the air, they headed across the rocky terrain.

Along with Jillian Massey and Ethel Cassidy, she picked out a favourite spot to sunbathe on Carrigeen Bay. They had the sandy beach all to themselves, which suited them fine. Howth Head, plainly in view across the narrow stretch of water, allowing them to make out the detail on the West Pier, was far enough away from prying eyes to offer them a sense of privacy. They were content to get into their bathing costumes, soak up the sun and indulge in a little gossip. Later they would prepare a picnic but for now, they could relax and enjoy the tranquillity. In the distance, she could hear the fading sound of Jamie as he roared with laughter every time the two adults swung him in the air.

Jillian Massey seemed unable to snap out of the bad mood she had displayed on the journey over, barely speaking, barely civil. She spread a towel on the sandy beach, stripped, put on a two-piece swimsuit, applied sunscreen, covered her eyes with Ray-Ban shades and allowed her body to relax in the heat.

Usually, Ethel brimmed with inconsequential chatter, engaging her friends in a multitude of subjects, few of any importance – mostly stories about her twin sister or other members of the orchestra and their offstage antics but today she remained subdued. As soon as Maeve became pregnant with Jamie, she quit the orchestra but she had been kept up to date on the happenings of her ex-colleagues by Ethel. Whenever she needed a babysitter, it was to Ethel she first turned.

She had become part of the family. More often than not she joined Todd, Jamie and herself on family outings.

'You're very quiet today, Ethel,' Maeve remarked. 'There's nothing wrong, I hope?'

'No, no, not a bother; I'm fine.'

'You don't sound fine to me. Come on: you can tell me. What's the matter with you?'

'Oh dammit! What the hell am I saying, of course I'm not fine – and everything's the matter with me. All right, you're going to find out sooner or later anyway. I had the most awful row with Marina last week.'

'I don't believe you. You and Marina are so close. Whatever could have brought about such a thing?'

Ethel remained quiet for a moment before answering. 'It was a personal thing – completely my fault as it happens.'

'Then where's the problem? Tell her you were in the wrong, shake hands and put the nonsense behind you.'

'I can't.'

'Don't be silly, Ethel, of course you can. This weekend, when you're performing in the Concert Hall, tell her you were a silly goose, that it was all your fault; it's as simple as that. If I know Marina, she'll hug and kiss you and forget the whole thing.'

'I can't do that.'

'What? Why ever not?'

'Because Marina has quit the orchestra. She's gone to England.'

'Quit the orchestra? Gone to England?'

'Yes, Maeve, she's gone to an uncle of ours who lives in Liverpool; he's looking after Marina until she gets her own place.'

'I still can't believe this is happening – it's all so sudden. And you say this is the result of a row between the two of you?'

'I don't want to talk any more about it right now, Maeve, if you don't mind. I'm sick to death of the whole thing.'

Maeve decided to let the matter rest for the moment. Later, when they got off the island she would bring up the subject again, see if there was anything she could do to put matters right. Meanwhile she was determined to absorb the sun's tingling warmth on her body. In a bid to get more colour on her stomach and chest, she pulled down the top part of her one-piece bathing suit to her waist. She would cover herself properly again as soon as she heard Jamie returning with the two men. Exposing her breasts in front of the men posed no problem for her but she felt self conscious about doing so in front of her son. Looking at her watch, she estimated that they would not be back for at least another half-hour. That would give her enough time to get a little tan but was short enough to avoid burning.

Glancing at Ethel, it surprised her to see that her friend had not bothered to slip into her swimsuit. Obviously she was even more troubled about the row with her sister than Maeve had suspected. Ethel, who, of the three of them, paid least attention to warnings about the sun's harmful rays, was usually the first to discard her clothes. On a previous trip to the island, Ethel insisted they should skinny-dip and had been quick to lead by example. She might not have been the prettiest of the three of them but there could be no doubting that she had the best figure. This factor had been amply borne out by the attention Todd and Fergus had given her while they were splashing about in the water. Both men had had erections while indulging in the aquatic horseplay and it had been obvious to the two wives where the stimulus had come from.

Looking at Ethel now, Maeve attempted to snap her out of the poor mood. 'Come on Ethel, get out of that dress; it's a beautiful day, enjoy the sunshine while you can.' she said.

'What? Sorry, I was miles away; what were you saying?'

'I was just wondering why you hadn't got into your swimsuit.'

'Ah, I couldn't be bothered.'

'Well, that makes a change.'

'What do you mean by that?' Ethel's voice had taken on an edge.

'Nothing at all, my dear, nothing.'

A silence ensued followed by soft sobs from Ethel. Maeve sat up, shocked by the sadness overwhelming her friend. 'There, there, Ethel, come on now; this row with your twin is not the end of the world.'

'It's not Marina I'm thinking about; it's something else. But don't worry, I'll be fine, OK, I'm fine.'

'No, Ethel, you're not fine. It's patently obvious that you're unhappy about something. If it's not Marina, then for God's sake tell me what it is that's making you so miserable.'

By this stage, Jillian had taken note of what was happening and sat up. She looked at Maeve with raised enquiring eyebrows over her Ray-Bans but remained silent. Ethel shot darting glances at her two friends, a look of consternation on her face, before jumping to her feet and running along the sand towards an incline of stone outcroppings.

'I'll follow her,' Maeve said to Jillian, 'I've never known her to act so strange.'

Ethel sat at the base of the sun-warmed rock formation, head buried in her hands, sobbing quietly, quivers going through her body. Maeve moved quietly to her side and sat down on an adjoining rock. She said nothing, waiting instead for Ethel to decide she wanted to talk. It only took a few minutes before she was rewarded for her patience. Ethel lifted her head, brushed her hand across her eyes to dry the tears and attempted a smile. 'You're not going to believe this,' she said, the words catching in a sob in her throat, 'but the truth is – the truth is, I'm pregnant.'

'What? But? But you don't – '

'I know what you were going to say, Maeve, I don't have a boyfriend. You're right, I don't have a boyfriend. But I have girlfriends – and they have husbands – and I, stupid, dim-wit that I am, allowed myself to get pregnant by one of them.'

Maeve shook her head, dispelling memories of events that had happened twelve years earlier. She did not want to dwell on her past life. Much better to live for today, she told herself, better to forget the past and the pain, forget the regrets and the recriminations. After all, that was why she had come to London, that was why she had sought refuge in the big city. Only pleasant things were supposed to happen to her here. That was the way she liked it and that was the way she wanted it to stay. Looking at her watch, she realised she had only another hour to wait before the man in her life enfolded her in his arms and made all the bad things go away.

13

According to Wilson's secretary, a woman named Bernie Collins, her boss was in Edinburgh. At least that was what she told Emma. 'He'll be there for a few days to sort out planning procedures in connection with the new hotel he has bought over there.'

'I wanted to talk to him about the statement he has just issued to the media,' Emma said. 'Perhaps you could let me have a telephone number where I could contact him.'

'I'm sorry, Ms Boylan, but Mr Wilson left strict instructions that he didn't wish to talk to the media until he attended to his business in Scotland. I can, however, give you the telephone number of his solicitors if that's any help.'

'No, that won't be necessary, I'll wait until Mr. Wilson finds the time to talk to me. If you do happen to contact him in the meantime, perhaps you'll let him know that Emma Boylan from the *Post* wishes to talk to him. OK?' Emma put the telephone down and looked at the written statement in her hand. Wilson's office had made the same statement available to every branch of the media in the country in response to Johnny Griffin's press reception. In it, Wilson formally rejected the allegations made against him. The charges were, according to the statement, nothing more than a tissue of lies, a fabrication, an opportunistic attempt to turn a good deed by him – he admitted giving the youth a lift in his car – into something that never happened.

The statement, though short on detail, gave Emma the impression that Wilson was serious about confronting the issue. From experience, she knew that people who were sure of their ground gave little away, whereas those who were lying through their teeth gave buckets of details. Nevertheless, she decided to reserve her judgement on the issue until she had an opportunity to interview both Todd Wilson and Johnny Griffin.

The day before, after recovering her car from the clampers and getting back to the *Post*, she had contacted the Paramount Hotel and asked to be put through to Marina Cassidy. No one of that name had been registered at the hotel she was informed. Emma insisted there must be a mistake, 'I've seen the woman walk through your lobby with my own eyes,' she told the person at the other end of the telephone. After much persuading, Emma managed to get the reservations manager to check it out. This enquiry got her nowhere; no lone female reservations had been made for the past two nights. Emma had hung up at this point. Ever since, she had endeavoured to discover where the elusive woman might have gone. If she wasn't a guest in the hotel, and that appeared to be the case, then what was she doing there? Had Marina Cassidy attended the press conference? Emma didn't think so; she would have noticed a woman of such striking countenance.

And yet, the more she thought about it, the more she became convinced that there had to be a connection between Johnny Griffin's press briefing and Marina Cassidy's appearance in the hotel. Accepting that she had lost her opportunity to talk to Marina, Emma concentrated instead on other avenues of investigation.

Earlier in the morning she had made attempts to line up an interview with Johnny Griffin but her efforts had come to naught. Griffin's phone – the number listed for his parent's home – had been switched to a recorded message that advised callers wanting to talk to Johnny to contact Ormsby & Neville, his solicitors. Obediently, Emma did as directed. It turned out to be a waste of time and effort. 'We are keeping Mr Johnny Griffin incommunicado until a date is fixed for a hearing,' a recorded message informed her, adding that further information could be obtained by pressing the star button and dialling the digits 304, where a Mr James Norton of Ormsby and Neville would take the caller's number and get back to them. Emma slammed the phone down. 'Thanks but no thanks,' she said aloud.

Having little choice in the matter, she decided to put the Johnny Griffin sex molestation affair on the back burner and get on with something else. Sitting at her desk, she opened the envelope that Connolly had sent her by courier. It contained copies of the crime scene photographs taken at Ethel Cassidy's house and the pictures taken inside Jamie Wilson's bedroom. They had been on her desk since the previous morning but she had not had a chance to study them until now. Even though Connolly had shown her the original photos two days previously, they still had the same breath-stopping effect on her. The graphic images of death were too horrible to contemplate. Her focus shifted to the close-up photographs of the collage of newsprint cuttings pasted on Jamie's wall, or to be more precise, the two cuttings that had been removed from the wall. If Connolly's so-called experts were right, the frag-mented bits of type read: 'Ireland's Eye Tragedy.' It wasn't much to go on but it was something. She decided to check out microfilm files of every publication for the past six years. Her decision to trawl ten year's publications was based on Jamie's age. He had been eighteen years of age when he decided to leave this world behind, so it would be unlikely that anything before the age of seven or eight would be of any great interest to the boy. If nothing startling turned up in the microfilm for that period she would have to consider looking at earlier editions. Sighing, she hoped that would not be necessary.

Before going to the archival room, she decided to have a quick word with Bob Crosby. She showed him the photographs and pointed out the partially obliter-ated headline she was attempting to chase down. 'I can't recall, offhand, any tragedy that happened on Ireland's Eye,' he said, studying the photographs. 'Mind you, there was a famous murder trial way back in the 1850s concerning the death of a young woman on Ireland's Eye but it's not very likely that young Jamie Wilson would be too concerned about that.'

'No, I don't think so either; but, tell me, what happened?'

'Well, now, Emma, I know you think I'm a bit of a dinosaur but what I'm talking about happened about a hundred and fifty years ago. I do remember reading an account of the event. Let me see now. It concerned an artist who liked to travel across to the island to paint the scenery there. What's this his name was? Ah yes! Kirwan; aye, that was the name, I'm almost sure. Anyway, a boatman from Howth would bring him across in the morning and return to ferry him back in the evening. Kirwan's wife would sometimes accompany him to the island, taking the opportunity to sunbathe while your man got on with his painting. This was all very fine and dandy until one particular day when the boatman returned in the evening to bring the pair of them back to the mainland, he discovered that the artist's wife had gone missing. After a prolonged search, they found her in an area known as the Long Hole. Her dead body lay on top of an altar-like slab of granite, a spot known ever since as the Body Rock. Apparently there were scratches on the face and blood coming from a gash on her breast but in the subsequent inquest a verdict of accidental death was recorded. That should have been the end of the matter but un-fortunately for Kirwan it didn't end there. The rumour mill went into action.'

'Nothing changes,' Emma said. 'So what happened?'

'Well, from what I remember reading, Kirwan was an argumentative individual who had a habit of getting up people's noses. Some of his neighbours with a grudge against him put it about that the artist had murdered his wife and had murdered other people before her. The rumours turned nasty when it was discovered that Kirwan was a bit of a lad. It turned out that he had a mistress with whom he had seven children.'

'What? Well, that makes a change; the mistress was the one stuck at home with the kids while the wife sunbathed.'

'I hadn't thought of it like that, Emma, but yes, I suppose it was a bit that way. Anyway, the authorities at the time took the rumours seriously enough to arrest Kirwan. The trial that followed turned out to be something of a cause célèbre in Victorian Dublin with no less a personage than Isaac Butt leading his defence.'

'The same Isaac Butt that we read about in our history books, the one who championed Home Rule for Ireland?'

'Yes Emma, the very man. He was able to prove that Kirwan had never murdered anyone and he exposed the rumours as nothing more than malicious gossip. But even with the defence of such an eminent barrister, Kirwan was still found guilty. Back then they didn't pussyfoot around; once found guilty, the penalty was death. There were many who felt the trial had been a terrible miscarriage of justice. It was subsequently discovered that Kirwan's wife had a history of poor health and was prone to fits. Her own father, it transpired, died from a fit. During the trial, the world's leading expert on forensic science, or whatever passed for forensic science at the time, concluded that the woman's death was not as a result of a homicidal drowning or suffocation but rather the result of a fit. Witnesses testified that they had seen her on different occasions convulsed in a fit. After several appeals for acquittal, Kirwan's death sentence was commuted to one of life imprisonment. That in itself proves they were unsure of the conviction. If he was guilty, they should have carried out the death sentence; if he was innocent he should have been set free. Instead they went for the worst of both worlds: life. Like I said, back then "life" meant exactly what it said.

'Kirwan continued to assert his innocence over and over again but nobody wanted to hear, at least nobody who could do anything about his predicament. After serving twenty-six years, mostly in Spike Island prison, the judiciary of the day, knowing full well that a miscarriage of justice had taken place, released him. But not wanting to lose face, and not prepared to give him the pardon he deserved, they insisted that he be deported to America. He died there a month later, a broken man.'

'And that really happened? Emma asked.

'Yes, it's all documented somewhere, court records, the whole lot. Sad story. Visitors to Ireland's Eye still visit the Long Hole in order to get a look at the infamous Body Rock. Over the decades it has taken on mythical status with stories being told of sightings of the ghost of Kirwan's wife. However, Emma, all of this is very unlikely to have anything to do with what you're looking into.'

'You're right Bob, I think I'll just work my way back through the years for the present, see if I can find some connection a bit more recent than the mysterious death of Kirwan's wife.'

'The best of luck to you Emma. Remember, what you're looking for could be anywhere; not necessarily a daily edition. It could be an article in one of the evening papers or a Sunday paper, a magazine; it could have appeared in an early edition and subsequently been dropped in a later one. You'll pardon me if I use the old cliché, but you my dear girl are looking for the proverbial needle in the haystack.'

'Jeez, thanks boss, I don't know what I'd do without your encouragement.'

'Anytime, Emma, you know me.'

Maeve forgot her annoyance as soon as she saw him. He looked a little tired, she thought, but his smile and his embrace left her in no doubt that he needed her as much as she needed him. 'I've booked a table for two in Le Gavroche,' she told him between kisses. 'We'll have to leave straight away if we want to get there by 8 o'clock.'

'Ring them; try and get them to change it to 10 o'clock instead. I've just flown in from bloody Africa and what I need right now, a damn sight more than food and wine, is a bit of love and affection, so come on let's do what we do better than anybody else.'

'Whatever do you mean?' she asked in a mock serious voice, as she loosened his tie and began to unbutton his shirt. 'You're not referring to the wonderful work we do for the starving people of the world by any chance?'

'No, I'm bloody-well not,' he said with mock annoyance, his hands busy undressing her, 'I'm talking about good old-fashioned sex, the oldest game in the book and still by far the best.'

'Don't you think I'd better ring that restaurant,' she asked, standing completely naked beside him, 'before the games commence.'

Fergus smiled, looked down at his aroused man–hood and said: 'Here, why don't you make a trunk call while you're at it.'

Two hours and ten minutes later, Maeve Wilson and Fergus Massey sat opposite each other in one of London's finest restaurants. They had ordered a taxi after their lovemaking to take them from the Cadogan to Upper Brook Street. Regarded as the high temple of haute cuisine, Le Gavroche, with it's sophisticated, clubby ambience, had played host to Maeve Wilson and Fergus Massey on their occasional odysseys from the real world. It was the sort of restaurant where, if you needed to look at the prices, you shouldn't be there.

Maeve had taken special care with her appearance and felt comfortable with herself. Fergus, who looked good in anything, as far as she was concerned, had made that little extra effort to cut a dash with his ensemble. It had been almost six months since they last dined there, so it came as a pleasant surprise that the maître d' should remember them. As on previous visits, the restaurant was busy and retained that special air of exclusivity that made Le Gavroche so special. They were given a corner table that allowed them to see the action all around them while, at the same time, being quiet enough to allow them to hold a conversation in little more than whispers. After studying the wide choice of culinary delights on the menu, written entirely in French, Maeve ordered supreme of chicken on char-grilled vegetables and red pepper cous-cous. Fergus, who invariably plumped for fish, choose sautéed scallops in a soy and spice sauce along with crisp, fried vegetable strips.

The food, when served, lived up to the high expectations they associated with the chic Mayfair restaurant. Maeve, who did not consider herself the greatest wine connoisseur in the world, though she could distinguish a New World sauvignon from a European one or a Burgundy from a Bordeaux, choose an expensive 1996 Ch Margaux from a daunting selection of 800 wines. Fergus had insisted she do the choosing but appeared to regret his little act of social grace as soon as he tasted the claret. She could tell by the expression on his face that he wanted to make some unfavourable comment but, not wanting to appear priggish, remained silent on the subject.

On special nights like this, it was usual for both of them to steer clear of happenings that affected their day-to-day involvement with SUCCOUR or anything remotely connected with their works for the Third World. Several other subjects were also avoided on these occasions. No reference was ever made to Jillian, Fergus's late wife or the circumstances of her death. Neither did they talk about Ethel Cassidy or her involvement in the past with both Todd Wilson and Fergus. In essence, they made small talk, whispered sweet nothings to each other and conserved their energies for lovemaking. Until this occasion, their make-believe world had worked fine but it was obvious that things had changed. Neither of them could totally ignore the dark clouds hovering above them. Even allowing for their plush surroundings and the gourmet food so lavishly plied, it would have been impossible for either of them to pretend that Jamie Wilson had not committed suicide or that Ethel Cassidy had not been murdered. On top of that, both of them were aware of the sexual harassment allegations being levelled against Todd Wilson. But it was a report in one of the 'scandal' weekly magazines that forced them to acknowledge the real world.

'Did you know that the *Dublin Dispatch* has a piece on the stolen funds taken from our Ethiopian operation in Tigray and Wollo?'

'No,' Maeve said, surprised by the news and even more surprised that Fergus should break their unspoken rule not to discuss business matters at times like this, 'When did this happen?'

'Today's publication. A journalist I know got in touch with me while I was still in flight, told me about it.'

'But why would the *Dublin Dispatch* want to report it in the first place? I don't understand. I thought they only went in for dirt, muckraking, innuendo, scandal and that sort of thing; why would they want to report on a robbery that took place half way across the world, for God's sake?'

'Because they're suggesting that the robbery might not have been a robbery in the strict sense of the word; they're suggesting that the affair might have been an inside job.'

Maeve rolled the stem of her wine glass between finger and thumb; all thoughts of savouring the delights of her meal having suddenly evaporated. The food and wine in front of her would now be consumed as though she were on autopilot; her mind wholly engaged on Massey's revelations. 'Where could they have got such an idea? This is very serious; we must put out a statement immediately.'

'No, I don't agree,' Fergus said. 'As long as it stays in *Dublin Dispatch* it'll attract little attention. If we issue a statement it might give the story legs. By ignoring the report, we show our contempt for the article. As to where the news came from, I think I know the answer. The Irish Aid section within the Department of Foreign Affairs have been informed that we're embroiled in a dispute with the office of the United Nations High Commissioner for Refugees. They know we're at loggerheads with the Commissioner over who should accept responsibility for the loss of the stolen money.

And we both know that Foreign Affairs are currently hung up on demanding scrutiny and accountability of charity agencies, both domestic and Third World. So they've sent an observer to look into the matter for themselves.'

'But why would they want to do that? What business is it of theirs?'

'You have to remember, they gave us the guts of two millions pounds in grants last year.'

'Oh, I see,' Maeve said, putting her wine glass down with a little more force than was necessary, 'because there's public cynicism and suspicion of all agencies, they want to be seen to cover their arses, right?'

'That's it exactly. It's my belief that the person they sent to inspect our station in Korem has been talking out of turn.'

'But, even if that's true, even if the person they sent out to investigate the matter is a blabber mouth, I still don't see where they would get the idea that the robbery was an inside job.'

'Well, the *Dublin Dispatch* points out that the money had already been paid over to SUCCOUR by the UN at the time of the raid. It is therefore our responsibility. They've got their facts all wrong as usual but I don't think it would be wise to rush into print with a statement just yet.'

'You have a point. But if it should get into the mainstream media we shall have to come out with a strong denial.'

'I agree. And now, after the bad news, I have some

good news. Do you want to hear it?'

'It will want to be very good news to lift my spirits after what you've just told me; but go on, tell me.'

'The UN Secretary-General has agreed to open our new hospital station in Tekeze officially in three months time. It'll attract world attention and will be a reminder to our supporters of the great work you do. You'll appear on world TV news shaking hands with the secretary-general, a mighty boost for your profile and that of our organisation. And there's more. You're about to be invited to a reception hosted by Queen Elizabeth in Buckingham Palace later this month which she is holding to honour humanitarian aid workers.'

'You're serious?'

'Damn right, I'm serious; now, let's finish up here and get back to the Cadogan. The night is young and I feel a flow of energy making its way up my inside thighs.'

'Oh, so that accounts for the look on your face.'

'And what look would that be?'

'Difficult to describe. Let me see. Ah yes, I'd say you have the look a cat might have in a fishmonger's shop; a mean and hungry tomcat, a thoroughly bad creature.

'I see, Maeve, and what about you? For someone who is supposed to be such a paragon of virtue, you can be a right little devil.'

14

'Yippee, yah-hoo,' Vinny yelled in delight, holding Emma by the waist and swinging her around in a circle, her feet sweeping inches above the ground.

'Put me down, put me down, you great raving moron,' Emma said through yelps of laughter.

'This is the best news in the world – you – pregnant, I can't believe it. Yippee, yah-hoo – you a mother – me a father, a dad, for God's sake. There's no chance – no fear that the gismo you used could get it wrong?'

'No, at least I don't think so; but hey, Tarzan, will you put me down and stop yelling before you wake everyone in the whole building. Hey, don't forget you're holding two people in your arms now.'

'Oh, damn, you're right, I shouldn't be swinging you around. Wasn't thinking – might do some damage. Here, you must sit down!'

Vinny put his wife down so that she sat on the side of the bed and he proceeded to lie flat on his stomach on the floor. Resting his chin on her bare feet, he grinned stupidly up at her.

Earlier, dressed in shorts and open shirt, Vinny had been busy brewing coffee in the kitchen when Emma called him back into the bathroom. She showed him the pregnancy kit and announced the results she had got from her urine test. She had sat on the stool by the side of the bath, studying his face for reaction. She need not have worried. He felt an immediate surge of joy. It was then that he had grabbed her in the wild display of excitement, brought her into the bedroom and swung her around in circles.

Now, looking at her from floor level, Vinny caressed her leg with his hand, a look of wonderment still dancing in his eyes as he tried to come to terms with the good news. 'What surprises me,' he said, 'is that it happened so soon. Just think – a Spanish conception.'

'Ah, but that's where you're wrong; I'm not so sure it happened in Spain.'

'Not in Spain – don't be daft – of course it . . . '

'No, listen, Vinny, you see, well, my periods are late. I've lost count of the days since the wedding and all the excitement – and it's only four weeks since – since Spain. So that got me thinking'

'Emma, what are you trying to say?'

'Remember our weekend in Kilkenny about a month before the wedding? Well, we weren't exactly – careful – you know. We got a little carried away – went a bit overboard, took a chance, so – '

'You're pregnant from that time?'

'I think so but I don't know for sure – '

'Well, it doesn't matter Emma, it's still the greatest news – in fact it's even better news. It means we won't have to wait as long – and it makes your decision about work that bit easier.'

'What? Sorry, what do you mean?'

'I mean, now that you're pregnant, the question of continuing with the murkier side of investigative journalism no longer arises.'

'It doesn't?'

'Well no, of course not, it couldn't. It's a question of protecting our baby. You can't do that while chasing the bad guys – no contest there – I mean, it couldn't be more black and white.'

'Not to me, it isn't,' Emma said, growing more irritated with every word from Vinny's mouth.

Vinny looked at her, surprised at her reaction. 'You're not – you're not seriously thinking of continuing to –'

'Look, Vinny, I'm sorry but I think you're going way over the top on this – you sound so old-fashioned, like someone from the Victorian age. OK, all right, I'm pregnant, it's a fact – that's great, and I'm happy. But the world doesn't have to stop spinning because of it. I can't wrap myself up in cottonwool for nine months or eight months or whatever time is left. I have a life, I have a job, I have – '

' – you have a husband who loves you, that's what you have. You have friends who are concerned about your safety, but more importantly, you have a baby on the way – an unborn baby who – '

'For Christ's sake, Vinny, give us a break! Come down from the pulpit; this is getting way too heavy.'

'Well, damn it, it is heavy. You're about to bring another human being into the world. I don't think life gets much heavier than that. You have a new responsibility now – we both have. Surely to God, you see that – you wouldn't want to endanger our child.'

Stung by Vinny's remarks, Emma opened her mouth to say something but thought better of it. She did not want to argue the matter any further, deciding she needed time to think the situation through for herself. In the meantime she would give her husband the reassurance he sought. 'I'll let nothing happen to interfere with the safety of the baby – your baby – our baby. I promise. OK?'

'OK – good.'

'After all, I'm thirty-three years of age – getting on – the old biological clock is ticking away and all that.'

'Well thank God we got that settled. I'm glad, I'm really glad. But look, Emma, I never wanted you to drop your career altogether – I just thought that – '

'It doesn't matter, Vinny; it really doesn't matter; we both want what is best.'

'Exactly, that's what I was trying to say – that's all that matters.'

'And just to be sure everything really is OK, I need to go to Dr O'Sullivan today; get him to confirm the news; find out how long I'm pregnant.'

Less than one hour later, sitting at her desk, Emma attempting to concentrate on her work but continued to think about what Vinny had said to her. It was ironic that only two mornings earlier she had told Bob Crosby that she was handing her notice in to quit. What if he had accepted her notice? She thought about that for a minute. It certainly would have brought a whole new dimension to her argument with Vinny. Being out of work would have made it very easy to stay at home during the pregnancy and that was exactly what she did not want. Vinny, she felt sure, would have considered her mad if she attempted to look for a new job at such a time. Well, that had not happened, she thought happily, and now she was determined to work all the way through the pregnancy. She smiled to herself. Maybe she would give birth to the baby right here in the newspaper office.

Her thoughts returned to the work in hand.

She had spent two hours sifting through old editions of the *Post* on microfilm the previous evening in her efforts to find a reference to the torn piece of newsprint taken from Jamie Wilson's wall. All she got for her pains were two aching eyes. It depressed her to think about the further hours still required on the monitor to get through the enormous volume of text that existed in the files. It was a daunting task but she told herself it would be worth the effort if she turned up anything that gave a clue to Jamie's frame of mind before he took his life. More importantly, it could shed some light on why Ethel Cassidy had been murdered.

In that connection, Bob Crosby had brought to her attention a matter concerning Jamie's mother, Maeve Wilson. Returning to her office after her session in front of the viewing monitor, she found a copy of the *Dublin Dispatch* on her desk. Crosby had left the publication open and had circled a small article with his trademark day-glow green marker. According to the piece, Maeve

Wilson's organisation, SUCCOUR, had been robbed of £85,000 in Africa some weeks earlier. The unnamed writer of the article reported that the recently bereaved Maeve Wilson had sent her projects manager, Fergus Massey to Ethiopia to sort out the problem. Emma could not make up her mind how seriously to take the story. The *Dublin Dispatch* was not a reliable publication, a factor evidenced by the amount of apologies they were forced to carry on a weekly basis. That, and the fact that several cases of libel had gone against them in recent court cases, greatly weakened their credibility. And yet, Emma considered that this article had a ring of truth to it. She decided it might be worth investigating the matter further and made a mental note to contact Mary Dalton, an old friend of hers, who worked in the Department of Foreign Affairs. With a bit of luck, she would find out what, if anything, lay behind the article. She was in the process of searching for Mary's number when her phone rang.

'Hello,' she said into the mouthpiece.

'Emma, is that you?'

'No, it's Ma Baker,' she joked, 'of course it's me, Vinny.'

'Wasn't sure I'd get you – thought you might be out –'

'No, I'm stuck here for the moment – so much work to do – why are you calling?'

'Just wanted to say sorry about this morning. I know I sounded like I was laying down the law but I was being stupid – said all the wrong things.'

'Yes, you were a right royal pain in the backside

and no mistake but I forgive you. I'll stand by you, as the song puts it: 'cause after all you're just a man'. Now, Vinny, can I get on with my day's work or was there something else?'

'Well, yes, actually, I wanted to remind you not to forget to see Dr O'Sullivan.'

'God, you're gas, Vinny, you're like an ould woman. Of course I'm going to see him. I have an appointment for 2.30 this afternoon in his clinic.'

'Will you let me know straight away if – if, you know – '

'Of course I will.'

'Will he – the doctor that is – will he confirm straight away – for sure if you are – '

'I don't know, Vinny. I imagine he'll need to know the date of my last period to establish the likely date of birth, do some tests – urine, blood, that sort of thing but as I've never been pregnant before – '

'Me neither,' Vinny said, realising immediately how stupid he sounded. 'Hah, what I mean is, I've never been the one responsible for getting someone in your – our situation before.'

Emma laughed into the phone. 'Vinny, you're an awful eejit, do you know that.'

'Of course I do, why else would I have married you. But seriously, Emma, call me the minute you know anything.'

'Yes, darling, you'll be the first to know, I promise.'

'Good, good. Oh, yeah, there's one other thing: I contacted my father and arranged for him to have dinner with us tomorrow night – along with your parents – you know, tell them the good news.'

'Ah, God, Vinny, I haven't had a minute to contact Mum or Dad yet with all that's happening. But I suppose there will be no problems. Where will we meet?'

'I thought we might try the Riverrun Room in the Smithfield Court; what do you think?'

'Ugh, I don't know; that's Todd Wilson's new hotel. What made you pick it? I've written some unflattering things about Wilson's choice of location. Could be awkward if I bump into him there.'

'All the more reason to check it out. I've heard the food is very good but to tell you the truth I wanted to see a collection of paintings on display there; the ones I told you about seeing in Midland Antiques on the day I bought the Harry Clarke, remember?'

'Oh yeah,' Emma said, unable to recall the conversation. 'What's so important about them?'

'Oh, nothing, nothing at all except that they're a fine collection and I thought Ciarán would love to see them.'

'Right, all right, that's settled then but listen Vinny, don't book until I contact my parents, okay?'

'Sure, see you Emma. Don't forget to let me know as soon as you know anything – from the doctor.'

'Good-bye Vinny, see you this evening.'

Emma hung up the phone and smiled to herself. Vinny's attitude always made her smile but since she told him she was pregnant he had taken on the role of mother hen. She looked at her watch and decided it was time to make a move. She would look at some more microfilm. Maybe this time she would get lucky.

Ciarán Bailey squinted his eyes, grimaced, lifted his right foot slightly off the ground and let rip with a bowel-breaking fart. 'Good arse,' he said with evident satisfaction, moving quickly away from the fouled air and returning to his small kitchen where Vinny sat sipping a cup of tea. 'D'you know what I'm going to tell you, son?' he said. 'I feel fully qualified to sit in that famous black chair they used to have in Mastermind on the television and answer questions on my chosen subject – the life and times of artist, Harry Clarke (1889–1931). I've spent the last few days researching his work, putting together a chronological framework on his output and I can tell you this: he had a short but prodigious life.'

'So why then, d'you think, he's so neglected?' Vinny asked.

'Hard to say exactly but it's probably because of Joyce, Wilde, Beckett and the like. You see the problem is, people tend to see Ireland's cultural renaissance in purely literary terms.'

'That's true enough,' Vinny agreed, 'and then of course, you have to take into account the very nature of Clarke's chosen media; to view stained glass art, you need to visit the architectural site.'

'Aye, but luckily, in the case of your purchase, *The Angel of Peace and Hope*, I've unearthed evidence that proves it is authentic. The full-scale cartoon of the window was drawn by Clarke himself in the year 1918.'

'I still can't believe I picked it up for such a small amount of dosh. I'd say we're looking at a national treasure here; maybe we should get in touch with the National Gallery or the Municipal. What d'you think?'

'You are joking,' Ciarán said. 'I wouldn't give them shaggers the steam of my piss; they're the same dumb feckers who wouldn't give Clarke the light of day when he was alive.'

'Ah, come on, Dad, we're hardly talking about the same crowd. It's well over seventy years since the Irish Government rejected the Geneva Window.'

'It's a long time ago, right enough, no denying that, but the shame of it still rankles with me. First, the Free State government commissioned Clarke to produce a work on the theme of Irish Literature for the League of Nations building in Geneva – this was back in 1926 – and then, when they saw it, they rejected it.'

'Why exactly did they reject it?' Vinny asked, even though he knew the answer, having heard his father tell the story many times in the past, but unable to resist the opportunity to let the old man give vent on one of his pet hobby horses.

'Humph, they decided that the bottle of Guinness depicted in O'Casey's Joxer panel might give foreigners a false impression of the Island of Saints and Scholars.'

'They must have had better reasons than that to reject the work, surely,' Vinny suggested, knowing what would follow.

'Oh, yes, Cosgrave's government had other objections of equal gravity. Synge's Playboy was, they claimed, depicted wearing tight breeches that showed him to be a little too virile, and the female's clothing in the Gilhooley panel, they suggested, was too transparent. Back then, it seems men were not supposed to have pricks and women no breasts or – God forbid – nipples. Holy Catholic Ireland, me arse! Philistines, the whole bloody lot of them. And, if you think that's not bad enough, Clarke's widow was forced to refund the payment for the work to the state after his death in 1931. Can you credit that?'

'They were a right bunch of gombeens, all right,' Vinny said.

'That they were,' Ciarán agreed with a sigh, 'that they were.'

'Talking of great artists, I thought you might like to see a collection of eighteen century paintings I saw on the same day I bought the Harry Clarke?'

'Sounds interesting; where are they?'

'They're hanging in the new Smithfield Court.'

'A hotel? No, I don't think I'll bother.'

'Well, you're going there anyway. That's where we're having the meal I told you about. I've arranged for Emma's parents to meet us there for dinner tomorrow night.'

'That sounds like it could be a bit of fun.'

'Yes Dad, it will be a bit of fun but I want you on your best behaviour in the restaurant. No farting, belching or telling risqué stories, OK? Remember, Emma's parents are going to be there.'

'Huh, will you listen to him; I'll bet a pound to a

penny that Emma is not badgering her Ma and Da to be on their best behaviour in front of me. Anyway, son, you're wasting your time; you see, at my time of life it's a bit late to begin watching my p's and q's. Tell us though, what exactly is this dinner in aid of?'

'Curiosity killed the cat – you'll find out when we get there.'

'Oh, so I'm right, there is a reason.'

'Dad, honestly, you're impossible. Just have patience, wear your Sunday best clobber and all shall be revealed soon enough.'

15

Even a city like London had its quiet moments. Such a thought had never occurred to her before. It was 4.15 in the morning. Maeve Wilson lay awake, her mind alert, at odds with her exhausted body. The curtains shifted gently against the bedroom's tall casement windows, an early morning breeze buffeted the rich fabric as it made its way through the open fly-section. Beside her, Fergus Massey slept, his body moving in undulating rhythm to the sound of his low, almost musical, snoring.

Twenty minutes earlier it had been a different story. Lost in some nightmare, shouting unintelligible words, he had suddenly sat bolt upright and backed his body rigidly against the bed's headboard, a look of horror on his face. His arms flayed about like a man drowning, his mouth opening and closing as though unable to breathe. Her attempts to pacify him, to tell him he was only dreaming, were of little avail. He pushed her away forcibly, staring through her with hostile eyes. Then, as suddenly as the episode had begun, his body relaxed once more, his eyes closed and his breathing difficulties eased. Holding him in her arms, she had soothed him, like a baby, back to peaceful sleep. It wasn't the first time she had known him to have such a nightmare but she knew from past experience, he would be unable to remember any of it the next morning.

Carefully, she laid back the cover and eased her legs on to the floor, hoping her movement would not disturb his sleep. For a few seconds she sat on the edge of the bed, her weariness all-encompassing. A faint headache made its presence felt. She would have to take two Anadin Extra; they always worked for her at times like this. Plush carpet pile met her feet as she stood, put on her dressing-gown and moved stiffly towards the bathroom. Her thoughts remained with the man sleeping in the warm bed she had just vacated.

Some time before Fergus's nightmare had disturbed her sleep, their love making had been energetic, maybe too energetic. Gratification of the flesh had been achieved, though in a primitive, wanton sort of way. It was as if they were both unconsciously trying to exorcise the host of demons that clung to them wherever they went, an all-invasive stranglehold that refused to allow them escape from a haunted past.

He was still asleep, that suited her. She needed time and space to herself to think, time to unravel the half-formed thoughts playing silly buggers with her mind. Reflected light from the street lamps cast a soft yellowish glow on the objects and furniture in the darkened hotel suite and almost succeeded in lulling her brain into a false calm. Visiting the bathroom, she answered nature's call, flushed the toilet and hoped the gurgling sound did not travel to the bedroom. She rummaged about for her Anadins and found them eventually in her toilet bag. Stupid place to put them, she told herself. Like a sleepwalker, she moved into the lounge in silence. It was too quiet. She turned on the radio, keeping the volume low, and pressed the buttons that changed the waveband frequencies. After rejecting two phone-in talk shows, she found a classical music programme to her liking. She moved to the drinks cabinet, opened its door and blinked as the harsh white light from its interior hurt her eyes momentarily. Her throat felt dry but she did not want an alcoholic drink; she'd had too much of that earlier in the night. She poured herself a glass of mineral water, washed down the two headache tablets and continued to drink from the glass until it was empty. Feeling better, she sat on the most comfortable couch in the room, wrapped her dressing-gown around her legs, brought her knees up to her chest, hugged them and allowed her thoughts to return once more to the man sleeping in the adjacent room.

For the umpteenth thousandth time, she asked herself the same question: how was it that she had ended up with her husband's best friend as her lover? And for the umpteenth time, she found herself unable to come up with a satisfactory answer. She thought about her husband, Todd, and sighed. What a predicament to find herself in. Although the two men confided in each other – they had, after all, been friends since college days and still retained a close business relationship – Todd remained unaware of Massey's liaison with her. She preferred not to think about the consequences should he ever find out. How had it all happened? Why had life's strange twists and turns woven such a web of complicity for her. Thinking about this, she tried to hold back the tears forming in her eyes but could not. Even the beauty of Beethoven's Violin Concerto playing softly on the radio failed to deliver the sense of escapism she desired.

Thoughts of her son, and the short life he had lived demanded her attention. Since Jamie's funeral one question, along with all the others, bothered her greatly: had he discovered that she was having an affair with Fergus Massey? Had someone told him? Ethel Cassidy, she suspected, had a shrewd idea that something was going on between the two of them, but did she ever voice her suspicions to Jamie? Unlikely. Thinking about the close bond that had existed between her son and her one time friend, Ethel Cassidy, never ceased to cause her pain. From the radio, she could hear Schumann's Symphony No 1 but her thoughts, for once, not soothed by the sweet 'Spring' music, insisted on travelling back to a period of time in her life when she, and her friends, had been pulled apart in such drastic fashion.

Ethel Cassidy sat on the boulder at the base of a weather-worn outcrop, shaded from the sun by its amorphous rock mass, her eyes still red from tears. She avoided eye contact with Maeve. Instead, she gazed across the stretch of water that divided Ireland's Eye from Howth harbour and the mainland. Sounds of gulls, squawking as they glided through a perfectly clear blue sky, sounds of the soft perpetual murmur of waves advancing, breaking and receding on the shore, served to accentuate the awkward silence between the two young women. It had been several seconds since either had spoken. Maeve eventually broke the spell. 'I don't understand any of this, I don't know what to say.'

'What is there to understand? What is there to say?' Ethel asked cynically. 'It's all very simple really. I did something stupid, very very stupid; I went and got myself pregnant.'

'Yes, yes, that's what you said, but – well the thing is, I'm trying to understand your remark about who was responsible. Maybe I picked up what you said wrongly – I don't know – but you mentioned something about girlfriends who had husbands – are you saying that – that someone's husband is responsible for – for – ?'

'For making me pregnant; that is what you're asking, right?

'Well, yes, it's a damned odd sort of thing to say. Myself and Jillian are your friends – and we've both got husbands. Are you suggesting that – that – ?'

Ethel was about to answer but stopped when she saw Jillian Massey approach. Jillian had slipped a towelling beach wrap over her swimsuit but continued to wear her sunglasses. Seeing the distressed look on Ethel's face, she turned to Maeve for an answer. 'What's the matter with her?'

'I think it might be better if I let her tell you herself,' Maeve said a little testily.

Nobody said anything while Ethel's gaze appeared to fix on Howth's sea front, a sad wistful expression on her face. Out to sea, a ferry ploughed its way from Dun Laoghaire harbour on its way to Holyhead, yellow-beaked gulls bobbing on the boat's white swell. Jillian, not getting a reply from either of her friends, shrugged her shoulders, removed her sunshades and sat down beside Maeve. 'Will someone, for Christ's sake, tell me what's the matter?'

'An awful lot's the matter,' Maeve replied, 'Ethel's sister has left the orchestra and gone to England, but that's only the half of it. Ethel tells me she's pregnant.

The shock on Jillian's face quickly turned to a sneer. 'Marina gone to England? Ethel pregnant? Pregnant? Well, I'll be damned.' she said, giving a sceptical lift of her eyebrows. 'Maybe you'll tell me what the trick is; maybe you'll tell myself and Fergus what we're doing wrong while you're at it. Huh, I don't know why you're so upset. I'd give anything to be in your place.'

Ethel turned to look at Jillian, her face a mask of desperation. Her mouth attempting to form words, her lips trembling, but she seemed unsure of what she should say. Instead, she began to sob again. Maeve stood up and walked towards the water's edge. She had only made a few strides when she wheeled around with a petulant jerk of her shoulders, clamped her hands on her hips in an expression of irritation and addressed Jillian. 'Our good friend Ethel here tells me that she has been made pregnant by the husband of one of her girlfriends, no less.'

It took a second before the import of Maeve's words fully registered with Jillian. In that moment, as she marshalled her thoughts, a seagull swooped low above the outcrop where Ethel sat, its raucous cry punctuating the heavy silence between the three friends. When Jillian spoke, her voice had taken on a bitter edge that neither Maeve or Ethel had heard before. 'Are you by any chance accusing my husband, Fergus,' she asked, 'or are you accusing Maeve's husband of fathering this child that you are expecting?'

'I'm accusing myself, no one else. Now leave me alone both of you; go back to your precious husbands.'

'I'm not going anywhere until I get some answers,' Jillian said, almost shouting. 'You were the one to start this. I demand an answer. I want to know if you are accusing my husband of getting you in the family way. A simple yes or no will suffice.'

Maeve's question was even more direct. 'Have you and Todd been having sex?'

'Leave me alone, I don't have to answer either of you. I refused to answer Marina and I refuse to answer you. If you're both so unsure of your darling husbands, why not put the question to them; see what they have to say for themselves.'

Maeve and Jillian reacted with fury to this remark. Jillian attempted to grab Ethel and knock her off the rock but slipped and fell in the process. She cut her knees on a pile of sharp-edged stones at the base of the outcrop. By the time she recovered and picked herself up again, Ethel had begun to move from one rock to another, climbing higher up the rock front, using her fingertips and toes to strive towards the summit some twenty feet above her. Jillian set out after her with Maeve in tow. 'Come back down here and don't be stupid,' Jillian shouted. 'Where the fuck do you think you're going?'

'Go away! Go away, both of you, you hear? If you don't leave me alone I'll jump! You hear me? I said I'll jump, kill myself!'

'Yeah, go ahead, jump, huh; the only jump you're good for is the one that gets you knocked up,' Jillian said, steadily making her way towards Ethel. Maeve tugged at Jillian's beach wrap. 'This is all wrong,' she gasped. 'Let's get down from these rocks; they're dangerous. Let's get back on the ground and talk about the situation. We're friends; we can sort this thing out.'

'Friends, my granny's big fat arse!' Jillian shouted over her shoulder to Maeve, 'I don't call someone who accuses my husband of screwing her a friend.'

'She hasn't accused Fergus of . . . or Todd.'

'She hasn't denied it either,' Jillian shouted back. By now Jillian had got to within arms reach of Ethel. Maeve edged her way back to the base. 'Come back down here both of you,' she shouted as she watched Jillian reach out and grab Ethel. In a blind panic, Ethel kicked out at Jillian with the heel of her foot, attempting to free herself. The blow caught Jillian on the side of her head. Jillian screamed. Her hand shot to the spot where she had been hit. She lost her foothold. In horror, Maeve watched as her friend fell backwards from the rock face. Maeve's scream echoed the falling woman's terrified wail. Jillian landed awkwardly on her back, one leg twisting back underneath her. The side of her head caught the sharp edge of rock. Maeve ran towards her, still screaming. One look at Jillian's face told her the worst.

Maeve's thoughts re-emerged from the painful journey through the tunnel of time. She wiped the tears from her eyes. Although twelve years had elapsed since the awful day on Ireland's Eye, she could still picture the face of her dead friend. So much had happened in the intervening years, so very much. But with all that had happened since that tragic day, she still found it difficult to figure out how Jillian's husband had found his way into her bed and into her heart.

Todd Wilson's flight back from Edinburgh to Dublin had given him time to think about the predicament he found himself in. He had sorted out the difficulties that had arisen in connection with The Thistle and Rose. Sorting out planning irregularities and meeting with the various authorities that had a say in his develop– ment plans for the hotel had been a welcome diversion from the domestic strife currently bedevilling his life. It bothered him to know that Maeve would have read about the sexual harassment case being brought against him by Johnny Griffin. Even allowing for the rough patch their marriage had hit in the past few years, he felt sure she would not believe him capable of such sordid behaviour.

Waiting for the Edinburgh luggage to arrive on the carousel in the arrivals area, he spotted Fergus Massey some distance away. Massey, in conversation with two men, stood to one side of a group of passengers who had flown in on the Heathrow flight and were now busy collecting their luggage. Todd's attention was distracted momentarily by the arrival of his own luggage but having retrieved it, he approached his long-time friend. Massey's two companions had taken off before introductions could be made.

'Hello, Fergus,' Todd said, taken aback by the two men's sudden departure. 'Good to see you: what y'doing here?

'Todd, hey, this is a surprise. I'm back from a spot of business in London. Where are you coming from yourself?'

'I was over in Edinburgh for a few days; had to sort out a few bits and pieces that were causing problems with the Thistle and Rose, nothing serious though. Tell me, who were the lads talking to you? Hope they didn't run off on my account?'

'No, not at all, Todd; they're part of my crew for next month's yacht race around Ireland. They were telling me about a few difficulties they're experiencing with the boat.'

'Glad to see you don't let work get in the way of your sailing.'

'It's important to make time for the things that are important, Todd.'

'Well in that case, maybe you'll have time for a coffee

with me, Fergus. There's a few things I'd like to run by you – if you have the time, that is.'

'Yeah, sure, why not. There's a café on the departure floor.'

They found a space and chatted amiably over coffee and scones, getting the small talk out of the way before moving on to more serious topics. Todd discussed the problems he was experiencing over the Johnny Griffin business and asked for Fergus's advice on how best he should tackle the case. Fergus nodded gravely as he listened to his friend go through his list of woes. When Massey spoke, his advice could not be more clear-cut. 'You should hire the best firm of PR people available.

'Public Relations? I don't think so, Fergus. That lot are all spin and no content, spouting out pure waffle that nobody really believes. I'd have thought it more important to hire the best firm of solicitors available.'

'You already have the top legal people on your side, Todd. The problem is: this case against you won't come to court for ages. That gives the press all the freedom in the world to declare open season on your reputation.'

'Nothing new in that. It's been open season on me for as long as I can remember; shit, I often think I've become the nation's favourite blood sport. If you were to believe that bitch from the *Post*, Emma Boylan, you'd think I was public enemy number one.

'Exactly, Todd, which is why you need public relations. Your accuser, Johnny Griffin has already hired a PR firm; you must do the same. That way you can bring the media on side. They're a pack of vultures and must be fed. To read their stuff you'd think butter wouldn't melt in their mouths, that they were lily-white paragons of virtue, but they're not, Todd: they can be bought just like everyone else. So, you must wine and dine the bastards, send them presents, appeal to their vanities, wipe their arses if necessary but get them on your side.'

'Somehow, Fergus, I can't see Emma Boylan falling for that sort of patronising crap, can you?'

'Ah, I wouldn't be so sure, Todd. In her case maybe you could try a little *pubic* relations.' Todd did not find the remark funny but laughed along with Fergus anyway. Fergus wasn't finished on the subject of Emma Boylan. 'She's a woman – and you know what women are like, clitoris all-sorts, a little bit of what they like goes a long way.'

'I'm not so sure I agree with you on that score. That sort of thing might work for you; women are putty in your hands; they go weak at the knees for you, but I'm not in your league when it comes to the flattery business. So, that being the case, what do you suggest?'

'You're probably right, Todd; bullshit won't wash with this Boylan dame, and I'll have to admit she's unlikely to lust after your body, so you'll have to take the straight talking approach instead. Contact her yourself, say you read her articles and would welcome an opportunity to show what an up-front decent bloke you are. Invite her to stay for a weekend in one of your hotels, free of charge of course, and while you're at it, take out a series of advertisements for your hotels with the *Post* – a big spend – and there won't be a peep out of that lot. It's called public relations, Todd, and believe me it works.'

Todd nodded, finding his friend's advice to be well worth considering. The two men chatted about how to go about finding the right PR firm before Todd brought the subject back to his wife. 'I know this is awkward for you Fergus, what with you and Maeve working for the same organisation, but can you tell me where she is at the moment? It's most important that I talk to her. Have you seen her recently at all?'

'No, I haven't seen her since she came back to the office after the funeral for a few hours. I've been over in Ethiopia since then – flew back via London to do a spot of business – so I've not laid eyes on the good woman.'

'When do you expect to see her next?' Todd asked, knowing how pathetic he sounded.

'As a matter of fact I'll see her in two days time. We have a policy in SUCCOUR always to have a photocall when our trucks depart or arrive back from their Third World destinations. It's good PR.'

'You really are big into the PR angle.'

'Yes, Todd. I tell you it's your only man. It's especially important in my case; it lets the good people of this country know what their contributions have achieved.'

'Tell me, which port will the lorry come ashore?

'Rosslare Harbour. You want me to give her a message from you?'

'No, Fergus, I'll go down there myself; it's high time the two of us met face to face.'

16

The Smithfield Court Hotel felt justifiably pleased with itself for having had the foresight to incorporate an art gallery in its foyer structure. Named the Dedalus Gallery, after James Joyce's character from *A Portrait of the Artist as a Young Man*, it comprised a spacious area off the main lobby that doubled as an outsize anteroom for the hotel's bars and restaurant.

As a first-time visitor to the gallery, Vinny was impressed. Along with his father, Ciarán, and his father-in-law, Arthur Boylan, he studied the paintings with varying degrees of enthusiasm. He had already acquainted himself with some of the works when he visited the Midland Antiques shop but seeing them properly displayed in such sumptuous surroundings imbued the collection with a more positive sense of their worth.

Vinny's father Ciarán, inspected the paintings with the keen eyes of an expert. Next to him, Arthur Boylan, gazed at the elaborately framed canvases with bored detachment. He pondered on the length of time it was taking his wife Hazel and his daughter Emma to do whatever it was women usually did in the powder room. Never one for hanging around hotel lobbies, even one as grand as the Smithfield Court's, he liked to get into the bar for a few drinks before the meal.

'Well, what do you think of the paintings?' Vinny asked his father. Ciarán acknowledged the question with a nod of the head, too intent in scrutinising the pictures to make verbal comment. His eyes lingered on an unsigned painting that showed a family group of five young men standing behind a seated woman, all of them dressed in the best of eighteenth-century finery. 'This is a version of one of Romney's greatest works, The Beaumont Family,' he said at length, 'but one I haven't seen before.'

'It's probably a copy,' Vinny suggested. 'Why would he paint two versions of the same family? Could it be the work of one of his apprentices, a reworking of Romney's original.'

'No, it's definitely the work of Romney himself; his brushwork is unmistakable. Quite remarkable, really. Did you know that in his day – back around the 1790s or thereabouts – he was considered to be on a level with Reynolds and Gainsborough?'

'And was he?'

'Well, no, not really but he was still a great artist. I suppose he might have lacked the depth and substance in his art that we associate with his two illustrious contemporaries but I'll tell you this, Vinny, he's still a damn sight better than a lot of the chancers who call themselves artists today.'

As father and son discussed each painting in turn, Arthur Boylan listened to their observations feeling at a loss to comment on the merits or otherwise of their discourse because of his lack of expertise on the subject. For all he knew, they could have been talking absolute balderdash and nonsense, though he had to admit Ciarán's comments sounded well-founded and impressive. Nevertheless, he was glad when the ladies finally emerged from the powder room.

The meal in the Riverrun Room, a spectacular restaurant that used portraits of literary characters from James Joyce's writings for its decorative theme, was proving to be a great success. For the most part, the success was due to Ciarán Bailey's loquacity, lubricated in generous measure by red and white Chateau Vignelaure, and delicious food. Emma and her mother, Hazel, both chose the chef's recommendation for the day – succulent salmon trout, flavoured with lemon and flaked with mashed potatoes and parsley; Vinny choose sole on the bone; Ciarán went for the supreme of chicken and Emma's father, Arthur, ever the straight laced solicitor, insisted on a well-done sirloin steak.

Before the meal began, Vinny passed around the photographs he had taken in Spain on the honeymoon. Each picture was greeted with the appropriate oohs and ahs and good-humoured banter. In one particular photograph, a shot of Emma sipping a glass of red wine, she bore a striking resemblance to her mother, a fact that everyone commented on. Hazel Boylan, a good-looking sprightly woman with a short pageboy hairstyle, looked far too young to be Emma's mother and reacted with delight when Ciarán made flattering remarks to that effect.

Vinny was pleased with the effort his father had taken to dress for the occasion; compared to Arthur Boylan's safe three-piece blue-grey suit, Ciarán's ensemble represented the height of sartorial elegance. Wearing a multi-coloured cravat, white shirt, tweed jacket and cavalry twill slacks, he looked every inch the country squire. Only his Vandyke beard and longish hair gave evidence of his artistic status.

After the dessert had been served, a waiter, responding to a cue from Vinny, brought a bottle of Bollinger Grande Année 1988 and fresh glasses to the table.

'I would like you all to join Emma and me in a special toast,' Vinny announced, as the champagne cork popped and their glasses filled with the fine golden liquid. Emma got up from her place at the table, moved to Vinny's side and placed one arm around his waist. 'Vinny and I,' she said, 'are proud to announce that we are soon to become parents.'

Even the restaurant staff joined in the round of applause and the cheering. Emma and Vinny kissed each other to expressions of delight from the others at the table. Arthur Boylan ordered King Edward cigars for the men. The celebrations continued unabated until well after midnight by which time they, in marked contrast to Emma and Hazel, were showing signs of their alcohol intake. It was not until all the other diners had gone home that Vinny brought up the subject of Emma's role as a mother and how he had advised her to take a break from her work with the *Post*. With the effect of his prodigious alcohol consumption colouring his speech patterns, he talked about the dangers his wife had been subjecting herself to in recent times. 'It's my opinion,' he stated, 'that a mother-to-be should not be involved in the shady shenanigans of murders and the likes. Emma and me have had a bit of a barney, or heated words if you prefer, on the subject so I'm hoping that you, her closest friends, her kith 'n' kin, so-to-speak, can drill a bit of sense into that pretty-little-head-of-hers and get her to see a bit of sense, get her to see that what I'm saying is right. Right? I want you to convince her to take it easy. What do you say, eh?'

Ciarán, who had not seen his son this inebriated in a long time was about to ask Emma for her view on the subject but gave way to Hazel when she opened her mouth to speak.

'I agree with Vinny wholeheartedly,' she said firmly, 'Emma's first priority is to safeguard the welfare of the new life growing inside her. Giving up her job for a few months should be the least of her concerns. Besides, it'll do her good to get away from all that dreadful crime stuff she writes about in her paper – such ghastly people.'

Vinny, standing unsteadily on his feet, held out his glass to Hazel in a display of support and removed a half smoked cigar from his mouth. 'I couldn't agree with you more, Hazel,' he said, his speech slightly slurred, before turning his attention to Emma. 'That's the best course of action all around, definitely the best course of action. Right, we're all agreed on that, aren't we, Emma?'

Emma made no reply.

'Yes, we both agree with Hazel,' he continued, taking another mouthful of champagne, 'Emma will put her investigative journalism career on hold for the moment – until the happy event, that is – and do something a little less dangerous.'

This announcement was greeted with general enthusiasm.

'Vinny's absolutely right, my dear,' Arthur Boylan said to his daughter, through a haze of cigar smoke. 'Not the sort of place for a young woman in the first place, if you ask me, especially a pregnant one.'

'It's great news,' Hazel said, 'I'm proud of you, Emma. I can look forward to being a grandmother now without having to worry about the riffraff you're forced to rub shoulders with.'

Ciarán, who had been watching Emma's reaction to what was being said, noted her silence and saw the look of concern on her face. 'Well now, Emma,' he said. 'Looks to me like everyone here has decided on your future plans – and I'm thinking that maybe it's about time we heard what you think yourself.'

Before Emma could answer, Vinny interrupted. 'I told you, Dad, Emma and I have decided – '

'No, Vinny,' Emma cut in, almost shouting. 'We have not decided on anything. You may have decided. Mum and Dad may have decided but Ciarán is right: nobody seems too bothered about what I want.'

'But – but this is not – not – ' Vinny stammered.

'I don't understand,' Arthur said, 'I don't understand at all.'

'What are you saying – ' Hazel asked, with a bewildered expression on her face.

'She's being damn silly,' Vinny said, gesticulating with a cigar in one hand and a glass of champagne in the other, spilling some of its contents on to the floor as he did so, 'you're being – '

'I've had enough of this,' Emma said, unwilling to listen to another word from her husband. She stood up from her chair, walked around to where Vinny sat, took the cigar out of his hand and dumped it into his champagne glass. 'I'm going for a breath of fresh air,' she said. 'My baby's health is in far more danger from the smoke in this room than anything that might happen in my line of work as an investigative journalist.' Without another word, she walked out of the restaurant.

The Admiral Bagnall Hotel in Rosslare might not be in the same class as the Smithfield Court but the view it afforded its guests was infinitely better. Sitting in the hotel's lounge, sipping a mineral water, Maeve Wilson glanced through the huge plate glass window that acted as the lounge's front wall, and looked towards the ferry terminal. Putting the glass down, she massaged her temples with the ends of her fingers and lapsed into thoughtfulness. She had arrived two hours earlier in Rosslare aboard the Fishguard ferry and would have to wait another hour before the La Harve ferry pulled alongside the pier. When it did she would have to be ready to welcome home the SUCCOUR lorry from its latest mercy trip to Ethiopia. Like all aid and mercy agencies, her organisation, SUCCOUR was feeling the effects of a dwindling money supply. Public sympathy had been stretched to breaking point. Commentators on radio and television as well as the press were keen to highlight the millions of pounds being spent on arms by Ethiopia's own government. Given this background, it had become something of an uphill struggle to appeal to people's generosity. It was a far cry from how it used to be.

Back in 1984, Maeve had been going through a particularly bad patch in her marriage. Jamie had begun attending kindergarten and she found herself alone in the big house with nothing of any great interest to occupy her. She was young, attractive, a woman in the prime of life but already she had begun to ask herself: is this all there is? Seeing Todd's morose face each morning across the breakfast table had the effect of irritating her. Their once monthly session of love-making – if what they did in bed could be dignified by that term – had become something of a chore to be endured rather than enjoyed. But it wasn't just that the enjoyment had gone out of their lovemaking – it had never been great to start with. It was more a question of life having nothing to offer her. She no longer played the violin; she seldom met her friends from those days with the orchestra. There were plenty of social outings on offer but they were always connected to Todd's business and always populated by his friends.

She was, in a word, bored. She needed an outlet for her energies.

About this time, she had heard Bob Geldof's passionate appeal to everyone looking in on the famous Live Aid concert to send in some 'fucking money' to help the starving people of the Third World. Geldof's pleading and the multiple pictures of starving children spliced together to the Cars song, 'Who's Gonna Drive You Home', had a powerful effect on her. She wanted to help. Everyone wanted to help. But nothing would have happened if Todd hadn't unintentionally spurred her into action.

A packet of condoms, of all things, had forced her into making the biggest decision of her life. She had found them in Todd's pockets at a time when he was fully aware that she was on the pill. For once, she didn't even bother to confront him on the issue of his infidelities. She decided to get as far away from the problem as she could. Going to Africa seemed like a good idea. Ethel Cassidy, her long-time friend had agreed to look after Jamie in her absence.

Arriving in Addis Ababa for the first time as a mercy volunteer, her outlook on the ways of the world changed in the most profound way. Not sure of what to expect she journeyed overland with three other volunteers for 300 miles northwards through mountainous terrain, awed by Ethiopia's vast emptiness, until she arrived in the town of Korem in the province of Wollo, just below the border with Tigray.

Feelings of loneliness, of missing Jamie, were ever present but within days, when confronted by the human catastrophe all around her, these self-obsessed thoughts lessened considerably. Nothing could have prepared her for the shock of seeing so many sick and malnourished families. It was as though all the suffering of the world had been consigned to this one area of crumbling thirsty earth. All around her she was confronted by the stench of disease and poverty. How could a merciful God – the one the nuns had told her all about in school – allow the painful cries of children, little more than living skeletons, to go unheeded?

She had at first been totally overwhelmed by the scale of the suffering, but with experience she had learned to subdue her emotions in order to get on with her work. And she did work. She threw herself body and soul into the task at hand with a zeal that she never would have believed she possessed. She attended the sick; people suffering from pneumonia, measles, whooping cough and the ever-present relapsing fever. Relapsing fever was the most vicious killer among the adults she had attended. Transmitted by lice or ticks, the infectious disease induced vomiting, violent shivering, delirium and, in the end, merciful release. It had been her job to comfort these people who lay in their own diarrhoea, their bodies crawling with lice. She administered oral rehydration salts and intravenous dextrose wherever she could but many continued to die. She attended skeletally thin children, their skin pulled tight over cheekbones and shoulder blades that threatened to cut the skins of their backs; children too sick to wave away the flies on their faces. The hell that the nuns talked about in her school days paled when compared to this experience.

After eighteen months of work at hell's front line she returned to Ireland, a born-again human being. Seeing Jamie was wonderful but even more surprising to her, she found it in her heart to welcome Todd back into her arms. But the experience in Africa meant things would never quite be the same again. Her exploits there did not go unnoticed by the Irish media. She was invited to appear on several television and radio talk shows. Full-page features in magazines and newspapers were loud in their praise for what she had done. Hers was an interesting story to tell; the glamorous musician who had put her violin aside in order to bring comfort to the sick and hungry of the Third World. Within six months she had, along with Todd and his friend Fergus Massey, and the encouragement of the whole nation, set up her own organisation. SUCCOUR was born.

Older and wiser now, she sat in the lounge of the Admiral Bagnall Hotel wondering how it had all gone so flat. The glory days of the pioneering amateurs had vanished like a whiff of morning mist. Foreign aid had become big business. Her early success had a lot to do with the energy she employed in megaphone lobbying on behalf of the Third World poor. She had provided a wonderful image to the public of herself as a selfless and heroic woman helping the less fortunate of the world. It was an image that allowed her to become a major player in the business.

The smile that Fergus Massey's approach brought to her face vanished the instant she noticed Todd walking behind him. A subliminal expression in Massey's eye told her: don't blame me, I had nothing to do with this. His words, when he spoke, gave a very different impression, his inflection attempting, but failing, to convey an air of conviviality. 'Hi, Maeve, will you just look at who I just happened to bump into!' Before Maeve could open her mouth to reply, Todd cut in. 'Ah, so this is where you've been hiding,' he said, attempting light-hearted banter but sounding even less convincing than Massey. 'Well, you know what they say: if Muhammad won't come to the mountain then the mountain will have to come to Mohammed.' His false laugh was met with stony silence. In this moment of acute awkwardness, the two men sat down opposite her.

'What brings you here, Todd?' Maeve asked.

'We need to talk.'

'Here?'

'Well, I've tried to talk to you ever since – '

'Sorry, I've been – I've been busy.'

'No, Maeve, you've been avoiding me. A lot of things have happened since Jamie's death. We are – we're his parents.'

Maeve made no reply. Massey, his embarrassment evident, stood up. 'If you'll just excuse me for a moment, I need to go to the little boy's room.'

Free of Massey, Todd fixed his wife with a stern stare. 'Jesus Christ, Maeve, what the hell is going on? Our son takes his own life; everything we both worked for is falling apart and you pull a disappearing act on me. What the hell are you playing at? The media are crawling all over me, trying to crucify me. They're dragging up old business deals I conducted years and years ago. And, as though that were not enough, they're trying to make out that I'm some sort of pervert. Have you read what they're saying about me?'

Maeve nodded but held her counsel.

'All of a sudden, I'm supposed to be a goddamned fucking queer. How about that? Can you bloody well credit that.'

Maeve's smile was not pretty. 'And you'd like me by your side, is that it?' she said, making no attempt to mask her cynicism. 'You'd like me to confirm that you are strictly heterosexual; a macho man, a woman's man! Is that it?'

'I think it might be beneficial to both of us to be seen to stick together at a critical time like this.'

'Look, Todd, I really don't know where you're coming from with this but if it's an affirmation of your manly prowess that you want, I should remind you that it's at least six years since we attempted anything of that nature. If memory serves me right, you were unable to rise to the occasion at the time. A flat, flaccid performance as I recall, not what I'd call a ringing endorsement of your manliness.'

'You really are a bitch, you know that?'

'Yes, I suppose I am. Well, at least it's nice to hear there's no doubt in regard to my gender.'

Todd held his hands up in a gesture of peace. 'All I'm saying is that a show of solidarity would be good for both of us. Show the world that in spite of what has happened to Jamie, in spite of that awful tragedy, we're brave parents, willing to fight adversity together. United, we can take on the media, let them see we're a unit, let them see we're not prepared to put up with all this crap they're throwing at us.'

'You'll pardon me if I've got this wrong Todd, but aren't you the one in trouble with the media?'

'Yes, that's true but we're both targets. It's almost as though someone is deliberately setting us up. Your organisation has come in for some stick in the media of late on account of some missing funds. So you see, my dear, we could both do with each other's help.'

Maeve was about to react to his words when Fergus Massey returned to his seat. 'I hate to interrupt this cosy little chat between husband and wife,' he said, glancing at his wristwatch, 'but our lorry should be rolling off the ferry in the next ten minutes or so. Time we got down to the harbour while some daylight remains to welcome our hero home. You're welcome to string along if you'd like Todd; the three of us can have a drink afterwards. What do you say?'

Before Todd could decline or accept the offer, Maeve made her feelings abundantly clear. 'Sorry Fergus, but I don't want Todd next-or-near the photographers when they start clicking their cameras in front of the lorry. Right now, SUCCOUR can do without being associated with someone who stands accused of dodgy business dealings and having a liking for pretty boys.'

Todd leaped to his feet and grabbed Maeve by her shoulders. 'What sort of bitch have you become. I'm beginning to think that maybe you're the one behind all the shit that's happening to me. Maybe you're the one . . .'

'Stop it, both of you,' Fergus yelled as he attempted to disentangle Maeve from her husband. All three of them were shouting ugly insults at each other when the hotel manager, accompanied by a well-dressed man in grey pinstripes, approached them. 'Excuse me,' the manager said, 'could I interrupt for a second?' Todd, Fergus and Maeve fell silent and glared at the two newcomers. 'This gentleman here,' the manager said, indicating the man beside him, 'wishes to have a word with Mrs Wilson.'

Maeve squinted her eyes as she looked at the man. He was tall, over six feet, and wore a felt hat. She put his age somewhere in the mid-fifties and thought he had a kindly face. 'What can I do for you?' she asked politely.

'I wish to give you something,' he said, taking a large white envelope from his inside jacket pocket. 'It's a subpoena for you, Mrs Wilson.'

'A subpoena? What on earth for?'

'It obliges you to attend an all-party government committee who are investigating financial irregularities that have arisen in connection with certain aid agencies.' Without another word, the man placed the envelope in Maeve Wilson's hand, tipped his hat with his index finger, turned on his heel and walked away.

Stunned by what had happened Maeve looked to Massey, who seemed to have paled during the exchange, for some sort of explanation. But it was Todd who reacted first. 'Now, maybe you'll listen to what I'm saying, Maeve. Now maybe you'll believe me when I say there's a conspiracy to destroy us. Someone is trying to screw both of us.'

'No, Todd, I don't think so,' Maeve said, her voice shaking with rage, 'I think this is all your doing. I think you've set this whole thing up to get me back on your side, to help you save your own skin. That's what this is.'

17

Emma watched the digital display on the electronic alarm clock blink its way forward to 7.30 am and reached out to cancel the chimes before they began. Gingerly, she eased her body from between the sheets and headed straight for the bathroom. After responding to nature's first call she entered the shower, turned on the water, adjusted the temperature and let the spray of warm water pelt her body. It felt good. Although she had restricted herself to only a few sips of wine, her head was not in the best of shape. She pressed her forehead gently against the cold tiles of the shower wall and let the water splash on her hair and trickle down her face. Slowly, but surely, she was coming alive, her body clicking into 'on-mode'.

Aware of time pressing on, Emma dragged herself out of the shower and towelled herself dry, catching her reflection in the full length mirror as she did so. She was shocked to see two swollen eyes looking back at her; the result of residual smoke beneath the eyelids from the night before. The cigar smoke was to blame for that. The mirror inspection confirmed that no perceptible change had taken place regarding the size of her stomach and breasts. It was too soon to notice any outward signs of pregnancy. Apart from a slight heartburn each morning for the past few weeks and the feeling of nausea she sometimes experienced while driving in heavy traffic, no other pregnancy-related sickness worth talking about had bothered her. She prayed that this happy state of affairs would continue in the months ahead.

After drying her hair, she slipped into one of her more elegant linen suits, drank half a glass of orange juice, made a cup of instant coffee and toasted one slice of bread.

Vinny was still asleep when she tiptoed out the front door and made her way to the lock-up where the Volvo was stored. Vinny, she suspected, would have a sore head when he woke up later. He had eaten, drunk and smoked too much the previous night and had only himself to blame for the state he was in. She regretted her own behaviour towards him but felt within her rights to make up her own mind in regard to her job. Was she being stubborn? Yes, she had to concede that one but the combined opposition to her continuing in investigative journalism served to push her in that direction.

Another milestone of sorts had been established when they got home: for the first time since their wedding day, Vinny had gone to sleep without bothering with the familiar kiss and cuddle. She would have probably rejected it anyway, giving her mood at the time, but it rankled with her that he hadn't even made the effort. It should not have come as a surprise, after all, they had barely spoken on the way home from the Smithfield Court. She drove, he sulked. Watching Vinny crawl into bed, both socks still on his feet, his shirt half off, half on, brought a smile to her face in spite of herself. For the first time since her wedding day, she had truly felt married.

Bob Crosby waylaid Emma on the way to her office and insisted that she accompany him to the advertisement department on the second floor. 'There's something I think you ought to see,' he said, taking her by the elbow and ushering her into the advertising manager's office. 'It appears that one of the people you have been writing about is so enamoured of your literary skills that he has decided to spend serious money with the *Post* on an advertising campaign.'

'What are you on about?'

It was the Advertising Manager, Tommy Byrne, peeking at her from over his half-rimmed glasses, who answered her question. 'An eight-inch double on the front page every Friday for six weeks and a series of four half-page ads – in full process colour, no less – over the next three months, that's what it's about.'

'Will someone please tell me what this has to do with me?'

'Todd Wilson, would you believe?' Crosby said. 'Hilton and Hogge Advertising Agency have just booked, out of the blue, an advertising campaign for Wilson's hotel group. The front page, eight-inch-doubles are for his Budget Inns and the half-pages are for the five star Smithfield Court and his other four star hotels. So, how do you like them apples?'

'I'm flabbergasted,' Emma responded. 'It's all so – well, so obvious. I mean, surely Todd Wilson could not be so stupid or so naive as to think this newspaper would ever allow its editorial integrity – its objectivity – its independence to be influenced or deflected because someone decides to throw some serious money our way.'

Bob Crosby smiled, amused by Emma's verbal elevation of the ethics within the *Post* and winked at Tommy Byrne. 'If we were to apply such lofty ideals regarding all our advertisers, we probably couldn't afford to bring out the newspaper at all.'

'Come on, Bob, you're not seriously telling me that Wilson's big spend on advertising will have a bearing on what we say in editorial,' Emma asked.

'No, of course not, just winding you up a bit,' Crosby said, smiling. 'I wouldn't hesitate for a minute to expose the likes of Wilson even if he took out ten times the space he's already booked – provided of course we had any real evidence that he had broken the law.'

Back in her own office, Emma began the boring task of examining more of the prints taken from the archival newspaper pages, still hoping to find a clue to the Ireland's Eye reference contained on the cutting that had been pasted to Jamie Wilson's wall. It seemed like a hopeless task. She was about to put a call through to Detective-Inspector Connolly, to check if he had unearthed anything further on Ethel Cassidy's murder, when a call came through to her from the switchboard. 'Who is it?' she asked.

'I don't know. Some fellow – won't give his name, says its important that he talk to you. You want me to get rid of him?'

Emma thought for a minute. 'No, better put whoever it is on to me.'

The next voice Emma heard sounded vaguely familiar.

'Is that Ms Emma Boylan?' a man's bass voice asked.

'Yes, Emma Boylan speaking; who is this?'

'Hello Ms. Boylan. Todd Wilson here. Glad I caught you.'

'Todd Wilson? You're Todd Wilson?'

'Yes, Ms Boylan. I thought it was time you and I had words.'

'I see,' Emma replied, 'and what exactly brought on this sudden urge to talk to me.'

'I got the distinct impression from reading your articles that you were, shall we say, casting aspersions on my business ventures.'

'I see. Well, you know what they say, Mr Wilson – if the cap fits, etc, etc . . . '

'Well, in my case the cap does not fit. I am most concerned about the false impressions you are giving to your readers.'

'I don't believe I've given any false impressions to anyone.'

'Wrong! But look – look; I'm a reasonable man. I want no problems with you or your newspaper. I could sue you for defamation of character and win the case but it doesn't take a genius to figure out that the ensuing publicity would be bad for my business. So, Ms Boylan, I've come up with another suggestion . . . '

'I'm listening.'

'Meet with me. Let me put my side of the story to you. I promise to answer any question you put to me. I'll tell you what it feels like to lose a son, I'll talk about my marriage – whatever it takes. I just want an opportunity to put the record straight, nail some of the lies that are currently doing the rounds. What do you say?'

'I'll be happy to take you up on the offer. Where and when?

'Well, I thought it might be a good idea to meet in my home in Howth. Less likelihood of being bothered by anyone. Would that suit you?'

'Sounds fine to me. What time?'

'Let me see, say 8 o'clock this evening. Would that be okay?'

Emma glanced at her diary. 'Yes, Mr Wilson, that will be fine; I'll see you at your house at 8 o'clock. There's just one thing.'

'And what's that?'

'I'd like to bring my photographer along with me.'

'Whatever for?'

'It would help the article, show you in your own home – the human side of Todd Wilson as opposed to the business side we're more accustomed to seeing; what do you say?'

Wilson thought for a few seconds before replying. Emma could hear him breathing as she held the phone to her ear. It was obvious to her that he had not expected this request from her.

'Yes, all right,' he said at length. 'I'm not keen on the idea of photographers invading my privacy but on this occasion, as a concession to you, I'm prepared to make an exception.'

'Fine, Mr Wilson. I'll see you at 8 o'clock then.'

The Schoolhouse Hotel, in Northumberland Street, overlooking Mount Street Bridge, suited Emma and Vinny admirably because of its close proximity to their apartment. The building, a handsome redbrick retained lots of Victorian Gothic flourishes and a miniature turreted tower that dated from the time of its original incarnation, St Stephen's School. It was Vinny's contention that the pint of Guinness served in the Inkwell Bar was the best in the city. The bar itself, once the school's assembly hall, evoked the era of boys in short trousers and blazers, and girls in gymslips. In keeping with this theme, timber beams and floors, wainscoting, bound books and teachers caps and gowns were in evidence throughout the bar. And yet, in spite of this memorabilia from the '30s and '40s or maybe because of it, Emma and Vinny felt the Inkwell Bar represented, for them at least, one of the city's more pleasant venues in which to unwind, have an unhurried drink and a pleasant chat.

Without Vinny by her side for once, Emma sat among the lunchtime throng, sipping from a glass of mineral water. A quick glance at her watch told her that her guest was ten minutes late. But no sooner had she checked the time when she spotted Mary Dalton making her way into the bar. As she was almost six feet in height it was hard to miss her, with long tresses of red hair flying in all directions as she pushed her way through the lunchtime 'dot-com' clientele, her eyes, distorted behind thick lenses, sweeping left and right as they sought to pick out Emma. Partially hidden behind a beautiful carved staircase that led to a gallery lounge above the bar, Emma waved frantically in an effort to catch her attention. As soon as their eyes met, Mary Dalton attracted the attention of the whole bar by letting out a whoop of elation. Beaming with delight, she poured out apologies for being late, while at the same time, being effusive in her praise of Emma's looks and clothes.

With compliments returned in equal measure from Emma, they ordered lunch – both opting for the sirloin of beef – and a half-bottle of house red. They indulged in an unrestrained exchange of gossip about acquaintances they had known since student days. In between salacious chit-chat they found time to talk about each other. Emma's pregnancy took pride of place but only just: details of Mary's most recent sexual encounter with a married man came a close second. According to Mary, the man represented testosterone on tap. When Emma questioned the wisdom of having an affair with a married man, Mary claimed that having it off with an 'unavailable' guy was the best part about the relationship. According to her, he was only marginally better-looking than the Notre Dame hunchback, Quasimodo, was a right 'know-it-all' and deadly boring to boot. She was glad not to be the one who had to face him over a bowl of cornflakes every morning. Through fits of laughter, she explained to Emma that his only virtue lay in his ability to provide pleasure unlimited. He was powerfully endowed, had stamina and finesse in that department, and 'got the fuck out of my face after shagging me senseless.'

'But doesn't it bother you that he has a wife?' Emma asked.

'Not particularly. Quasimodo claims his wife no longer wants sex from him, says she's probably a closet lesbian.'

'Ah, come on Mary, pull the other one. He must be really stupid if he believes that.'

'He's not stupid, Emma,' Mary said, pretending to be serious, 'As a matter of fact he's a member of Mensa, has an IQ of 150 or something. He only loses it when it comes to sex – it's his Achilles heel.'

'Then Quasimodo's got more anatomical problems than his hump to worry about; his Achilles heel is attached to the wrong end of his leg.'

They had finished eating by the time Emma managed to get Mary off the subject of sex and on to the main purpose of their meeting: information. Mary Dalton worked as a secretary with Foreign Affairs and Emma hoped to glean some inside information on the recent inquiries her department were making into the financial transactions connected with Third World aid agencies. After skirting the subject for a few minutes, Emma decided to get to the point. She told Mary about her recent investigations into Todd Wilson's business activities and explained how she now wanted to widen the scope of her enquiry in order to probe the activities of his wife and her involvement in SUCCOUR. Mary, having got assurances from Emma that she would never divulge the source of her information, had quite a lot to say on the subject.

Maeve Wilson, according to Mary Dalton, had become so successful in building up SUCCOUR and attracting publicity for herself and her organisation that she had become the subject of frequent attacks from within the ranks of her own peers. Plans were afoot in diplomatic circles to have the Queen's invitation to Maeve Wilson cancelled. Foreign Affairs, her own department, she confided, were the prime movers on this issue. When Emma queried the validity of such a move, Mary Dalton had no hesitation in providing a rationale. 'A strong feeling exists,' she explained, 'that Maeve Wilson should not be singled out for this supposed honour, not when there are several other unsung heroes, all more deserving of recognition. Giving this sort of royal esteem to Maeve Wilson is like waving a red rag in front of a bull as far as the rest of the aid agencies are concerned.'

'But I thought Maeve Wilson was universally loved,' Emma said.

'By the people of the country, yes. They see photographs of her standing in front of her aid trucks or tending to starving children in Ethiopia; they see her on the top television chat-shows; they see the good work she is doing but they do not see the in-fighting that goes on behind the scenes between the various aid agencies. Believe me Emma, you'd hardly credit the viciousness that exists between the so-called charitable institutions as they fight each other for their slice of the action. Starving children, humanitarian aid is purely a business as far as they are concerned. And toughest among them in this scramble for supremacy is Maeve Wilson.'

'I'm astonished,' Emma said.

'Most people would be if they knew the truth. Did you know that the Irish Association of Non-Governmental Development Organisations recently excluded SUCCOUR from membership?'

'Why was that?'

'As the agency charged with streamlining a joint response to famine and global disasters, they were unhappy with Wilson's 'solo-runs' believing her not to be a team player. Her competitors in the aid-agency world have mounted a campaign in recent months to draw attention to SUCCOUR's funding.'

'Funding?' Emma asked. 'What do you mean?'

'Huge criticism has been heaped on how Maeve Wilson presents her agency's accounts. In particular, the costs for operating expenses and salary are lumped into the £8.5 million figure listed as 'relief and development expenditure.'

'In other words,' Emma said, ' we're not told how

much of the money SUCCOUR collects goes into Maeve Wilson's pocket.'

'Right. Which is why the Department of Foreign Affairs, which doled out two million pounds last year to SUCCOUR, is poking its nose into her finances.'

Emma wanted to hear more but Mary Dalton insisted she had to get back to work or there would be hell to pay. Reluctantly, Emma allowed her to go but felt well pleased with what she had heard. She paid for the two lunches, hugged her friend goodbye and thought about how this new information fitted in with what she already knew about Maeve and Todd Wilson. It told her nothing that connected either of them to the murder of Ethel Cassidy but, if nothing else, it made her think about Maeve Wilson in a whole new light.

18

Two autumnal landscapes and a winter scene, re-
miniscent of those snowy images of coaches and horses
so beloved of Christmas cards, stood in a clear space
at the base of the wall in Ciarán Bailey's studio. Standing
back from the three canvases, Ciarán and his son looked
for some redeeming feature in the works of art. Ciarán,
with head and shoulders bent forward, one hand
unconsciously scratching his backside, studied the
works intently. 'We might make a few shillings on the
frames,' he informed his son, 'but as for the paintings
themselves, well . . . '

Vinny smiled and nodded in agreement with his
father. He had bought the three paintings in North's
Antique Rooms, a scruffy little shop near the corner of
Wood Quay and Winetavern Street, for no other reason
than the worth of their frames. With an eye to current
trends, Vinny was aware how much seventeenth- and
eighteenth-century carved wooden frames were
fetching in sales. 'With a little restoration to the
giltwood, the frames will fetch at least twice what I paid
for them,' Vinny said, 'and the canvas could come in
useful enough for one of your masterly recreations of
'old masters'. What do you think?'

'Um, you could be right at that, son.' The smile on

Ciarán's face and the mischievous twinkle in the corner of his eye signalled the birth of another one of his flirtations with 'master-art' forgery. 'Aye, indeed,' he said, 'the bit of canvas might come in handy right enough.'

The two men talked about paintings and famous forgeries with Ciarán delighting in describing how he sometimes managed to recreate the chemistry of the pigments that were used before the mass-manufactured variety came in tubes. 'The old masters really were on top of their craft, you know, not like the daubers who call themselves artists to-day. There was no popping down to the local art suppliers for tubes of paint and ready framed canvases for them boys; they had to create their own colours, stretch and treat their own canvases. It's just a pity that the highlights achieved in flesh tones by those old methods cannot be reproduced by using to-day's metal based ingredients. For those subtle flesh tones, the old masters went to enormous lengths; they'd spend days grinding oyster shells into fine powder and then, using their own semen, they would turn it into paste.'

'You serious?' Vinny asked, wondering if his father was winding him up, 'they'd use their own semen?'

'Well, that's the story but I suppose sometimes they'd enlist the aid of their young apprentices, get them to take themselves in hand, toss their contribution into the mix.' Ciarán laughed. 'Some of those old masters might better be described as old masturbators. Still, you have to hand it to them – if you'll pardon the expression – all that trouble just to achieve one special effect.' Ciarán stopped talking for a few seconds, pulled at his earlobes and regarded his son with a mischievous twinkle of the eye. 'On the subject of paintings, forgeries, fakes and the like, I've got a bit of news that might interest you. Tell me, have you ever heard of a crowd called Jamboree Productions?'

Vinny thought for a second. 'Yes, I've heard of them. They're one of the better independent television production companies. Why do you ask?'

'Oh, its just that they're planning a special pro-gramme on Ireland's art galleries. They're going to look at some of our most famous paintings and question their authenticity.'

'Who told you all this?'

'An old friend of mine by the name of George Laffin. I rang him this morning at his home in London to talk about your Harry Clarke drawing; he's one of the people responsible for getting the Wolfsonian Foundation in Miami, Florida, to take an interest in Clarke's Geneva Window. Anyway, it turns out that Jamboree Pro-ductions have asked him to contribute his expertise to their programme. He's agreed to come and have a look at your *Angel of Peace and Hope* when he gets here. I'm looking forward to meeting him again; the last time we met was back in 1988 at the Fine Art Society's exhibition in London. We went on a pub crawl after the show and got totally rat-arsed. We were lucky not to end up in the nick. A young police man caught the two of us emptying our bladders down a drain grill on the side of a street. George talked the copper out of taking action, blabbered on to him about being guilty but insane, said he was only trying to hold his own and that surely that wasn't a crime. He yapped on and on making no sense, talking absolute gibberish, until the copper called us two old farts and told us to be on our way. Jeez, what a laugh we had.'

'Well, keep him sober when he comes over here, at least until he's had a chance to examine my Clarke drawing.'

Vinny wanted to hear more about George Laffin and was annoyed when the telephone interrupted their conversation. Ciarán answered it.

'Oh, hello Emma. Yes, it's me, Ciarán. Thank you! Yes, yes, good to hear from you too. I'm fine thank you. Yes, yes, I really enjoyed the meal last night; drank a bit too much but sure, what the hell! Yes, he's here, hold on a sec and I'll put him on to you.'

Vinny took the phone from his father, making a puzzled grimace on his face as he did so. 'Hello, Emma, this is a surprise. I didn't expect to hear from you, thought you'd never want to talk to me after my behaviour last night.'

'I think, maybe, we were both a little bit out of line last night so let's forget it – you're sorry, I'm sorry. We'll forget it.'

'Yeah, sure, that's OK with me,' Vinny said with evident relief, 'so tell me, how did you know where to find me?'

'I tracked you down; tried the apartment; tried

North's Antiques before guessing you might be at the shop.'

'How's the bump?'

'Our future son or daughter will not thank you for referring to them as a bump, but to answer your question: the bump is fine.'

'Good, so, nothing's wrong?'

'No, nothing's wrong but something has come up. Todd Wilson made contact with me today. He has agreed to talk to me about all that's been happening of late. I'm meeting him in his house in Howth at 8 o'clock this evening so I'll be late getting in. I'm putting the story together for the morning edition so I'll have to go back to the office before I make it home.'

'I hope to God you know what you're doing,' Vinny said, apprehension creeping into his voice. 'It all sounds a bit much to me, especially now. You really ought to be taking it easy – in your condition, you know.'

'Ah Christ, Vinny, we've been down this road already. I'm pregnant, that's all. It's not a disease; it's a condition that millions of women find themselves in every day; it doesn't mean the world has to come to a stop.'

'I know all that, Emma, but I still worry.'

'Well, don't Vinny. You're an awful ould eejit, you know that. I'm being very careful so there's no need for anyone to worry. I'll telephone you later tonight at the apartment and let you know when I'll be home. OK?'

'Fine, I'll be waiting for your call, oh yea, one other thing –'

'What's that?'

'I love you, Emma.'

'And I love you too. Say 'bye to your Dad for me.'

'Will do, 'bye.' Vinny said, hanging up the phone and shaking his head. Emma, he decided, knew what she was doing, she knew how to take care of herself and had done so long before he came on the scene. He smiled – you're right Emma, I'm a right ould eejit.

Matt Dempsey eased the semi-automatic gear change down a notch and allowed the Mercedes-Benz Actros to slow down as he approached a bend on the road just south of Naas town. Hauling a trailer filled with white, electrical goods, he was on the final leg of a journey that had taken him halfway around the world and back. The recently constructed bypass, skirting the town of Naas allowed him avoid what had for years been a bottleneck and meant he would reach the depot in Celbridge within the hour. Once there, he would leave his truck and head for the village of Leixlip. That was where he shared a mews with his girlfriend. With a bit of luck and not too many traffic hold-ups, he would get there by 6 o'clock that evening.

Ever since his departure from Rosslare Harbour for the continent of Africa, seven weeks earlier, one thought more than any other remained foremost in his mind: his return to his girlfriend. It was, he had told himself several times, far too long a period for a full-blooded twenty-eight-year-old male like him to be away from Fidelma Roper, the first love of his life. His truck, he cheerfully acknowledged, came a close second.

A lot had happened in those seven weeks, some of which he did not quite understand. He encountered little difficulty on his outward journey. After the obligatory SUCCOUR photocall in front of the Rosslare/Cherbourg Ferry and receiving last minute instructions from Maeve Wilson and Fergus Massey, he negotiated the Actros up the ramp and on to the boat. Over sea and land he stuck to familiar routes, routes he had mapped out for himself on previous trips to Ethiopia.

Driving through France represented the first leg of his land trek. With more and more of the old French Route Nationals barring trucks he took the N158 out of Caen and headed for Bordeaux via Alencon, Le Mans, Tours, Poitiers and Angoulême. He was careful at all times to keep his tachograph records in order – never exceeding the daily driving limit, taking his forty-five minute break every four-and-a-half hours – and monitoring his speed limiter. Crossing the Pyrenees into Spain, he set out on his favourite stretch of the journey. He spent most of his sleeping periods on the cabin's bunk mattress but preferred to get a good night's sleep in the comfort of a proper bed whenever the possibility arose. In Madrid, one of his overnight stops, he had taken time out to buy Fidelma a present – yet another doll to add to her growing collection – before pushing further southwards through Córdoba, Seville and Cadiz.

By the time he sailed from Cadiz to Tangier in Morocco he had fully psyched himself for the marathon journey through Africa that lay ahead. Passing through

Marrakesh never failed to fill him with a sense of its mystique, with its shimmering light and open-air markets piled high with rugs, woodwork, jewellery and leather. On a previous journey he had bought a jacket in the Place Djemma el-Fna for Fidelma. She adored it and swore to him it had the softest leather in the world.

With a hint of spice still in his nostrils, he left Morocco and the Atlas mountains behind and headed for the mighty Sahara Desert, a true test for the 12-litre V6, engine that throbbed beneath his body, and a true test of his own stamina. With experience, he had become familiar with all the different countries border crossings and ever wary of the over-zealous officials who manned them. He made sure to have all the proper documentation to hand. Likewise he knew where to stay overnight and where not to stay overnight.

Entering Algeria on the road connecting Oujda and Tiemcen he experienced a frustrating day's delay at a checkpoint, consigned to his cab, but once through he thundered past vast plains, deserts, shanty towns, villages, cities and towns, on his south-easterly journey. Through Niger and into Nigeria, between the equator and the Tropic of Cancer, it got pretty hot, but the air conditioning in the cab did its job most efficiently.

No matter how many times he travelled through the African Continent he would never get used to its vast mysterious wilderness or the fact that each new day dawned over an ever changing landscape. All breath–taking. His journey took him past sweeping sand dunes, waving grasslands, sprawling savannahs, cool and misty highlands, hot and humid lowlands, and forests that were damp and dripping. As he encountered each new vista, he wished Fidelma could share the experience with him. He imagined making love to her underneath skies that stretched with blue forever or beneath star-filled nights where a background web of exotic sounds and smells would take their passion to new heights. He made up his mind; yes, someday he would definitely bring her with him. Fidelma, who cherished animals – she once owned three cats and a puppy – would have a chance to see, first-hand, the most awesome wildlife spectacle in the world.

Trucking through the Sudan on the penultimate leg of his trek, his Actros was forced to slow down to a crawl at times while negotiating unsurfaced dirt tracks and highways that had been washed away by recent rains. In the large urban townlands of Khartoum, he encountered uniformed soldiers belonging to the Revolutionary Council. Representing the people who had seized power in 1989 in a military coup, they looked anything but friendly to Matt. When they saw his Irish passport, however, they cheered and saluted him, gesturing to their guns. Not understanding their tongue, but reading the body language, he assumed they were telling him they approved of Ireland's armed struggle. Finding his most approving expression, he waved back at them and was, much to his relief, allowed to continue on his way.

Three weeks and two days after leaving Rosslare Harbour, tired and thirsty, dreaming of cold pints of

Guinness and making love to Fidelma, though not necessarily in that order, he pulled the truck into a space in front of the SUCCOUR clinic and warehouse in Korem. Signs of the recent famine were everywhere to be seen, though Korem had managed to avoid the worst extremes of the hardship. Even so, there was evidence of misery everywhere he looked. Long before his approach to Korem, he had seen rows of desiccated carcasses, hide-covered bones of cows, sheep and goats. In the villages he could not help but notice how skeletally thin the children were, with their tiny necks supporting heads that looked too big for their bodies. They stood on legs no thicker than sticks, looking at him through half-opened eyes, wondering perhaps if he could ease their suffering. Deeply moved by their plight, he hoped that his container might add some small measure of relief to what was obviously a disaster.

Two days later, the goods from his container emptied – a quantity of high-energy cereal, skimmed milk and vitamins, second-hand medical equipment given to SUCCOUR by hospitals who had upgraded their technology, blankets, clothing, numerous different medicines, immunisation kits, and all manner of preventative healthcare aids – he waved a sad good-bye to Ethiopia and set out on his long journey home.

Hauling an empty trailer all the way to France, he made good time and managed to gain a day on what the same outward segment of the journey had taken. In Bordeaux, he picked up a load of white electrical goods, mostly deep freezers, the sort used in supermarkets, along with some cold storage units and chest freezers. It was here that he encountered the first hiccup in an otherwise smooth operation. Normally he would drive his truck into the appropriate bay, wait while the goods were being loaded, sign the proper documentation, and be on his way. On this occasion he was obliged to allow another driver take his truck to a warehouse while he remained in an office. When he protested, he was informed that this was how they operated and if he didn't like it he could take his truck and leave without his load. Reluctantly he acceded to their demands.

In Cherbourg port, having almost forgotten the incident at the loading bay, he was stopped by customs and asked to open his trailer. He watched nervously as customs men with sniffer dogs inspected his load, fearing that concealed drugs might have been planted inside the electrical goods. That would explain why such an odd procedure had been adopted when the goods were being loaded. His fears were unfounded. Within seconds, he was given the all-clear. A burly customs officer explained to him that they had been looking for illegal immigrants. Ever since fifty-eight dead bodies had been discovered in the back of a sealed container coming through Dover, inspection pro–cedures had been greatly increased. Matt knew that France, a country with a ruthless record when it came to drugs, had, until that unfortunate tragedy, been almost blasé about illegal immigrants. Fellow truckers had told him that in France he was more likely to be dealt with reasonably if caught with half a dozen people hiding in his truck than would be the case if he were caught with cannabis in his sports bag. He was glad to see that things had changed for the better.

And then, coming off the ferryboat in Rosslare Harbour, the same thing happened again. Once more, customs officers, along with their sniffer dogs, inspected the contents of his truck. It had been a more thorough search than the one in Cherbourg. They opened all of the freezer units and checked carefully behind panels and lids. The cab and under-trailer came in for particular scrutiny.

He had just received the all-clear when Maeve Wilson and Fergus Massey appeared. They shook his hand, congratulated him on a job well done and posed for photographs in front of the truck.

That had been late yesterday evening.

Now, one day later, as he neared his home depot he still wondered why his truck had been singled out for special attention by the customs people. At the time, the SUCCOUR logo had been prominently displayed on all sides of the vehicle. After spending a night in Mrs O'Hare's guesthouse in Wexford, and sleeping on till midday in an effort to shake off his exhaustion, he was enticed by Mrs O'Hare to eat a large breakfast. It tasted good. He smiled to himself, thinking, the wonders of the world are all very fine but there was something very special about being back on the old sod. Feeling invigorated, he thanked his hostess, telephoned Fidelma to let her know he was home and headed for his Actros. After removing the SUCCOUR logos from the truck, he climbed into the cab and began to make his way to the Celbridge depot.

He was less than half a mile short of his goal when the accident happened.

19

'Maniac,' Emma shouted as a car shot out from Todd Wilson's driveway, almost colliding with her Volvo, missing her by the merest fraction of an inch. The offending vehicle moved so fast that she had not time to recognise the driver or to establish whether or not there were passengers in the car. By the time she recovered sufficiently from the shock, the speeding car had turned a corner and disappeared. 'Did you see that?' Emma asked her passenger, Ronan Long.

'Did I what? Fuckin' near shit myself, I did. Bloody headcase; driving like that. We could've had a serious accident.'

'Don't suppose you got a look at the driver?'

'No chance. I just saw the car coming for us; put the heart crossways in me, it did. Might have been a woman though, come to think about it; yeah, something tells me it might have been a woman.'

'You're sure that's not just your prejudice talking.'

'No, no, swear-to-God. Something tells me it was a woman behind the wheel.' He smiled before continuing, 'And that's not just because I think women are such shitty drivers.' Emma, about to quote statistics that proved women drivers were superior to men, thought better of it and shook her head. She knew from past

experiences that arguing with a self-confessed chauvin-
ist like Ronan Long was a futile exercise. She was never
too sure how serious to take Long's sniping at women
and suspected he said the things he did more for the
hell of it than for any firmly held conviction he might
have had. As a staff photographer with the *Post*, she
had worked with him on many consignments and had
always found him most professional, personality and
snide comments aside.

Still a little shaken, Emma pulled into Todd and
Maeve Wilson's driveway. Checking her watch, she
noted that her arrival was a little premature, ten
minutes to be exact. Todd had been specific about the
time, eight o'clock he had said. 'I think we should wait
here in the car for a few minutes,' Emma told Long,
'we're a bit on the early side and besides I need to get
my breath back after what's just happened.'

Ronan Long, agile and restless by nature, was in no
mood for remaining in the car a minute longer than
was necessary. 'No, let's get out, stretch our legs; I can
take a few exterior shots of the house. It's one helluva
pile and no mistake. I'd say you'd need a right few bob
to live in a place like this.'

'Well, now Ronan, it's a safe bet that neither Todd
or Maeve Wilson are exactly on the breadline.'

As soon as Emma and the photographer stepped
out of the car, Todd Wilson, behind the wheel of an XJ8
Jaguar Sapphire, pulled into his driveway. 'Glad you
could get here,' he said in welcome, getting out of his
car. He shook hands with Emma and acknowledged

Long with a curt nod of the head.

Emma, who had met and interviewed Todd Wilson in the past, had never seen the man look so tired. Heavy jowls sagged on an alabaster-like face, his trademark moustache took on the appearance of a theatrical prop and the black bags beneath his eyes added to the impression of weariness. His knotted tie hung loose and pushed to one side, his undone shirt collar button allowing a tuft of unruly chest hair to protrude in its stead. Pushing his stocky frame towards the house, Emma could not help but notice that his suit – probably one of those expensive jobs made to measure by one of the top tailors in Dublin or London – was creased and rumpled and looked as though he might have slept in it. Emma was about to tell him about the car she had seen dart out of his driveway when she stopped in her tracks. Wilson, too, froze in mid-stride. He held up his hands in horror. 'Oh, shit no,' he moaned, 'I don't believe this.' Like Wilson, Emma and Long stared at the bright pink aerosol message covering most of the front door:

WILSON'S
FAGGOT LAIR
KILLER-PERVERT

For a moment, all three of them stood there not saying a word. Ronan Long was first to revert to type, pointed his camera at the graffiti and rattled off frame after frame in quick succession. 'No, you can't do that,'

Wilson shouted to the photographer, moving in front of the offending words. Long lowered his camera in compliance; it didn't bother him, he had taken all the shots he needed.

Wilson was about to use his key to open the door when he noticed the broken lock and splintered jamb. 'Good Jesus, I've had a break-in,' he said in a hoarse whisper, pushing his way into the house. Emma and Long followed. It was immediately evident that the aerosol artist had got there before them. With no regard for the decorative splendours of the Wilson household, graffiti defaced the hallway, staircase and first landing.

'I think it's time you talked to the cops,' Emma advised, as she took in the garish mess that was everywhere in evidence. The words all followed a similar pattern to that on the door, words like 'cock-sucker', 'wanker' and 'dung-pusher', liberally illustrated with crude representations of male genitalia. Wilson's face, chalky white to begin with, now took on a sickly grey, green pallor. 'They've been upstairs,' he said, terror in his voice, 'Christ Almighty, they've been up to Jamie's room.'

He began to make his way up the stairs, each step seeming to take great willpower. Emma, followed by Long, made her way up the steps behind him. At that moment, Emma would have sworn Wilson had become oblivious of her and Long's presence. Like someone sleepwalking, he moved across a wide, carpeted landing before stopping in front of a partially opened door. For a moment it looked as though the man was about to faint. Unsteadily, he placed his hands on the door jambs. A body-wrenching sigh escaped his lungs. His eyes stared in stupefaction at the pink aerosol letters on the door:

I saw what you did to Ethel Cassidy, your whore.
I saw what you did to the boy.
Arse to arson, there is no escape.

Emma moved up behind him without saying a word. She read the message and heard the dreadful sighs coming from Wilson. No words were spoken for several seconds.

What happened eventually surprised Emma.

Wilson turned to look at her, his eyes wide open, unblinking, as though locked in some unimaginable terror. 'Push the door open,' he ordered her in a voice that no longer sounded like his own, 'look into the room for me – tell me what you see.'

Emma reached out her hand. She pushed the door open. The room inside was dark. In the few seconds it took to adjust to the darkness, they all gasped in horror. A body hung suspended by a rope from the ceiling. An exposed rafter beam creaked as the body swayed gently in the disturbed air current.

Todd Wilson screamed.

20

Things had quietened down considerably by the time Detective Inspector Connolly arrived. His response to Emma Boylan's telephone call had been rapid – city centre to Howth in fifteen minutes. Even allowing for sirens blaring, that was remarkable. With his sidekick, Sergeant O'Rourke, a thin, angular man in his late twenties, Connolly spent a minimum of time inspecting the aerosol messages inside and outside Wilson's house, before concentrating his efforts on the bizarre scene that confronted him in Jamie Wilson's bedroom.

Todd Wilson continued to stare with incredulity at the life-size mannequin hanging from the ceiling beam. Someone had taken the trouble to dress the flesh-coloured dummy with great care. One wrist had been draped with an expensive bracelet and the feet had been forced into a pair of fashionable high-heeled shoes. The mannequin's head, bereft of any facial features, had been adorned with an auburn coloured wig.

Todd Wilson sat on the side of Jamie's bed, shoulders slumped, forearms anchored to his knees, face waxen, the skin beneath his eyes purplish, moving his head slowly from side to side. 'I don't believe this,' he said, muttering the morose mantra over and over again.

'Be thankful it's not a real body hanging up there,' the detective said. 'This is the work of some cruel prankster, some weirdo, a sicko with a grudge against you. It's awful, I agree, but it could have been worse, yes?' Failing to elicit a coherent response, Connolly proceeded with caution, his voice patient, his manner polite, 'I don't suppose you have any notion of who or what might be behind this – this elaborate prank?'

'I know exactly who's behind it,' Wilson snarled.

'You do?'

'Yes, damn it,' Wilson shot back, shaking his head emphatically. 'My wife, the most venerable Maeve, saviour to the world's poor and wretched; she is the one who set this up.'

Connolly furrowed his brow. 'Your wife? I see. And what makes you think this is the work of your wife?'

'Everything. I'm married to the woman for Christ-sake, I know how she operates. The messages, the clothes, the whole caper; all her handiwork. I recognise the clothes on the mannequin; they belong to Maeve.'

'That doesn't necessarily mean she's responsible for this.'

'Oh, she did it all right, you may be sure of that.'

'Seems a bit improbable to me,' Connolly said, caressing his chin between index finger and thumb. 'Your wife would hardly need to break in the front door of her own house to gain entry, now would she?'

Todd nodded his head in answer but made no audible reply. He was evaluating what Connolly had just said, attempting to collect his thoughts, trying to organise his thinking. 'She may not have done this herself, not physically that is,' he said after some consideration, 'but I'm absolutely sure she's behind the whole sick episode.'

'So, you're saying she got someone else to do this for her, is that it?'

'Yes, I suppose I am. No, damn it, I don't know. I just don't know any more.'

'OK, Mr Wilson, I understand, this is a difficult time for you; we'll leave it for now. I'll take a full statement later – see if we can make any sense of all this.'

Emma, who had been listening to the conversation wanted desperately to get more information from Wilson, but she could see from his demeanour that her requirements would have to wait, and ditto for the interview he had promised.

Connolly moved downstairs, beckoning Emma to follow him as he did so. Relieved to get away from Jamie's room, he sat on the overstuffed couch facing the lounge's bay window. Trappings of wealth were everywhere to be seen but his thoughts were resolutely fixed on the scene he had just witnessed on the floor above him. Slouching against a profusion of cushions, with both hands pushed into in his trousers pockets, he regarded Emma with a questioning stare. Emma said nothing, waiting instead for him to begin the conversation.

It would be dark within the hour. Daylight crept stealthily from the room leaving ever longer shadows looming in its wake. Looking out the window, she could make out the shape of Ireland's Eye in the distance. A Martello tower, erected on the north west tip of the island to guard against invasion in the Napoleonic wars, stood nipple-like on the rocky outline, the scene beginning to fade as it merged and melted into the encroaching dusk. The view reminded her of the press cutting that had gone missing from Jamie's wall. So far, neither she nor Connolly had provided any real clues as to what the connection might be. A chastening thought occurred to her: what if there was no con-nection, no connection at all. She dismissed the thought.

Looking back to Connolly's brooding presence, Emma wondered if perhaps similar thoughts were going through his head. His face, its features accentuated by the half-light, never looked more perplexed to her. He remained ill at ease, uncomfortable in this opulent setting. 'Makes you think, doesn't it,' he said, his eyes frisking the objects in the room, 'all this wealth, money, extravagance, and what has it brought them?' He answered the question himself. 'Nothing as far as I can tell, nothing but misery and pain.' He paused for a moment before returning his gaze to Emma. 'Tell me something, how did you happen to be here for this?'

Emma told him about her appointment with Wilson and how, on her arrival, she had narrowly escaped being hit by a car as it darted out from the Wilson's driveway.

'Interesting.' Connolly said, puckering his lips, 'I imagine that whoever drove that car is our culprit, wouldn't you say?'

'Yes, it certainly looks that way.'

'And you say you didn't get a look at the driver's face?'

'No. It all happened so fast. Ronan, my photographer – you met him upstairs – thinks it was a woman behind the wheel but he's not a hundred percent sure.'

'Great, just great. So, let's see, we have a top investigative journalist and a newspaper photographer coming face-to-face with a driver and neither of them can even tell whether it was a man or a woman. Zero marks for observation, Emma.'

'No need to sound so smug; you weren't there. We were so busy trying to avoid being hit that all we saw was just a blur.'

'So, there's nothing to suggest that this lunatic driver that you describe might have been Maeve Wilson?'

Emma thought for a second. She tried to recall the moment of near impact, attempting to dredge sub-liminal images to the surface of her mind. 'Listen, I know I said I didn't recognise the driver but at the same time I'm almost positive it wasn't Maeve Wilson. The more I think about it the more I'm convinced that the person behind the wheel might have been a man. I wouldn't swear but I'm almost sure he wore a hat. Yes, definitely a man's hat, with the brim pulled down on the forehead.'

'Sounds to me like someone determined not to be recognised. Could be anyone. I'm sure a businessman like Todd Wilson has made lots of enemies over the years.'

'I'm sure he has,' Emma agreed, 'but it's obvious from the aerosol messages that whoever dressed and hung that mannequin from the ceiling knew about Ethel Cassidy's murder as well as Jamie's suicide. That should narrow down the list of suspects considerably.'

'You're thinking it could be Ethel Cassidy's sister maybe, what's her name; Marina. Wearing a man's hat is the sort of obvious ploy someone would use to stop observers from recognising them.'

'Yeah, it could be her I suppose,' Emma agreed without conviction, 'and you're right, it could be a woman disguised as a man. But where does that get us? I keep wondering how that good-looking fellow, Fergus Massey fits into things; he's involved in Todd Wilson's business dealings and he's also one of the head buck-cats in SUCCOUR but somehow or other I can't see him involved in this sort of prank. There's something immature about what's happened here. That's why I think it could be that fellow, Johnny Griffin, the one bringing the lawsuit against Wilson. What d'you think?'

Connolly considered what she had said for a moment, his mouth creating its habitual puckered expressions before speaking. 'I don't know, I really don't.' After a longer than usual pause, he smiled. 'There's always the possibility that Wilson could be right,' he said, enjoying the thought. 'His own wife could be the one behind all this – though somehow I doubt it.'

Their conversation went round in circles, getting nowhere, until finally they agreed that they simply did not know who or what was behind the elaborate set-up. Parting, they agreed to get in touch the next day, 'We can swap notes,' Connolly offered, 'see if we can make some sense of this thing.'

'Sure,' Emma agreed, 'talk to you tomorrow.'

Tomorrow, it was almost tomorrow, quarter of an hour to midnight to be exact. Emma finished her piece for the next day's edition, satisfied that she had a respectable, if not spectacular, front page story. Of more interest to her was the press cutting that Connolly had sent by courier to her. It was a photo copy of one of the missing articles from Jamie Wilson's wall, the selfsame article she had expended so much energy looking for. She had fully believed the missing press-cutting would clarify why Jamie had committed suicide and throw some light on who, or why, Ethel Cassidy was murdered. It did none of these things. If anything, it added to the mystery.

Tragedy on Ireland's Eye

A group of day-trippers to Ireland's Eye, taking advantage of the current fine spell of weather, were sunbathing on Carrigeen Bay, a favourite spot with visitors, when a freak accident occurred. Mrs Jillian Massey, wife of well-known business man, Fergus Massey, fell from the rock where she had been lying in the sun, and struck her head against a sharp outcropping. Mr and Mrs Massey had gone to the small island with their friends, Todd Wilson, prominent entrepreneur, his wife Maeve and family friend Ethel Cassidy. The shocked party accompanied Jillian off the Island but she was declared dead on arrival at St Vincent's Hospital.

The article went on to tell about the murder that had taken place at the Body Rock on the island a hundred-and-fifty years earlier, information Emma had already heard from Bob Crosby. But the report did contain some very interesting information. For one thing, it made a direct link between Ethel Cassidy and the Wilsons. Not only that but Maeve Wilson's colleague in SUCCOUR, Fergus Massey had also been present on the island that day; his wife had died in the accident. Emma read the short article several times trying to tie it into present circumstances but could make no significant connections. And yet, Ethel Cassidy had seen fit to tear this from the wall while Jamie Wilson hung from a rope above her. Emma put the photocopy into her files, disappointed that it had not helped her solve any problems but resolved to think about it further .

She was about to tidy up her desk when Long pushed into her office with three glossy prints in his hand. Emma was impressed with what she saw. 'Only problem is,' she said, 'which one to use. They're all very good.'

'Yeah, that's what I thought myself,' Long agreed,

without the slightest hint of modesty. 'They're little dingers, minor works of art; might even persuade readers to read the boring old text you write to accompany them.'

Emma was used to Long's teasing. 'You're full of shit, Ronan, you know that!'

'Yeah, you've told me often enough. And now if you've finished with this bag of excrement, I'm going home to get some kip. If you've any sense, you'll do likewise.'

Looking at her watch, Emma realised how right Long was; it was time to go home. She began to clear the day's accumulated clutter from her desk when she noticed a yellow sticker attached to an article on the morning's issue of the *Post*. She could tell that Bob Crosby, who had a habit of popping into her office from time to time, had resorted to his old habit of leaving hand written messages. The article with the Crosby's sticker had a headline, which read: 'Truck driver arrested on drugs charge after freak road accident.' Emma had glanced at the story earlier that morning when scanning through the paper but didn't bother reading past the first paragraph, drug seizures not being a subject she normally covered. But now, she read it carefully:

Gardaí, investigating an accident in County Kildare between a lorry and a JCB, were surprised to discover a cache of hidden drugs at the site. At about 6.30 pm Mr Matt Dempsey, the driver of the lorry, was travelling along the Celbridge Road, coming from the Naas direction. He had passed Backweston Farm, a property owned by the Department of Agriculture and Food, when he swerved in an attempt to avoid colliding with a JCB that approached from a side road. Details are, as yet, unclear but it appears that the lorry, in negotiating its manoeuvre, collided with the back of the JCB. The lorry then skidded out of control. It careered on to the road's lay-by, hitting a large pothole before ploughing through an embankment and ending up in a roadside field. Gardaí at the scene discovered that the lorry had been carrying ten kilos of cannabis. A spokesman confirmed that drugs, with a street value of £100,000, were concealed inside the lorry's tyres. This discovery had been made because one of the tyres carrying the drugs had burst in the course of the accident. Personnel from the Gardaí Drug unit were immediately called to the scene and Mr. Dempsey has been escorted to Lucan Garda Station where he has been charged with offences against the Drugs Traffic Act. In a brief statement to reporters, Dempsey said he was totally innocent of any wrongdoing, insisting that he could shed no light on how, or where, the drugs had got into the lorry's tyres. Mr Dempsey will remain in custody until a court hearing is set. The accused, along with his lorry, had arrived back in Rosslare Harbour after travelling over-

she imposed on herself. Here she was, sitting at her desk just shy of midnight, putting a story about the Wilson's to bed instead of putting herself to bed. Some choice: cold type and printer's ink or a warm bed and a husband to snuggle up against. What did that say about her priorities? This was her life, she reassured herself. She enjoyed her job, no, she loved it. She felt at home in the *Post* building. Even now, listening to the sound of the huge presses as they made their familiar, comforting rumbling noise down in the womb of the building, she was glad to be a small part of the team that brought the news to the public every day.

Most of the other journalists on her floor had gone home for the night but down the hall from her office, telephones continued to ring at the newsdesk. The night editor along with his skeleton staff were all set for the graveyard shift. Sometimes the best new stories broke in the early hours, new scandals emerged, waiting to tantalise readers the next day.

She could hear echoes of printers yelling at each other, laughing at dirty jokes, whistling and slagging each other good-naturedly, as they worked. Like demonic midwives, clad in grease stained blue overalls, they fussed about the great Heidelberg press, moni-tored its progress, as it laboured to deliver the *Post*'s latest edition.

All she wanted now was to get home, go to bed and get some sleep. She hoped that Vinny would still be up. Tired and all as she felt, she wanted to run to-day's events past him, see if he could help clarify her mind on what exactly was going on with the Wilsons. And while he helped unscramble her thoughts, she hoped he might rustle up a little late-night snack – maybe a cheese and onion sandwich with vanilla ice cream to follow.

21

Flight FR 444 out of Dublin spent twenty-five minutes air bound before touching down on the runway of Liverpool Airport. Sitting next to a window, to the rear of the left wing, Emma could have seen the Irish Sea if she had bothered to look down. Once or twice her eyes did catch sight of the sun's midday reflections dancing on the ocean's surface beneath the Fokker 50 but her thoughts remained resolutely anchored back in events that had taken place in Dublin over the previous couple of days.

So much had happened in such a short time that it was difficult to take it all in; so many things she had wanted to do but, for one reason or another, could not. It was this inability to be in several places at the same time that she found most frustrating. She had wanted to talk to the lorry driver, Matt Dempsey about his role as a courier for the SUCCOUR organisation but he remained temporarily out of reach, in the custody of the Gardaí in Lucan. Charges were being brought against him but she had no doubt he would be allowed bail in the next day or so and allowed freedom until his case came before the magistrates court. She would endeavour to meet with him as soon as she returned from Liverpool.

She had also failed to make contact with Todd Wilson. More than ever she had wanted to go ahead with the interview he had promised. Wilson, it appeared, had gone to ground, hiding away from the glare of publicity her article had generated. Ronan Long's stark photographs coupled with her text, describing the hanging mannequin in Jamie Wilson's bedroom and the ugly graffiti adorning the house, had created a most dramatic front-page spread for the *Post*. It had rekindled accounts of Jamie's suicide. It focused fresh attention on Wilson's business ethics and raised questions about Maeve Wilson's aid work in Africa.

Getting in touch with Maeve Wilson proved to be as impossible as ever. Emma had phoned and left several messages with her Dublin office but received no feedback. Equally, Fergus Massey had not bothered to return her calls. It prompted Emma to wonder what exactly all of these people had to hide. Even Johnny Griffin, the young fellow bringing the sexual harassment case against Todd Wilson, had made sure he was unavailable for comment.

Unexpectedly, it was Detective Inspector Connolly who came to her rescue. While investigating the break in at Todd Wilson's house he had promised Emma he would contact her the following day, and true to his word he had done just that. Their telephone conversation had gone on at length about the strange happenings in Wilson's house but it was his news about Ethel Cassidy's sister Marina that prompted the positive line of action she had now embarked upon. According to the detectives, Marina Cassidy had been spotted in Dublin Airport on the same night that the break in occurred, boarding the last scheduled night flight for Liverpool. He invited Emma down to his office in the Phoenix Park Garda depot and allowed her to view the video footage captured on the airport's security cameras. She had no difficulty recognising Marina Cassidy. 'Leaving the country so soon after what happened in Todd Wilson's house,' Connolly remarked, 'makes you wonder if she could have been the culprit, doesn't it?'

Although not convinced by Connolly's reasoning, Emma was nevertheless forced to look at events from a new perspective. Believing Ethel Cassidy's murder to be intrinsic to whatever lay behind the extraordinary list of unexplained incidents surrounding Todd Wilson, Emma had decided to act on her gut feelings. With painstaking patience, she had spent the best part of the day attempting to dig up information on Ethel Cassidy's elusive twin. She knew, courtesy of Connolly, that both sisters had once been members of the Dublin City Orchestra. It wasn't much to go on but it did at least give her a starting point. Making contact with members of the orchestra had not been easy but she had managed to track down some of the musicians. Not that her endeavours yielded much; those she talked to had joined too recently to have known either of the Cassidy sisters.

As she was on the point of giving up on the quest, making her last telephone call, her luck changed for the better. Kay McSweeney who played violin with the orchestra until her retirement two years earlier, remembered them. 'Two nicer girls you could never hope to know,' she enthused, 'and talented too, especially Ethel. Both their lives seemed to fall apart when Ethel became pregnant. The poor dear wasn't married at the time but typical of her thoughtful nature, she left the orchestra rather than cause a scandal for her fellow musicians.'

'Do you know what ever became of Ethel Cassidy's baby?'

'I'm not sure. God's truth, I'm not sure. There were whispers doing the rounds in the orchestra at the time – ugly rumours. It was said that Ethel got rid of her baby.'

'You mean she had an abortion?'

'God help us, but yes, that's what was said but I for one never believed that; Ethel was not that sort of person.'

Emma allowed Kay McSweeney to reminisce about her time as a violinist in the orchestra and talk about how well she knew Ethel and Marina Cassidy. Her voice, when she talked about recent events took on a sad tone. She had attended Ethel's funeral, she told Emma, expressing her horror for what had happened to her one-time colleague. 'I sympathised with Marina at the graveside but, what with her terrible grief and all that, I don't believe she remembered me at all.'

'Do you know where Marina Cassidy lives these days?' Emma asked.

'I'm not sure, to tell you the truth. When she left the orchestra, about the same time Ethel became pregnant, she went to live with some relatives in Liverpool. We exchanged Christmas cards and postcards for three, maybe four, years but you know how it is, we lost contact after that. I do know that she got a job teaching music over there but I've no idea what she does for a living these days. I sent her a Mass card for Ethel but I can't be sure if she got it or not.'

'Do you still have the address from the time she first went to Liverpool?' Emma asked.

'Yes, yes, I have. I held on to the old postcards – wanted to hold on to them as a keepsake.'

And now, a day later, with the sound of the aircraft's two Pratt & Whitney engines whining in her ears and Marina Cassidy's address, taken from a postcard several years old, in her hands, Emma was about to land in Liverpool airport. From there she would begin her search to find the one person she hoped could shed light on Ethel Cassidy's murder.

The timing could not be more synchronous. While Emma made her way into the arrivals area in Liverpool airport, her husband Vinny, along with his father, stood at the arrivals barrier in Dublin airport. According to the information on the monitor suspended from the ceiling, flight EI 163 from Heathrow had landed. The two men smiled brightly when George Laffin walked into the Arrivals area, pushing a trolley laden down with cases.

Vinny's first impression of the man's appearance reminded him of an erratic compass: it was all over the place. George Laffin was a walking contradiction. On one level, he could pass for a family doctor, while a less charitable appraisal might see him as an ageing Hollywood matinee idol. Wearing a lightweight straw-coloured suit, a multicoloured waistcoat, and a polka dot bow tie, the art expert certainly cut a dash. At sixty plus, his face, though not handsome, was interesting in a lived-in sort of way, his strong features and hooded eyes accentuated by a full head of snow-white hair, tied at the back in a ponytail.

'Hello there, you old reprobate,' Ciarán hollered, shaking his hand firmly. 'It's good to see you; God, but you're a sight for sore eyes.'

'Likewise my dear fellow, likewise Ciarán,' Laffin said, his cultured British tones ringing out above the airport din. 'I'm jolly pleased to see the authorities have not locked you up yet for all those fake masterpieces you've foisted on the unsuspecting public.'

'Shush for God's sake, will you, or you'll have me arrested on the spot,' Ciarán said, pretending to be scared. Vinny, watching the two men enjoy their reunion decided, that since his father had apparently forgotten he was there, to introduce himself. Because of Laffin's forthcoming television appearance, there had been mention of him in the weekend supplements that now came free with all the main newspapers. One commentator who had seen Laffin on some BBC chat show described him as a *rara avis*, a spontaneously witty man who could talk knowledgeably, without being boring, on the subject of fine art. Apparently, he had caused consternation in British art circles by claiming that the National Gallery's famous Rubens painting, *Samson and Delilah*, was a fake. Vinny stuck out his hand in welcome. 'I'm pleased to meet you, Mr. Laffin. My name is Vinny, my father has told me so much about you.'

'Delighted to meet you, dear boy,' Laffin said, clasping his hand firmly, 'I had no idea this old codger had it in him to produce such a fine handsome specimen of manhood.'

Pushing their way from the Arrivals to the car park the two older men continued to abuse each other verbally with good-humoured witticisms while Vinny, unable to get a word in edgeways, set about packing the cases into the back of his Citroën.

The next few days he felt sure would be a lot of fun.

22

Emma asked the taxi driver to wait a few minutes. She had found the address where Marina Cassidy lived more than ten years earlier and was about to discover whether or not she still lived there. Eccles Place, a quiet residential cul-de-sac to the west of Woolton, looked like a typical old-fashioned middle-class address to Emma with its neat rows of redbrick two-storey houses and meticulously cultivated front gardens. She walked up the garden path to No 23, stood for a moment in the doorway, took a deep breath, and pressed the bell. Nothing happened. She pressed the bell a second time and waited. Looking at her watch she noted that the time was 4 o'clock. Perhaps she's still at work, Emma thought, and berated herself for not having the sense to leave her visit for later that evening, after 6 o'clock maybe. That way she would have a better chance of finding someone home. About to turn away and return to the taxi, she heard a noise from inside the house. A surge of excitement shot through her. The door swung open. Her face dropped. The person standing in the doorway, staring enquiringly at her, was a middle aged man. 'Can I help you?' he asked pleasantly.

'Yes, I hope so,' Emma said, 'recovering from her disappointment, 'I was wondering if Marina Cassidy lives here?'

'No, no one of that name lives here I'm afraid, luv,' he said. 'You must have the wrong address.'

'You're probably right – and I'm sorry to have bothered you. It's just that the person I'm looking for once lived here. I was hoping, foolishly as it turns out, that she hadn't moved. I'm not sure what to do now, you see. It's really important that I find her.'

'You're Oirish, luv,' he said, smiling, an expectant look in his eyes.

Emma reciprocated with a demure smile, wondering what being Irish had to do with anything. Not having the obligatory red hair and freckles, perhaps he expected her to hike her skirt above her knees and break in to a high-stepping *Riverdance* routine. He was, she could see, a handsome athletic six-footer, dressed in sport shirt, denims and trainers, and was flashing flirtatious eyes in her direction.

'Yes, I'm Irish,' she said, giving him no encourage–ment, but remaining pleasant, 'I came over to Liverpool especially to talk to Marina Cassidy. Tell me, have you been living here long, I mean in this house?'

'Five years. Tell you what, luv. I can get in touch with the bloke who sold me the house. He might know where she's living now, might keep records, you never know. Is there somewhere I could get in touch with you if I dig up anything?'

'That would be most helpful, yes.' Emma said, handing him her business card. 'I'm staying in the Adelphi Hotel. I'll be there at least until tomorrow. If you do come up with anything you can contact me there.'

'Fine, I'll do that – but don't set your hopes too high, it's a long shot at best. OK, luv.'

On her trip back to the city centre, Emma, feeling despondent, thought about what she would do next. Kay McSweeney had given her the address of the school where Marina had given music lessons. Somebody there, she felt sure, would surely remember the good-looking Irish girl who worked as a music tutor.

All that would have to wait until the next morning, she decided, knowing that classes would be over for the day by now. She sighed, resigned to the fact that she would have to spend a night in Liverpool, a city she had never been to before, in a hotel where she knew no one. She had chosen the Adelphi on the recommendation of Bob Crosby. Bob and his wife had stayed there a number of times and heaped praise on the place, referring to it as a relic of old decency. It was the only place, he confided to Emma, where he could strip off and use the sauna, solarium and jacuzzi without worrying whether or not someone from the Irish media might be in the vicinity waiting to poke fun at his portly figure. The thought of Bob Crosby in the all-together brought a smile to her eyes.

She would, for once take it easy. With little fear of being contacted by her office, she would relax and enjoy all the comforts that the hotel had to offer her. Besides, with a baby inside her to think about, being shamelessly pampered for one night would do both of them the world of good. The taxi slowed down for the evening traffic in Lime Street before pulling into Ranelagh Place and stopping in front of the imposing Britannia Adelphi building. Emma got out, paid her fare, and made a promise to herself that tomorrow she would track down Marina Cassidy with renewed vigour.

Fergus Massey looked up from the letter he was reading. 'You're not going to like this,' he said. 'They've postponed your visit.'

Perplexed, Maeve Wilson's hand shot out and grabbed the letter from his hand. 'What visit? Who are you talking about?'

'According to that letter – it's from the Department of Foreign Affairs – they have had communications from the British Foreign Affairs Select Committee advising them that your visit to Buckingham Palace has been cancelled. In diplomatic-speak, they say your visit is deemed inappropriate at this point in time and therefore postponed indefinitely.'

Maeve began to read the letter. 'They can't be serious?'

'Oh, they're serious all right. As you can see, it's all there in black and white; it's got the government's embossed gold harp on the top of the letterhead; I'd call that serious enough.'

'But why? I mean, why are they doing this to me? They were the ones responsible for sending the invitation in the first place. They don't even give a reason.'

'They don't have to give reasons but I think it's fairly obvious why this is happening.'

Maeve Wilson threw the letter down and looked at him with raised eyebrows. 'Obvious, you say? Not to me it isn't. Any trouble we might be experiencing with the organisation had got nothing to do with Buckingham Palace for God's sake. Somehow, I can't see the Queen of bloody England reading the Irish newspapers and nudging the Duke with her elbow and saying: 'Hey, Philip dearest, did you see what they're saying about Maeve Wilson in the "Mick" papers.'

Massey smiled at her almost perfect mimicking of the Queen's voice. When he spoke, he affected a most serious tone. 'It's got nothing to do with the Queen.'

'Who then?' Emma asked.

'Camilla Parker-Bowles,' he replied, trying to hold a serious face but not succeeding, 'I'm sorry Maeve, I couldn't help that. It's just that I'm trying to come to terms with your picture of the Queen and Prince Philip chatting about what's in the Irish papers.'

Now they were both laughing. 'So, it's our own buggers in Foreign Affairs putting the boot in,' Maeve said, becoming serious again. 'What I don't understand is why. Why are they gunning for us – for me in particular?'

'We've made enemies by being more successful than most of our longer established colleagues in the aid business. You look and sound a damn sight better than any of them so they want to pull you down.'

'Nothing new there; it's been like that since day one.

Why have they waited till now to do something about it. What has sparked this war?'

'You mean the summons to appear before the investigative committee and the publicity about the lorry?'

Maeve nodded her head grimly. Sitting behind her desk in the Dublin office of SUCCOUR, she had asked the receptionist to hold all calls. Fergus Massey in response to her telephone call the previous evening had agreed to see her this morning. He had driven up from his country residence in Abbeyleix for what she had termed a 'crisis meeting'.

On arrival, half an hour earlier, they had discussed her subpoena. Massey's assessment of this situation failed to relieve her anxieties. They both needed to face certain facts, he told her, and went on to clarify their position in regard to the forthcoming investigation. Their books had anomalies, he admitted, while assuring her that there was nothing that a little creative accountancy wouldn't put right.

Ordinarily, Maeve would have accepted his re-assurances but on this occasion her concerns were far from eased. 'This business with the lorry – and the drugs – worries me' she said, handing Massey a copy of the previous day's *Post*.

'Bad break,' he conceded, giving her a glum look. 'I've already read the article and I agree, the timing couldn't be much worse.'

'You can say that again,' Maeve said with a sneer, 'Emma Boylan's attempts to link us to the driver makes me very nervous.'

'Yes, but her piece contains no facts; it carries no real conviction. As far as I can tell, this journalist Emma Boylan has a fixation about Todd Wilson and his business ethics; she's like a terrier with a bone, just won't let go. In an effort to make a name for herself, she's dogged his tracks for months now, writing all sorts of scurrilous articles, but she hasn't laid a glove on him yet. And now, she's trying to get to him – through you – but it's not you she's after; you're only incidental to her main focus of attack, and that remains Todd Wilson.'

'I suppose you could be right. All the more reason why I want to keep my distance from Todd. I'm still trying to figure out how Emma Boylan happened to be at the house for that weird mannequin business.'

Massey smiled. 'It's my guess that Todd invited her there – part of his new charm offensive with the media. Unfortunately for him, the whole thing blew up in his face.'

'Any idea who could have been behind the whole charade?'

'You mean it wasn't you?' Massey asked, grinning from ear to ear.

Maeve was not amused. 'I'm hardly likely to do something as stupid as that in the very same room where – where Jamie . . .'

'I'm sorry, I'm really sorry, Maeve, I wasn't thinking, that was out of order, quite unforgivable.'

'It's all right, Fergus. I shouldn't be so jumpy, I'm

sorry. It's just that I can't even think about the house without picturing poor Jamie. That's the real reason I haven't set foot in the place since his death. I just can't bring myself to go there, be reminded of him or remember the way it used to be.'

'It also means you don't have to face Todd.'

'Yes, there's that to it too but with the way things have developed, it's just as well. All this media exposure on Todd could have disastrous consequences; it's bound to reflect on me sooner or later.'

'No, Maeve, I wouldn't worry unduly; if we remain calm, refuse to get caught up in the controversy, this thing will probably all blow over – a storm in a teacup, nothing more. It'll be all right in the end, trust me.'

'I hope you're right,' she said uneasily.

It was a bit like being caught up in a whirlwind. Vinny's two days of driving for his father and George Laffin had left him reeling. The two older men had decided on an exhaustive pilgrimage to the sites where Harry Clarke's works were on display. Because Laffin's involvement with the televised arts programme would not commence for another two days, he teamed up with Ciarán for, what he termed, a self-indulgent orgy of art appreciation. His excuse, not that he needed one, was that he wanted to talk about Irish art when he appeared before the cameras and to do so, he needed to absorb what the country had to offer.

Vinny's role was more straightforward: he was their driver. With Emma out of the country for a few days, he jumped at the chance to accommodate the two men. To visit all the places on their list, they would have needed the services of a helicopter and a week to spare, instead they had to make do with his Citroën 2 CV6 and a curtailed itinerary crammed into two days.

Dublin city and county proved to be the easy part; first a visit to Bewley's cafe in Grafton Street where they sat beneath Clarke's Order of Architecture window, followed by a visit to the Hugh Lane Municipal Gallery of Modern Art in Parnell Square. A specially constructed blackened booth in the gallery allowed them to view *The Eve of St. Agnes* under the best possible conditions. Clarke's pictorialisation of Keats's poem illustrated, in twenty-two leaded panels, the story of Porphyro's wooing of Madeline and how, on the eve of St Agnes, he answers her prayers by entering her bedchamber and slipping her away from her father's castle. This exquisite window served to whet their appetites to see more of the artist's work.

They travelled to Holy Trinity Church in Killiney to view the stained-glass window depicted in the cartoon Vinny had recently bought. Together, they studied the masterpiece in detail, admiring the angel's ashen face, its tapering fingers and sumptuous gold-pink wings, and the overall androgynous quality evident in the work. Vinny felt a lump in his throat as he allowed the full power of Clarke's stained glass to swamp his vision.

After Killiney, the Clarke pilgrimage continued unabated as Vinny headed south for Cork, stopping in Ballylooby and Cloughjordan on the way. In between visiting the various churches, they made an equal number of stops in nearby public houses – ostensibly for the use of their toilet facilities – but in reality to sample the hard liquor they sold. Vinny found it difficult to keep up with his travelling companions' rate of alcohol intake, drinking half a pint of Guinness for their every measure of Irish whiskey. After five such stops he had little choice but to switch to mineral water.

In Cork City, they visited the Crawford Municipal Art Gallery and the Honan Chapel in University College Cork. It was late evening before the three men, weary from their travels, and not helped by alcohol consumption, checked into Jurys Hotel for the night.

The following morning, much to Vinny's surprise, Ciarán and George had beaten him to the breakfast table. Not yet 7.30 am, and the two old boys were wide awake, putting away a full Irish breakfast with evident relish, while engaging in a most animated conversation between mouthfuls. Vinny was even more astonished when George Laffin informed him that he had gone for a swim in the pool and had 'worked-out' in the hotel's leisure centre for half an hour before eating.

Feeling anything but well himself, his head sore from the intake of Guinness the previous day, Vinny managed to get away from the city centre before the morning traffic build-up reached its peak. Temporarily shutting out the conversation of his two passengers, his thoughts returned to the telephone call he had made from his bedroom to Emma in Liverpool. She had admitted that morning sickness had made an unwelcome appearance. 'It's not as bad as I thought it would be,' she had said reassuringly, accepting at the same time that she would need to take a little lie-in until she felt ready to face the world. Vinny, who never considered himself the best at saying the right thing in situations of this nature, was glad when Emma brought the call to an end. Before hanging up, she told him that she hoped to return from England that evening and promised to ring him when she knew for sure what her plans were.

Pulling into Killaloe, County Clare, to see the Presentation window in the local Catholic church, Vinny thought he noticed the car's clutch acting up a bit but hoped it was just his imagination. He tried to remember the last time he had the Citroën serviced but couldn't. One thing was certain: it was way overdue.

It was 5.15 in the evening by the time Vinny drove into the basement car park attached to Huband House, relieved to have completed the marathon trek. Laffin announced that next day, providing Emma had got back, he would be their host at a meal in the Smithfield Court. Although Jamboree Productions, the television company looking after his stay in the country had not booked him into the Smithfield Court, he had been intrigued by what Ciarán had told him about the collection of paintings on view in the hotel and wanted to see them for himself. Vinny wanted to visit the hotel for an altogether different reason. He wanted to lay the ghost that haunted him ever since his last visit to the hotel. Like some dark shadow following him, his memory of that particular evening refused to go away. He had behaved in an unacceptable manner then and had, by his foolish actions, greatly upset Emma. For days he had thought about how he would put the matter to rights and now finally, he had the answer. George Laffin's invitation would give him an opportunity to make it up to her.

23

After talking to Vinny, Emma replaced the phone, slipped quickly out from beneath the sheets and stood uneasily on the floor. She knew she was going to be sick. Scurrying to the bathroom, she sank to her knees and retched into the toilet bowl. Five minutes later, just as she began to wish she were dead, the heaving eased. Feeling fractionally better, she got off her knees and waddled unsteadily to the sink. Water! She needed water to rinse her mouth. Running the cold tap, she made the mistake of glancing at her reflection in the mirror. A frightened yelp escaped from her throat. Shocked by the chalk-white face staring back at her, she shook her head, brought her hands to her cheeks and attempted to massage some life into the wan visage. It worked. A trace of colour enlivened her face. Relieved to be back from the undead, she poured herself a glass of water and rinsed her mouth.

She felt almost human again. Almost. But she did not feel quite up to facing the day yet. Not just yet. Getting back into bed became an irresistible urge. Five minutes, she decided; that was all the time she needed to get her head and body working in harmony again. She covered her head with blankets, found her most comfortable position and willed herself to feel better.

One hour later, at 10.15 am, Emma sat down to coffee and toast in the hotel's bright breakfast room. She felt good as new again. While sipping her coffee, she studied the Liverpool street guide she had picked up at reception when she first arrived in the hotel and attempted to locate Rodney Place. According to Kay McSweeney, Marina Cassidy worked as a music teacher in St Catherine's Comprehensive School when she first went to Liverpool. That was over twelve years ago and Emma knew that a lot could have happened in the intervening years. But, in the absence of more current information, it was worth trying. Rodney Place, the school's address was, according to Kay, just off Rodney Street.

A young waiter, seeing Emma study the city map, approached her and asked if he could help. Glad of any assistance, Emma asked if he could tell her how to get to Rodney Place.

'It's easy enough to locate,' he said, taking the map from her and using a pen as a pointer. 'If you are coming from the Leece Street direction, you will see a small side street to your left immediately after the car park, just about there; you can't miss it,' he said, making a small 'x'-mark with his pen, 'and if you take a second left-hand turn about fifty yards further on you will find yourself in Rodney Place.'

'Thanks, you've been most helpful. You seem to know your city very well.'

'Yes, I suppose I do rather, most of it anyway. I used to knock about with some mates from John Moore's

University in Rodney Street some years back but I haven't been to that neck of the woods in yonks.'

'Don't suppose you know where St Catherine's Comprehensive School is located?'

'Yes, funny you should ask, I do. You can't miss it. It's an old drab-looking building with blackened redbrick walls and big black windows; looks like something out of a Charles Dickens novel. You'll see it as soon as you move into Rodney Place.'

Emma thanked the young waiter, finished her coffee and toast and ordered a taxi. Within half an hour she found herself being driven into Rodney Place by a man with handsome features and wearing a white turban that put her in mind of the actor Omar Sharif. 'What building are you looking for, lady?' he asked, looking at her reflection in his rear-view mirror.

'St Catherine's Comprehensive School.'

The taxi driver pulled his car to a stop and pointed to several large hoardings that stood in front of a building site. 'This is it,' he said, 'and you must be one of the architects. Anything you build on the site of the old school has got to be a damn sight better than the monstrosity you just pulled down. The site-manager's office is to the left; that is who you want to see, yes?'

Stunned by what confronted her, Emma was incapable of saying anything for a moment. When she did speak, she used just one word to sum up her annoyance: 'Fuck.'

'Here?' the taxi man asked, turning his head around to look at her directly for the first time. 'You came here to fuck?'

'No,' Emma said crossly, 'I want you to get me the-hell out of here and back to the Adelphi Hotel. OK?'

'Is no problem, lady,' the taxi man said, shrugging his shoulders as he executed an erratic U-turn in the street. Neither Emma nor the driver spoke a word as they headed back the way they had come.

Her first morning in Liverpool was, Emma acknow-ledged, turning out to be a proper pain in the arse.

He is finally home. Fidelma undresses slowly in front of him, her eyes beckoning him to do the same. Somewhere in his subconscious he can hear his name being called.

'Will you wake up out-a-that,' a man's voice shouts.

He knew that voice; it belonged to Sergeant O'Meara from the Lucan Garda station. But why would the Sergeant bother him here at home?

'I've a bit a good news for you, me boy-o,' the Sergeant said, shaking Matt's shoulder, 'though God knows you don't deserve it.'

Reluctant to let go of the dream, Matt tried to focus on the erotic thoughts still fluttering through his consciousness, aware of the rampant desire in his body screaming for release. He sat up, blinked his eyes and pushed the Sergeant's hand from his shoulder. 'What?' he asked, not fully sure if he was awake or still dreaming.

'Ah for the love a God, will you wake up and not be actin' the eejit; I want a word with you.'

Fully awake now, Matt sat up on the bench where he had unintentionally dozed off. The previous night sleep had proved elusive and yet, having dressed and eaten a frugal breakfast, he had drifted into a deep slumber, half-sitting, half-flying, on a hard bench. He was, he realised, still in his cell at Lucan Garda station.

'Your bail money has been posted,' the Sergeant told him. 'So as long as we hold on to your passport and you agree to present yourself here at the station on a daily basis you're free to be on your way. You might as well make the best of it because you're looking at a long prison stretch for your crime.'

'I committed no crime,' Matt said defensively. 'I'd no idea there were drugs contained in my lorry.'

'Someone else put them there, is that it?'

'Yes, I've been set up.'

'Aye, that's right me boy-o, same ould story you all have. You an' all them other drug dealers are as innocent as the driven snow. My arse, y'are! Scumbags like you make me sick, d'you know that, destroying the youth of this country. So, come on with you now; get out of me cell before I puke me guts up looking at the likes-a-you.'

Knowing it was pointless to protest his innocence to this particular officer, Matt made his way out of the cell, collected his few belongings at the front desk and headed out into daylight.

He had three weeks of freedom before he stood trial, three weeks to discover who had set him up and why. He intended to make good use of that time. First, he would spend some time with Fidelma. His recent spell of deprivation on the sex front needed urgent attention. That represented number one priority. More than anything in the world he needed her love. But after that he would stop at nothing to find out who was behind his drug bust. His employers had paid his bail money, or at least he assumed they were the ones who had coughed up the £25,000, so he would start with them.

Emma's day in Liverpool had taken a dramatic turn for the better.

On return from her fruitless journey to Rodney Place, she found that a message had been left in her room. The words, written on a plain postcard, were short and to the point:

Ms Emma Boylan:
Meet me in the Walker Art Gallery at 4 o'clock this evening.
Marina Cassidy

Having established that the Walker Art Gallery was within walking distance of her hotel, Emma decided to explore the city centre in the hours available before her rendezvous. After a spot of window-shopping in the Cavern Walks area, she soon tired of the trendy clothes displayed in the boutiques and shops there. She was impressed by the city's architecture where, unlike Dublin, old buildings had been successfully refurbished rather than reconstructed. Everywhere she looked there were reminders of the city's most famous sons, the Beatles. Emma, never the greatest Beatles fan in the world, preferred instead to stroll along the waterfront in and around the Albert Dock area. She had seen pictures of the granite Liver Birds that adorn the clock tower on television programmes from time to time but had not, until now, realised how much they dominated the skyline and gave focus to the Albert Dock development. What had once housed a collection of warehouses for cotton, tobacco, wines and spirits had been redeveloped to include tastefully designed bars, restaurants and galleries.

Getting away from the hustle and bustle that was Albert Dock, Emma wandered through Chavasse Park and found herself in the pedestrian area of Whitechapel before finding a quiet café in Queen Square. She ordered a coffee and took time out to formulate the questions she would put to Marina Cassidy when they met later that day.

On the dot of 4 o'clock she made her way up the colonnaded steps of the Walker Gallery and entered its vast interior. Her immediate thought was: how in God's name am I supposed to find anybody here. Looking at a diagram of the floor plan did little to help. She would just have to visit each gallery segment in turn and hope that Marina Cassidy showed up before she overdosed on culture. She joined in with the flow of visitors and viewed everything from early Italian and Flemish works to Rubens, Rembrandt and Degas. Even to her untrained eyes, she had to admit that the paintings were awe inspiring and for once she wished she shared Vinny's appreciation of the fine arts.

While in Room 11, the Impressionist and Post-Impressionist area, a picture titled *Interior at Paddington*, by Lucian Freud, an artist she had never heard of, caught her eye. The composition – a bespectacled, young man wearing a gabardine-like overcoat, standing behind a sinister looking pot plant that might have been a yucca – made her feel uneasy. While trying to discover what it was about the painting that bothered her, a voice from behind made her jump. 'I always stop at that painting too,' the speaker said. 'It makes my flesh creep.' Emma wheeled around. It was, as she expected, Marina Cassidy. Emma held out her hand in welcome. 'How did you know me?' she asked.

'Oh, it wasn't too hard; I saw you at Johnny Griffin's press conference in Dublin. You sat at the back observing all. But you missed me; all the time I was observing you and everyone else there.'

'I did see you later,' Emma said, 'when you walked through the hotel's lobby. I wanted to run after you but I was having a spot of bother with the people who had clamped my car.'

'Yes, I saw that too but I didn't want to talk to anyone at that stage. That was why I got out of there fast.'

'And how did you know I was staying in the Adelphi?'

Marina Cassidy gave a little laugh. 'Easy,' she said, her whole face transformed by the smile, 'it was my partner you spoke to when you visited Eccles Place. I live there with him; his name is Danny Jackmann.'

'He was a most convincing liar,' Emma said, smiling herself.

'Yes, I have him well trained. He knows how much I value my privacy and screens all callers.'

'But you've decided you want to talk to me?'

'Yes, Emma, I've read almost everything you have written about Todd Wilson. You appear to be the only journalist around with the balls to question him.'

'I'll take that as a compliment.'

'I meant it that way, Emma; the only trouble is: you don't know the half of it.'

'I know that you told Detective-Inspector Jim Connolly that Todd Wilson was responsible for your sister's murder.'

'Yes, I believe he was behind the fire in her house – the fire that burned her to a cinder – but, the truth is: Todd Wilson killed my sister several years before the fire.'

'I was hoping you'd talk to me about that,' Emma said.

'Yes, it's time I talked to someone who is willing to listen, time someone heard the full story. But not here. If you like, we'll go for a drive to Southport. We can walk along the beach there and talk all we like with nobody to bother us.'

'Sounds fine to me,' Emma said.

24

Making small talk at first, the two women accessed the other's temperament as they attempted to establish a rapport. Marina talked about Liverpool and the part of the city they were now in: Southport. According to her, Napoleon III built the grands boulevards in Paris after spending an enjoyable holiday in the Merseyside resort of Southport. The emperor, she informed Emma, was so taken by the sweeping panorama of Lord Street, Southport's tree-lined boulevard, that he decided to recreate a similar vista in Paris.

In what seemed like an excuse to avoid broaching the subject they had come to discuss, Marina, adapting the role of an enthusiastic tourist guide for the resort, continued to extol the virtues of her adopted city. Walked past the botanical gardens and on to the golden sands, Emma gazed towards the water in the distance, only half aware of the dim outline of a ship making its way slowly up the Mersey. She wondered how much longer Marina would shrink from mention of Ethel or the relationship her twin sister had with Todd, but she decided not to push things.

Even though it was a pleasant afternoon, they found themselves virtually alone on the beach. Apart from an elderly man taking his dog for a walk, they had the place to themselves. The sun reflected brightly on the sand and a slight breeze, buffeting off the gentle waves, fanned late-afternoon warmth on to their faces. Marina appeared to have relaxed, sometimes dragging a foot in the sand the way a child might do. She smiled when Emma related the episode that brought her to St Catherine's. Marina explained that she had left 'Cat's Com' several years earlier and now gave lessons in Liverpool's Institute of Performing Arts, a Fame—type of establishment where all disciplines in the field of modern entertainment were catered for.

After a long pause, when it seemed to Emma that Marina had become lost in some private world of her own, she stopped walking for a moment and gazed out across the water. 'You want to know why Ethel Cassidy was killed,' she said, not looking at Emma, 'and you want to know what part Todd Wilson played in her murder? Yes?' Before Emma could reply, she continued. 'I'll tell you, Emma. But before you can begin to understand why things turned out the way they did, I need to fill you in on a few details.

'My twin-sister Ethel and I were close; as close as any two sisters could be. As children, we had an idyllic upbringing in Cooraclare, a small town in West Clare. Our house rang with the sound of music. Both my parents and my grandparents were fine musicians. Ethel and I played fiddles, concertinas and any other musical instruments we could lay our hands on from the time we were old enough to hold them.

'My parents are dead now but the love of music they

instilled in me remains to this day. My father in particular was regarded as a fine musician. He played the traditional airs popular in West Clare with the best of them but he also took a keen interest in other music forms. He liked American blue-grass music and the Cajun tunes from Louisiana. As far as he was concerned there was very little distance between the hills of Clare and America's Appalachian mountains. One minute he'd be extolling the virtues of local hero, Elizabeth Crotty, and attempting to play *The Wind That Shakes the Barley* or *The Reel with the Beryl* in her style; next minute he'd move on to Bill Monroe's *Kentucky Waltz*. He simply loved all music and sometimes even had a go at Mozart's *Eine Kleine Nachtmusik*. Dad encouraged us to develop our technique and entered both of us in competitions in all the County Clare and All Ireland Fleadhs. We were something of a sensation in trad-itional music circles back then, known as the Cassidy twins, playing jigs and reels in local dance halls and concerts. At an early age, both of us won All Ireland medals and later, when we were a little older, were awarded bursaries to study music.

'We started in the Royal School of Music in Dublin on the same day. Maeve Finan – later to become Maeve Wilson – also began. Ethel and I formed a friendship with her almost immediately and we remained friends right through our college days. After we qualified, the three of us were accepted as members of the Dublin City Orchestra. It didn't pay very well and we were always skint, always short of rent for the flat we shared in Stamer Street. To earn an extra few shillings in our spare time, the three of us, along with a guy named Tom Foxe formed a string quartet. We put on a good show, musically speaking, and picked up a residency spot in the old Hibernian Hotel in Dawson Street. As far as technique was concerned, Ethel and I were better violinists than Maeve but she outclassed us when it came to interpretation, expression and flair. Not that there was any jealousy among us as far as the music was concerned. No, it was something else altogether that brought about dissent in the camp.'

Emma listened without once needing to interrupt or probe. Like the waters of the Mersey moving swiftly before them, Marina Cassidy's torrent of words flowed steadily onward, one detail overtaking another, rippling like lapping waves from her mouth. Her face, as she spoke, had taken on an impassive look, almost as though she were locked in some sort of time warp. It was only when she broached the subject of Todd Wilson that any degree of animation showed in her face, her expressions taking on an increased look of loathing.

'I still remember the first evening Todd Wilson and Fergus Massey made their appearance in the old Hibernian,' Marina said, a slightly strident timbre evident now in her voice. 'Christ, I even remember the tune we were playing as they took their places at a table in front of our platform: 'Send in the Clowns' – how appropriate can you get? It was hard to miss them; Fergus Massey, tall and dashing, impossibly good looking, a fleece of stylishly toffee coloured hair to his collar, and on his arm, the graceful Jillian Harrington, then his fiancée, later to become his wife. Todd Wilson accompanied the beautiful couple. Accompanied by a dolly bird, he represented the other end of the 'looks' spectrum: stocky build, handlebar moustache, pinkish skin, arrogant demeanour and brash manners.

'All three of us girls were smitten by Massey's good looks straight away. No point in denying it. To young impressionable girls just out of our teens, as we were at the time, he represented the most perfect specimen of manhood we'd ever seen. Ethel was less successful than the rest of us at hiding her feelings; she confessed to me how much she lusted for a man like that. I was not unaffected myself but I had enough sense to dismiss any such fanciful notions of romance; I thought of him in the same way as today's teenagers think about film stars, footballers or pop stars: all right as a pure fantasy lover but not someone you gave any serious consideration to.

'Maeve, unlike myself and Ethel, openly allowed her feelings to show. She serenaded their table to the exclusion of all others in the dining room, moving her body sensuously in rhythm with the melodies gushing from her violin. A Stradivarius in the hands of a virtuoso could not have expressed more eloquently, the passion, the sexual hunger and the wanton needs she felt that night. It was a shameful display – and quite beautiful all at the same time. Only problem was: her dexterity and soul-bearing pavane ignited a fire in the wrong person. Yes, you've guessed it: Todd Wilson responded to her overture.

'In the weeks that followed, Maeve responded to Todd's courtship but only in order that she could get near to Fergus Massey. Of course she never admitted as much to us but we could see the way she looked at Massey. Because of Maeve's involvement with Todd, myself and Ethel, as her closest friends, were invited to lots of parties, boat trips and the like. Invariably, Fergus and Jillian Harrington would also be part of the scene. It was a strange sort of period in our lives. We were young, a bit wild, and thought the world was our oyster. With the sort of abandonment that only youth embrace, we partied too much, stayed up all night, lived life to the full, drank too much vodka and occasionally got stoned out of our tiny minds on cannabis. In the midst of all this madness, for madness it surely was, Fergus Massey qualified to the Bar and took silk. A few months later he married Jillian. Todd Wilson was best man at the ceremony and of course myself, Ethel and Maeve attended as guests. It was a great day and we all got totally piss-eyed. But what I remember most about the day was how Maeve and Ethel, after all the guests had gone home, draped their arms around each other and cried their eyes out.

'Things settled down for a while after the Massey marriage. Old man Wilson passed away leaving everything to Todd. The father had owned a string of turf accountant shops and operated on-track betting stands in all the main horse and greyhound racetracks throughout the country. On top of that, the old boy had bought up two small hotels and a couple of pubs, and had done well for himself wheeling and dealing in land speculation. No shortage of money there but not an awful lot of class. This bothered Todd and he set about upgrading the business. He built up the turf accountancy business by opening high-street shops left, right and centre, and then, when the time was right, sold that part of the business to some British concern and made a fortune in the process. He invested the money wisely and managed to increase the family fortune left to him by leaps and bounds. But the thing he wanted most, the respectability he craved, still eluded him. Maeve, for her part, fooled herself into believing she loved him. Long before he had amassed all this money, he asked her to marry him. She was stupid enough to say yes.

'From the start, the marriage was on shaky grounds. Well, anyone could have told you that'd be the case. Even before they got married, I could see their relationship was all wrong – a bit like that of a dog and a lamp post – with Maeve being the lamp post. It only survived because of the friendship between the Wilsons and the Masseys and the fact that myself and Ethel remained close – maybe too close. We were big into late-night parties – we were continually on the piss and there seemed to be an unending supply of cannabis on hand. Sometimes we would head off in the Wilson boat for Ireland's Eye and spend the night there. There was a spot there called the Long Hole that had hidden caves and a waterbound altar called the Body Rock. I remember once we got really out of our skulls drunk and played a practical joke on Massey – put him on to the Body Rock and pretended to go away. Poor Fergus, he cursed us to hell and back; swore he'd kill us but eventually saw the funny side and laughed himself sick with the rest of us. These mad trips eased off a bit when Maeve became pregnant with Jamie but even during this period we still managed to get up to high jinks.

'On the night that Maeve gave birth to Jamie in Holles Street, Todd was on Ireland's Eye with Fergus, Jillian and Ethel. I was not there on that occasion but Ethel told me afterwards that she had got high as a kite, went skinny dipping with the others and allowed Todd to have sex with her. I was shocked. Jesus, can you imagine, I couldn't believe my ears; I mean, she didn't even like the man, never mind the fact that he was married to her best friend.

'I thought Ethel's indiscretion was a one-off flight into madness and had no reason to believe otherwise until the day, seven years later when she told me she had become pregnant. Todd Wilson, she confessed, was the father.'

Marina's flow of words stopped. Tears misted her eyes. Emma suspected that whatever came next would be even more painful for Marina to relate than what had gone before. During the silence, Emma thought about Ethel Cassidy and the awful death she had met. Although she had never met her, listening to her twin sister talk so vividly about events from the past took on an eerie aspect of transgression into the spirit world. She felt the hairs on the back of her neck stand up. Her thoughts were interrupted when a nervous little laugh came from Marina. 'Let's get out of here,' she said, almost as though she too had suddenly become frightened. 'Let's go back to the city and have a coffee or something.'

'That's fine with me,' Emma said, not sure how to react.

'I want to tell you the rest,' Marina said, 'but I'll feel better sitting down. There's a nice little pub I know in Lord Nelson Street; we'll go there.'

It was after 6 o'clock by the time they got to the Nelson's Rest. It was a charming old-fashioned pub complete with dark wooden beams and brass orna–ments. If it were not for the incongruous, one-arm games machine with its gaudy colours and pinging sounds, the place could have belonged to an earlier time. Propping up the counter, a small group of after-work office workers were deep in conversation regarding the exploits of the city's two premiership football clubs, Liverpool and Everton. Emma and Marina found a cosy alcove and ordered coffee and ham sandwiches. They made small talk at first, contented to sip coffee and eat before embarking on another trip into the past. When Marina took up the story of her sister Ethel again, Emma could see pain etched in her face.

'We had the most serious row in our lives,' she began. 'I called her a slut and she called me a cold-hearted, tight-arsed frigid bitch. This from twin sisters who loved each other. At first she refused to tell me who made her pregnant. We were living together in the same flat in Stamer Street that we had shared with Maeve before she married Todd. For some weeks before our blistering row, I had an idea Ethel might be carrying on with a married man. Ethel liked men and she liked her sex. I did too but I was a lot more choosy about who I allowed into my bed. I suppose, compared to her I did appear frigid. Ethel brought the weirdest collection of men you could imagine back to the flat. You know the sort – arty-farty types, no-hopers who thought they were gifted as writers, painters, sculptures, musicians or the devil knows what. They sponged money from her and drank every drop of booze we brought into the flat. I don't think any of them had any real talent – except for shagging their brains out, that is. I would hear them in the room next to mine, humping away like there was no tomorrow, grunting and groaning like bloody animals.

'One night after performing in a gala concert in aid of Third World relief, Ethel returned to the flat with me straight after the show. I could tell from her strange downbeat behaviour that something serious was amiss. When she told me she was pregnant I went crazy. I'm not proud of how I reacted but I was so annoyed with her. She admitted she had been seeing a married man but refused to say who he was at first. Me, stupid naive dimwit that I was back then, never suspected, not for a minute, that it could be Todd Wilson. When she finally admitted he was the one, I went ballistic, totally ape-shit. If Todd Wilson had been near me at that moment I would have torn him apart with my bare hands, limb from limb and I would've danced on his bones. As it was, I slapped Ethel across the face, she belted me back and we called each other the most awful names imaginable.

'The next day, I quit the orchestra and took the ferry across to Liverpool. My dad's brother, Uncle Tom owned the house in Eccles Place then, and I went to him. He welcomed me with open arms and helped get me an interview for the job in St. Catherine's Comprehensive School. I hated those first few days in Liverpool and missed my friends back in Dublin. But more than anything I missed Ethel. We had never been parted before and I realised for the first time how close we really were. But I was proud back then, stupid really, and I stubbornly refused to contact her. I was miserable. I wanted to say how sorry I was for saying all the horrible things I had said. I wanted to let her know that I was prepared to help her through the difficult times she faced. Unfortunately, I did nothing.

'I was less than a week here in Liverpool when she contacted me. The news couldn't have been worse. She had gone to Ireland's Eye with the Wilsons and Masseys for an afternoon's spot of sunbathing. She told Maeve Wilson and Jillian Massey about the row she had with me. Naturally enough, they wanted to know what brought it about. After some probing from them, she admitted she was pregnant and gave that as the reason for our split-up. Maeve and Jillian wanted to know who the father was. For obvious reasons, Ethel couldn't divulge the name but when the women pressed, she said something snide about how they shouldn't be so smug when it came to their own husbands' fidelity – something along those lines. Needless to say, Jillian and Maeve didn't take too kindly to this slur. They saw red. A three-way row broke out. It had tragic consequences. Jillian fell from a rock face – she had been trying to catch Ethel – and bashed her head against a rock in the process. It was an accident but Jillian died. I am a bit unclear as to what followed in the immediate aftermath; Ethel could never bring herself to talk about it. Suffice to say she landed on Uncle Tom's doorstep three days later.

'She was in terrible shape. She told me the dreadful story about what had happened on Ireland's Eye. We hugged each other, we bawled our eyes out crying, we promised we would never fight again. Unfortunately, we did fight again – almost immediately. She wanted an abortion; I wouldn't hear of such action. I said I could get her a job here; said we could play music together; said how the two of us could bring up the baby when it arrived. I argued with her, told her how we could make a new life for ourselves in Liverpool, explained to her how no one knew us here and how no one would ask any awkward questions. She would have none of it. She showed me a wallet stuffed with money, given to her by Todd Wilson, she told me. In the end, I agreed to help her. I had no choice. She said she was going to go through with it, with or without my help. It was the darkest hour of my life. There isn't a day I go through since then that I don't ask myself if I couldn't have acted in a different way, found some way to talk her out of what she did. I cried, she cried, we both wept until there was no more tears left to fall but we still went through with the awful deed.'

Marina stopped talking when she noticed Emma had begun to cry. It was only when she noticed Emma caressing her stomach that she understood. 'You're pregnant?' she asked Emma.

'Yes, I am. I'm sorry, I just . . .'

'Jesus, Emma, I'm sorry. I had no idea. I never would have told you that story if I'd known. Shit, I'm really sorry.'

'It's all right, Marina, honestly. You couldn't have known. Besides I did ask you to tell me the story. I'm all right now, honestly.'

Marina ordered two fresh cups of coffee and chatted about inconsequential things until she was sure the awkward moment had passed. It was Emma who brought the subject back to Ethel Cassidy, assuring Marina that she wished her to go on with the story. But the momentum had been broken and Marina finished with a curtailed account of what happened.

'Three weeks after the abortion, Ethel returned to Dublin. I should have gone with her but I didn't. Our Uncle Tom, who knew nothing about what Ethel had done, became ill soon after that. God's curse seemed to be on us at the time. Tom was diagnosed with

Alzheimer's disease. I decided to stay with him, look after him. The poor man died eighteen months later. I've lived in the house ever since.

'Nothing was ever the same between myself and Ethel after the abortion. I could never come to terms with the course of action she decided on – still haven't to this day. I still loved Ethel but when I discovered she had given up the violin and had gone to work in the Wilson household as babyminder and gardener, I lost all faith in her. The whole thing was beyond my comprehension. How could she do something like that?'

'Did you ever find out why she went to work for the Wilsons?'

'If you mean did she ever tell me, the answer is no. I do have a theory however. You want to hear it?'

'Yes, sure.'

'I believe Ethel was consumed by guilt after the abortion. Knowing that Jamie Wilson was half-brother to her terminated baby – both of them sharing the same father – Jamie had somehow taken the place of her lost baby. In him she had found a channel to lessen her guilt, to fool herself into believing that by loving him she could somehow absolve herself from the consequences of her actions here in Liverpool, make amends for her crime. I believe that's why she went to work for the Wilsons, to be with Jamie, but I never got the chance to put it to Ethel. In the years that followed we had less and less contact with each other.'

'When did you last talk to Ethel?' Emma asked.

Marina thought for a few seconds before answering.

'Not long before Jamie Wilson's suicide, less than two weeks before Ethel's murder.'

'She wrote to you?

'No, she telephoned me. I was amazed when I got the call; we hadn't spoken to each other in over a year. She told me that she no longer worked for the Wilsons.'

'Did she say why?'

'No. I asked of course but all she would say was that it hadn't been pleasant and that the past had come back to haunt her.'

'What did she mean by that?'

'I'm not sure. I pushed her for more information but she insisted she couldn't discuss it over the phone. She wanted to know if I could visit her, said she desperately needed someone to discuss her problems with before they got out of hand. I asked her, rather unkindly, I'm ashamed to say, to stop dithering and to give me some idea about what she was on about. It had to do with Jamie Wilson, she said after much prodding.'

'The problem had to do with Jamie Wilson,' Emma said. 'And this was only a week or so before the boy . . .'

' . . . committed suicide,' Marina said, finishing the sentence for her. 'That's the part that still haunts me. I feel so guilty; I should have gone to her straight away, don't you see, but I didn't. If I had, then maybe none of this would have happened.'

'And she gave you no inkling as to what exactly the nature of the problem was with Jamie?'

'She cried when she talked about him. It was hard to make sense out of her words and I missed most of what was said. Jamie had met a lovely girl in college, she said. I made that much out through the sobs and they appeared to be doing a line together. I remember the girl's name; it had such a nice heavenly ring to it, Angela Devine. Honest. I swear, that was her name. Anyway, Jamie had never been so happy, according to Ethel. Then, if I understood her properly, his father had gone and spoiled everything. I asked her what she meant by that but I couldn't get a proper answer. She was more or less incoherent. Several times she said: "He's told the boy, the bastard has told the boy the truth. He's destroyed Jamie and turned him against me; he's ruined everything!"

'I decided to go to Ireland and get to the bottom of things, sort out whatever mess my sister had got herself into. Trouble is: I left it too late, didn't I. Story of my frigging life; never there when she needed me. I had to arrange things at work, get time off, get someone to stand in for me, the usual sort of things, things that seemed important at the time but of course, as events turned out, they weren't.

'I didn't know it at the time but Ethel was already dead by the time I boarded the plane to come to Dublin. My twin sister had looked for my help and I'd failed her. How do you think that makes me feel, eh? So, a little late in the day, I've decided to do something to avenge what happened to her. The only reason I've told you all this is because I want you to help me destroy the monster, Todd Wilson.'

25

His much anticipated reunion with Fidelma did not turn out to be anything like what he had envisaged. To his astonishment, she was cross with him. He couldn't believe it. Instead of welcoming him back in her arms, smothering him with kisses, tearing his clothes off and jumping in the sack to make love, she decided to take issue with him. Questions; she wanted answers to questions. He was having none of it. 'Ah, come on Fidelma, give us a bleedin' break for Christ's sake,' he pleaded, but the lady was not for turning. Never mind sweet entreaties like – 'Oh, you poor dear, what have those awful people tried to do to you!' Never mind – 'Let's make love, Matt; you can tell me later about all the other unpleasant stuff.' It wasn't enough that the cops should have bombarded him with questions about his lorry and the drugs; it wasn't enough that he had to appear before a magistrate like some common criminal to protest his innocence (unsuccessful as it turned out), but now Fidelma had jumped on the bandwagon. Like some Gestapo inquisitor in a scene from an old movie, she interrogated him.

It took him the best part of an hour to convince her that he had been a blameless victim in everything that had happened. At last, her expression changed, her smile let him know that he had been fully reinstated in her affections. But the longed-for lovemaking still didn't get under way. This time he was responsible for the impediment. He sulked. He was the injured party. What sort of girlfriend could ever believe that he could possibly have been involved in such shady shenanigans in the first place? That's what he wanted to know. He felt most aggrieved; it was all so terribly unfair.

The stand-off lasted a full two minutes before Fidelma began to laugh. Matt held out for a further ten seconds before the petulant pout turned to a grin and he too creased up in laughter.

The lovemaking that followed was good, prolonged, relentless but not as good as Matt had anticipated. Nothing could have matched the fantasy routine he so vividly envisioned in his mind during his time abroad on his travels. Lying together, temporarily exhausted after their amorous exertion, they heard the doorbell ring. At first, both of them ignored the intrusion, pretending not to hear it. But the caller persisted. 'I'll get it,' Fidelma said finally, 'more than likely it's me they're looking for.'

'Probably some toyboy you picked up while I was away in Africa,' Matt joked, making no attempt to stir himself.

'Yeah, you're probably right,' Fidelma replied, playing along with the joke, as she pulled on her panties and dressing gown, and slipped on her bedroom slippers. 'I'll tell him to buzz off with himself – explain that my real stud has returned – and then come back and see if you can still measure up to the task in hand.'

'Oh, ya durty filthy little slapper,' Matt said through yelps of laughter. 'Have a heart, girl; don't you know they didn't feed me half well enough in Lucan cop-shop for this kinda crack.'

Fidelma was still smiling as she pulled the bolt back from the front door and opened it. The smile faded immediately. Two men, wearing ski-masks grabbed her. She screamed. A gloved hand applied to her mouth cut the scream short. Pushed in the back, she went sprawling off-balance and on to the floor. Her face took the full brunt of the fall. Blood splattered from her nose. Before she knew what was happening, a hand grabbed the hair of her head and yanked her to her feet again. Terrified, her face cut and bloodied, her dressing gown flopping open, she managed to ask the question: 'Who are you?'

'We have a little business with your boyfriend,' a gruff voice said from behind a ski mask. 'We need a few words with him.'

'He's not here,' she snapped. Wrong answer. The brute force of a slap across the face knocked her sideways.

'You're a lying little slag,' the same gruff voice said as he pulled the dressing gown down on her arms, exposing her breasts. 'You see, my small-titted tart, we had your precious lover boy followed. We know he's been here banging the arse of you for the past few hours.'

As she fumbled to cover her nakedness, Matt came

rushing from the bedroom. 'What-the-fuck's . . . ' was all he managed to say before the intruders rushed to grab him. Totally naked, Matt attempted to kick out at them. His effort was futile. One of the masked men caught his foot, jerked it high into the air, knocking him backwards onto the floor. Simultaneously, the other attacker's thick-soled boot connected with Matt's exposed scrotum with all the efficiency of a club head smacking a golf ball off its tee. Matt's fractured scream pierced the air as his hands shot, belatedly, to shield his testicles. Doubled up in agony, groaning like some wounded animal, his eyes searched frantically for Fidelma. Shocked by the sight of her bloodied face, his own pain temporarily pushed aside; he resolved that no further harm should come to her. But he had not reckoned with the brutality of the attackers. His thoughts now focused on Fidelma's welfare, he struggled to his feet and was about to go to her when both intruders launched into a frenzied attack on him. He was repeatedly kicked, punched, head-butted and clobbered about the head before getting a rabbit punch on the back of the neck.

Fidelma rejoined the fray. Fearing for Matt's life, she leaped to his side and cradled his battered head in her hands. He was, she could see, only semiconscious. 'You bastards, leave him alone,' she screeched, finding a resolve she didn't know she possessed. 'Why are you doing this to us? Who the hell are you? What do you want from us?'

'Your friend here has been a bit careless with

someone else's property; cost our boss a lot of money. We're going to teach him a lesson. So, unless you'd like your teeth in a bag, I suggest you cooperate with us.'

'What do you want?' Fidelma asked.

'Get him into his clobber; we need to take him to meet our boss.'

'I'll do nothing for you. I want you both to get out of here this minute.'

'Look, slurry puss, we can take him with or without his kit. The choice is yours. But if you don't dress him, me and my buddy here will fuck you, good-looking – both of us at the same time – you know, the old meat in the sandwich trick, so what's it going to be?'

Fidelma had no need to think about his proposition. She took the threat seriously; the brute meant what he said. The second attacker, the one who had not bothered to speak once throughout the ordeal, had begun to caress his crotch. 'OK,' she said, 'I'll get Matt into his clothes, but let me tell you . . . '

'Yeah, blah, blah, bloody blah; we know all that, you'll do the devil and all. Save your breath 'cause you've got no say in the matter. Do what you're told. Be quick about it and we might just allow you to stay breathing.'

Fidelma retrieved Matt's clothes from the bedroom and managed with great difficulty to get them on to his bruised body. During this awkward operation, Matt moaned in agony each time she forced a leg or an arm into a sleeve or trouser leg. With the task complete, the attackers pushed her aside and grabbed Matt from beneath his arms and hauled him towards the front door, his feet dragging along the floor. 'If you contact the cops,' the gruff voice warned, 'you'll never see limp-dick here alive again. You've already used up all your own lifelines, bitch. Next one is his, OK? You phone a friend or say one word to anyone, the game is over for Mattie-boy here. If you're stupid, open your trap to anyone, we'll be back to get you. We'll hump you from here to Kingdom come in ways you can't even begin to imagine. Then we'll inject a little HIV infected blood into you just for the fun of it. You got that?'

Fidelma watched as the front door slammed shut in her face. Matt was gone. She was alone. Feeling numb, she sank to her knees, then flopped down on the floor and began to shiver and shake. 'Dear Jesus, what am I supposed to do,' she implored, seeking guidance from a God she had abandoned many years earlier.

No response came to her pleading.

George Laffin and Ciarán Bailey were on their second drink by the time Emma and Vinny made it back from the airport to their apartment. Emma, whose flight from Liverpool had been delayed by half an hour, could have done without the task of entertaining visitors as soon as she got home. Even as her plane touched down in Dublin Airport, her mental faculties continued to review her encounter with Marina Cassidy back in Liverpool. Coming to terms with Marina's accounts of how Todd Wilson had destroyed Jamie and Ethel Cassidy, was difficult to fully absorb. The whole thing was so fantastic. The more Emma tried to make sense out of what she had heard, the more confused the whole affair became. If, as Marina maintained, Jamie was central to what had happened, then maybe she should try to track down this girlfriend with the heavenly sounding name, find out if she could shed any light on events leading up to Jamie's death. It would probably prove to be a waste of time but you never could tell; maybe the girlfriend would give her some insight into Jamie's behaviour that put a whole new spin on things.

Seeing Vinny at the airport, waiting for her in the Arrivals lounge, was like a breath of fresh air. It forced her to put Ethel Cassidy's murder, and Todd Wilson's part in it, on temporary hold. As always, Vinny cheered her up with his lively banter as he drove through the city and made it to Huband Place. It was when he informed her that George Laffin and Ciarán Bailey were waiting for them in the apartment that her spirits floundered. With all that had happened in the past few days she had forgotten about Vinny's arrangement to join the two men for a meal in the Smithfield Court. The timing could have been better, she thought, but decided not to voice her lack of enthusiasm. Remembering how things had turned sour on their last outing in the same hotel, she was determined not to spoil things for Vinny, on this occasion.

Emma greeted Ciarán with her usual fuss while conferring celebrity status on George Laffin. As ever, Vinny was amazed at his wife's resilience. Watching the way she put the two older men at ease made him feel good. George Laffin was beguiled by her and chatted like some long-lost friend. She laughed heartily at his risqué stories and surprised him by countering with a few funny anecdotes of her own. Effortlessly, she guided him on to the apartment's small balcony off the living room. Holding on to their drinks, they both leaned against the rail and took in the view of the water tumbling over the nearby lock gate. When Emma asked him about his role in the proposed television documentary, he was happy to enlighten her. 'The programme plans to feature the recently opened new extension to the National Gallery of Ireland. They've shot a short film showing some of the major exhibits, including the recently discovered Caravaggio, and all I have to do is throw in a sort of educated commentary, that sort of thing.' While he spoke, he watched the dark water of the canal move lazily from Huband Bridge on to Mount Street lock, observing a swan as it drifted gracefully on the water's surface. Emma too, was taken by the peace and serenity the canal presented but the moment of sublime bliss dissipated when Vinny approached to remind them it was time to go to the Smithfield Court.

In a smooth operation, the main course appeared in front of them: paupiettes of sole with leek and ginger for her, and for Vinny, lightly grilled sea king scallops napped with pink peppercorn cream. The two older men, who couldn't be bothered to look at the menu, ordered sirloin steaks, boiled potatoes and lashings of fried onions. Vinny, who had chosen the wine, watched bemused as the wine waiter, with much ceremonial fuss, presented a bottle of German Kabinett to George Laffin for approval, in the mistaken belief that he was hosting the meal. 'The wine, sir,' he said with toffee-nosed smugness, 'our Rödesheimer Berg Rottland, Riesling 1994.'

George, tipping a wink to Vinny, brought the waiter down to earth by indicating with a hand gesture that Emma would inspect the label. Emma smiled knowingly at George, looked at the label and nodded her approval to the waiter. Somewhat chastened, the waiter poured a measure of wine into Emma's glass for her to taste, only to discover he had been wrong-footed again; on this occasion the lady wished her husband, Vinny to do the tasting.

After this spot of mischievous fun with the wine waiter, they enjoyed their meal, the topic of con-versation concentrating on the absence of the eight-eenth-century collection of English paintings from the hotel's Dedalus Gallery. Much to Vinny and Ciarán's disappointment, the collection of eighteenth-century paintings had been replaced by an exhibition featuring works by fifty twentieth-century British artists, along with self-portraits by the artists. When Vinny spoke to the hotel manager on the matter, he was informed that the collection he referred to had been shipped across to their sister hotel in Edinburgh. According to the manager, this was hotel policy; there would be, he claimed, an ongoing exchange of paintings between the different premises owned by the Wilson group.

Notwithstanding this disappointment, the visit to the Smithfield Court was turning out to be well worthwhile. The meal had been a great success, thanks mainly to the non-stop flow of stimulating conversation generated by George and Ciarán. For Emma, it provided an opportunity to unwind and take it easy, relax, enjoy the food and the company while preserving her energy. She declined the wine and the offer of an after-dinner liqueur, content to watch her three male companions indulge themselves by ordering vintage port. Vinny, having learned his lesson from his last occasion in the Court, was careful to limit his intake of alcohol and not to order cigars.

On the way out of the restaurant Vinny pressed a ten-pound note into the wine waiter's hand. The waiter, who had earlier written off his prospects of a tip and had, in all probability, dismissed Vinny and his party as a bunch of cretins, now swallowed his breath as his Adam's apple bobbed up and down in an attempt to express gratitude.

Vinny was still smiling as he made his way through the hotel lobby, on the way to the exit, when he stopped dead in his tracks. Paul Newman, the man who had sold him the Harry Clarke drawing, was making his way through a door that led to a private office to one side of the reception area. Vinny felt absolutely sure that Newman had recognised him but instead of an acknowledgement, the dealer quickly turned his face away, as though not wishing to be seen. Newman, who had been accompanied by another man, disappeared from view, leaving Vinny to wonder what could have prompted such strange behaviour. Noting Vinny's sudden immobility, Emma cast her eyes to where he was staring. She saw nothing except a closed door with the word 'private' written on it. 'What's the matter, Vinny?' she asked, trying to read the puzzled look on his face.

'Odd,' was all he said at first.

'What the hell's got into you, Vinny?' she pressed.

'Odd,' he said again, pointing to the door. 'I've just seen Paul Newman, the guy who sold me the Harry Clarke drawing go through that door with another man. The funny thing is: I know he saw me – recognised me – but he tried to hide his face from me. Now, why would anyone want to do that?'

By now, George and Ciarán had joined Emma and Vinny in the centre of the hotel's foyer. 'Is there some sort of problem?' George asked.

'No, not really,' Vinny replied. 'It's just a bit of a coincidence, that's all. The art dealer who imported the paintings we wanted you to see in the gallery here – the same fellow who sold me the Harry Clarke – well, I've just seen him with another man here in the hotel.'

'So?' George asked, 'what's so remarkable about that?'

'Oh, nothing, nothing at all, except – except that he acted as though he didn't want me to see him here.'

Emma had by now switched to investigative mode. 'Can you describe the man who was with this art dealer fellow? Could he have been Todd Wilson, by any chance?'

Vinny thought for a moment before replying. 'I couldn't say, Emma, I only saw his back – besides, I was concentrating on Newman.'

Without warning, Emma strode away from her three companions and approached the reception counter. She informed the receptionists who she was, adding that she was from the *Post*, and asked if she could see Mr Todd Wilson. On being informed that he was not on the premises, Emma pointed to the door behind the reception area and said she had seen him go through it a few minutes earlier. 'I'm afraid you're mistaken, Madam,' she was told, 'I can assure you, Mr Wilson has not been here at all this evening.'

'Then, who was it I saw?'

'I have no idea, Madam,' the receptionist said with a finality that let Emma know further information would not be forthcoming.

Returning to the others, Emma related what she had learned before all four of them finally headed in the direction of the exit. Like her companions, Emma remained oblivious of the CCTV camera above them, and to the fact that two men were watching intently as a monitor recorded their every move.

26

Six male politicians, all decked out like tailor's dummies, sat around the stately mahogany table, each busily shuffling papers, each filled with a sense of his own importance. They were charged with the task of looking into allegations of abuse and financial irregularities in Third World aid agencies. The room in which this enquiry was taking place befitted a building designated to house the Irish Parliament, its scale and grandeur a lasting legacy to the talent of its architect Richard Castle, who in 1745 built it for James FitzGerald, the twentieth Earl of Kildare.

Usually the general public would run a mile rather than listen to the wall-to-wall waffle generated in the course of such hearings but to-day was slightly different. Because of Maeve Wilson's enforced appearance, and because of her high profile in the media, the proceedings commanded considerable interest. A television crew, some radio personnel, a select gathering of press reporters and political correspondents sat at a discreet distance from where the deliberations were taking place. Like her colleagues in the press, Emma Boylan tried to avoid these public inquisitions whenever possible but made an exception on this occasion. Having the opportunity to see and hear Maeve Wilson in action was reason enough to ensure her attendance. With a little luck, she might get an opportunity to talk to her, ask a few questions, maybe even get a few answers.

It was almost lunch hour by the time any real business got under way. Maeve Wilson, along with the chief executives of the country's other three main aid-agencies, was introduced by the committee chairman to the other members. In turn, all four made opening statements. Maeve Wilson chose to speak last. Her résumé of SUCCOUR's record in the fight against suffering and disease in the Third World sounded most impressive to Emma's ears. With Fergus Massey by her side, Maeve Wilson came across as a woman of substance, someone who had the welfare of those in need at heart. Speaking in subdued tones, her words tripping off the tongue with an ease that belied the nervous vein throbbing in her neck. She traced the history of her organisation from its inception to its present day status, alluding occasionally to specific projects that had saved the lives of countless hundreds of people in Ethiopia, people who, she claimed, would otherwise be dead today.

Although Emma's appraisal of Maeve Wilson continued, she occasionally switched her attention to Fergus Massey. In the course of her work as a journalist she had come into contact with Massey on a few occasions. But it was only since her meeting with Marina Cassidy in Liverpool, only after hearing about the relationship that existed between Massey, Todd Wilson and the Cassidy twins, that her interest in the man had grown substantially. Glancing at him now, she could not be indifferent to his striking good looks. Emma had come across his name with some frequency while researching her articles on Todd Wilson's business activities. From the sketchy details she had uncovered, it appeared that Massey had contributed sizeable financial contributions to projects headed up by Todd Wilson. Throughout these early years, it was apparent that Massey's main interest lay in sailing and flying. But then, unusually for him, he took an active interest in the SUCCOUR agency. Although Maeve Wilson had been the prime mover in setting up the aid-agency it had been Massey's money that had got the project off the ground.

Looking at how Massey and Maeve Wilson reacted with each other, as they faced the politicians, Emma wondered if their relationship might be more than just a business arrangement. They looked so incredibly good together. Bearing in mind what Marina had told her about the wild times Massey enjoyed two decades earlier, a time when Maeve and Ethel Cassidy positively drooled over him and availed of every opportunity to be in his company, it was only natural to wonder if any of these feelings survived down through the years.

Emma's chain of thoughts was interrupted when the chairman brought proceedings to a temporary halt. It was lunchtime. Business would recommence at 3 o'clock that afternoon.

The morning had been a non-event as far as Emma

was concerned. She had learned nothing that she did not already know. She was debating in her own mind whether or not she should bother coming back in the afternoon when she found herself walking next to Maeve Wilson and Fergus Massey. Like everyone else attending the hearing, they were headed for the car park at the rear of Government Buildings. Never one to miss an opportunity, Emma introduced herself to them and asked if they would mind if she asked a few questions. Maeve Wilson smiled her best professional smile but declined the request, claiming she had an appointment somewhere else and was already a few minutes late. Emma was about to try again when Fergus Massey stopped in mid-stride and turned to face her. 'When do you gutter-snipe hacks get off harassing people, eh?' he asked, 'I know who you are and what you have been writing in that rag of a paper you work for. As far as I'm concerned you are not worthy to breathe the same air as the good decent people you dare to criticise.'

'Sorry,' Emma said taken aback but recovering quickly, 'but who are you referring to – these good people that I have criticised. Who exactly do you have in mind?'

'I see,' he snapped, fixing his eyes on Emma, 'dumb as well as irresponsible, are we? You know damn well I'm talking about Todd Wilson. The pathetic muck-raking you have been doing is nothing short of disgraceful.'

Emma was incredulous. She wanted to cut across his aggressiveness, rebut his assertions but Massey preempted her. 'Well, let me tell you,' he said, his voice remaining low but the tone undeniably belligerent, 'Miss Guttersnipe, you are barking up the wrong tree when you attack my friend Todd Wilson; he is a decent man doing a decent job for the betterment of this country of ours. Whereas you, and the worthless rabid newspaper you work for, are nothing but scum of the earth.'

'I beg your pardon . . . ' was all Emma managed to get out before being subjected to more of Massey's invective. 'Why don't you do something useful for once in your life!' he continued, 'Why don't you use your talents, meagre and all as they might be, to discover who is behind the conspiracy that is actively working to destroy Todd Wilson.'

Emma opened her mouth to reply but Massey and Maeve Wilson had moved away before she could speak. She took a deep breath and exhaled. She stood immobile, trying to gather her thoughts, attempting to recover from the whirlwind of abuse that Massey had visited upon her. Forced to revisit the oft-repeated Shakespearean quotation: 'All that glitters is not gold' Emma realised that Fergus Massey's aplomb and glittering smile were nothing more than a shallow mask, a cloak to hide an ugly nature.

The face looking back at Fidelma Roper from the hand-mirror bore little resemblance to the one she had grown familiar with over the past twenty-four years. Her nose looked as if it had been flattened by a heavyweight boxer's fist, the area beneath the left eye was blackened and the eye itself was half closed. The rims of both eyes were red and puffed from constant crying. Her bottom lip, distorted by a series of inflamed cuts, looked ugly and raw. The outward signs of what had happened to her did not fully reflect the state of shock and fear she felt inside. She had tried to sleep during the night but recurring nightmares insisted that she face her tormentors over and over again. She had screamed, cried, tossed and turned until finally, towards dawn she had managed to get a few hours uninterrupted sleep.

Already late for work, she phoned her employer to say she was not feeling well and would not be in for a few days. She had no intention of letting her friends in Hewlett-Packard see her face in its present state; the global provider of computing and imaging solutions would just have to try and muddle on without her for a few days.

But the state of her face and her absence from the workplace were of little consequence when compared to her worries about Matt Dempsey. Where was he? Was he alive or dead? She had hoped against hope that he would return home during the night. He did not. Why hadn't he contacted her? Surely whatever business his abductors had with him couldn't be taking that long? Jesus, anything could have happened to him. She tried to rationalise the thoughts rushing around her head, think things through. The two brutes who had taken him away had warned her not to tell anyone about what had happened if she wanted to see him alive again. Were they serious? Were they bluffing? Shit, she didn't know. In her confused state of mind after their departure she had complied with their orders.

After a night of torturous deliberations she felt less inclined to believe their threats and more fearful of what might happen to Matt if she didn't do something. Who should she contact, that was the uppermost consideration in her mind. He had just been released on bail by the Gardaí, the same Gardaí who believed he was into drug trafficking. She couldn't imagine them getting too excited about his abduction. They would probably think it was a ruse to avoid his obligation of checking into the station every day during his bail period. Bastards. She believed him when he insisted he had nothing whatsoever to do with drugs but now she was faced with a dilemma: Who to trust? Who to contact?

Wearing only a dressing gown, she walked about the living room aimlessly with a mug of instant coffee in her hand and a vacant look in her eyes. For the past two years she had shared this small two-storey mews with Matt. Until yesterday it had never crossed her mind that anything untoward could ever happen to shatter the sense of security the place offered. This was the idyllic place where they shut the world out; it was the place where they made love, where they felt free and uninhibited in each other's company. Her collection of dolls from around the world had grown considerably in the space of the two years and had become the focal point of their lounge. This morning, she felt their tiny eyes upon her; it was as though they expected her to do something about what had happened. 'I'm thinking, I'm thinking,' she said to the collective eyes, instantly realising she was losing it, talking to inanimate objects. First sign of madness, she told herself. The latest doll remained in its special presentation box. Because of its association with Matt, she doubted if she would ever add it to her collection. It would depend entirely on what happened to Matt.

It was another hour before she made a decision on what to do. After looking in the telephone directory, she contacted the Lucan Garda Station.

27

Emma was back in the Dáil building by 3 o'clock, feeling much better. Exposure to fresh air during the lunch break had done wonders for her. She made a resolution not to let anyone get under her skin during the afternoon session, no matter how obnoxious he or she might become. Notwithstanding this pious aspir–ation, the proceedings managed to put a damper on her newfound benevolence. What she was hearing was dull stuff indeed. Facts and figures were exchanged in a lacklustre fashion, the ebb and flow of questions and answers, conducted at a snail's pace, induced barely concealed yawns.

It was only when Maeve Wilson's turn came to quantify the remuneration she and her fellow directors paid themselves that the proceedings sparked into life.

Committee member Michael P. Wall decided it was time to score a few points at the expense of Maeve Wilson. In the course of a longwinded exchange, he remarked that Maeve Wilson's salary seemed unusually high to him. Maeve took exception to his supercilious tone and stopped him in mid-flow. With her nose up-tilted exquisitely as though offended by some obnox–ious odour emanating from his direction, she insisted that he justify his remark. Not expecting this comeback,

Wall, a wiry little ferret of a man in his late thirties, whose movements appeared jerky and slightly uncoordinated, had some difficulty finding the words he needed to make his case. 'Well,' he said, after going through a series of extreme facial expressions, 'let's take an example, shall we. Let's take the case of Whitty and Bowes, one of this country's most successful wine, spirit and tobacco distributors. You would agree with me, Mrs Wilson, would you not, that they are very successful?'

'If showing a huge profit is an indicator of success, then yes, they are successful,' Maeve replied. 'What is your point?'

'My point is this: their stock shares have increased by at least 10 per cent each year for the past three years . . . and yet, their chief executive's salary comes to less than yours. You would agree, would you not, that any fair appraisal of what Whitty and Bowes' chief executive earns and what you earn is . . . shall we say, out of proportion.'

'Yes, I agree with you,' Maeve said, taking everyone in the room by surprise, 'I agree that there is an imbalance between the two sets of salary. In my capacity as chief executive of SUCCOUR, I have saved the lives of thousands of people who without the intervention of my organisation would probably have died.' She paused for a second to let the significance of what she had just said register, before continuing. 'On the other hand, the chief executive of Whitty and Bowes has, through the distribution of wine, spirits and tobacco, probably caused the deaths of thousands of people foolish enough to consume his products. So, yes, there is an imbalance: Whitty and Bowes' Chief Executive is overpaid; I am not paid enough.'

It was arrogant stuff from Maeve but it put the politicians on notice that they would have to try a lot harder if they hoped to make a case against her. Emma, who had enjoyed the exchange, decided that the initial P in Wall's name stood for Piss-artist. In the cross-examination that followed, Maeve continued to get the better of the exchanges. She produced storyboards that showed areas in Ethiopia where her aid agency had undertaken projects to alleviate suffering. Supplementary storyboards were produced to show, by way of graphics, how various medical equipment and emergency first-aid clinics had been deployed in the most neglected areas. Price tags had been cleverly attached to each display to show where money had been spent. From the expressions on the politicians' faces, with the notable exception of Michael Pissartist Wall, it was clear that Maeve Wilson had gone a long way to allaying their fears in regard to the funding of her aid operation.

At 5 o'clock, the chairman brought proceedings to a halt. The hearings, he announced, would continue the next day when closer examination of financial accounts would be on the agenda. It meant that the principals of the aid agencies would not have to be present, the more detailed number crunching being assigned to their top accountants and financial advisors.

Leaving the chamber, Emma noticed Fergus Massey and Maeve Wilson making their way towards her. She took a deep breath. Oh, God, Massey is going to give me another earful. Maeve stood in front of her, smiled and said: 'Mr Massey has something he'd like to say to you.'

Emma objected. 'Well, I'm not so sure I want to hear what . . . '

Massey interrupted her. 'Look, Ms Boylan, I want to apologise for what I said to you earlier today, I was way out of line.'

'Yes, Mr Massey, I believe you were. What you said about . . . '

Massey cut across her again. 'What I said was wrong, you're quite right, I totally accept that. My only excuse is that I get so mad when I see someone like Todd Wilson being castigated for wrongs he did not do. I was wrong to strike out at you Ms Boylan. My behaviour was inexcusable; I know your job is to report the news – and I was wrong to have a go at the messenger. It's whoever's behind the message that should get the bollocking, not you. I'm sorry.'

'Apology accepted,' Emma said, 'but maybe you'd like to give me the benefit of your thinking in regard to who you suspect is behind this so-called conspiracy to destroy Todd Wilson.'

Massey flashed her his most dazzling smile. 'I'd rather not say at this point. I have one or two theories but I'll hold my counsel until I'm more positive about my facts.'

'That's a pity,' Emma said, determined not to be brushed aside by his smile, 'because if we were to pool our inform ...'

'I'm sorry, Ms Boylan, I've got to go.'

Emma was left standing with Maeve Wilson while Fergus Massey dashed off in the direction of the car park. Maeve shook her head in mock exasperation. 'He's still annoyed with me for getting him to apologise to you; men can be such a pain in the neck when they chose to be.'

'Yes, I know exactly what you mean, I'm married to one.'

They both laughed. It was as though some bond of sisterhood had been established. Taking advantage of the moment, Emma decided to press forward with her own agenda. 'Would you have the time to talk to me? There's a few questions I'd like to ask, and ...'

'No, sorry, I really have to be somewhere in ...'

'Please.'

Maeve smiled and nodded submissively. 'Very well, then, after Fergus's behaviour, I suppose I owe you that much. Let's get away from here, go somewhere and have a coffee.'

The Shelbourne Hotel, on the corner of Kildare Street and St Stephen's Green North, only a few hundred yards from Government Buildings, provided their refuge for coffee, biscuits and a chat. Emma would have preferred to interview Maeve, run through a question-and-answer session, but it was obvious from the moment they sat down in the comfortable seating in the hotel's front reception area, that Maeve wanted to keep their exchange on an informal chat basis.

It was only to be expected that Maeve would talk about her work in the Third World, but Emma did manage to steer the conversation on to more personal matters. Sympathising over the recent death of her son Jamie, brought about a motherly response from Maeve that was in stark contrast to the snappy business-like image Emma had seen her display at the all-party committee hearing. Maeve talked about Jamie with great fondness, recalling anecdotes from his school and college days, reliving special moments between mother and son, moments of tenderness that brought a mist to her eyes. In the course of conversation, Emma let slip that she was pregnant, expecting her first baby. This revelation brought further discussion on the joys of motherhood with Maeve becoming quite animated as she recalled the highs and lows of her own pregnancy.

They had poured themselves a second cup of coffee before Emma had the opportunity to introduce Ethel Cassidy into the conversation. Maeve did not appear to have any problem discussing Ethel and talked freely about the close relationship that had existed between her one-time housekeeper-cum-gardener and her son Jamie. 'You and Ethel,' Emma said, 'were members of the Dublin City Orchestra at one time. Why did you both give it up?'

A frown appeared on Maeve's face. 'When I became pregnant with Jamie, Todd insisted that I take a break from work. I didn't agree. I wanted to continue with the orchestra until the last minute but I did something I would never do now: I gave in to Todd for the sake of peace. I had always intended to go back to the music but as things turned out it just never happened.'

'And Ethel?' Emma asked, trying to sound casual, 'Why did Ethel leave the orchestra?'

Maeve shifted uneasily in her seat. It was apparent that she was uncomfortable with where the conversation was heading. For a few awkward moments it looked as though she would not reply at all but finally, after toying with her coffee cup, she spoke. 'I don't like to speak ill of the dead, but I'm afraid Ethel was the author of her own misfortunes. She was forced to leave the orchestra because of an accident of her own making. It's a long story and I don't have time to give you all the background but essentially, my husband Todd was involved in an argument with Ethel that went disastrously wrong. It happened at a very troubled period in Ethel's life, a time when she felt she needed the comfort of a man. Unfortunately, the man she hit on turned out to be my husband. It was a disastrous situation all round. Now, I'm not going to tell you that Todd was whiter than white when it came to his interest in the opposite sex, God knows his exploits in that direction are well enough documented but I can assure you he had no interest whatsoever in Ethel.

'Ethel could not accept this rejection and on one occasion, under the influence of too much alcohol, she attacked Todd physically, threatening to kill herself if he did not leave me and live with her instead. Todd had never heard a more absurd suggestion. He told her she was stark raving mad to suggest such a thing. On hearing this, Ethel's attack on him intensified, forcing Todd to defend himself. This was when things got out of hand. Todd, who sometimes does not know his own strength, pushed her away from him more forcefully than he had intended to. She fell heavily and hurt her left hand. Phalanx damage, the doctors explained at the time. Apparently, she had chipped the bone between the second and third knuckle of the little finger. The outcome for Ethel was disastrous; she never played the violin professionally after that day. She still had the ability to play but her confidence as a serious musician was shattered and she hated the thoughts of playing badly.

'Todd had no choice but to tell me what had happened. I was furious at first, a natural enough reaction, you'll agree, but after carefully considering the implications of what had happened, I decided that Todd should pay to have the best specialists look at her hand. Everything that could be done was done but as I said, she never played professionally again. Without the violin she had no way of making a living so I suggested to Todd that we take her on as housekeeper until she found some better employment. Todd was dead against the idea – created ructions – but I insisted. You see, I knew how fond of Jamie she was and that the boy needed someone to look after him when myself and Todd were not at home.

'Since earliest childhood days, Jamie suffered some breathing difficulties and was prone to allergic reactions. Because of this he was prescribed anti-histamines and put on a restricted diet. In his early days in national school, his allergic reactions to food and air pollutants caused a series of minor upsets. You know what small boys are like; they want unrestricted play and fun. Poor Jamie. Ethel took it upon herself to administer adrenaline injections and other prescribed medication. In spite of his problems, Jamie managed to have a happy childhood and developed normally in every other respect. In the months and years that followed, Ethel, when she wasn't tied up with looking after him, discovered a talent for gardening. She was damn good at it, too, and even if Todd didn't agree with her way of doing things, she stayed on. She even played the violin for Jamie when he had difficulty sleeping. Because of his condition, his breathing sometimes became irregular at night. At times like that Ethel would sit by his bedside and play soothing melodies or read story books until sleep overtook him. She instilled a love of music in him and even greater love of books.

'She was doing a fine job – everyone thought so. I thought so but Todd just couldn't get along with her at all. In the end, just before the . . . the tragedy, the two of them had a major disagreement. Todd had just bought Jamie a top-of-the-range computer with DVD unit, CD writer, scanner, colour printer and the devil-knows-what else, when Ethel took issue with him. She accused Todd of buying Jamie's affections – of never being with the boy when he was needed. The row got out of hand. The upshot of it all was that Ethel lost her job.'

Emma wanted to know more about Ethel Cassidy and was about to frame a question when the sound of a mobile phone brought their conversation to a halt. At first Emma thought it was her phone but discovered she had neglected to switch it on after her lunch break. Maeve Wilson extracted a mobile from her clutch bag and pressed it to her ear. After a series of barely audible yeahs, ums and OKs she made a kissing sound with her lips and put the mobile back in her bag. 'Look, Emma, I'm really sorry but I have to . . . I have to run along. I enjoyed our little chat and I hope everything goes well with you over the next few months. Have to rush. We'll talk again. 'Bye.'

And that was it. Maeve Wilson was gone. Emma resumed her seat. She cursed whoever had invented the mobile phone. Just when she was about to get the full story as to why Ethel Cassidy had left the Wilson's, the damn bleeper sounded. Damn, damn, damn! There were a number of messages stored on her own mobile phone but she resisted the urge to hit the playback button. She wanted a few minutes to allow her brain to assimilate all that she had heard from Maeve Wilson, to put a structure on what she had learned.

It intrigued her that Maeve should have told her about the rows between Ethel and Todd. The first row had brought about the end of Ethel's musical career, the last row had cost Ethel her job. Emma found it interesting that Maeve should neglect to make any reference to Ethel's unwanted pregnancy. There were so many things that didn't add up. Todd Wilson had, according to Maeve, knocked Ethel down, damaged her hand, and then looked after her medical expenses and gave her a job in his house. It was even harder to understand why Maeve Wilson would encourage her husband to employ a woman who was, supposedly, besotted by him. Surely, that didn't make sense. But the big question remained: why was Ethel Cassidy murdered three days after the boy's funeral?

Emma shook her head admitting defeat. She had more questions than answers. She had several theories, a hundred-and-one scenarios but nothing she could totally believe in and certainly nothing she could go to print with.

Before leaving the hotel, she decided to listen to the recorded messages stored on her mobile phone. Vinny had contacted her twice. Assuming the role of mother hen, he wanted to know if she was feeling well . . . and would she ring him back. Emma smiled in spite of herself. She really did love Vinny and appreciated his concern for her well-being. She sometimes wanted to scream at him, tell him to stop being a fusspot but the truth was she loved him, she loved him more than she would ever be able to let him know.

Bob Crosby had called her and asked her to get in touch with him. She looked at her watch. It was almost

6 o'clock; he would have to wait until next morning.

The final message had come from Detective-Inspector Connolly. He sounded peeved and wanted her to contact him without delay. Emma considered ringing him there and then but changed her mind. She felt tired, bone-weary. She just wanted to go home, flop into an easy chair, throw off her shoes and chill out for a few hours. With a bit of luck Vinny would rustle up some grub and later . . . and later they would make love.

28

Vinny insisted that Emma remain on in bed until she felt better. He had brought a light breakfast to the room but she hadn't felt like eating anything. Even the freshly squeezed orange juice he had made failed to entice a positive response. 'You go,' she told him. 'I'll be OK in half an hour, honestly Vin. Go on . . . meet George. I'll call you on the mobile as soon as I feel a bit better.'

He gently felt her stomach, a newfound morning ritual, kissed her goodbye and reluctantly set off for the Merrion Hotel. In the course of a telephone call the previous day to George Laffin, he had arranged to pick him up there this morning at 8.30 am. On the short drive to the hotel he thought about the unborn son or daughter who would one day call him Daddy. It was a concept he had some difficulty in coming to terms with. Birth, he readily accepted, was a miracle, a truly wonderful miracle, but as a man, he felt his role in the period leading up to the birth was unfairly minuscule. There was, he could see, great joy for the woman during these months, a joy that the male could only guess at, but there was also a less pleasant side to pregnancy, a side that he could do nothing about – even if he wanted to.

He had gotten used to Emma's morning sickness

but he still hated to see her go through such an unpleasant experience. She had been totally exhausted the evening before when she came home from the office but he knew better than to ask her to ease up on her workload. Instead he had cooked chicken fricassee for them both, uncorked a Chardonnay and later, after he had tidied the kitchen, sat down with her in front of the television to watch a video. For what must have been their third or fourth time they sat through all 218 minutes of *Once upon a Time in America*. Both of them loved the old Robert DeNiro epic, Emma for the storyline, he for the soundtrack.

George Laffin was already waiting on the front steps of the Merrion Hotel by the time Vinny got there. As ever, George seemed in the best of spirits as he took his place in the passenger seat. Looking more like a tourist about to take a trip down the River Nile than a drive to Ireland's misty midlands, George's ensemble could best be described as 'designer casual'. His straw-coloured, linen suit, ruffled handkerchief sprouting over the breast pocket, open-neck, button-down shirt and violet-tinted sunglasses, together with his fleece of long white hair and ponytail, ensured that heads turned to look at him. Loquacious to a fault, his stream of anecdotes, exquisitely exotic, helped take Vinny's mind off the slow moving bumper-to-bumper traffic that had become so much a part of Dublin's morning traffic in recent years.

'You seem a bit preoccupied,' George said to Vinny. 'Nothing the matter with that good lady of yours, I hope?'

'No, George, but thanks for asking. Emma did have a little touch of morning sickness earlier but she'll be right as rain after a lie-in.'

'She's a wonderful woman, Vinny – very bright – very beautiful. You're a lucky man to be married to her. You make a fine couple.'

Vinny, always uneasy when being complimented, groped for an appropriate reply. 'You never took the plunge yourself?' was the best he could come up with.

'You mean marriage? No, Vinny, I did not. I often thought it must be rather wonderful to have a wife of one's own. But somehow or other that was not in the gift of life for me.'

'How do you make that out?' Vinny asked.

'Simple, dear boy, I wasn't cut out to be a lady's man. I discovered that at a very early age.'

Ever since Ciarán had introduced his elderly friend to him, Vinny had wondered about George's sexual proclivities. It wasn't that it bothered Vinny one way or the other – it didn't. He liked to think he had a broad acceptance of people's sexual leanings but he couldn't help thinking that George might be teetering on the edge of gay. Determined not to air his half-formed suspicions, Vinny somehow allowed his tongue to get away from him. 'Did you ever . . . what I mean is, y'know, girls . . . did you ever go out . . . ?'

'As a matter of fact I did, Vinny. One time and one time only I went out with a young lady. The episode coloured the rest of my life as far as the fairer sex is concerned. I was sixteen – or was it seventeen? – at the time. Anyway, I accompanied this young lady to a theatre – a Noel Coward comedy, if memory serves me right – and afterwards to a meal in a rather posh restaurant. Because my money was in short supply in those days, I picked the cheapest item on the menu and rather hoped my companion might do likewise. Alas, she did not! Fortunately, I scraped enough coins together to meet the bill but the poor chap who served us is still waiting for his tip. I drove her home – I had borrowed a friend's Morris Minor for the occasion – and she invited me into her house for a cup of tea. I duly obliged, thinking it churlish to do otherwise, and followed her into a darkened living room. The young lady – her name was Lillian – explained to me that her parents were asleep and that switching on the lights might wake them.

'No further mention of the tea was made as she eased me on to a rather over-stuffed settee, placed her arms around my neck and proceeded to kiss me full on the lips. This was an altogether new predicament for me and I began to tremble in fear, not knowing what the proper response ought to be. I had never been kissed by a woman before, well, except by my mother, that is, and of course that didn't count – my mother had never attempted to stick her tongue down my throat – so I found myself in a state of great agitation. At this point Lillian attempted to effect a horizontal position on the settee while manoeuvring me on top of her. Damned awkward, I can tell you; I was so clumsy, all elbows, knees and feet. My every instinct urged me to run screaming from the house but thinking that this might be the norm for such encounters, I resolved to see the thing through come hell or high water.

'The lady was by this stage quite excited, her tongue flicking in and out of my mouth like a jackhammer, one of her hands guiding mine on to her breast while in a simultaneous motion, her other hand fumbling with my fly. I lay there in the darkness, petrified, dashed if I knew what was coming next. I felt slightly flattered, thinking that I was somehow responsible for eliciting such a strong response from Lillian – or was it Gillian – I am not absolutely sure. The young woman was by now gasping as though she were having difficulty in breathing, her body tossing and writhing in violent spasms as her hands pounded into my back. I was thankful she had abandoned her search for my 'family jewels', for to tell you the truth, my manhood had by then shrivelled to embarrassing proportions. I decided, there and then, that if this was what love was all about, I wanted none of it. I managed to disengage myself from her flaying arms and heaving thighs, but in doing so I crashed to the floor, my backside knocking a vase of flowers off a small occasional table. The ensuing noise was enough to wake the dead. That was bad enough but to make things worse Lillian – yes, that was her name – had by now gone into a right old frenzy, gasping like a wild animal, her feet kicking out wildly at the end of the settee.

'In a flash, the lights came on in the room. A red-faced man, dressed in blue striped pyjamas, looking for all the world like John Bull's bulldog, barged into the room followed by a dumpy little woman in a great flowing night-dress. 'Quick, wife,' the man bellowed back to the woman, 'get the inhaler, our Lillian is having another one of her asthma attacks'.

'Unable to move with fear, I watched as the woman held a mask to her daughter's mouth, conscious only that Lillian's breast lay fully exposed. Within a few moments her breathing returned to normal, the cue for her father to turn his focus on me. "Get out of this house, you dirty filthy scoundrel," he roared, grabbing me by the hair of the head and pulling me to my feet before forcefully propelling me towards the door. Well, needless to remark, I had absolutely no desire to argue with the man. Scurrying with great haste to the exit, I felt the full force of his bare foot connect with my posterior, whereupon my trousers, unzipped and unbuttoned courtesy of his nimble-fingered daughter, dropped to my knees, tripped me up and sent me sprawling to the floor. I wanted to die there and then from embarrassment. In the most ignominious manner you can imagine, I crawled on all fours out of the house while Lillian's father continued to rain kicks on my exposed backside.'

George had just about finished his account of his first adolescent encounter with the opposite sex when Vinny heard his mobile phone ring. It was Emma calling. Much to Vinny's relief, she let him know that she was feeling better and ready to face the world. 'After you left,' she told him, 'I dozed off for a while . . . can't have been long, maybe half an hour, anyway, Detective-Inspector Connolly phoned me and woke me up.'

'Well, he had no business ring . . .'

'No, it's all right Vinny. I'm glad he woke me; I feel grand now, honest. Talk to you later. OK?'

'Yeah, fine Emma. See you this evening. Love you.'

'Ditto.'

Vinny switched the mobile to mute. Satisfied that Emma was feeling much better, he could now listen to George Laffin without worrying about her at the same time. George continued to tell tales from his past, at ease in Vinny's company, taking full advantage of his captive audience of one.

Jamboree Productions, the people making the television documentary, had given George a day off and Vinny had offered to bring him to the Midland Antique shop in Durrow. Since witnessing the strange behaviour of its proprietor Paul Newman in the Smithfield Court two nights earlier, Vinny's curiosity had got the better of him. He wanted to know why Newman had shied away from him. He wanted to know what he was doing in the hotel in the first place and who was the person with him.

But there was another reason he wanted to visit the Midland establishment and it was this second reason that had appealed to George Laffin. Vinny had heard from one of his contacts in the fine-art trade that Midland Antiques had acquired an original illustration by Jessie Marion King. Vinny, a long time admirer of the Scots artist's work, had copies of some of the Art

Nouveau designs she had produced at the turn of the nineteenth century but had never got his hands on an original. Vinny was pragmatic enough to know that big profits could be made from the limited supply of her original drawings that existed. If Newman had an original, then he would very much like to buy it.

George Laffin who shared Vinny's fondness for Jessie Marion King, owned a pair of silk curtains she had designed when she was a student in the Glasgow School of Art. For this reason he jumped at the chance to join Vinny on his expedition; opportunities of seeing original work by her were rare enough.

Both men were to be disappointed.

According to the woman who greeted them in Midland Antiques, Mr Newman was not available. 'He's gone across to England this morning to look at some paintings,' she informed them. Vinny explained that he had recently bought a drawing from Newman and had come, along with his friend George Laffin, to see a Marion King illustration. The woman, a featureless creature in her mid-to-late-forties, never offered her name to the men but Vinny suspected she might be Newman's wife. Speaking with a flat Midland accent, she told them she knew nothing at all about the illustration they were talking about but invited them to poke around and look at all 't'other yokes' on display.

In silence, they browsed about the showroom. The woman turned her attention to a tall German man who was busy looking at a rosewood fall-front desk with brass handles. With a strong German accent, he referred to the item as a *secrètaire à abattant* as he lowered the writing surface and examined an array of pigeonholes and tiny drawers. While this inspection was in progress the woman continually stole glances at Vinny and George. Aware of this scrutiny, both of them looked half-heartedly at everything on display, barely glancing at display cases, inlaid firescreens, leatherbound books and the like. They found nothing of interest and decided to head back to the city. It was while they were saying goodbye to the woman, whose name they still didn't know, that Vinny spotted something with the corner of his eye. A number of framed canvases lay against a wall, their plain backs visible through the covering sheet of clear plastic.

Vinny experienced a sense of *déjà vu.*

'Is it all right if we have a look at these paintings?' he asked the woman.

'Oh, you can look all y'want but t'won't do you no good. They're already sold. They're going to Todd Wilson's hotel in Castlepollard later to-day; only came back from Scotland yesterday, they did.'

Cautiously, Vinny pulled away the plastic covering and angled the frames so that he could see the front side of the canvases. Immediately, he could see they were the same pictures he had seen on his last visit to Midland Antiques, the same paintings he had seen displayed in the Dedalus Gallery a week later. Vinny gave George a conspiratorial wink before asking him what he thought of the collection. George, could see that what he was looking at were the paintings Vinny and Ciarán had describe so enthusiastically to him a week earlier.

They examined each of the paintings in turn without further comment before, once again, taking their leave of the woman. Neither spoke until they were well away from Midland Antiques. 'What the hell is going on with those paintings?' Vinny asked. 'They're travelling over and back across the Irish Sea like ping-pong balls.'

'Yes, that's a bit odd. But there's something else you ought to know about those paintings: they have quite a history. Back in the 1980s most of what we've just seen were in private collections in the north of England. A handful of rich landowners and successful indus-trialists bought them as investments. You see, Vinny, back in the 80s there was a sort of vogue for British portraiture of the late eighteenth century. Those who couldn't acquire them by legitimate means found other ways to get them. A spate of great art robberies took place around this period and forced the so-called patrons of the arts to take drastic measures to protect their investments. One of the ploys they used to outwit the thieves involved having copies made of the paintings.

'I see,' Vinny said. 'They would hang the copies on their walls for their friends to admire while having the original paintings - for their investment - locked away safely in a vault somewhere.'

'Yes, that was the idea ... and it worked up to a point. Except that, as in the case of the paintings we have just looked at, sometimes more than one copy was created. Not only that, but the artist who painted those extra copies was none other than the legendary Frederick Cabanel.'

'I've heard of him,' Vinny said. 'Didn't he do some time in prison for passing off fakes as originals?'

'Yes, that's the man. He was a rare genius, a descendant of the great French artist Alexandre Cabanel. As an artist Frederick had the respect of his peers but he could barely earn enough from his work to put bread on the table. So, when he was approached by unscrupulous dealers and offered huge sums of money to paint copies, he obliged. He was good though, too damn good. Even the experts couldn't tell his fakes from the originals.'

'So you're saying, in effect, that the pictures exhibited in Todd Wilson's hotels could be fakes. Is that it?'

'If it were just a case of fakes, Vinny, I wouldn't mind so much. But it's a darn sight more serious than that. The people behind these paintings present a serious problem.'

'How do you mean?'

'The gang behind these fakes are vicious thugs who will stop at nothing to hide their real trade - drugs. Using *objets d'art* is a favourite ploy. With paintings it's straightforward enough; they hollow out cavities in the main frames or the interior canvas stretcher frames and conceal the drugs therein.'

'But that would mean that Todd Wilson is involved in drug smuggling.'

'That does seem rather unlikely, Vinny, but you never know. Wilson might not be aware of the status of these paintings; it's possible he is being duped. It could well be that our missing friend Paul Newman is the one running the racket on this side of the Channel.'

Vinny laughed. 'Ah, no, George, I find it hard to believe he could be the brains behind such a scam.'

'But why, Vinny? You saw him in the Smithfield hotel trying to hide from you. That sounds rather fishy to me.'

'Hm. I see what you mean. Maybe I misjudged the fellow. I just didn't think he was bright enough or cunning enough to be a villain. What do you think we should do about it?'

'I suggest you go to the police, Vinny.'

'Yes, I should . . . but I think I'll let Emma know first, she's already working with Detective Connolly on the Todd Wilson thing; might be best if we let her deal with this.'

'Sounds like a good idea to me,' George said.

29

Connolly offered Emma a cup of tea and a biscuit but, unusually for him, he kept the usual pre-meeting chitchat to a minimum. This morning the detective was determined to get down to business straight away, an approach that did not suit Emma. For once, she could have done with being eased into the fray. She felt decidedly fragile. Even though she had recovered from her early morning bout of nausea, she had not touched the breakfast Vinny had prepared for her.

To compensate for how she was feeling she had spent a little extra time putting on her face and selecting her wardrobe. After an exhaustive trawl through her clothes, she selected a neat suit as the most sensible choice. Today, simplicity had won out.

Hair and make up had taken a little longer.

She ran a brush through her abundance of light brown hair and cursed when some of her gold-tinged ringlets rebelled against her best efforts to make them conform, stubbornly insisting on popping out like springs from an discarded mattress. Her face with its fine skin and striking bone structure, something she inherited from her mother, had for once, decided not to rise and shine. All her skills and artistry in make-up were called upon. Only after infinite patience and a little more foundation, powder, rouge and lip-gloss than usual did she consider her face just about presentable to the world. But her eyes, thank God for her large grey-green eyes, they represented her best feature and had not let her down.

A mirror inspection had given her confidence to face the world. But now, with Connolly glaring at her, she doubted whether her exterior shell would be enough to get her through the day.

'You haven't been straight with me, Emma,' Connolly said, the edge to his voice unmistakable.

'What are you getting at, Detective-Inspector?' she asked, tempted to ask if he had got out the wrong side of the bed this morning but reflecting on her own less than joyful morning, dismissed the thought. Better to play it straight, she decided. 'It might help, Detective, if you were to tell me what's eating you.'

'Well for a start you and I were supposed to have an agreement. You remember? We agreed to abide by Bob Crosby's compromise rules, right? I'm supposed to tell you what I know; you're supposed to tell me what you know.'

'I thought we had been doing that,' Emma replied rather lamely.

'Well, I've been doing my bit. I told you about Marina Cassidy being spotted in Dublin Airport.'

'So?'

'I have discovered that you took a flight to Liverpool. You should have told me, Emma.'

'What? I have to tell you when I make day trips to

England to do a bit of shopping?'

'Ah, come on Emma, please don't get smart with me. You see, we followed up on Marina Cassidy ourselves. I sent one of my best men over to get a statement from her. She told us you'd already been there. You should have told me, Emma.'

'You're right,' Emma said, sounding suitably chastised, 'I should have but I don't see what good it would have done. All I got was background stuff. I still don't know who's responsible for Ethel Cassidy's murder and I found nothing that advances the case against Todd Wilson.'

'Well, it might surprise you then to discover Marina Cassidy was definitely in Wilson's house.'

Emma raised her eyebrows. 'I find that very hard to believe.'

'You can believe what you want,' Connolly said, shrugging his shoulders. 'That's your prerogative. But fingerprints we took from Wilson's house match a set we got from our trip to Liverpool.'

Emma could not hide her surprise; she fully believed Marina had nothing to do with the bizarre mannequin hanging incident in Wilson's house. What she was now hearing from Connolly cast doubt on the validity of all that Marina had told her. 'I see,' was all she said.

Connolly frowned. 'I'm not sure you do see. We have been doing some checking up on Marina Cassidy and have discovered she is a frequent visitor here. She was in this country three days before Jamie Wilson committed suicide. She was also here when her sister

Ethel was burned to death.'

'You're not seriously trying to insinuate that she had anything to do with Jamie's or Ethel's deaths?'

'No, but she's been over and back a lot, and knows a damn sight more about what's going on than she's letting on.'

'Well, for what its worth, I think Marina loved and admired her twin sister Ethel very much. On the other hand, she makes no bones about her loathing for Todd Wilson. She blames him for everything bad that has happened to Ethel. But to suggest she could be in any way involved in what's happened to Jamie or Ethel is just plain bonkers.'

'Maybe, maybe not. There's something not right here, something we're all missing – and Marina Cassidy is part of it. I'd like you to tell me everything you found out from her.'

Emma thought about his request for a moment. Trying to second-guess Connolly was never easy but she felt sure he wanted to discuss some other aspect of the case with her; he just needed to know she was being straight with him before he opened up to her. Weighing up the situation, she decided to give the detective a full account of her conversation with Marina Cassidy.

Connolly listened intently, nodding his head occasionally, but never interrupting. When she had finished, the detective changed the subject again without commenting on what he had just heard. 'Did you know that Todd Wilson's wife, Maeve – she of saintly virtues – uses Leinster Road, Rail and Sea Hauliers to transport her goodwill cargo to the Third World – and that one of these lorries was discovered to be carrying drugs on its return journey to this country.'

'Yes, I read about it,' Emma said, 'but according to SUCCOUR, they just hire the lorries. It's reasonable to accept that Maeve Wilson can't be responsible for what some driver might decide to pack on his homeward journey.'

'That's exactly what I thought, Emma, but a few strange things have been happening that make me uneasy. The driver of the lorry in question got out on bail two days ago. Some anonymous benefactor paid the money. We're trying to establish the identity of whoever paid the bonds money but I fully expect it will turn out to be the haulage company itself in some guise or other. Now if it turns out that either Todd or Maeve Wilson is behind the payment, then we have a serious situation on our hands. My colleagues in Lucan Garda station confiscated the driver's passport and on top of that, he was ordered to report into the station every day.

'And you're now going to tell me he hasn't showed, right?'

'Right, Emma, but it's a bit more serious than that. The name of the driver caught with the drugs is Matt Dempsey. He lives with his girlfriend, Fidelma Roper, in the village of Leixlip. He's been driving lorries for three or four years; she works for the Hewlett-Packard people as a programmer or technician or something like that. Anyway, she contacted the local Garda yesterday and reported that her boyfriend had been beaten up and abducted by two masked men. When the Leixlip Garda discovered that Matt Dempsey was on bail for suspected drug smuggling, they immediately contacted the boys down the road a few miles in Lucan. Their first reaction was that Dempsey had done a runner. It was a natural enough conclusion to jump to; after all Dempsey was, in all probability, facing a long stretch in jail. But when they went to interview his girlfriend, they changed their minds. Seems the girl had been badly beaten. There were bloodstains all over the place. It turned out that most of the blood belonged to Dempsey.'

'Sounds like someone is determined to take this driver out of the equation,' Emma said. 'Someone sure as hell is afraid of what he might say.'

'The question is who,' said Connolly. 'Maeve Wilson's organisation would suffer irreparable damage if Matt Dempsey were to point the finger in her direction. Equally, if Todd Wilson were to be linked to a drug scandal on top of all the other accusations against him, it would force him to resign from the chairmanship of some of his companies.'

'Would you mind if I talked to the driver's girlfriend? I might find out something that your boys missed.'

Connolly hesitated for a second before answering. 'If you promise to keep it low – and report any findings of interest to me. No more trying to go it alone like you did in Liverpool. OK?'

'Yeah, fine, I promise if I find anything of importance I'll let you know.'

'Good, then we both understand each other.'

'Indeed we do,' Emma said, 'and to show my good faith, I can give you some information in connection with dodgy paintings that are doing the rounds of Todd Wilson's hotels.'

'Dodgy paintings?'

'Yes, paintings that are used as a cover for drug smuggling.' Emma told the detective what she had learned from Vinny and George Laffin. When she had finished her account, Connolly nodded his head and raised his eyebrows. 'Interesting,' he said, 'very interesting; it might turn out to be something and then again it might be nothing at all. I'll have it checked out . . . keep an eye on this fellow, Paul Newman. If he brings any more works of art into the country we'll nab him and strip his paintings down to his canvas. Nice one, Emma.'

'Thanks, Jim,' Emma said, for once using his first name, 'you see, I really am all in favour of cooperation.'

Locating the Leixlip mews where Matt Dempsey and Fidelma Roper lived took a little longer than Emma had bargained for. The place had grown so big. Once a sleepy little village on the banks of the Liffey, Leixlip now had a population of 20,000 and was expanding at an alarming rate. As a child, she remembered her father bringing her to Leixlip Castle, former home of the Guinness brewing family, for a special fête day. Back then, with a population of less than a thousand, the village consisted of one street, a winding river, two awkward bridges, two churches, two pubs and half a dozen quaint little shops.

Apart from the two awkward bridges, one at either end of the village, little remained of those fond childhood vignette images she had retained ever since. Like most villages on the outskirts of Dublin, the latter decades of the twentieth century had demanded a huge price in the name of progress. A proliferation of American hi-tech computer companies had transformed the area from being a dormitory overspill for Dublin city commuters to what many people thought of today as Ireland's version of Silicon Valley.

Motoring up the steep Captain's Hill, going north from the village, Emma found her way to Heart Lane, a small road running parallel to the main Galway–Dublin railway line. To get to the two-storey mews Emma drove along a private driveway, past the shell of an old abandoned manor house and down a gravel pathway that ran through an apple orchard. It occurred to Emma when she saw the mews that it had probably served as an outhouse for the manor building in the more grandiose days of its prime.

She parked her Volvo 360 GLT and studied the building for a moment before getting out of the car. All seemed quiet. Emma found it difficult to believe this small mews could possibly be home to an international drug smuggler. If it was, then the suspect, Matt Dempsey, hadn't exactly splashed out on worldly possessions.

Emma pressed the bell push. A faint melody of chimes sounded from inside the house. Getting no response, she tried it again a further three times. Taking in the scenery while she waited, she noticed a reflection of sunlight from one of the windows in the old manor house. It was as though a mirror had swivelled and caught a momentary flash of sunlight. Although the windows were all boarded up, fragments of glass still remained in the rotting frames, but Emma didn't think these jagged fragments could achieve the affect she had just witnessed. Not only that but she felt sure there was a slight movement from inside the darkened shell of the house. Could someone be watching her? Had the light bounced off a pair of glasses or binoculars?

Or was it all in her imagination?

There was certainly no sign of life there now. Still pondering whether her mind was playing tricks on her, she heard a woman's voice coming from behind the mews' closed door. She spun round, faced the door and listened.

'Who's there?' the voice asked.

'I'm Emma Boylan, investigative journalist with the *Post*. I'd like to talk to you if that's OK? Please.'

'The press? No, no, sorry, please go away, I don't want to see anyone from the press.'

'I've been talking to the Gardaí and they've told me what happened to you and Matt. They said it was OK for me to call and see you. Honest, you can check with them if you like. You're Fidelma Roper, right? I only want to help you.'

There was silence for several seconds before Emma heard the sound of a bolt been pulled across on the inside of the door. A small opening appeared. Emma could not hide the shock she felt at seeing the young woman's face. 'They really did work you over,' she said. 'It looks painful as Hell.'

'You want to see it from my side,' Fidelma Roper said, attempting a smile but failing to even come close. Hurriedly, she ushered Emma into a small sitting room, nervously bolting the door behind her. 'You'll have to forgive my rudeness, keeping the door shut in your face but I'm a bag of nerves since they took Matt away. You see, they said they'd kill him if I told anyone about what happened. I didn't know what to do . . . I was going frantic, terrified to do anything. In the end I rang the . . . I had to tell someone. At first they thought I was making the whole thing up, trying to concoct a story for Matt's sake. It was only when they came here and saw the state I was in that they believed me. I'm still not sure if I did the right thing or not.'

'You made the right decision,' Emma said, trying to find comforting words for the young woman. Fidelma Roper, she could tell, was on the verge of hysteria. Wearing no make up, with eyes that were red from crying, and a face that had turned black and blue from cuts and bruises, the young woman sat down and faced Emma. A collection of dolls, all different, each miniature model dressed in the distinctive costumes from around the world, adorned the small living room, their smiling faces and sparkling eyes appearing to mock the sad visage of their owner. 'Maybe you should get away from here for a few days,' Emma suggested. 'Go to a friend's house – or your parent's, maybe – wait until you get some news.'

'I thought of doing something like that but . . . well, the thing is, I felt I should stay here in case Matt came back or tried to get in touch.'

'Does he have a mobile phone?'

'Yes, but he left it here. They dragged him out of here practically unconscious so . . . '

'And do you have a mobile phone?'

'No, I mean yes; yes I have one. I hardly ever use it. Matt gave it to me as a present last Christmas.'

'So, Matt could get in touch by calling on either of the mobiles or by using your landline.'

Fidelma frowned. 'I've thought of all that,' she said, trying to hold back the tears, 'but wherever they're holding him, they're not letting him near a phone. I know Matt, he would contact me if he had the chance.'

'Did Matt talk to you about the drug bust he was involved in.'

'Yes, he told me everything he knew about it. Matt had nothing whatsoever to do with that, he hates everything to do with drugs, would never in a million years willingly get involved in anything so stupid. But I know that the two brutes who bundled him out were involved in the affair.'

'How do you know that?'

'Because as they were bashing Matt, they shouted

something about it being his fault for losing some valuable property belonging to their boss – said he had to be taught a lesson.'

'Have you contacted Matt's employers?'

'Yes, after I talked to the cops I called them. Fat lot of good it did me. I was put through to some manager fellow . . . can't remember his name, said there was nothing he could do – end of story. I knew from his attitude that he didn't want to know; probably thinks Matt imported the drugs and deserves what he's getting.'

Emma continued to talk to Fidelma, trying to discover anything that might help her establish who might be behind her boyfriend's kidnapping but it was obvious that the frightened woman could throw no further light on the episode. Emma advised her again to think about moving out of the mews for the time being but Fidelma wouldn't hear of such a notion. It was with a degree of unease that Emma took her leave of Fidelma, wanting to offer some reassurance or comfort but not being able to do so.

Driving away from the mews, Emma pulled to a stop outside the abandoned manor house. She was still curious about the flash of reflected light she thought she had seen from inside one of the windows. The remains of a stone wall ran alongside the gable end of the house, its fractured surface covered for the most part in weeds, ivy and broom. An old iron gate, rusted and warped, stood partially open, its base obliterated in a tangle of wild grass and thorny shrub.

Emma got out of her car to take a closer look. She stepped carefully through the opening and followed a path that had been tramped out through the weeds. The path wound its way to the back door of the house, its contours dictated by the random dispersal of abandoned mattresses, rotting timber pallets, empty bottles, squashed beer cans and an assortment of rusting household goods. The old stone-built manor house appeared sombre and forbidden, its brooding bulk seeming to drain the colour from the sky above it. For no apparent reason, a sense of isolation enveloped Emma. Before getting to the back door of the house, she stopped in her tracks. Just visible through the bushes at the gable end of the house furthest away from her, she saw the shape of a four-wheel drive. The shock of seeing the vehicle in the house's overgrown garden forced her to an intake of breath.

Emma felt the hairs prickle down the back of her neck. The earlier feeling of isolation was replaced by a different sort of dread. There was someone in the house, she felt sure of it. The flash of light she had seen had not been a figment of her imagination. There really was someone lurking in the darkness behind the partially boarded window. And that someone had spied on her as she visited Fidelma Roper. Feeling suddenly scared, Emma made her way over to the four-wheel drive, all the time concerned that she was probably being watched. A black Land Cruiser, its fresh tyre marks in the vegetation showing the route by which it had entered, stood parked between two clumps of bushes. She made a mental note of the registration number and decided to get back to her own car without delay. If the Land Cruiser was owned by the people who had beaten up Fidelma and kidnapped Matt Dempsey, she wanted nothing to do with them. It wasn't that she considered herself a coward but, over the years, she had developed a healthy regard for self-preservation. It was one thing to be brave; it was another thing altogether to be stupid.

As the reflection of the old manor house disappeared from her rear-view mirror, she thought about Fidelma Roper and the dangers she might be exposed to. It seemed highly possible to Emma that the same people who had attacked Fidelma and Matt could now use the old manor to keep watch on the mews. It could even be possible that they were holding Matt prisoner inside the walls of the old building. The more Emma thought about this idea the more convinced she became that she was not reading the situation correctly. Why would someone go to the trouble of kidnapping Matt and then hold him in captivity within sight of where they had taken him from the first place? It did not make sense.

There was, she realised, another alternative: perhaps the Gardaí were responsible for the presence in the old house. Maybe they were observing the mews in case the kidnappers returned. She would report to Connolly as soon as she returned to her office. He would soon tell her whether his colleagues from Lucan station had set up a surveillance operation or not. If they had, then

Fidelma Roper had nothing to worry about, but if the presence in the house had nothing to do with the Gardaí, then something would have to be done about protecting her.

30

Vinny had decided not to leave the apartment until Emma was ready. It was past noon by the time they got in their cars and exited the basement garage space beneath their apartment. The morning sickness that had played havoc with Emma's system for the past ten days decided to take a day off; it was not nearly as bad as she had come to expect. She had felt well enough to sit in front of her PC monitor to check incoming e-mail and send replies where warranted. The daily chore of clearing correspondence out of the way without having to be at her city desk represented one of life's more recent improvements. Emma embraced all aspects of the new technology and modern communications; with online access to her computer in work, her office hours had become far more flexible of late.

Her telephone call to Connolly had given her cause to worry. The detective confirmed her worst fears in regard to Fidelma Roper's safety. The Lucan Garda station, he informed her, had not sanctioned any surveillance operation in the abandoned manor house that faced Fidelma's mews. The question remained: who exactly had been in the house? After listening to Emma's report on what she had discovered on her visit to the building, Connolly promised to look into the situation straight away. He asked if she could meet him for lunch to discuss the situation in more detail and she had agreed. They would meet at 1 o'clock in the Grafton Room Restaurant on the second floor of the St Stephen's Green Shopping Centre.

Vinny could not help but overhear their telephone conversation about the men who had abducted Matt Dempsey. It concerned him that Emma might be exposing herself to unnecessary danger. With as much diplomacy as he could muster, he attempted to point out the risks she was taking. He stressed the fact that she was dealing with thugs, brutes who thought nothing of beating up people to within a hair's breadth of their lives. She dismissed his concerns with one of her favourite finger flicks. 'I'm a big girl,' she said, determined not to let herself become embroiled in an argument, 'and I know how to look after myself and besides . . .'

'It's your job, I know, I know,' Vinny said, knowing better than to argue with that sort of logic.

Observing Emma in his rear view mirror as she negotiated her Volvo up the car park's exit ramp behind his Citroën, Vinny could not help but smile to himself. She was so busy checking her make-up in her rear view mirror, something she did every time she got in her car, that she did not see him looking at her. As habitual as a snooker player chalking his cue, Emma never failed to make this last-minute mirror inspection at the beginning of each journey.

But Vinny's smile soon disappeared.

He had only driven twenty metres along the street and was about to shift into third gear when the clutch failed to engage. He tried again without success and was forced to switch off the ignition. Emma, not expecting this sudden halt, managed to hit the break in time to avoid crashing into his rear bumper. Another car, a maroon coloured Toyota Camry, surprised by Emma's sudden stop managed to avoid impact with her rear bumper by mere centimetres. Making a shamefaced grimace, Emma waved an apology to the driver, a red-haired woman with tinted glasses, who acknowledged her contrite gesture and drove on.

Vinny got out of his car, walked back to her and explained what had happened. Seeing the look of concern on his face, Emma resisted the urge to have a go at him over his beloved Citroën. Although fifteen years old, the two-tone cream and burgundy car was in reasonable good condition, but close inspection of the mileage clock would show the digits were on their second count.

After pushing the Citroën back to the curb, Vinny joined Emma in the Volvo and finally headed for the city centre. 'Damn it,' Vinny said. 'I thought I noticed the clutch acting up a bit while I was driving George Laffin and Dad on their Harry Clarke pilgrimage . . . and I meant to get it checked out but forgot all about the damn thing.'

Although the post midday traffic was heavy they still managed to make it to Leeson Street in less than ten minutes. Observing the time on the dashboard,

Emma was delighted to note that she would have time to spare before her lunch appointment with Connolly; it would allow her to have a quick look at the baby clothes in Mothercare.

Vinny got out of the Volvo at the Earlsfort Terrace and Lower Leeson Street junction, his intention to walk through Quinn's Lane and on to Donnegan's garage in Mackies Place. He had dealt with Paddy Donnegan, a huge giant of a man who hailed from Cavan originally, for more than a dozen years. It was Donnegan who had sold him the second-hand Citroën in the first place – and he trusted the big mechanic completely. Donnegan had recently serviced the car so that it would pass its road worthiness test. It came through the test but the exercise had cost him almost a thousand pounds. It now looked like he would have to fork out more money to keep the old girl on the road. For the first time, Vinny wondered if he shouldn't think seriously about getting a new car. He would hold off any such decision until after he talked to Donnegan. The car's fate would depend on his assessment of the situation.

Watching Emma pull away from the curb and into the traffic, Vinny noticed another car darting out from the kerbside and forcing its way into the line of traffic behind her. Other motorists, annoyed by the car's impatient entry into their lane, blasted their horns as they braked to avoid collision. Thinking to himself that this was how road-rage incidents occurred, Vinny took a second look at the driver in the offending car.

He froze.

It was the same driver he had seen earlier pulling out behind Emma when the Citroën's clutch failed. He was positive; there could be no mistake. The car, a maroon-coloured Toyota, driven by a redheaded woman wearing tinted glasses, was definitely tailing Emma. He needed to warn her but she had already passed through the lights on the Earlsfort junction and had moved on to St Stephen's Green North, passing by the Department of Justice building. He had to warn her somehow. Bumper-to-bumper traffic was slow but even so, she would approach the Harcourt Street junction with the Green within two or three minutes.

Frightening thoughts shot through his head. The conversation she had had with Connolly earlier that morning fast-forwarded through his brain; he had heard her describe what had happened to Fidelma Roper; he had heard her tell the detective about being watched from an old manor house.

Emma could be in real danger.

Every nerve ending in his body screamed a warning. He had already started to run as he attempted to formulate a plan of action. Cursing himself for leaving his mobile phone in the Citroën he tried to think of a solution. She had planned to park in the St Stephen's Green Shopping Centre car park, that much he knew. It wasn't that far away, quarter of a mile, maybe less, but he was on foot, she had the benefit of a car. He tried to think. Usually a queue formed to gain entry to the car park there; he hoped that would be the case today, with any luck today's queue would move at a snail's pace. It was imperative that he get to her before she got out of her car – a daunting task but he had to give it a try. If he ran fast and cut through the park, taking a diagonal path that would bring him out at the Fusiliers Arch on the Grafton Street corner directly opposite the shopping centre he might be in time.

Strollers in the park stared in wonder at Vinny as he pounded his way along the curving pathways, often ignoring the Keep-off-the-Grass signs, ploughing through the formal lawns, hopping across flowerbeds, taking advantage of any short cut that might quicken his progress. Out of breath and gasping for air, he stopped for a second on the humpback bridge that crossed the duck pond, wiped the sweat from his eyes and forehead, before setting off again at full tilt.

All the time, in the back of his head, he was hoping against hope that the traffic might slow down Emma's progress sufficiently to allow him to get to the shopping centre's multilevel car park in time for her arrival. He made fast and furious calculations. She would have to turn left into King Street, pass by the Gaiety Theatre to get to the car park's entrance in Lower Mercer Street. This was at the rear of the shopping centre and should, if Vinny's calculations were correct, delay her for a minute, maybe two. Oh, please God, he prayed, let there be a traffic snarl-up there today.

His journey was taking too long.

He cursed. Panting and puffing, he swore as the pedestrian lights beside the Fusiliers Arch refused to turn green, favouring the steady stream of cars instead, blocking his progress. Still on red, he bounded into the traffic lanes, waving his arms in the air like a demented juggler, forcing motorists to jam their brakes to the floor as he pushed perilously across the street. Ignoring the angry motorists who had joined in an unholy symphony of horn blowing, Vinny made it to the pavement on the far side and darted through the people moving about on the circular entrance space to the centre.

Startled shoppers dodged out of his way as he ran the length of the ground floor to where the escalators were situated. Taking two steps at a time, he made it to the first floor in a matter of seconds. *Oh, God, let me be on time.* He had mounted the steps that would take him to the next floor when he heard a commotion above him.

A single scream rang out.

A woman's scream. The sound of running feet. The disturbance, he could tell now, was at the base of the top-level escalator. This was the escalator that led directly from the car park area. Vinny knew with the sort of certainty that defied logic that Emma was in serious trouble.

Blindly, furiously, he scrambled up the mid-level escalator, taking huge steps as he made his way to where a crowd of people had gathered. Voices shouted in panic, 'Get a doctor! Hurry, the woman's hurt! Someone, quickly, call an ambulance. She's bleeding badly! Move back, move back, give her room there, come on, move back . . . .'

Now Vinny could see her.

'Emma! Emma! Oh, Jesus Christ, Emma!' he said, his voice a hoarse whisper. 'What have they done to you?' He pushed his way to where she lay and fell to his knees beside her. He could see the gash on her nose and forehead and the blood that covered most of her face. Her feet, pressed against the guardrail of the stairs, had forced her knees up towards her chest. Blood covered both her knees and ran down her legs. In a state of absolute panic, Vinny took hold of her hands and looked into her face. Her eyes were glazed. Her features distorted in pain. But she was conscious. She recognised him. The strength of her grip surprised him as she moved his hands on to her stomach.

Vinny tried to speak but had difficulty finding words.

'Emma! Oh God, Emma! This . . . this is terrible! Terrible but we'll get help to you in a few minutes. Hang in there! Hang . . . '

'Vin . . . Vin . . . I love . . . Vin. Vinny, my baby – It's safe; it's safe! Vinny, Vin . . . '

'Thank God! Oh, thank God! I thought that . . . I was . . . afraid that . . . ' But as Vinny tried to comfort her he became aware that she had slipped into unconsciousness.

Her skin felt cold. She breathed deeply and evenly. Her eyes opened. *Where am I? What time is it . . . what day of the week is it?* There was no way of accounting for time. Emma did not know how long she had been in her present state of mind, a sort of celestial dimension where activities appeared to stretch, merge, warp and shatter, where physical appearances from the real world were only distantly graspable. *What's happened?* With a supreme effort, she tried to focus her mind, put a construction on events and come to terms with her current situation.

The escalator, yes, I remember parking the car, walking to the escalator... a push, yes, then tumbling down, hitting off the steel edged flight of steps, seeing the giant sunlit glass atrium flash on and off with dazzling speed, pendants and shop signs revolving round and round, still falling, hurting, sharp darts of pain, my body bouncing into shoppers on the descending escalator. Why did I fall? Did I slip? Did someone push me? I don't know. Blood, God almighty! Yes, blood everywhere, blood on my face, blood in my eyes, a sea of blood. Falling, tumbling, falling, stopping abruptly, the world funnelling into a black vortex, people surrounding me, a forest of legs, elongated arms, distorted hands reaching down to me, and then a face, a familiar face... Vinny's face. His mouth, opening and closing. I can't make out what he is saying to me... can't remember... but a persistent thought overrides the pain: how handsome he looks! What a beautiful man Vinny is! All of a sudden it's important that he should know of my feelings but my mouth won't work, won't form the all-important words. His face swims out of focus, the world swims out of focus. There is nothing, a void, no sounds, nothing. A blackness descends – darker than the darkest night.

Consciousness of a kind returns. Trolley wheels squeak as she travels through long corridors, through sets of swinging doors, into an alien world inhabited by people wearing white coats, green coats, face masks, starched uniforms. 'Give her some analgesic to ease the pain,' a disembodied male voice shouts, the words echoing in the depths of her head. Pain? Yes, she is aware of pain, but it is a far away thing, tearing at her in a different dimension. Vinny, still holding her hand, gently squeezes her fingers, as he explains to someone that his wife is pregnant. Wooziness from the ad-ministered sedation allows her to drift away into crazy tormented dreams.

Later, how much later she could not tell, she became aware of bandages swathing her forehead, her hands and her knees. It was only when she attempted to move her legs that the restrictions on both knees made themselves manifest. She felt drowsy and sore; her body a collection of ugly bruises and lacerations. But above any other discomfort, the need to know about her baby was paramount.

'Emma, you're awake again,' Vinny said. 'How do you feel now?

'Vinny . . . Vinny, how long . . . how long have I been here? My baby! Is my baby all right? Where am I?

'You're in the Dublin Central General Hospital and this is your second day. You took a nasty fall but according to the doctors there's no immediate danger to the baby. Nothing's broken – cut forehead, bloody nose, nothing worse. They tell me you'll be fine in a day or so. They were worried at first about the baby's safety but it turned out to be a false alarm. But just to be on the safe side they are going to carry out a few further tests.'

'Oh, thank God, thank God! I thought for one awful moment . . . oh Vinny, I thought such terrible thoughts! But, all is well, all is well.' Emma tried to smile but failed. 'Listen Vinny, I don't mind ending up with a boxer's nose, but right now I need to pee very badly. I'm bursting! Can you get a nurse or someone to get me a bedpan or whatever it is they use before I wet the bed.'

Wanting to help but feeling inept and awkward, Vinny glanced around the small sterile cubicle not knowing exactly what he was looking for when much to his relief the door to the room opened.

'Here's Dr Pattison,' he said to Emma. 'She's been looking after you for the past few – and doing a great job, if I may say so.'

Dr Pattison favoured Vinny with a kindly smile as she made her way to Emma's bedside.

'How are you feeling, Emma?' she asked, the soft lilt of her Donegal accent soothing and warm.

'I don't know Doctor, you tell me,' Emma answered. 'I'm not sure how I feel right now – except to say that I need to piddle real badly.'

'We'll do something about that presently, Emma, but I'm afraid you'll have to hold on to it for a while longer; we want to carry out an ultrasound examination on your tummy first and we must have a full bladder for that.'

'Has this something to do with my baby, Doctor?'

'Yes, it's just a precaution. There's been a small blood trace so we don't want to take any chances.'

Before Emma could ask any further questions, hospital orderlies entered the room and wheeled the bed into the corridor. 'This shouldn't take too long,' Dr Pattison said to Vinny, 'I suggest you wait in the visitor's lounge until we're finished with the test.'

'You don't think there is anything . . . wrong with . . . you know . . . '

'Well, Mr. Bailey, I think everything is fine but we'll soon have the answers one way or the other.'

In the visitors lounge, Vinny sat awkwardly on a most uncomfortable chair, his shoulders slumped, a day's growth of beard on his face, his mouth tense and his brow furrowed. He picked up a well-thumbed copy of Time and flicked through it without registering what was contained in the pages before replacing it where he found it. A clock on the wall let him know that he had only been there ten minutes; it felt like an eternity. Through huge glass doors he watched absentmindedly as a stream of people – doctors, nurses, nuns, patients in dressing gowns, visitors and orderlies – passed by in an unending procession. Other people, sitting quietly in the bench-chairs set around the visitors lounge, lost in their own private worlds, glanced wearily at him from time to time but kept their distance. In the corner of the room, a television set showing MTV remained mute and completely ignored.

He opened his Silk Cut pack and extracted a

cigarette. He looked at it before putting it between his lips. Emma hated to see him smoking but this was an emergency; she would understand, he felt sure. Before striking a match to light it, an elderly man sitting across from him cleared his throat to attract his attention. The man, pointed to the No-Smoking sign; then, in a gesture worthy of mime artist, Marcel Marceau, wagged his index finger in censure. Vinny looked at the man, forced a quick artificial smile in his direction, cursed him silently and put the cigarettes back in his pocket.

He was about to leave the lounge and look for a safe place to light up when he heard his name being paged over the intercom. Going immediately to the information desk, he was directed by a receptionist to a bank of telephones nearby and told to pick up phone 3. 'Hello, this is Vinny Bailey,' he said expectantly into the receiver.

'Vinny, this is George Laffin here; I've just been talking to Ciarán; he told me the news. I can't believe it. I'm stunned, absolutely stunned. How is the dear girl? Please tell me everything is OK.'

'Thanks for calling, George. I'm not sure how things are with Emma. They're doing tests as we speak.'

'What kind of tests, may one ask?'

'Something to do with . . . I'm not exactly sure what. An ultrasound examination. It seems they found some trace of blood. I'm so sick with worry, trying not to think the worst. Y'know . . . '

'I'm so terribly sorry about all this but, please God, it will turn out to be all right.'

'I tried to stop it you know – really tried. Just couldn't get there in time! The bastards pushed her before I could get to her. Jesus, God . . .'

'What? You mean it wasn't an accident? But your father, her parents – they think . . .'

'I haven't told them yet. They're frantic enough as it is. No point in burdening them with all this until we're sure Emma is all right.'

'Yes, yes, I can see that . . . you're probably right. I'll call you tomorrow, Vinny. I'll be with the Jamboree Productions people; we're having a dry run at the programme. I'm sure things will be better by then. Give Emma all my love. Tell her she's in my thoughts.'

'Thanks George, I'll do that.

As Don O'Carroll, chief gynaecology consultant to the Dublin Central General Hospital, left the room, Dr Pattison gave Emma's hand a little squeeze of comfort. 'Losing your baby must seem like the end of the world to you right now,' she said to Emma, 'but no permanent damage has been done and there's no reason why you can't become pregnant again.' Emma stared back at the doctor but made no attempt to reply. The doctor nodded sympathetically as she watched the wad of tissues being squeezed in Emma's hands. 'I'll send in your husband now if you like,' she said as she turned to leave the room. She had reached the door before Emma spoke. 'Please Doctor, I know how anxious he must be . . . but, but I would prefer . . . I need, that is . . . to be left on my own for a little while.'

'I understand,' Dr. Pattison said, noting that tears were now falling freely from Emma's eyes. 'I'll look back in ten minutes; we'll see how you are feeling by then. OK?'

'Yes, that will . . . that will be fine, thank you, Dr. Pattison.'

Alone now, Emma pushed her head back into the pillow; emotionally exhausted. A pain, more mental than physical, rocked her body. Nothing as bad as this had ever happened to her before. She wanted to scream but could not summon enough energy to give vent to her feeling.

Her baby was dead.

The unthinkable had happened. The gynaecologist had tried to explain what had happened but his words were as meaningless as her very existence seemed to her now. The gynaecologist's small unblinking dark eyes had looked straight into hers as he mouthed words, sprinkled with technical terms that to her represented little more than abstract sounds; explanations about uterus haemorrhage, pneumothorax, feotoplacental perfusion, severe trauma and suspected perineal weakness – just meaningless utterances. No matter how she reshuffled the words and considered their possible meanings, only one truth remained: her baby was dead. Dead. The ultra-sound scan had established the absence of any heartbeat in the foetus. The thing inside her that should have been her baby would be removed from her body in a D and C procedure within the hour.

Emma held the wad of tissues to her eyes, attempting to regain her composure. It was no good, she continued to weep uncontrollably. What would she say to Vinny? He had seen the danger all along, had warned her, had begged her to be careful. Her own parents had voiced their concern, as had Bob Crosby and the detective, Connolly. The whole goddamned world, it seemed to her now, had screamed its warning but she had remained deaf to it all, believing she knew better than the lot of them. Why, in spite of all this advice, in spite of all the warnings, had she persisted in believing that she was above the weaknesses of others . . . that she was wiser, more intelligent, and less susceptible to such adversities? Christ, what grand conceit. How could she ever look Vinny in the eyes again! How could she live with the awful pall of guilt that cloaked her like some living corpse?

In the midst of her depression she began to mouth the words of the 'Hail Mary'. As a lapsed Catholic, it had been a long time since she had prayed, but now the words, coming involuntarily to her lips, brought a strange kind of comfort to her. She was halfway through repeating the entreaty to a God she wasn't sure existed when slumber blotted out the awful reality all around her and ushered in a period of peaceful oblivion.

31

Johnny Griffin switched on the car's main beams and turned the key in the ignition. The 24-valve V6 engine of the Nissan Maxima roared into life instantly. With the enthusiasm of a Grand Prix racing driver in a warm-up session, he pumped the accelerator pedal in a series of quick successive foot stabs. The response, like some monstrous growl from the depths of the jungle, filled the night air with a restless energy.

Sitting in the passenger seat, his girlfriend, Sarah-Jane Keegan, was not impressed, either with the surge of power coming from beneath the car's bonnet or by the macho antics being displayed by Johnny. 'Are you sure you're fit to drive?' she asked. 'You're way over the limit, you know.'

'Yeah well, fuck it, what the hell, I don't have a full driver's licence either but who the hell's going to bother us at this hour of the night.'

Earlier in the evening, a totally sober Johnny had taken the greatest care while driving his father's Nissan the twelve miles from Castlepollard to the town of Mullingar. He had arranged to meet Sarah-Jane in Baggot's Town House, a pub frequented by the young set, situated off Austin Friar Street. For Johnny, getting permission to use the car had not been easy. Only after much arguing had his father allowed him to borrow the Maxima. It was a first, but the ould fellow – the title he conferred on his father – attached certain conditions. Johnny had to give a solemn promise to take good care of the car: 'Top it up with super grade unleaded, keep well within the speed limits and, above all else, promise not to consume any alcohol.' Johnny had never the slightest intention of observing any of these conditions, especially the one concerning drink; he truly believed he could hold his liquor as well, if not better, than the next man.

Having a car at his disposal for the first time had made him feel good. In the hotel lounge, he had ordered shots instead of the beer he usually stuck to. Sarah-Jane, sharing in his excitement at first, had two measures of brandy and ginger ale but switched to mineral water when she became alarmed by his consumption of Paddy whiskey. It was almost 1 o'clock in the morning by the time the two of them returned to the car.

Driving out of the midland town, Johnny ignored the thirty-mile speed restriction and took pleasure in smoking the wheels as he shot forward from the few traffic signals he bothered to heed. The sign for Dublin flashed past as Johnny accelerated hard over the flyover that brought them on to the dual carriageway that bypassed Mullingar town. He flashed a broad grin at Sarah-Jane as the tyres bit into the road surface and pushed him into the back of his seat. The powerful engine's torque catapulted them forward. 'Now we're sucking diesel,' he shouted, feeling exalted by the anticipation of the open, almost empty road ahead of him. As the slip road from the flyover merged with the dual carriageway, he flattened the accelerator and yelped with pleasure. 'This fuckin' beauty can climb from zero to sixty-two miles an hour in less than ten seconds; did you know that?' he said excitedly. 'Fuckin' ace or what!'

Sarah-Jane couldn't care less about the car's capabilities but she was concerned about her boyfriend and his ability, or lack of ability, to drive. 'Johnny, slow down for God's sake! You'll have us both killed.'

'Afraid?'

'No, I'm not afraid,' she lied. 'I just think you should slow down a bit.' But she was afraid. Right now, she was afraid of him. She lied to him as she had lied to her own parents earlier in the day. She had been afraid to tell them the truth, knowing full well they would not allow her to stay out for the night if they knew she was with Johnny. Telling them that she was staying over at her friend Cathy's home had secured her freedom. Her parents knew Cathy Perry, her pal since schooldays, and had no reason not to trust the two seventeen-year-olds on their own. But now, sitting next to Johnny, she was sorry she had lied to her parents. She made a further attempt to get him to slow down. 'Johnny, please be careful; it'd be terrible if something happened to your Dad's car.'

He grinned, an ugly upward distortion of the mouth. 'Jayzuss,' he said, 'the old shite didn't want to give it to me at all; made me promise this, that and t'other. Honestly, I could have thumped him. What he didn't know was that I was going to take it one way or t'other, with or without his permission.' All the while Johnny spoke, he watched the curve of the rev counter needle climb. In quick succession, he crashed through the gears, pushing finally into fifth, his foot jammed to the floor, the speedometer showing eighty, eighty-five, ninety, ninety-five.

Sarah-Jane knew that in his present inebriated state of mind, her appeals to slow down would more likely bring about the opposite result. She had never seen him quite like this before, a crazed look on his face, a frightening sneer that dared the night to stop his race. She was scared but she knew better than to admit as much to him. Glancing at him now, as the faint glow from the instrument panel silhouetted his stubbled cranium, she saw its shape transmogrify into a skull. She looked away, dismissing the macabre vision. 'I still don't understand why you should have to meet someone at this ungodly hour of the night,' she said, trying to make sense of a conversation they had had earlier in the pub but more importantly, trying to blot out the deathly vision she had just imagined. Engaging him in conversation, she hoped might help divert his mind from the car's performance and get him to slow down to a reasonable speed.'

'Wasn't my idea,' he said, pushing ever faster. 'This detective fellow I've talked to – his name's Connolly – he said he wanted to meet me in the Burlington Hotel at 2.30 am this morning, said it would be well worth my while, said he wanted to talk about this court action I'm taking against Todd Wilson.'

'But, why so late at night?'

'I don't know . . . less people around I suppose. Probably wants to offer me a bribe. Doesn't want any witnesses – some sort of shit like that.'

'And if he tries to bribe you, will you take it?'

'If the price is right, yeah, of course I'll take it.'

'What would you consider right?'

'Ten grand for starters but I'll look for more, a damn sight more. Todd Wilson is loaded; that fat bollix wouldn't miss ten grand – that's just pocket money to the likes of him.' Johnny eased back a fraction on the throttle, fished a dented pack of Rothmans from his jacket pocket, extracted a cigarette and depressed the car's lighter mounted on the dashboard. Up ahead he could see a few vehicles bunched together as they slowed down to 30 miles an hour to pass through a single lane traffic calming system. According to the road sign, they were approaching the town of Kinnegad.

Sarah-Jane held the bright red coils of the lighter to his cigarette as he motored through the almost deserted main street of the town, impatient to get on the open road again, impatient to pass the few cars holding up his progress. He was half way through the town when his mobile phone rang. 'Hello, he said, pressing it against his ear, 'who's this?'

'Where exactly are you?' a voice asked.

'Ah, Detective Connolly, is that you?' Johnny said.

'Yes it's me. Now, can you tell me exactly where you are?'

'Don't worry. Keep your shirt on. I'll be in the Burlington in time. I'm passing through Kinnegad at this moment, coming to the roundabout on the new bypass, OK?'

'Fine, just checking. See you on the dot of two-thirty.'

Johnny put the mobile down in the space beside the gearstick as he exited the roundabout. 'Silly bastard, afraid I wouldn't show up. Wilson must be shitting himself. Well, the price for my cooperation has just gone up a few thousand quid . . . I'm in the driving seat now.' He laughed a maniacal guffaw. 'Hey, Sarah-Jane, d'you get it? I'm in the driving seat.'

'Yes, that's very funny, Johnny,' Sarah-Jane said, almost in tears.

Picking up speed again, Johnny raised his arm and hit the button that opened the sunroof, letting in a blast of cold night air. Sarah-Jane's protest was drowned by the incoming roar as she hit the button to quickly close the roof again. Johnny laughed at her discomfort and pressed a CD he had brought along into the in-car-entertainment unit, determined to extract every possible ounce of pleasure from the car. With the heavy metal sound of Korn belting out 'Got the Life' from the surround-sound speakers, Johnny pushed the speed up until he was passing the ton mark.

Speeding through the night, passing through the townland of Moyvalley on a straight stretch of road, a new track had just started on the CD when Johnny spotted something that seemed to appear out of nowhere, coming in his direction on to his side of the road. He eased his foot slightly on the accelerator and flashed his lights. 'Get on to your own side of the road you dopey-looking shitearse,' he shouted, his words barely audible above the aggressive din coming from Korn's 'Falling Away from Me'.

Sarah-Jane heard the fear in Johnny's voice, and sensed him flinch. Now, she too stared at the road ahead.

There were headlights coming straight at them. Blinding white beacons that refused to dip, closing in fast on their side of the road.

'A fuckin' lorry! Get off the road,' Johnny screamed.

His foot dived for the brake pedal but he knew it was futile; he was too late. Ear-splitting noise exploded inside his head. Intense light blinded him.

In an instant, the noise ceased.

He floated above the Nissan, saw how it began to break apart, saw Sarah-Jane thrown into the air like a cabbage-patch doll. He could see her face so plainly, her eyes wide with fear, her face a frozen mask of terror. He wanted to call out to her but she disappeared from sight.

It went quiet.

Everything moved in slow motion below him; the Nissan crumpled like an accordion as the lorry's radiator grille pushed the car's engine inwards. He could see no driver in the lorry's cab. Like some magical display, the Nissan's windscreen cracked and frosted into a thousand pieces. The whole window unit collided with other items, all of them spinning like a juggler's props through the air. Korn's CD glided like a frisbee past his eyes, clear enough to read the lyric titles printed on its surface. The car's doors opened, buckled and broke away from the vehicle's main frame, the seats tumbling and turning in a crazy uncoordinated dance.

Unbelievably, the night had turned into a hot summer's day. A bright shimmering haze enveloping what remained of the lorry and car as the two vehicles fused and melted into one another, the kaleidoscopic effect spoiled only by an incongruous smell. What was that smell? He knew that smell; yes, it was diesel. A loud boom sent vibrations cresting through the air. A dazzling display of flames shot into the sky and buffeted the air beneath him with an invisible blanket of intense heat. The lorry's cab burned like a torch as its trailer jack-knifed and slid off the road, mowing a roadside hedge of bushes clean away from its roots as it did so. Paintwork on ripped sections of the car's bodywork bubbled and sent multicoloured flames shooting out into spectacular fan-like shapes.

Johnny could feel the heat now. It was time he moved away from his position above the conflagration. But something was stopping him, holding him sus-pended above the shimmering scene. He could see Sarah-Jane lying in a ditch. Her head turned to look at him, her mouth opening and closing, calling for help but making no sound, no sound at all. Balls of fire rained down all around her. He tried to lower himself, reach out his hand to grab her but instead of descending he began to move in the opposite direction. Faster and faster he soared into the sky until he reached a vanishing point of white light.

And then, a vast nothingness.

Sarah-Jane Keegan was alive but unconscious. On her way to Mullingar County Hospital by ambulance, the medical attendant by her side put her odds of survival as poor to non-existent. Both legs had been broken, her neck had been twisted and it looked as though her spine might have been damaged. She would have to wait until the hospital had time to examine her to find out if the injuries really were life-threatening. Multiple cuts and abrasions scarred the rest of her body with the exception of her face, which miraculously had escaped without a scratch.

Lying unconscious, she could not have been aware of how her boyfriend, Johnny Griffin, had fared. Under the circumstances, it was just as well. Unlike her, he had not been thrown from the car on impact. By the time the ambulance and fire brigade had arrived on the scene, he was already dead, his body burned beyond recognition.

Apart from the grisly findings in the car, something else disturbed the Gardaí who were first to arrive on the scene. No body had been found in the cab of the burned-out lorry. Not only that, but they discovered a steel bar wedged against the steering wheel. They were only guessing but the inescapable conclusion was that the lorry had been primed to continue along a fixed route until it crashed into something. It was beginning to look as though the crash might not have been an accident as they had first assumed. But it was too early to draw any serious conclusions in that regard; the forensic people would have to examine everything in minute detail before establishing what exactly had happened.

Initial inspection, however, suggested that the driver had somehow managed to escape from the vehicle before the impact. This prompted a search in the vicinity of the crash for a missing driver, presumed injured, but no such person was found. A more thorough search would be carried out at first light. The absence of daylight hampered investigation into tyre marks on the road's surface but even under arc lights, it was possible to establish the fact that the lorry had been travelling on the wrong side of the road.

32

A herd of Friesian cows grazed the lush pasture that bordered the Boyne, unconcerned by the lone figure, clad in white jumpsuit and trainers, who was sitting by the river's bank. Sunlight reflections, like a scattering of multi-faceted diamonds, bounced off the river's surface as its flow hurried by over a stretch of rapids on its way towards the village of Slane. Across the river from where Emma Boylan sat, newly planted woodlands and an old arbour formed a screen that hid all but the uppermost part of the eighteenth-century Slane Castle. The castle, famous in recent times on account of its association with major outdoor rock concerts, did nothing to disturb Emma's tranquil scene today. Only the soothing echo of running water and the barely audible sound of grass being scooped into the animals mouths as they lazily ate their fill, drifted on the air. The earthy smell of the freshly chopped grass along with the slight breeze blowing upstream had the desired calming effect on her nerves.

In an effort to get away from the incessant telephone calls, Emma had come down to the riverside. She had followed the pathway that ran past her parents' home, through a series of sloping meadows, before it snaked its way alongside the river's steep banks. Never before in her life had it seemed so important to her to find some space all to herself. In the three days since leaving the hospital, she attempted to hide away from the world in the house that had served as a cocoon in her childhood days. This plan might have worked except for the fact that too many people knew she was there.

They all meant well and she was grateful for their thoughtfulness but no words, no matter how well intentioned, could ease the awful emptiness she felt inside. Her parents were wonderful; they took such pains to avoid using any expressions that might remind her of her recent loss but the look of concern ever present in their eyes never allowed her to escape from the guilt and loss that hung over her.

Vinny too, was wonderful; she could see how hard he tried to hide his own hurt while offering her every support and encouragement. Never once did he so much as hint at attribution of blame or responsibility for what had happened. Maybe it would be better, she thought, if he did come out and accuse her, have a blazing row, clear the air, but for the moment at least, she carried enough self-blame in her head to be going on with.

Bob Crosby's telephone calls – the only ones she bothered to take, the only lifeline with the real world – were a welcome relief. With a delicacy she did not associate with him, he talked about her tumble on the escalators and told her about developments in regard to the follow-up operation. Crosby had learned from Connolly that a red wig and a pair of spectacles had been found near the scene of the crime. It meant that the woman driver Vinny had described, the person tailgating her, was in all probability, a man and not a woman. The detectives investigating the incident had looked at videotapes recorded by the in-store security cameras and identified the redhead as he – if it was a he – stalked Emma. What the cameras failed to pick up however, was the bit where Emma's attacker cast aside the disguise and melted into the general throng of shoppers.

Crosby had brought her up to date with the happenings at the *Post*. His reports from her place of work had the effect of shifting attention away from her own personal problems but it was a fleeting respite and it failed to ignite any desire in her to get back to work. As the bulk of a blue-and-white cow moved nearer to her, its tongue reaching for grass within inches of her feet, she tried to think about her future with the *Post*.

It was while trying to make sense of these thoughts that she felt a presence behind her. Thinking it might be her mother, she turned her head to look and was surprised to see Detective-Inspector Jim Connolly gazing at her. Emma had spoken briefly to the detective in the aftermath of the accident – a jumbled con-versation, abstract questions, fragmented answers, incoherent words – but she had not had any contact with the detective since leaving the hospital. Looking at him now, she couldn't make up her mind whether she resented or welcomed the intrusion.

'How are you, Emma?' He asked, moving over to sit beside her. 'Your mother told me I'd find you here. I hope you don't mind me coming?'

Emma shook his offered hand in welcome. 'Detective-Inspector, what a surprise. I'm feeling much better. Thanks for asking. Must be something very important to bring you all the way down to Slane. You've discovered who pushed me, right?'

'I wish! No, I'm afraid we haven't got a fix on your attacker yet but we're hopeful.'

'Hopeful?'

'Yes. We're examining video footage from the store's security camera and with a bit of luck we'll nail the bastard who pushed you. You heard about us finding the wig and glasses, I suppose?'

'Well now, I've tried to keep myself incommunicado these past few days. I've not bothered with the radio or the television. I've switched off my mobile phone and asked Mother to hide away the newspapers ... but there's no escaping the real world: Bob Crosby has brought me up to date. So, without wishing to appear rude, what brings you here?'

'Why Emma, I came to see how you are, of course.'

'And ... ?' Emma prompted.

'And to let you know that I followed up on that business about those suspect paintings you were on about. I tipped off my friends in Customs and Excise. Yesterday evening they stopped Paul Newman coming through customs and confiscated his collection. You were spot on, Emma. They found illegal drugs hidden in cavities hewed out in the frames. Never would have found them if they hadn't been tipped off. Newman is now in custody. He's refusing to talk to us. We've already confronted Todd Wilson. He disclaims any involvement, maintains he franchises the display areas in his hotels. His only involvement in the operation is that of rent collector, or so he'd like us to believe. As long as Newman keeps his mouth shut it's difficult to get to Wilson.'

'Well, I suppose you could call that progress of some kind,' Emma said, 'but I know you didn't come all the way down here just to tell me that.'

'No, Emma, you're right. The truth is, I wanted to see if you were well enough to . . .'

'Well enough to what?'

'I wanted to make sure you were strong enough to talk to me about what happened to you. You see, there've been some other, more disturbing developments in regard to this whole Todd Wilson investigation. But if you'd rather wait until you're feeling a bit stronger, we can put this off for another time.'

'Well, to be honest I was trying not to think about all that stuff . . . but seeing as how you're here, you might as well tell me what's the latest. Have you managed to locate Fidelma Roper's boyfriend yet? What's his name? Matt Dempsey?'

'That's part of what I wanted to talk to you about. Matt Dempsey has not reported back to Lucan Garda Station in compliance with his bail conditions. At this stage I'm inclined to believe he has been abducted. I don't think he's done a runner. We checked out the old manor house in Leixlip and discovered it had been used to spy on Dempsey's mews. There is another inescapable implication arising from all this that might possibly concern you.'

'Concern me?'

'Yes, you see, whoever was there on the day you visited Matt's girlfriend is now aware of your identity – knows you're involved in the case.'

'Yes, that's a reasonable assumption. I told you already about seeing movement inside the house while I stood on the mews doorstep.'

'I think that might explain why you were attacked in the St. Stephen's Green Shopping Centre.'

'What? You're serious?'

'Of course, I'm serious, Emma! That's why I'm here. Let me tell you something else that has a bearing on all this. You know about the action being taken against Todd Wilson by Johnny Griffin?'

'Yes, of course; sexual harassment; Griffin claims that Wilson did a little male bonding of the unwanted variety. What about it?'

'There's no easy way to tell you this: Johnny Griffin was killed last night in a car crash. A lorry ploughed head-on into the car he was driving, crushed it beyond recognition and set it ablaze. Dreadful scene. It's in today's papers but his name has not been released yet. He was so badly burned that his identity has only been established in the past hour. Initial investigations suggest that it wasn't an accident – that the crash was planned. To make matters worse, Griffin had a passenger with him, a young girl – her parents have just been informed – just seventeen years; she's badly injured, still unconscious. We hope she might be able to tell us what happened when she regains consciousness . . . if she regains consciousness. There's another thing about the crash that's bothering the local investigation; the lorry driver – the one who crashed into Griffin's car – has disappeared. The suggestion is that he jumped from the cab before the impact but a search has turned up nothing. It's as though he was spirited away, I tell you, it's weird.'

'I'm speechless,' Emma said, taking a deep breath. 'What the hell is going on?'

'A good question, Emma. What is going on? There's the question of young Jamie Wilson and the strange collage of cuttings on his wall. What drove him to take his own life? Then we have Ethel Cassidy – her house set alight. Her body burned to death, murdered in the most horrible way imaginable. Next we have Matt Dempsey: kidnapped, still missing, and now we have what looks like the murder of Johnny Griffin. Another fire, another body burned to death. All these incidents are connected directly or indirectly to Todd Wilson. On top of that, we have you, Emma. You've been prominent in your investigation into Todd Wilson's business affairs, and you too, met with an accident that could have been fatal.'

'It was fatal,' Emma said. 'My baby was killed.'

Silence followed. Emma wiped away a tear from her

cheek. Connolly moved closer to her, put his hands on her shoulders in a reassuring gesture. 'I'm sorry Emma. I'm really sorry.' He allowed Emma her moment of silence before speaking again. 'That's why I'm here, Emma. I think you could still be in danger. There's something more to this case than meets the eye. I'm not sure exactly what it is . . . but I think you should be very careful until we establish what the hell it is we're up against.'

'Well, he's unlikely to get to me down here in Slane – unless he comes swimming up the Boyne.' It was a feeble attempt at humour and it failed to elicit a smile from either one of them. 'Are you going to bring in Todd Wilson?' Emma asked.

'I'm going to talk to him, yes, but as of this moment all we have are suspicions. I can't charge him unless I've hard evidence and . . . the truth is; we have nothing on him at all. We're stymied.'

'Tell me, Inspector, do you really believe Todd Wilson is behind what's happening?'

'Yes I do. I can't see what other way there is to read it.'

'So, you're saying that . . . that Todd Wilson is going around killing people.'

'Well, yes, Emma, when you put it like that I know it sounds crazy but, crazy or not, that's the way it's beginning to look. Like you, I think his business ethics leave a bit to be desired but for the life of me, I can't think of anything he's done to make him take such drastic action.'

Emma thought for a moment, a faraway look in her eyes. 'Neither can I,' she said, 'but if it's true, then he's responsible for the death of my baby. If that turns out to be the case, I'll kill him with my own bare hands.'

'No, Emma, you won't do anything of the kind. In spite of the dreadful experience you've had, in spite of your terrible loss, you'll remain the professional that you are. Your objectivity is what sets you apart from your colleagues in the media – that won't change.'

Emma started to cry.

A docile cow poked its head between Emma and Connolly's feet to scoop a mouthful of grass, oblivious of the powerful emotions being experienced by the two humans. Connolly remained silent, not wanting to intrude any further on Emma's grief, thinking he might have been wrong to burden her with so much un-pleasant news so soon after her dreadful ordeal. Emma dried her eyes and looked into the detective's face. It was as if she sensed the thoughts going through his head. 'I'm glad you came to see me,' she said, 'and I appreciate that you have been so open with me. You've provided the jolt I needed to get my head back on straight. I've tried the old ostrich trick, buried my head in the sand and found it doesn't work, I'm only fooling myself.' She stood up, took a last look at the Boyne's rolling water before turning to face Connolly. 'Let's walk back to the house and see if there's anything we can do to get to the bottom of this thing.'

'I think that maybe you should give yourself a little more time. I think that . . . '

'No,' Emma said forcefully, 'it's about time I stopped feeling sorry for myself . . . time I took responsibility for what's happened . . . time I got off my backside and did something useful instead of moping around. I'm going to find out, once and for all, what Todd Wilson is up to.'

33

On his arrival at the hotel it became apparent to Vinny that he would have to sit through the TV4 half-hour arts documentary before George would accompany him on the journey to Slane to see Emma.

Sipping a glass of white wine – George had a bottle of Macon Lugny served in his suite – Vinny watched the programme unfold. On the television screen, George looked younger than he did in real life. His long white hair, normally all over the place, had benefited from the make up department and the lines in his face had all but disappeared due to the benign effect of a soft lens camera.

Exhibits from the new enlarged National Gallery of Ireland appeared on the screen while George delivered a bright and entertaining commentary on each work of art in turn. Even though Vinny was familiar with the exhibits, he still found George's expert knowledge of art most interesting. With perfect ease he took the viewer on a tour of the gallery's fine collection, making the point along the way that Ireland, as a nation, ought to be grateful to George Bernard Shaw for enriching the gallery by bequeathing the royalties from some of his literary works. His words breathed life into the masterpieces, adding facts, informed opinions and anecdotal comments when he considered it necessary while allowing other paintings to speak for themselves.

As the end credits rolled, Vinny clinked his glass against George's and congratulated him on a fine piece of work well done. George seemed happy enough with how the programme had turned out but seemed, for once, reluctant to launch into an overblown verbal dissertation on his contribution to the project. He got out of his seat, switched off the television and looked at Vinny with a pained expression. 'I say, Vinny, are you sure that bringing me to Slane to see Emma is such a good idea?'

'What's brought this on, George? You said yourself, this being your last day in Ireland, you'd like to see her.'

'Yes, I know I did, but I've been thinking; after what she's been through, the last thing she needs is to have an old fart like me visit her.'

'Don't be silly, George. Emma would never forgive me if I let you leave the country without saying goodbye to her. Besides, it'll do her a world of good to spring this surprise on her, it'd bring a smile back to her face. If anyone can do it, you can.'

'You're sure, absolutely sure?'

'Yes, George, I'm telling you, she'll be thrilled . . . and you'll be doing me . . . and her a big favour.'

'Fine then, we shall go to see her together . . . but shouldn't we ring her or something first, let her know . . . ?'

'And spoil the surprise; not likely! Besides, she has

her mobile switched off and I'm still driving her car . . . so she's not likely to be going anywhere, is she?'

'Very well then, if you insist. Let's go.'

Connolly's car was not the smoothest when it came to negotiating corners, a fact Emma discovered as her body slithered on the bum-sliding vinyl-covered passenger seat. 'So Marina Cassidy has popped back into this country,' she said, trying to ease the pressure the safety belt had asserted on her left shoulder.

'Yes, she was picked up on the surveillance cameras at Dublin Airport two days ago. I only found out yesterday.'

'And you've no idea where she's staying?'

'Afraid so; gone to ground, damn it. I didn't expect her to come back. And, not expecting her to show, I didn't see any point in leaving instructions with the airport security boys to detain her.'

'Any idea why she's returned?'

'Your guess is as good as mine, Emma, but it's got to have something to do with recent events. I'll be honest with you. I don't like it. If she contacts you, I want you to ring me immediately.'

Emma nodded but remained silent. Like the detective beside her, she had a bad feeling about this new development. Was Marina a harbinger of sinister deeds to come? She didn't need to be reminded that nasty events seemed to follow on the heels of her last appearances.

Connolly dropped the subject of Marina Cassidy's

reappearance and returned to the subject of Johnny Griffin's fatal crash. He thought Emma's insights into Todd Wilson's murky business dealings might help shed some light on the situation. On this occasion she was of little help. For the past week she had purposely shut her mind off all aspects of her investigative work. But listening to Connolly now, she found herself wanting to catch up with the latest developments.

She shuddered as she visualised the scene of Griffin's death. If he was murdered, and Connolly certainly seemed to believe that was the case, then there could be little room for speculation in regard to who perpetrated the crime. Only one person stood to benefit from Griffin's death: Todd Wilson. It seemed to Emma that Wilson was prepared to go to any lengths to protect his reputation.

Did that mean he wanted to kill her too?

During the course of their journey from Slane, a constant flow of calls had been transmitted to Connolly via his radio phone, all of them to do with on-going police inquiries. Emma had got used to the constant interruptions and for the most part ignored them. It wasn't until they were motoring along the Finglas Road, approaching Phibsborough on the outskirts of the city, that a call came through that captured her full attention.

'We have a reported fatality in the short-stay car park at Dublin Airport,' the disembodied voice on the radio phone announced.

'What are the circumstances?' Connolly asked.

'The airport police got an anonymous tip-off. The caller told them to check out a certain car boot, said it contained a dead body. They called in the local Gardaí to examine the car. While waiting for the Gardaí to arrive, the airport police establish that the owner of the parked car took a flight out of the airport earlier this morning and is booked to return later tonight.'

'What did the Gardaí discover when they arrived?'

'Well, this is all happening as we speak; it's only minutes since our lads arrived on the scene. They forced open the boot and found a badly mutilated body of a man. He'd been dead for some time; looks like he was hacked to death in some sort of savage attack.'

'Have they identified him?'

'No, not yet. Information is sketchy but they say he was probably in his twenties, maybe early thirties. The body was completely naked; there's nothing to help identify him. Right now the scene is being secured, awaiting the arrival of the state pathologist. This could take some time as both he and his assistant are out of the city on other assignments.'

'Did you say the airport police had established who owned the car?'

'Yes, that's why we thought you should be informed. The dead body was found in the boot of Todd Wilson's Jaguar.'

'Repeat that,' Connolly asked, a look of incredulity on his face.

'The car belongs to Todd Wilson.'

'Shit!' Connolly hissed, for once using an expletive.

'Yes, Detective-Inspector,' the metallic radio voice replied.

Eyeing Emma apprehensively, Connolly took a moment to reflect on what he had heard before speaking again. 'I'll be there in ten to fifteen minutes.'

'Right, Detective-Inspector, I'll let them know.'

Connolly closed the line and glanced at Emma. A look of dread crossed his face as he pulled the car to the side of the road and stopped. 'You heard all that?'

Emma nodded, feeling a growing sense of panic. Split-second, blood-red images of her own tumble down the shopping centre escalator flashed through her brain. 'Yes, I did . . . Wilson . . . I'm staggered,' she said, finding it increasingly difficult to catch her breath, pressing the palms of her hands against the car's dashboard in an effort to calm herself down. What she was hearing was too close to her own tragedy, too close to the recent horror visited upon her. 'We were just talking about Wilson,' she stammered, 'but Jesus, this . . . this is nightmare stuff. And the dead body . . . who?'

'I think we both know who it is,' Connolly said, his voice little more than a strangulated whisper. Emma said nothing, felt nothing except a chilling sensation. It was as though multiple ice-fingers were crawling all over her body. Connolly too sat mute, as though stunned. His knuckles showed white as his hands gripped the wheel of his car, his eyes squeezed shut.

It was several moments before his eyelids flicked open. And when they did he looked at Emma, his composure apparently restored. 'What you heard is confidential at this stage. I don't want you going into print with this yet. OK? I'm going to have to drop you here; you'll have no problem getting a taxi back to the city centre.'

Emma had been too shocked to even give a thought to how she should react as a journalist. But hearing Connolly's dispassionate voice brought her mind back into focus. In an instant she pushed her own very personal interests to one side and switched to 'working' mode. 'I'll make a deal with you,' she said. 'I promise to hold back on the story for the moment but, in return, I want you to take me with you to the airport.'

'You know I can't do that.'

'Fine. In that case you can let me out and I can phone in the story straight away.'

'You wouldn't.'

'Just try me.'

Connolly switched the ignition back on and began to edge his way out into the traffic. 'OK, you win. But I don't want people to see you getting out of my car.'

'With all hell breaking loose in the airport, who on earth is going to notice me?'

Connolly gave an exasperated sigh. 'Right, right Emma, I'm allowing you to come with me on this occasion but it's against my better judgement. Just don't get in my way. OK?'

'I'll let you do your job, Inspector; all I ask is that you allow me to do mine.'

'Shit,' Connolly said, using the same expletive for

the second time that day, this time giving full expression to the word.

34

Vinny was annoyed and pleased, all at the same time: annoyed because he and George Laffin had driven down to Slane only to find Emma gone from her parents home, pleased to discover that his wife had at last shaken off the inertia that had characterised her recent days.

According to Emma's mother, Hazel, her daughter appeared to regain her old spirit – miraculous was the word she used – and she had taken off with Detective-Inspector Connolly for Dublin in great haste. 'Let me see, it's four o'clock now,' she said, checking her wrist watch, 'you've missed them by about half an hour – perhaps a bit more.'

'Sounds like the old Emma to me,' George Laffin said, not showing any annoyance at having made the journey for nothing. On meeting Emma's mother he had immediately established a rapport, allowing his mellifluous tones to put her at ease, effortlessly engaging her in conversation.

Vinny, only half listening to the conversation between George and his mother-in-law, continued to ponder on the fact that Emma should have left without bothering to inform him. He seemed most agitated, unable to sit for more than a minute on any one chair, gesticulating with his hands as he spoke. 'I'm surprised we didn't see them somewhere along the road; I'm sure we must have passed each other.'

'Yes, Vinny, I'm sure we met and passed Emma on the way here,' George said calmly, 'but how were we to know she was travelling in some unmarked police car.'

'You're right. And I wasn't driving my Citroën – if I'd been driving that, she'd have spotted us for sure. Just as well I'm picking up my own car tomorrow. With Emma back in harness, she'll need her own transport.' A satisfactory smile brightened Vinny's face as he looked at Hazel. 'I don't suppose she told you where exactly they were going?'

'Only to say they were dashing back to the city.'

'Did she take her mobile phone with her?'

'Yes, but it's not working; the battery's dead as a dodo. She wanted to recharge it but discovered she'd left the charger thingamajig back in the apartment.'

'So, effectively, she's incommunicado,' Vinny said. He thought about this for a moment before turning to George. 'I know what we'll do; we'll head back to the apartment straight away. There's still time for you to see Emma before I take you to the airport.'

George threw in a note of caution. 'Assuming she'll be there, that is.'

'Of course she'll be there. Where else would she be?'

Connolly made his way through the tarpaulin cordon being erected around the crime scene and asked who was in charge. A uniformed member of the airport police introduced himself as Tom Madden and quickly brought him up to speed on the operation. Madden's men, with the assistance of two uniformed garda officers continued in their efforts to secure the crime scene and seal off the involved area from the public. Already they were running into problems from travellers who were being prevented from reclaiming their parked cars.

Taking charge of the operation, Connolly took a closer look at the body. The dead man had not been moved from its position in the boot of the Jaguar. Whoever had dumped him there had been thorough in the savagery they had inflicted on the body. From the angle of the head against the shoulders, Connolly could tell that the neck had been broken. Equally, he could tell from the impossible angle of the legs that they too had been broken. The total surface of the corpse was discoloured and covered in scrapes and bruises but it was the hands that brought an involuntary groan from him. 'Oh, sweet Christ,' he said, choking on his words, his stomach heaving. The dead man's two hands had been severed at the wrists and lay to one side of the body.

Two photographers from the forensic unit appeared on the scene as Connolly turned away from the ugly sight. The rest of the investigating team moved in and set about their business with quiet efficiency. It was a procedure becoming all too familiar to Connolly – they would subject the victim to a microscopic examination, using tweezers and a vacuum, checking for fingerprints, threads, hairs, anything likely to provide a lead. All findings would be carefully collated and labelled and taken to the forensic laboratory for further tests. Silent and grim-faced, Connolly allowed the team to set up their equipment, ever conscious of the stench of death hanging heavily in the air. Their first priority would be to record all angles and condition of the body, a factor he knew would be critical to the investigation, especially when it came to the litigation that would invariably followed on from such a crime.

Tom Madden interrupted his thoughts. 'We've got a picture of Matt Dempsey from the Lucan Garda on our computer screen if you'd like to see it.'

Connolly nodded, grateful for the interruption, and followed the Airport Security Chief as he made his way to an office in the main terminal building. Earlier, on his approach to the airport, Connolly had used his car radio to contact Lucan Garda with a request to send a photograph of Matt Dempsey to him via the Airport Police. It was just his bad luck that Emma Boylan should have been in the car with him at the time but under the circumstances, he had little choice. Boylan, as far as he was concerned, was a fly in the ointment. She knew too much. If she reported everything she knew at this early stage of the investigation she could seriously jeopardise the entire operation. But they had reached a sort of compromise. She had agreed to hold back on naming Todd Wilson as the owner of the car involved and not to refer to any links that might exist between the dead man and the recent drug bust involving Matt Dempsey.

In return, he agreed to inform her of up-to-the-minute developments, in as far as was possible, before the general media got in on the act. He had also agreed that she would get the OK from him to go public with the Todd Wilson angle before anyone else.

Inside Madden's cramped office, the airport's chief of security handed him a colour laser print that showed a head and shoulders shot of Matt Dempsey. Connolly had no doubt in his mind that the face looking out at him from the photograph was the same face that now lay battered, bruised and very dead in the boot of Wilson's car. A shudder ran through his body. He knew he was facing into a murder investigation like nothing else he had ever experienced before. Once the public discovered there was a connection between Todd Wilson and the dead man, the media would go into overdrive. The fact that Wilson's wife, Maeve, along and her organisation, had used the dead man to drive one of their truck loads of medical aid supplies to Africa would send shock waves throughout the whole aid-agency business. In the days ahead, Connolly had no doubts whatsoever, that both Maeve and Todd would be subject to a sustained onslaught from the media. Press, radio and television reporters would sift through every aspect of their lives with the intensity of scavengers tearing at the entrails of a dead carcass.

Using one of the telephones in the airport's main terminal building, Emma contacted Bob Crosby. His initial response of surprise and delight at hearing from her gave way to incredulity when she told him of her involvement with what was happening at the airport. Hinting at, but careful to avoid naming names over the telephone, she left her boss in no doubts as to the importance of the breaking story. In briefest detail, she told him about her journey from Slane with Connolly and how she had agreed with the detective to hold back on certain information. Crosby queried this at first but agreed with her actions when she clarified the situation. In response to her request, Crosby agreed to dispatch a photographer to the airport straight away and to have a laptop and a mobile phone delivered to her.

Before talking to Crosby, she had tried to contact Vinny. She knew he planned to travel to Slane to see her so it was important that she reach him before he set out on the journey. Hoping to catch him at the apartment she rang there first. There was no answer. Cursing softly to herself, she left a message for him on the answering service. Vinny, she hoped, would see the flashing red light. As soon as her mobile phone arrived from Crosby she would contact him again.

In the meantime she needed to get back to the car park, find out from Connolly if he had anything further to report on the murder investigation. The *Post* photographer should arrive any minute and, in spite of temporary restrictions, she hoped to be able to complete the first in a series of reports from the crime scene.

From what little Connolly had let slip, she knew that a press briefing would be announced soon, the venue to be the Garda headquarters in Phoenix Park later in the evening. This, she knew, was Connolly being clever. His intention was to schedule the briefing in the Phoenix Park at the very time that Todd Wilson's plane would touch down after its flight from Edinburgh. It meant that Wilson could be brought into custody for questioning without the glare of publicity. Not if I have my way, Emma said to herself. She would advise Bob Crosby to send someone else to the Garda press briefing while she, along with the *Post* photographer remained in readiness at the airport. Just when Connolly thought it was safe to sneak Wilson off for a spot of interrogation, she would pounce.

It was while driving out of the village of Slane, heading in the direction of Dublin, that Vinny first noticed the black Land Cruiser in his rearview mirror. Half listening to his passenger, George Laffin, who insisted on keeping up a running commentary on life's vagaries, Vinny made his way down the steep hill that led to the old multi-arched stone bridge that spanned the river Boyne, all the time observing the looming vehicle sticking close to his tail. He felt most uncomfortable. At times, the bull bars of the four-wheel drive moved to within inches of his back bumper. On the vehicle's bonnet, a large graphic depiction of a dragon, outlined in gold and silver, spewed brightly coloured flames down to the grill and front bumper. If the purpose of the dragon was to intimidate other road users then it had succeeded as far as Vinny was concerned. He tried to make out who was behind the wheel of the Land Cruiser but the vehicle's black tinted windscreen made it impossible.

On either side of the bridge, a set of traffic lights controlled a one-way counter-flow traffic system. This usually led to a traffic tailback while waiting for the opposite flow to complete its green light phase. Vinny hoped he would be held on the red light on this occasion; it would give him an excuse to get out and remonstrate with the driver behind. He did not want this to develop into a road-rage incident but he was determined to put a stop to the Land Cruiser's aggressive behaviour before it developed into some–thing like that. But fate, not on Vinny's side, ensured there was no delay; the lights remained green, leaving him little option but to proceed.

Half way across the bridge's span, Vinny felt his car being hit from behind; it was only a gentle nudge but the shock made his foot involuntarily press down on the accelerator. George Laffin stopped talking and looked at Vinny for an explanation. He got none. Vinny felt a prickling sensation on the back of his neck, his instincts now receptive to danger and fully alert. Picking up speed, he made it to the other side of the bridge and began the climb on the far side of the river. All the while the four-wheel drive loomed large in his rear view mirror. By now, George Laffin knew something was wrong. 'What's the matter?' he asked.

Vinny was about to answer when a motorcycle materialised from behind his car and began zigzagging in front of him. 'What in damnation is going on,' George Laffin asked a second time, his voice by now taking on a note of real urgency.

'I think we're in trouble,' was all Vinny could say.

The motorbike rider, dressed in black leathers and wearing a black visor, continued to weave dangerously in front of the Volvo. Vinny hit the brake pedal in order to avoid collision. Immediately, the Land Cruiser nudged his back bumper again. Quickly, Vinny pumped the accelerator. George opened his mouth to speak but, for once, seemed incapable of uttering a word. Vinny saw the fright on the older man's face. 'Don't worry George, we'll get these cowboys out of the way.' His brave words belied the panic he was feeling. He wasn't sure what to do. It was all happening too fast.

Whumph!

The Land Cruiser's bull-bar grill crashed into his bumper. He clung to the steering wheel, desperately trying to control the car. His foot slammed down on the accelerator. In that same split second the biker had chosen to slow down. The Volvo rammed into the bike. Vinny and George watched in horror as the bike shot into the air. The impact tossed the rider and his machine down the side embankment that sloped sharply down to the River Boyne.

Before the motorbike came to rest, Vinny's car was subjected to another massive impact from behind. This time, the Volvo lost contact with the road. Vinny and George were lifted into the air, their car spinning out of control. Vinny's hands gripped the steering wheel, his knuckles turning white from the pressure. The car plunged headlong down the side of the embankment. Like rag dolls, George and Vinny were thrown about as the vehicle thumped its way over hump and hollow. A bone-crushing bang brought the car to an abrupt stop.

Vinny blinked his eyes, shook his head, attempting to clear the chaos chasing about inside it. The Volvo had come to a stop, its front lodged deeply into a clump of bushes, its engine no longer running. An eerie silence hung inside the car. George, he could see, had his head pressed between his headrest and passenger door. A streak of blood issued from a gash in his forehead and trickled on to his white beard. 'George, George are you all right,' Vinny asked in growing panic.

A groan escaped George's lips. 'I'm fine, I'm fine Vinny . . . hard to kill a bad thing.' The relief Vinny felt was short-lived. Through the mud splattered wind-screen he could see down a steep incline of rough terrain that led to the river's edge. Halfway between the water's edge and his stalled car a motorbike lay lodged upon a pile of rocks. Some yards away a figure dressed in black leathers lay still on the ground. Vinny remembered the rider and the crazy manoeuvres he had performed only minutes earlier.

He was about to open his door when he noticed a figure scrambling down the embankment from the roadside. The black Land Cruiser, he could see, had parked by the side of the road above the approaching figure. Dressed in denim, the man, a tall athletic young man, hopped and jumped over the rough ground.

Before reaching the car, he covered his head with a white woollen balaclava and produced a handgun. 'Get out o' the fucking car,' he roared, pointing the gun in Vinny's face. Vinny stared at the weapon with disbelief. The gunman took a step closer. 'Get out o'the fucking car,' he repeated, his voice turning to a screech.

Vinny did not need to be told a third time. He pushed his door open, got out of the car and stood with his hands in the air. 'Who are you? What . . . what do you want?' Vinny asked, his voice sounding every bit as shaky as he felt.

'Get the woman out,' he yelled.

'The woman . . . what woman?'

'Don't fuck with me or I'll blow yer fucking head off. Now get the woman out o'the car . . . it's her we want.'

'Look,' Vinny pleaded, 'the person in the car is an old man, he's been hurt in the accident. I need to get him to a doctor.'

As Vinny spoke, George Laffin lifted his head from its hidden position by the door, blinked his eyes groggily and turned to look at the gunman. There was silence for a moment as the attacker looked askance at the white-haired man.

'This car belongs to Emma Boylan, the journalist, Right?' The gunman barked.

'Yes,' Vinny replied, 'but she's not here now . . . as . . . as you can see.'

'And who the fuck are you? Who's the ol' bollix?'

Before Vinny could answer, a Garda patrol car

screeched to a halt behind the Land Cruiser. The man holding the gun glanced around and immediately pulled the balaclava from his face. 'Get back in the bleedin' car,' he ordered, 'and keep yer trap shut or I'll shut it for good.'

Although Vinny could see a uniformed garda getting out of the patrol car in the background, he never lost sight of the gun pointing in his direction. He scrambled back into the driving seat with as much haste as he could muster and closed the door behind him. The gunman put the weapon away and turned his back on the Volvo. He then began to wave his arms frantically in the air as though looking for help and started to run in the direction of the approaching law officer. 'There's been an accident,' he yelled, 'you'd better take a look . . . looks bad; there's an ol' man badly injured,'

'What happened? Did you witness the incident?' the officer asked.

'Afraid not; I was driving by when I saw the car and the bike down by the river. The biker's injured . . . might be dead for all I know. The ol' man needs lookin' after. I'm goin' to call an ambulance from my car phone.'

There was a moment's hesitation before the garda replied. 'OK, all right, you ring for the ambulance while I take a closer look at the scene.'

Vinny heard the exchange of words and wanted to call out a warning but feared that if he did, the escaping gunman might use his weapon. By the time the garda had made it to Vinny's car the gunman was already climbing into his Land Cruiser. As Vinny explained to the officer what had happened, the four-wheel drive sped away. The policeman, to his credit, admitted he had been fooled by the charade. 'At least I got the registration of the bugger's jeep,' he said, by way of self-mitigation. 'Let's have a look at your friend here. He looks fairly shook up to me.'

George, hearing this exchange, put a brave face on things. 'Forget about me, Constable,' he said, 'I've got a scratch, nothing more. But I think you should have a look at that fellow lying down there by his motorbike.'

Vinny followed the garda down the slope to where the leather-clad figure lay. The garda officer, a beefy red-faced man in his forties, was experiencing some difficulty with his breathing. Climbing down steep banks was obviously not something he had encountered for a long time. He discarded the jacket of his uniform as each step down the embankment caused him increased stress. Sweat patches of growing proportions seeped out from under his armpits, changing his ultramarine shirt to an ugly slate grey.

To Vinny's eyes, the motorcyclist looked too still, one arm pinned beneath his body at a dangerous looking angle. A black visor covered the man's face making it difficult to gauge if he was alive or dead. 'I'll see if I can get a pulse reading,' the garda said, breathlessly. 'It might be dangerous to touch his helmet ... he could have sustained a broken neck. Gingerly, he lifted the man's limp wrist and felt for a sign of life. 'He's alive,' the garda said, 'can you believe it, he's still breathing. We'd better not move him. I'll call the ambulance; I presume our friend in the four-wheel didn't bother his barney to contact anybody.'

'You can bet on it,' Vinny said

'Might be best if yourself and your elderly friend went in the ambulance as well ... get yourselves checked out ... can't be too careful.'

'I'm all right, Officer, no damage at all, thank God but I think my friend George should see a doctor, get his cut dressed.'

'I agree, it doesn't look too serious but we'd better let casualty have a look at him just the same.'

'Right, you're right. Look, ah ... any chance you could get me some help to have the car towed back to the road?'

'No problem. I'll arrange that as soon as the ambulance arrives. And after that I'd like you to accompany me down to the station to make a statement. You got a good look at the other fellow's face, the one that got away, I mean?'

'Yes, I saw him all right. He was wearing a balaclava at first but he removed it when you showed up. I'd recognise him again if I saw him.'

'Good, I saw him too but it always helps to have a little corroboration; helps to nail blackguards like him. I already have his registration number ... not that it will do me much good; the shagger probably stole the vehicle in the first place.'

'Well, when the biker recovers you should be able to find out who exactly they are and what the hell they were playing at.'

'That, my friend, is exactly what I intend to do.'

Two hours later, Vinny was back in Emma's Volvo, heading towards Dublin. George Laffin sat beside him in the passenger seat, the plaster on his forehead the only evidence of the ordeal he had endured. While Vinny gave his statement in Navan Garda station, George's injuries were seen to in Our Lady's Hospital, nearby. The red-faced garda, whose name was Mahaffey, had, with Vinny's help, put names to both the motorbike rider and the Land Cruiser driver. Both had records. Both were wanted for questioning on a string of offences. According to Mahaffey, they were freelance 'heavies' willing to do anything for anyone providing the price was right. The biker had suffered multiple injuries in his fall but none that were life threatening; a garda officer sat by his hospital bedside, waiting to interrogate him as soon as consciousness returned.

It would only be a matter of days, Mahaffey assured Vinny, before the other blackguard was apprehended. 'We'll subject both of them to the full rigours of investigation,' he said with obvious relish, 'and within a short space of time they will cough up their guts . . . tell us exactly who is pulling their strings.'

Mahaffey had been most helpful. He had organised a tow-truck to pull the Volvo back on to the road. No serious damage had been inflicted on the car; a buckled front and rear bumper, a few scrapes here and there but nothing that would stop him from driving.

It was only now while motoring back to the city that

he realised how lucky George and he had been; it could have been much more serious. 'Just think, George,' he said to his silent passenger, 'Emma might have been the one in the car.'

'Thank God she escaped all that,' George said, 'after what she's been through ... what with losing the baby and all that ... well, let's just be glad she was spared that.'

'Amen to that.' Vinny said, refusing to put his worst fears into words. The attack on the car had been aimed at Emma; she was the one they wanted, that was what the gunman had said. Twice in a matter of days, attempts had been made on her life. It was a scary thought. The question was: who wanted her eliminated? Although Emma did not fill him in on all the details of her recent investigative work, he knew that she had been digging up some unpleasant stuff on Todd Wilson. Wilson's wife, Maeve and her organisation had also come under her scrutiny but surely, he reasoned, these were not the sort of people who went about trying to kill people. After what Emma had been through, he hated the thoughts of having to talk to her about what had happened to himself and George. Sooner or later he would have to bring up the subject, but he would prefer if it were later. He turned to George and attempted a smile. 'What Emma needs right now is a period of calm ... a complete break from all this sort of stuff. I'm just sorry you won't be able to see her before you grab your flight back to London.'

'Shame really,' George said, nodding his head, 'but

we have no choice but to go straight to the airport.'

'Tell you what, George; when we get to the airport, we'll telephone her at the apartment; that way you'll be able to say goodbye.'

'Good idea, Vinny. If I have the time, I might give Ciarán a call as well.'

35

Post photographer Ronan Long captured the sequence perfectly, his subject matter unknowingly complying with his wishes. Todd Wilson and Detective Inspector Jim Connolly, framed in the Nikon's viewfinder, made their exit from the airport's arrival area via a covered walkway that led to the short-term car park. Emma Boylan, moving at a discrete distance behind her photographer, watched as both men got into the unmarked garda car. A cordon erected close by blocked the view of Todd Wilson's Jaguar from prying eyes. Emma studied Wilson's expression. She wanted to scream at him, stop him in his tracks, force him to answer her questions. Did you murder the man in the boot of your car? Did you murder Ethel Cassidy? Are you the bastard who killed my baby? But she couldn't ask the questions and she couldn't show her presence here. All she could do was observe him. His face, beneath the scarce, slicked back hair, had lines and crevices that spoke volumes about the pressure the man had been under in recent times. But was it the face of a killer? Was he a monster? His jowls appeared more bulldog than ever, his eyes a little wearier, but whatever dark secrets lay beneath the fleshy folds of his face remained hidden.

Long continued to click frame after frame as Connolly reversed his car out of its space and headed away from the car park, Emma observed the low-key exit with a mixture of emotions. Wilson had not been placed under arrest, which meant there were no handcuffs. What a pity, she thought, visualising the impact such a photograph would have made on the front page of tomorrow's *Post*. Wilson was only being brought in for questioning, not being arrested. Emma knew only too well what that meant: Wilson could be questioned for up to forty-eight hours before a decision was taken to charge or set him free. Because of his high profile, the authorities would want to be absolutely sure of their ground before they applied to the DPP to bring charges against him.

One way or another, Emma had hold of a good story. But somewhere in the back of her head a gnawing thought tormented her; more a question really, or to be more precise, a series of questions: Why am I doing this? What are my motives? A good story? Justice? Revenge? She refused to contemplate the answers. She was afraid to face the truth, scared to acknowledge the malformed need for the retaliation struggling for release from the darkest regions of her mind.

Crashing a shutter down on these thoughts, she concentrated instead on the task in hand, reminding herself that she was, after all, an investigative journalist. And to be successful in that field, she knew from past experience, she must remain focused in her intent. That meant leaving no room for personal considerations of any kind. She was chasing a good story. No other considerations could be allowed to upset her objectivity.

While her media colleagues were sitting at a news conference in the Phoenix Park Garda Depot, being told that persons were being detained for questioning in connection with the discovery of a dead body in the airport car park, she had the inside track. Her report, when it hit the streets, would be picked up in all the TV and radio bulletins throughout the following day. The *Post* would have to be credited as the source for the story, a factor bound to bring a smile to Bob Crosby's face. The goodwill coming Emma's way wouldn't make up for the terrible time she had experienced recently but it would help get her life back on the rails.

Yet, just as the euphoria of the moment threatened to carry her away, her thoughts returned to Earth with a bang. She remembered the brutalised body of Matt Dempsey and sighed. Although she had never met Dempsey, she had met his girlfriend, Fidelma Roper. It was hard not to think of her now and to imagine the terrible anguish she must be suffering. With thoughts of her own recent misfortune never far away, Emma could identify with Fidelma; like her, she too was a victim. Both had been kicked in the teeth by life's cruel turns of fate. It just wasn't fair.

Emma decided not to let Matt Dempsey's name appear in print until she checked with Connolly that Fidelma had been informed of his death. It was, she knew, the very least she could do for the unfortunate young woman.

Accepting Long's offer of a lift from the airport back to the city centre, Emma had only strapped herself into the passenger's seat when she saw Vinny, along with George Laffin, attempt to move into the space Long was vacating. 'Let me out, let me out,' she shouted like an excited schoolgirl to the photographer. 'Look, it's Vinny, my husband Vinny. He's driving my car.'

Vinny had not seen her until she got out of Long's car and waved wildly at him. 'Hey, Vinny,' she yelled, 'what're you doing here?'

Vinny rolled down the window. 'I'm trying to park,' he said, bringing her Volvo to a halt in what had been Long's space. 'I might ask you the same question. What are you doing here?'

Before Emma could answer she noticed Vinny's passenger getting out of the car. 'George! How are you George?' she said, moving to greet him. 'Of course, I'd forgotten; this is your day for going back to England.'

George beamed with delight as he embraced her. 'Yes my dear Emma, I'm on my way back to London but I can't tell you how happy I am to see you before I go.'

Rocked from side to side in his bear hug, Emma noticed the plaster on his forehead. 'What happened your forehead? Don't tell me yourself and Ciarán got into a bar brawl?'

Vinny interrupted George's laughter. 'Let's move into the departure lounge; we can catch up on all that's happened there. I'll bring in George's cases, check them through and then we can grab a coffee before his flight is called.' Vinny hadn't yet told George about the gift that he and Ciarán had decided to give him. Father and son had, after a short discussion some days earlier, agreed to offer their friend the Harry Clarke drawing as a memento of his trip to Ireland, knowing how much Laffin would appreciate it and knowing the value he put on the artwork, a value way beyond its monetary worth.

Over coffee and scones, Emma told them about her trip back from Slane with Connolly and the subsequent discovery of a dead body in the boot of Todd Wilson's car. Telling them that the detective had just taken Wilson into custody for questioning brought her account to an end. Vinny and George had pressed for more details but she refused to elaborate and insisted instead in hearing what they had been up to. Vinny told her about bringing George down to her parent's house to say goodbye to her and went on to relate the episode about their off-road excursion. In describing the incident, Vinny had been careful not to mention the fact that the gunman had asked for her specifically. Even so, Emma was quick to conclude from what he told her that the attack was aimed at her. 'You were driving my car,' she said, 'the same car I drove parked in the St Stephen's Green Shopping Centre on the day I was pushed down the escalator. Whoever wanted me on that day is still after me.'

Vinny, hearing George's flight number announced on the speakers, used it as an excuse to change the subject. 'Come on George, that's your boarding call.' Accompanying Emma and George as far as the boarding gate, he produced the cardboard tube that housed the Harry Clarke drawing and presented it to George. 'Dad and Emma and I wanted you to have this as a reminder of the time you spent with us in Ireland. We hope you like it.'

For once, George seemed flustered. Awkwardly he unscrewed the plastic cap from the end of the tube and extracted the drawing. When he saw it he looked astonished. 'Goodness me,' he said, groping for words, 'I couldn't possibly accept such a gift . . . knowing the lengths you went to find this treasure in the first place, not to mention its worth . . . honestly!'

'We want you to have it,' Emma and Vinny said in unison, shaking his hands in turn. Emma kissed him on the cheek and noticed the tears forming in the old man's eyes. 'I'll never forget this trip to Ireland,' he said, 'and I'll never be able to repay the kindness you have shown me; believe me, I really do appreciate it.'

'It was our pleasure to have you,' Vinny said, putting the drawing back into the tube. 'Now get on that plane or they'll take off without you.'

Emma and Vinny continued to wave their goodbyes until George disappeared into the covered walkway that led to the plane. 'Right,' Vinny said, taking hold of his wife's hand, 'let's go home; we've both got a bit of catching up to do.'

'Sorry Vinny,' she said, 'I need to pop into the office for a few minutes first. There's a few bits and pieces I have to put to bed for tomorrow's edition. I hope you don't mind?'

Vinny smiled. 'I don't mind in the slightest,' he said, leaning over to kiss her, 'I'm just glad to see you back in the thick of things.'

Bob Crosby allowed his arms and hands take the weight off his body as he leaned heavily on the boardroom table. His legal team, Joe Hughes and Lionel Belton, had, after much discussion and four rewrites, given Emma Boylan's article for tomorrow's front page the all-clear. Crosby hated to let the legal boys loose on any story and only called them in on occasions when he absolutely felt a need for their scrutiny. It was his firmly held belief that given the opportunity they would put forward arguments why certain passages from the weather forecast should be dropped, but on this occasion he had no choice but to be careful. Severe repercussions would follow if he did not take this extra precaution on the Todd Wilson revelations. 'Thank you, gentlemen,' he said, dismissing the two solicitors. 'I'll sleep all the more soundly tonight knowing that the morning's front page has passed muster with you guys.'

Crosby read the article one last time and looked at the photographs that would accompany the text before leaving the boardroom. Glancing at his watch he noted that it was almost midnight. Pushing his bulk up two flights of stairs, he made it to Emma Boylan's desk just as she was about to leave for home. 'Glad I caught you, Emma,' he said, collapsing into a chair, trying to get his breath back. 'I just got the green light for your piece on Todd Wilson. The legal louts cut the balls out of it as usual but it's still going to cause a storm when it hits the street in the morning.'

'Jeez, Bob, you look as though you've just gone fifteen rounds in the ring with "legal". You're all out of breath.'

'Damn stairs!' he said, his breathing coming back to normal. 'I'm going to have to do some exercise. Anyway, your article has just gone to press. All hell will break loose tomorrow.'

Emma nodded her head in agreement. 'And your friend, Detective Inspector Connolly, is going to have my guts for garters.'

'Speaking of Connolly,' Bob said, a perplexed shadow appearing on his face, 'I heard a whisper about him earlier today that I can't quite figure out.'

'Oh?'

'Yes, I was chatting with Jack Robertson, editor of the Midland Times and he told me the oddest damn thing. Robertson is an old friend of mine; our friendship goes back to college days in Clongowes Wood. Jim Connolly was a student at the time and the three of us have kept in contact ever since. We swap tips from time to time in regard to shares on the stock exchange. Nothing big, mind you, but we've made a few killings – if you'll pardon the expression – over the years. Anyway, Jack was talking to me about the strange accident that killed that young fellow who brought sexual molestation charges against Todd Wilson.'

'You mean Johnny Griffin?'

'Yes, Johnny Griffin. His suspicious death represents a huge story as far as the Midland Times is concerned. Only natural, given that Griffin's family hails from the midlands. Anyway, Emma, in the course of their investigations into the accident, they had a reporter speak to Griffin's girlfriend. It appears she was lucky to escape from the crash with her life. For three days she remained unconscious in Mullingar General Hospital. Yesterday she regained consciousness and spoke for the first time about what happened on the fateful night. Among other things, she claimed that Johnny was on his way to Dublin to meet Detective Inspector Jim Connolly when he met his death. She claims that Johnny told her he was meeting Connolly in the Burlington Hotel and that the detective was going to give him thousands of pounds to withdraw his legal action against Todd Wilson.'

Emma sucked in her breath. 'What?'

'My reaction exactly,' Bob Crosby said. 'I simply don't know what to make of it. Why would Connolly agree to act as a go-between for Todd Wilson and Johnny Griffin? It makes no sense. When you consider that at this moment, as we speak, Connolly has Wilson in custody, questioning him on the discovery of a dead body in his car, it simply doesn't add up.'

'I agree,' Emma said. 'I don't have to tell you I'm not Connolly's biggest fan but I can't believe that story. Somehow or other Griffin's girlfriend must have got her facts wrong.'

'Either that or I've got my old college chum figured all wrong. I've been thinking about how he first asked me to get you to share information with him. You fought my decision like an alley cat. I thought I was clever, you know, appearing to give him a little in order to get a lot in return. Right now, I'm not sure who was fooling whom.'

Emma looked at her boss, staggered by what he was saying. 'You're not seriously suggesting that Connolly could be bent?'

'No, I'm not; but I'll admit that a doubt has been planted in my brain. He was the one you were going to meet in the shopping centre on the day you were attacked . . . he knew precisely when you would arrive there. It could be a coincidence of course, but . . . '

'No, stop this, Bob, I don't want to hear this. It's crazy – crazy! It couldn't be Connolly! It couldn't be . . .?'

'I want to believe that, Emma, but there's something else that bothers me about all this. I was telling you about how Robertson, myself and Connolly like to speculate on the Stock Exchange – nothing too serious, you understand – but all three of us have taken a bit of a hit in recent times with shares we bought in Wilson's companies. With myself and Robertson, our exposure is limited, not having invested a whole lot to begin with but in Connolly's case, his investment is more substantial. Robertson believes the detective is in deep. And, ever since your critical articles began to appear, the share price in Wilson's companies have dipped steadily. So, in essence, it's in Connolly's interest to see Wilson survive this onslaught of bad publicity and thrive again. All this is a bit far-fetched, Emma, and I'm not inclined to give the notion much credence. I don't believe Connolly would allow himself to become involved in anything as murky as this business with Johnny Griffin. I don't want to believe it, but, having said that, I suggest you keep a close eye on everything he does.'

'I've been doing that anyway, Bob, I always do. But surely Connolly will be taken off the case now that this accusation – the one made by Johnny Griffin's girl-friend, has been levelled against him.'

'Yes, you'd think so, but I suppose it depends on what Connolly's superiors believe. I mean, it wouldn't be the first time a good cop was accused of being bent. There's not a lot we can do about it right now so I suggest you go home, have a good night's … and be ready to join the fray tomorrow. It's going to be quite a day.'

'Yeah, right, Bob. Goodnight.'

36

Emma squinted. Pulling the curtains open, she allowed the early morning sunshine to blast in through the bedroom window, its slanted slab of saffron light illuminating the pillow where her head had been less than twenty minutes earlier. Already dressed and ready to confront whatever the day held in store for her, she listened to the radio, waiting for the news. The amorphous shape beneath the duvet that was Vinny brought a smile to her face. She watched for a moment. He stirred lazily but continued to keep his head hidden beneath the rumpled sheets, not quite ready to rise and shine . . . not just yet. And she was content to let him lie on.

The newsreader on Today FM let her know it was 7.30 am. Top news item concerned itself with the report on Todd Wilson's detention overnight in custody and the discovery of the dead body found in his car. Mention of the *Post* article was made and credit for the revelations were duly accorded to her. Soon, she realised, every branch of the print and broadcasting media in the country would be on to her, attempting to get their very own exclusive sound bite. Well, not today, she determined; no, today she had her own agenda to attend to and it didn't include feeding titbits to reporters who were too inept to create their own headlines.

Driving through Fairview on her way towards Howth, she wondered if Vinny had emerged from under the duvet yet. She thought about ringing him on her mobile but decided against it. Let him lie on if he wants to, she told herself, smiling. He had been so wonderful with her the night before. They had cried together, talked about their loss, cried some more. Comforting sounds, little more than incoherent whispers were shared. Arms entwined, they held each other close, close enough that their hearts appeared to beat as one. She could not let him inside her in the physical sense – she was still too sore from what had happened – but somehow they had managed to mingle and melt into each other in a blissful, exotic pleasure trip, a trip that took them to heights never before achieved.

Held up by stalled traffic, she wiped a tear of joy from her eye and gazed wistfully beyond Fairview Park, where flats of mud, sand and green algae remained wet and shiny in the wake of the outgoing tide. Out to sea, a fog bank had bedded down on the Liffey estuary, shrouding all but the top half of one of the chimneys of Poolbeg's electricity generating station, giving it the surreal appearance of a rocket in readiness for blast off. Another smile. Perhaps it was the phallic imagery or, more likely, a residue of pleasure from the amorous encounter of the previous night that brought her thoughts back to Vinny and his unselfish lovemaking. He had known instinctively how fragile she felt both physically and mentally and how, paradoxically, she needed him to commit his body and soul to her unconditionally. One did not always have to use a match to ignite a fire, a truism that Vinny patiently and devotedly set about proving.

The blast of a horn from the car behind snapped her thoughts back to reality; the traffic snarl-up had unblocked itself and she was free to move again. With an apologetic wave to the grim-faced man in the car behind her, she drove forward, wondering if the same driver had ever been lucky to experience real love and affection. No, she concluded, studying his face in her rear view mirror, he probably hadn't.

Twenty minutes later, Emma made it to the seaside village of Sutton, a mile short of Howth Head. According to the information she had received from Connolly on their first formal transfer of notes, Angela Devine lived with her parents at 17 Glencarraig Heights. Emma had intended to meet Angela earlier but with all that had happened, never got around to it. Marina Cassidy had spoken to her about Jamie Wilson's girlfriend on her recent trip to Liverpool. Could it be possible, Emma wondered that Angela Devine could shed light on why her boyfriend had decided to top himself?

17 Glencarraig Heights turned out to be a spacious bungalow with an unhindered view of Dublin Bay. Situated between the suburbs of Sutton and Howth, the area's demographics placed it among the wealthiest in County Dublin. A sandy-haired boy of ten or eleven, dressed in Pokémon pyjamas, answered the door. 'No,

sorry, my sister's not here,' he said in answer to her request to speak to Angela. An all-prevailing smell of burning toast had accompanied the boy to the door. 'D'you want to talk to my Mom?'

Before Emma could answer a woman wearing a silk dressing gown with a Japanese floral motif appeared at the door. Tall and lean to the point of anorexia, she gave Emma the benefit of a perfunctory smile. 'You were looking for our Angela?' she asked in a tired, put-upon voice that was redolent of too many cigarettes.

'Yes, I was hoping to have a word with her. My name is Emma Boylan; I'm with the *Post*.'

'Would this have anything to do with young Jamie Wilson's death?' the woman asked, leaning her lanky frame against the doorjamb, her hair hanging in limp strands about her face. 'It's just that I'm Angela's Mom and we've been getting a bit of bother since the terrible event.'

'I'm sorry to hear that, Mrs. Devine, but yes, I was hoping Angela could talk to me about Jamie Wilson.' Emma had to think quickly before continuing. She had a gut feeling that if she gave the real reason behind her visit, Mrs. Devine would not be forthcoming with answers. 'I'm working on an investigative piece on teenage suicides,' she lied 'and it would be a great help to talk to someone who was close to him. I believe Angela was his girlfriend.'

From beneath heavy eyelids, shrouded further by sunken, skull-like sockets, Mrs. Devine scrutinised Emma hard and unflinchingly before answering. 'Well now, girlfriend might be putting it a bit strong – they were good friends as far as I know, nothing more – but I can only tell you what I told the other people who called here to talk to her: she's out of the country at the moment.'

A shout from within the house interrupted Emma as she was about to speak. 'Hey, Mom, the milk is boiling over; it's all over the cooker.'

'Well, whip the saucepan off the cooker,' Mrs. Devine shouted back. 'I'll be there in a second.' She looked at Emma and shrugged her narrow shoulders. 'Sorry about that. Getting breakfast in this house is not for the fainthearted. Was there anything else?'

'I've called at a bad time, I'm sorry but I won't delay much longer. You said other people called to talk to Angela? When was this?'

'A woman called here yesterday wanting to talk to her; said she was a twin sister to Ethel Cassidy, the Wilson's housekeeper. The poor woman was burned to death in a fire recently. Jamie introduced Angela to her when he brought her to his home.'

Emma was taken aback that Marina Cassidy should call to see Angela Devine but decided not to push the subject any further. 'You said two people called; do you mind if I ask who the second caller was?'

'Oh, let me see now, that would've been about two, no, three days ago. A detective, he said he was. Big fellow. Can't remember his name.'

Emma sucked in her breath. 'Could it be Connolly?' she asked.

'Why yes, now I remember, you're right it was Connolly. At first I thought he said Connery, you know, like the actor Sean Connery, but he corrected me; said it was Connolly.'

Emma felt her stomach flutter. Two shocks in as many minutes. She wanted to scream 'What the hell is going on?' but she tried to hide her annoyance. 'Angela is out of the country, you said. When do you expect her back?'

'I'm not sure. She's on a literary tour of England with a bunch of her university friends. They're trying to visit as many places as they can associated with great writers. They're using a bus and staying in hostels so it's hard to keep track of where she is on any given day. Y'know, the sad thing is: poor Jamie Wilson was supposed to have gone with them, had his deposit and all paid up in full. Funny that. I mean, when you think of what he did, don't you think?'

'Yes, it's odd that he should have paid to go on a tour,' Emma agreed, 'especially if he knew he wouldn't be around when the time came to travel.'

'Yeah, that's what I can't understand. Such a waste of young life,' she said in an almost absent-minded manner, her skinny fingers stroking a chin that almost wasn't there. 'Look, I'd better get back to the kitchen. As for Angela, I expect she'll be home by tomorrow or the next day. You want me to tell her you called?'

'Yes, please, if you would,' Emma said, handing her a business card. 'Ask Angela to call me when she gets back.'

Further shouts from the kitchen brought the interview to an abrupt end.

Emma took her annoyance out on the gearstick of her Volvo as she drove away from the Devine household. The tranquil scene all around her was in stark contrast to the anxiety clogging up the further reaches of her mind. A cloudless expanse of sky with backlit gulls silhouetted against a sun that appeared to hover above the nearby Howth Head and Ireland's Eye, failed to brighten her spirits. Her doorstep interview with Angela Devine's mother had forced her to re-evaluate her thinking in regard to Marina Cassidy and question her assessment of Detective Inspector Jim Connolly. Was it possible, she asked herself, that both Marina and Connolly had played her for a fool? If the answer to that was in the affirmative, where did that leave her? And why did both of them want to talk to Angela Devine all of a sudden? Did they believe the young woman could tell them why Jamie Wilson had taken his own life? Could she also shed light on Ethel Cassidy's murder?

The proliferation of questions doing the rounds of Emma's head was getting her nowhere. One thing did become clear, however, she would need to talk to Angela Devine as soon as she got home – and preferably before Marina and Connolly got to her.

With less than half the freight container filled and medical-equipment donations down to zero, Maeve Wilson was left in no doubt in regard to the seriousness of the problem facing her. Under normal circumstances she would, at this stage, be making final arrangements to send the container on its way to Ethiopia. But the circumstances were anything but normal. Word had gone out to all the health boards, hospital and specialist clinics that all was not well with SUCCOUR.

Sitting at her desk, an array of newspapers spread out in front of her, Maeve was left in no doubts as to the causes for this state of affairs. Her own photograph and that of her husband had made the front pages of every national broadsheet and tabloid. Article after article tied her and Todd closer together than they had ever been in real life. Even though Todd was the one in custody, it didn't stop the reporters from taking sidelong swipes at her Third World enterprises. The fact that no connection existed between what she did and what Todd did appeared not to bother anyone in the slightest. Along with Fergus Massey, she was accused of allowing the financial side of the business to become sloppy and open to abuse.

Considering all the press and television coverage, Maeve understood why her most reliable donors were now questioning her bona fides. But while accepting that Fergus and she should have handled things more professionally, she was in no doubt where the real blame lay for her current difficulties: her husband, Todd Wilson.

Every article in every paper, every radio station and every television newscast posed the same question. How much did she know about her husband's business dealings? Now that he was helping the police with their enquiries into a murder case would she continue to head up her own Third World aid organisation? Would she stand by Todd Wilson? Maeve cleared the newspapers from her desk and dumped them in her bin. She was tempted to strike a match and set fire to them but resisted the temptation. Whoever said that all publicity was good publicity, she decided, was talking rubbish.

She had every right to be mad at Todd but for some reason she felt little or no animosity towards him on this occasion. It was one thing for her to berate her husband, she told herself – God knows, he deserved the lambasting she had showered on him over the years – but this media barrage of resentment linking him to murder was, in her opinion, unwarranted and unfair. Some of the coverage had found him guilty already. Maeve knew Todd's shortcomings better than most; she knew he could be unscrupulous in his business dealings, she knew about his womanising, his lying, his cheating, his meanness and a hundred and one other faults, some serious, some petty but she had no reason to believe that murder was among his vices.

Fergus Massey, who had phoned her earlier, told her he had set up an appointment to meet the Garda Chief Superintendent. According to Massey, talking to Connolly would be a waste of time. 'If you want action,' he had said, 'you have to talk to the top dog.' Massey continued to assure her that Todd could not possibly be involved in murder. The two men had known each other since college days and apart from a row over a silly prank at the Body Rock on Ireland's Eye, they had remained loyal ever since.

Considering the three-way relationship that had existed between them for so many years, she realised how each of them in turn deceived the other. In Todd's case she believed, rightly or wrongly, that his cheating and lying had been a feature of their married life from the beginning. Did that justify her adulterous affair with his best friend, Massey? And what of Massey himself? What sort of friend sleeps with that friend's wife? It all added up to a sordid set of circumstances, she realised. It was something that had developed of its own accord, something that had taken on a life of its own, something she had felt unable, and unwilling, to stop – until now.

With a newborn clarity, stunning in its intensity, she understood that she must support her husband, speak out on his behalf, let the world know that Todd Wilson was no murderer. But, another part of her brain, the part that housed her survival instincts, insisted that she do nothing.

There was something bugging Emma, a half-formed idea gnawing at the edge of her brain. It was something that Bob Crosby had said to her when he persuaded her to share the research notes she had made on Todd Wilson with Connolly. According to Bob, Connolly liked to dabble in stocks and shares. That in itself meant very little. But when put together with the interest he had shown in her notes on Todd Wilson's shareholding in various publicly quoted companies, it took on a new significance.

Sitting in front of her PC, she tapped into the Internet and searched the financial pages until she found what she was looking for. Tying the information coming up on the screen with the documentation she had unearthed in the company's office at the initial phases of her investigations into Todd Wilson, a picture of sorts began to emerge. Then, she hadn't known exactly what she was looking for, and had not picked up on something that seemed obvious to her now. Unaware of hours passing, she downloaded reams of financial information; she became more and more convinced she was on to something. Checking and double-checking her facts and figures to make sure she was not mistaken, she put the pile of photocopied documents to one side. One or two key elements remained to be clarified but to do so she would need the help of a hacker. Bob Crosby would never permit her to take such action but she would have no scruples about using such tactics. She needed certain information in regard to a specific offshore holding company if she was to prove beyond doubt that her instincts were right. And the only way to get that information would require an expert hacker. Gleefully, she rubbed her hands together and set about closing down her computer. She knew a self-confessed hacker.

But even without this information, even without all the answers, she felt confident that she knew who was behind the recent spate of 'accidents' and deaths. She knew the murderer's identity.

37

Marina Cassidy felt the smooth pebbles buffet her bare feet as she splashed through the rippling foam, her legs tingling from the wet spray. Making her way to the shore, holding both shoes in her hands, she climbed the slight incline of sandy beach and let out a yelp of delight. She had made it back to Ireland's Eye after an absence of more than a dozen years. The offshore island always looked its best in June and July, she remembered, especially when the long warm evenings remained bright almost to midnight. Even allowing for the length of time since she had last set foot on Howth's promontory and its islet, it still held a special fascination for her. She retained a vague memory of Todd Wilson taking her sister Ethel and herself around the peninsula all those years ago. Back then, before she had learned to hate him, Todd had been an informative guide, pointing out mysterious landmarks, recounting tales about haunted headlands with wondrous names like Gaskin's Leap, Piper's Gut, Puck's Rock and Black Jack's Well, areas that resonated with echoes of ancient druids, pirates and shipwrecks.

Being back after such a long time made her feel tipsy, made her want to yell and kick her feet in the sand. Light-headed from the short boat journey between Howth's West Pier and the island, she sat on a rock and absorbed the last vestige of heat from the slow setting sun. She was content to sit there soaking up the warmth, head tilted back, eyes closed, listening to breakers on the shore, until her boatman returned from his chore of berthing his small pleasure craft. The fact that she had just shared an extravagant meal and drunk a little too much alcohol with that boatman in the King Sitric, one of Howth's finest fish restaurants, added to her flightiness.

She had wanted to celebrate, and Fergus Massey had been more than happy to facilitate that celebration for her.

Todd Wilson was finally being brought to justice, reason enough for her to pop champagne corks. She had never forgiven Wilson for forcing Ethel to abort her baby in Liverpool all those years ago. In the difficult years that followed, Marina kept in touch with Fergus Massey, or to be more accurate, he had kept in touch with her. During those self-imposed years of exile, during the depressing periods when her relationship with her twin sister shattered and buckled out of shape, Fergus had provided her with a constant, reassuring link to her homeland. He would contact her at irregular intervals, have her meet him in a small private airstrip beside the Aintree race track. From there he would fly her to Weston Aerodrome, west of Dublin, in his Piper Warrior, have a meal together and later, book her into some luxurious hotel for the night. The following morning he would fly her back to Liverpool.

More recently, when Ethel had perished in the fire at her home, Fergus was the one who had contacted her, found a place for her to stay and vowed to help her discover who, or what, lay behind her sister's death.

And now, with Todd Wilson in custody, she felt that the task had been accomplished. She still hadn't got positive proof of course; she still couldn't tell who exactly had set the house ablaze but she had little doubt where the blame lay. Todd Wilson may not have struck the match himself but he gave the orders, of that she had no doubt. Knowing he was out of harm's way, in police custody, was enough to set her mind at ease.

She was still thinking about Todd Wilson and what he had done to Ethel when she heard Fergus Massey's feet crunching through the sand. He stood for a moment in front of her, studying her upturned face, before sitting down beside her. 'Brings back a few memories, eh?' he said.

'What does?' she asked absentmindedly, reluctant to let go of her own thoughts.

Massey grimaced, then smiled. 'This island,' he said, 'brings back memories . . . all those years ago.'

Marina nodded, her eyes still closed, inviting the last of the sun's warmth to penetrate her skin. With only the gull's cries to disturb the peace, both of them sat for several minutes enjoying the island's solitary atmosphere, listening to the waves gently lapping the shoreline and tasting the faint brine-laden breeze on their lips. Marina became aware of Massey's arm as it rested on her shoulder, his fingers gently caressing her skin. She liked the feeling. Massey leaned closer to her. 'I'd like you to look at something with me,' he whispered in her ear.

Marina stirred, opened her eyes, blinked against the light, and turned to look at him. 'Yeah, sure, Fergus. What do you want me to see?'

'You're probably going to think I'm a bit morbid, but . . . if you have no objection I'd like to visit the spot where Jillian met with her death.'

Marina, taken aback, tried not to show her surprise. 'Sure, it's only right that we should show our respects to the dead.'

Fergus nodded in agreement but made no immediate reply. He disengaged his arm from her shoulder, got to his feet and began walking towards the island's rocky escarpment. Marina slipped her shoes back on hastily and followed him. To one side of the precipitous formation a path of sorts forged its zigzag way to the top. 'We're going to have to climb up there,' Fergus shouted back to her. 'You feel up to it?'

'Yeah, sure, why not,' Marina answered back unconvincingly, looking down at her shoes despairingly.

The rocks beneath their feet were wet in places making their progress to the top slippery and dangerous. Fergus, first to complete the ascent, offered his hand to Marina and pulled her to the high ground. Getting her breath back, Marina took in the magnificent vista this vantage point offered.

'It's beautiful up here,' Fergus remarked.

'Breathtaking,' Marina agreed. By turning in a

semicircle she could see the distant peaks of the Mourne Mountains, Dublin Bay, its coastal towns and harbours glistening like pearls in the evening sun, Bray Head with its granite cross on the summit, the Wicklow Mountains, Lambay Island and far, far out to the east, looking to where the line between sea and sky dissolved, she could identify the faint outline of the tip of Snowdon in Wales.

Marina followed Fergus, walking a few paces behind him. Golden gorse, purple heather, ferns and multi-coloured wild blossoms, though beautiful, did little to ease her discomfort as she struggled in ill-equipped shoes to hold her footing in the rough terrain. By the time Fergus halted at the edge of an escarpment, Marina was puffing and panting like a marathon runner approaching the finish line, trying to catch her breath, glad to stop for a rest. Without looking at her, Fergus pointed to a jagged outcropping below him. 'That's where Jillian was killed,' he said, bitterness evident in his voice, something she had never heard in him before. Marina said nothing. She just stood there beside him, looking at the rock, occasionally glancing at the haunted look on his face. After what seemed like a lifetime of silence but was in fact no more than three minutes, Marina decided to move away from the spot. By now, the sun had begun its slow-moving descent to the horizon, taking some of the day's heat with it. Glancing back at Fergus, his stillness caused her to shudder. Best to leave him space to contemplate whatever thoughts are going through his head, she decided.

Twenty paces onward, she heard him come up behind her. The despondent face she had witnessed minutes earlier had mellowed into a cheerful countenance. 'Come on,' he said. 'I'll show you the Body Rock.

'The Body Rock?'

'Yes, you remember, Marina? We went there with Todd all those years ago – the famous rock in the tidal waters of the Long Hole, the scene of Ireland's Eye's best known murder.'

'Oh, yes, yes of curse. Todd brought us to see it in his boat.'

'His father's boat,' Massey said, correcting her.

'Yes, that's right, his father's old boat with the outboard engine. You and Todd were still bachelors at the time. Myself, Ethel, and Maeve came with the two of you to the island . . . got piss-eyed if I remember rightly. Todd insisted on bringing us to the Long Hole to show us the Body Rock . . . told a terrible story, before I passed out from the drink.'

'Do you remember the story?'

'Yeah, I think so. Let me see: some artist fellow was supposed to have raped and killed his wife, right? Her body was found on the rock – the Body Rock. The artist was found guilty. Wasn't that it?'

'Something like that. You want to see the spot where it happened?'

'I don't know . . . first time I went there I was under the influence. But yeah, fine, it should be interesting to see it in the cold light of day – or evening, even.'

'Great, great, come on, this is the perfect time to

see the rock. The tide is out which means it's visible. It's not often you'll get such a good opportunity to see it.'

'Yeah, all right Fergus, lead me to the Body Rock.'

Emma had made a coffee for Vinny and herself, and was about to sit down in front of the television to watch the evening's 9 o'clock news when Mrs. Devine phoned her. 'Sorry to bother you so late in the evening,' she began, 'but there's something I thought you might like to know.'

'You're not bothering me at all,' Emma said, wondering what revelation the gaunt woman had to impart that wouldn't wait until the next day. 'What is it you think I should know?'

'Remember the other day when you called; I told you about the detective that called to speak with Angela?'

'Yes; Detective-Inspector Connolly.'

'Well, that's the problem. The man who called to my door gave that name but I've just been looking at today's paper and I saw a picture of Detective Connolly. He's not the same man. Unless there're two Detective Connollys, he's not the one who wanted to talk to Angela.'

'You're sure about this, Mrs Devine?'

'Of course I'm sure; I wouldn't be bothering you otherwise. I'm just glad that Angela wasn't here when he called; he could have been anybody.'

'Did he look anything like the photograph you saw in the paper?'

'No, not really. The man I saw was a bit younger I'd say, definitely more handsome, dressed well, spoke well, seemed a decent sort . . . but nowadays you never know . . .'

Emma, believed the woman. It was obvious that her caller had impersonated the detective to hide his true identity. Emma thought she knew the reason why. Rather than pursue the subject any further over the phone, she decided to take a different tack. 'Any word from Angela about when she's coming home?'

'Yes, as a matter of fact,' Mrs Devine said, sounding surprised by the sudden change of direction. 'She rang me about two hours ago. She gets into Dublin Airport in the next hour or so. She's getting a taxi from there to take her home. I expect to see her a bit after 11 o'clock tonight.'

'Would you mind if I called to see her in the morning; it's most important that I check a few things out with her?'

'I don't know about that. She's going to be exhausted after all her travelling. Ring me in the morning – make that mid-morning – and we'll see how things are. All right?'

'OK. Fine, Mrs Devine, I'll do that. Thanks for calling me; I really appreciate it.'

Emma replaced the telephone and looked at her watch: 9.05 pm. Mrs Devine's call had intrigued her, especially the bit about Connolly not being Connolly. It fitted in with other information she had received earlier that evening when her computer hacker struck gold.

The top-grade files elicited and downloaded illegally added weight to the strongly held suspicions she already had in regard to who had called to the Devine household. If she was right, it confirmed her earlier conclusions about who had murdered Ethel Cassidy. And, if she believed that, if she were correct in identifying Ethel Cassidy's killer, the same killer had also been responsible for the other unexplained deaths. But did the list of evil deeds include her own recent mishap? Finding a convincing reason why the same killer should want to push her down a flight of stairs and run her car off the road stumped her. There was, she reflected, still a few pieces of the puzzle that didn't fit.

Angela Devine, she felt sure, might be able to help with the grey areas but she had no intention of waiting until the next day to talk to her. When Angela Devine arrived in Dublin Airport and came through the arrivals door in an hour's time, Emma would be waiting for her.

Connolly felt frustrated. He had, over the course of the day, spent five tough interview sessions with Todd Wilson and had got nowhere. Either Wilson was an exceptionally good liar or he really wasn't guilty of anything more than sharp business practice. Compounding his lack of progress, his colleagues in Navan Garda Station had informed him that they had got nowhere with the two men who had run Vinny Bailey off the road. Both were steadfastly refusing to say who hired them.

Three hours earlier, about six that evening, Connolly's firmly held convictions that he had the right man in custody took its first dent. CCTV video from the Airport Police showed the body of Matt Dempsey being put into the boot of Wilson's car by two shifty looking individuals. The quality of the tape was poor, making the action look at though it was shot in a snow storm. Even so, it was obvious that neither of the men captured on film could have been Wilson. Another video, better quality this time, its digital time clock attesting to the fact that it had been recorded several hours earlier, showed Wilson parking his car. Yet another piece of recorded footage, with perfect picture definition, showed Wilson boarding the plane for Scotland.

Connolly knew he would have to come up with something more substantial, something solid, if he was to hold Wilson in custody. His earlier interrogation of Paul Newman had been a waste of effort. The antique dealer refused to implicate Wilson in his drug importation scheme. It was obvious to the detective that someone was paying Newman to keep his mouth shut, paying him enough to risk going to jail. Connolly's frustration was at breaking point. If he could only discover who was bankrolling Newman, it would resolve so many things. But he didn't know who it was. That being the case, his investigation was going nowhere fast.

38

Marina could understand how the Long Hole had got its name. It looked as though some ancient deity had chiselled an oblong slab of solid rock from the earth, and left a great gaping hole in its place. Peering over the rim, Marina tried to make out the detail. At the bottom of the hole, water gently swirled around an enclosed space, lapped against the concave rock face, creating an eerie echoing murmur. The sensation reminded her of an almost forgotten sound, a sound she hadn't heard since holding a conch to her ear as a child. Then she had been told she was hearing the sea but this sound was louder, more insistent, more unearthly, more scary.

'We took Jamie here on the day Jillian died,' Massey said, making Marina emit a little start of fright. She hadn't noticed him moving so close beside her. 'Jeez, I'm sorry Fergus,' she said, 'but this place is giving me the heebie-jeebies.'

Massey ignored her comment. 'Of course, back then, back on that day myself and Todd took the boy here, the tide was fully in. You see that rock set in the middle of the water below,' he said, pointing to the base of the hole, 'that was completely submerged by the wash on that day. A pity, really. Jamie would love to have seen that.'

'That . . . that's the Body Rock?'

Yes, the very one. Let's go down and have a closer look at it.'

'Go down there? You're joking!' Marina said, unenthusiastically. But the look on Massey's face could not be more serious.

'Come on,' he urged, finding a ledge that wound its way down the steep rock face, 'we've still got an hour of daylight left. Remember, you were here before.'

'Yes, not that I recall a whole lot about it. I was piss-eyed at the time. It didn't seem half as frightening.'

Marina, slow to desert the high ground, watched him manoeuvring his body along a narrow ledge before she reluctantly decided to follow him. After a few feet of the decent, the spiral ledge became steadily steeper. Some portions of the slippery downward slope had handholds and metal wedges drilled into the rock face, presumably put there by some thoughtful soul to help frightened sightseers like her. These aids were of little comfort to Marina. Inch by inch, foot by foot, she managed to make it all the way to the base of the hole without mishap. Massey applauded her as she stepped on to the safety of a rock pile that bordered the pit's base, the sound of his hand clapping echoing ghostly against the towering rock face all around them. 'There now, that wasn't so bad, was it?' he said to her.

'Just tell me one thing,' Marina asked, trying to get her breath back. 'How are we supposed to get back out of here?'

'Easy, we take the low sea-level passage out through

the crevasse that leads to the sea. It's possible to walk out that way when the tide is out – as it is now. Otherwise, you'd need a boat.'

'So why didn't we enter by this sea-level passage?'

'What?' he said, laughing. 'And miss all the fun of climbing down the sides?' His mirthless guffaws ricocheted round the Long Hole, sounding not unlike Vincent Price's maniacal contribution at the end of the Michael Jackson song 'Thriller'.

Marina's thoughts became fixated on getting out of the place. The slowly encroaching darkness worried her. 'OK, Fergus, I've seen the Long bloody Hole; it's wonderful; it's great. As a desirable tourist destination, I'd rank it right up there with the Pyramids, the Eiffel Tower and the Taj Ma-fucking-hal but right now I'd like if you could get us to hell out of here, It's freezing my tits off.'

Again, Massey ignored her comments. 'You see the Body Rock over there,' he said, pointing to a huge block of black granite surrounded by a few inches of water, 'that's the very spot where they found the body of the artist's wife, back in 1852.'

Marina looked at the altar-like rock almost as though she expected to see a dead body there. A shiver ran through her body. 'Why on earth would she come here in the first place?' she asked, her imagination refusing to let go of the macabre image.

Massey shrugged his shoulders. 'Hard to say, really. She probably came here to find solitude. Her husband was a self-absorbed artist who liked to sit in front of his easel, paint whatever aspect of Ireland's Eye took his fancy, rather than pay any attention to her. She, poor thing, was left with little choice but to come here. Of course the geography of the place was quite different back then, easier accessibility for one thing, but it's easy to see why she would pick a place like this.'

'I don't know about that; it's not a place I'd choose . . . it's such a desolate spot.' Marina hunched her shoulders and shivered. 'So, who killed her . . . I mean, if it wasn't her husband . . . who else could have done it?'

'Interesting question, that,' Massey said, never taking his eyes off the rock. 'They found her lying on her back, partially naked. All the signs suggested sexual interference. There were scratches and bruises on her face and eyelids, on the insides of her thighs, and her breasts were badly cut and scarred, both nipples displaying evidence of bite marks.'

'Well, that exonerates the husband.'

'Sorry?' Massey said, finding it hard to believe anyone could be that naive. 'How do you make that out?'

'Well, if it was just a question of sex, a husband wouldn't need to go in for any of that rough stuff, would he? So, who did it?'

'Nobody knows for sure but there are a lot of theories on the subject. Todd Wilson once told me a story that had been passed down to him through several generations of his family. According to his tale, she came here to have sex with some smugglers who used the Long Hole as a base for their operations. If the story is to be believed, the woman liked a bit of rough trade and on the day in question things simply got a bit out of hand.'

'Sounds a bit implausible to me,' Marina said.

That's what I thought when I first heard it but I've changed my mind since. Todd, who has lived in this area all his life and knows the place like the back of his hand, took me down here one day – back when we were students – and showed me the potholes and caves where the smugglers hid their spoils. He took me through to the caves then ... which is more than he could do now, what with all that extra flab he's carrying. One of the caves connects right here in the Long Hole. Come on, I'll show you.'

Massey, not waiting for an answer, made his way around the base of the walls, climbing over boulders, moving upwards until he disappeared in through a slender gap in the rock face. Marina, standing alone and becoming more frightened by the minute, had no choice but to follow. Climbing over the sharp-edged rocks hurt her feet and hands, every discomfort encountered accompanied by a self-pitying cry of pain. I'm going to give Fergus Massey a piece of my mind when I get out of here, she swore silently to herself. She was forced to bend and contort her body in order to slip in through the fissure where Massey had disappeared. In an instant everything had gone dark. She was about to call out when she felt Massey's hand reach out to her. 'Here, grab my hand,' he offered, pulling her upwards. 'The next section is a bit tricky.'

Terrified now, wondering where she was heading, Marina began to sob. She screamed when Massey let go of her hand but ceased instantly when a bright light lit up her surroundings. They were standing in a cavernous space and Massey had found a torch. It took her several seconds to recover her composure and bring her breathing under control. Not saying a word, Massey moved in and out of great shadows, busying himself by lighting a storm lantern. With the extra illumination she got a better sense of her surroundings. Slime-covered rocks, dripping wet, formed a rough-hewed passageway that stretched past the light from the lantern and disappeared into a black void. A sour, damp smell, suffocating in its intensity threatened to induce vomiting in Marina. To both sides of the cave, rows of timber beams, like old railway sleepers, formed shelves against the wet walls. They appeared to be rotten, covered in mould and fungus, and were empty of any content. The temperature, in marked contrast to the atmosphere above ground, was close to freezing. 'I want you to take me out of here immediately,' she said to Massey, attempting to convey a no-nonsense order, but failing even to convince herself.

'No,' Massey said curtly. 'I brought you here to tell you a story, a story of treachery and deceit. A story in which you and your twin sister Ethel played a leading part.'

'What the hell are you talking about, Fergus?'

'I think it's about time you were told the truth about

the child you and your sister killed in Liverpool.

'Jesus, what is this?' Marina asked, trying to come to grips with what she was hearing. 'Ethel was pregnant with Todd Wilson's baby. He gave her the money to go to England for an abortion. I tried everything in my power to stop her.'

'You didn't try hard enough. And it wasn't Todd's baby.'

'Of course it was Todd's baby. You've said so yourself all those times we've met ever since. Both of us have worked together to make sure the bastard pays for what he has done. What the hell's got into you Fergus, you're beginning to frighten me.'

'Like your sister Ethel, you are a fool, Marina. You are a dumb stupid cow, right? You believed what you wanted to believe. Never once did you bother to discover the truth. As for Ethel, she was just a dirty slut. She was responsible for Jillian's death here on Ireland's Eye ... and then, with your help, she killed my baby.'

'Your baby? What the hell ... ?'

'Yes, it was my baby. I am the father of the child you both killed.'

Waiting in the airport's arrivals concourse, Emma checked the bank of suspended monitors for the tenth time in as many minutes. The word Landed flashed on and off, on and off, against the flight number she was interested in. She had no difficulty picking out the group of university students from the other passengers.

Having flown in from Stansted Airport, they were making their way from the baggage collection zone through the sliding glass doors that led to the public waiting area. Emma studied the group carefully trying to pick out Angela Devine. She made the connection easily enough. One of the group, taller than the rest, looked like a younger version of Angela's mother, though considerably better looking. She would never be described as beautiful but she had striking features. Rimless glasses accentuated intelligent eyes that seemed too large for her thin face. Long sandy coloured hair sat untidily on her shoulders, begging to be brushed and styled into some sort of shape. Dressed in jeans, T-shirt and trainers, she pulled a large holdall sack, complete with its own tiny wheels, behind her. Any doubts Emma may have entertained as to Angela's identity were settled when one of the students spoke to her and addressed her by her name.

Emma followed as Angela made her way to the exit and watched her hug and say goodbye to her companions before making her presence felt. Offering Angela a business card, she introduced herself and asked if they could have a few words together. Angela glanced first at the card, then at Emma. 'I know who you are,' she said, her manner friendly, 'I've read some of your articles in the *Post*, seen you on the television once or twice. What can I do for you?'

'I'd like to ask you a few questions about Jamie Wilson if you have no objections?'

Angela Devine gave a little sigh. 'Hmm, I thought as

much. To be honest, now is not such a good time. I'm dog-tired, absolutely bushed. It's been a long hectic day. I want to call a taxi, get home, have a shower and have some sleep.'

'Tell you what,' Emma offered, taking hold of Angela's holdall, 'I'll drive you home, save you the taxi fare. I promise to keep the questions to a minimum. What do you say?'

The expression on Angela's face said no but after weighing the situation for a few seconds, she gave the nod of consent.

Shreds of daylight clung stubbornly to the city skyline as Emma, along with passenger and luggage, departed the airport complex and headed for Sutton. The journey would be a short one so Emma lost no time in dispensing with small talk and moving on to what was uppermost on her mind.

'Did Jamie give any indication that he was unhappy – depressed?'

'Well, yes he did,' Angela answered uneasily. 'But, you see, Jamie was always unhappy about something or other. He bitched about his parents continually, called them strangers who sometimes lodged in the house. He bitched even more when they were there because all they did was fight with one another – the parents, that is. It was hard not to feel a bit sorry for him. All things considered, he was a nice fellow. He had pretty screwed up ideas about sex and sin – one and the same thing to him – but we got on fine . . . especially when the topic centred on books.'

'Towards the end, though, did you notice any difference, any personality changes?'

'Yes, unfortunately I did. I've thought of little else ever since . . . you know, wondering if I should have reacted differently, asking myself if I could have prevented what happened. Guilt, I suppose. You see, he came to me about a week before . . . before he did what he did. I'd never seen him so upset. He said we couldn't go on seeing each other any more. I couldn't believe it – we'd been getting on so well. I demanded an explanation. He refused. I kept on insisting.'

'And . . . did he tell you?' Emma probed.

'Well yes, eventually. He told me a strange story. I'm sorry, I can't tell you everything he told me; it would take all night but I'll give you the gist of it. OK?'

'Yeah, fine, go ahead,' Emma said, slowing down her driving, conscious of the fact that they were half way to Sutton.

'Someone came to talk to Jamie a few weeks before his eighteenth birthday and greatly upset him. You see, in the absence of his parents, he had become very close to the Wilson's housekeeper, Ethel Cassidy. In many ways she was his mentor. He adored the woman. Which was why he reacted so badly when this person who came to talk to him revealed a darker side to Ethel Cassidy.'

'Did he tell you what this dark side was?'

'Yes. This person who talked to Jamie told him that Ethel had once had a baby . . . and that she had gone to England to have an abortion. This really freaked Jamie – he was the most pro-life person I know – but when he was told that his own father had been responsible for making Ethel pregnant, he just couldn't get his head around that concept at all.'

'Yes, I can imagine how revelations like that could unhinge Jamie . . . but, well . . . ?'

'You still don't know why he ended our relationship, right?'

'Right,' Emma said, deliberately letting other cars pass her, trying to slow down the journey.

'To be honest,' Angela said, 'I didn't understand it myself at the time. It wasn't until the day after they found his body that I discovered the rest of the story. He posted me a letter, you see, on the very day it happened. Creepy or what? Anyway, in the letter he asked me to forgive him for what he had planned to do – said he cared for me greatly, thanked me for being his true friend. He gave me some other information of a very personal nature and included a photocopied document which he claimed explained his course of action . . . except that it didn't, not to me at any rate.'

'Can you tell me what was on the photocopy?'

Angela thought about this request for a minute before answering. 'No, sorry, Ms Boylan, I can't do that. Jamie requested that I keep it a secret, said I was the only one who needed to know the truth. I feel I ought to honour that wish.'

Emma would have liked to hear more but she was nearing Angela's home in Sutton. She didn't have time enough to coax further information out of her about the contents of the photocopy. 'Just tell me one thing, if you can,' Emma asked, pulling into the driveway to her house. 'Do you know the name of the man who talked to Jamie?'

'Yes, I do.'

'Can you tell me his name?'

'No, and that's two questions.

'OK! All right. Fine,' Emma said, but continued to ask further questions anyway. 'If I tell you who I think it was, will you nod your head if I'm right?'

Angela made no reply.

'Was it Fergus Massey? Was he the person who spoke to Jamie?'

Angela did not nod her head. But as she got out of the car, Emma could see tears forming in the young woman's eyes. It told her what she wanted to know.

Marina stopped screaming, stopped yelling for help. She had reached a point beyond fear, beyond terror. The portion of sky above her, the part defined by the Long Hole's surface aperture, had grown dark. Stars, like tiny pinpricks, twinkled forlornly from the heavens. Marina Cassidy knew she was going to die. The awful realisation had dawned on her a few minutes earlier when the first spray of seawater splashed her face. Blood from her wrists and ankles, flowing from burns and raw cuts inflicted by ropes that held her fast to the Body Rock, merged with the salty spray. If what Massey had told her was true, the water would completely cover her within the hour. Sometime before that happened, she would be dead.

39

Connolly glanced at his wristwatch and cursed silently. 9.30 am already. He had come to work without having breakfast, something he rarely did, and he had spent the last forty-five minutes interviewing Todd Wilson, getting nowhere fast, going round and round in circles. Wilson had the knack of getting right up his nose – always ready with an answer for everything.

Emma Boylan was waiting for Connolly when he returned to his office. His expression let her know that he was not in good form. 'Emma,' he said, trying to coax a smile to his face, 'tell me you've come to give me good news, tell me you've got something on Todd Wilson that will allow me to press charges.'

Emma shook her head and puckered her lips.

'I see,' Connolly sighed, reading the body language, 'so if it isn't good news, what brings you here?'

'I've had some serious thoughts on this case over the past few days . . . decided I'd like to run a few things by you – if you have the time.'

'Time I've got buckets of. Answers I've got diddly-squat. So, whatever you're selling, I'm likely to want to buy.'

'I've re-examined all Todd Wilson's company documentation. I've had a computer friend of mine, a dab hand at surfing the web, extract files from various offshore financial organisations and . . .'

Connolly interrupted her. 'You've used a hacker to illegally break into confidential files. Is that what you're telling me?'

'Do you want to know what I've uncovered or not?'

'Oh damn it, Emma, go on! Tell me. What've I got to lose.'

'I've discovered that Fergus Massey bankrolled Wilson's earliest business ventures. In fact, Massey was chairman of the board in most of Wilson's earlier enterprises.'

'You say "was". Does that mean he's no longer involved?'

'He's still involved but not to the same extent. In recent years, Wilson has bought out Massey's share-holding in one company after another. At this moment in time, Massey no longer holds the chairmanship in a single Wilson company. He's not even on the board of directors. He sold shares drip, drip fashion over the past decade. However, he went solo during this period; he invested considerable finance in a number of property ventures and sporting related enterprises. All of them have failed to make a profit. The truth is: Fergus Massey is strapped for cash.'

'He could have fooled me . . . certainly keeps up appearances,' Connolly remarked. 'He owns a big house, has boats, a private plane. How does he do it?'

'As far as I can make out, he is dependent on the

revenue he generates from SUCCOUR to fund his lavish lifestyle.'

Connolly whistled softly. 'You could have something, Emma. That organisation is coming under increased suspicion at the moment. You know what they say – no smoke without fire. Could Massey be on the fiddle, pocketing charitable donations for himself? And where does that leave Maeve Wilson? Christ, the implications are awesome.'

Emma hesitated a moment before continuing. 'I have to know something from you before I go any further,' she said, looking the detective straight in the eye, 'I need to ask you a few questions.'

'I usually do the asking around here,' Connolly said, peevishly.

'Nevertheless, I want some answers before I continue.'

'OK. Go ahead. It'll make a change if nothing else.'

'Tell me, Detective Inspector: did you attempt to see Angela Devine in the last week?'

'Angela Devine? Sorry, who's Angela Devine?'

'She was Jamie Wilson's girlfriend. But it doesn't matter, you've answered my question.'

'You have more?'

'Just one more. Did you know that Johnny Griffin told his girlfriend he was on his way to meet you on the night he was killed?'

'Huh! So, you found out about that. You're good, Emma.'

'Answer the question.'

'Yes, Emma, I know about that allegation. It's a load of horse manure. When Sarah-Jane Keegan – that's the girl's name – regained consciousness, she said Johnny was on his way to the Burlington Hotel to collect a bribe in order to drop his court action against Todd Wilson. He told her I was the go-between. Well, as it happens, I was in the company of the Chief Superintendent at a function in the Mansion House on the night in question. I had no contact with Johnny Griffin in regard to a meeting, good, bad or indifferent. But from what this unfortunate girl says, it seems Johnny actually believed he had spoken to me over the phone; he really thought he was going to meet me.'

'I think I know who fooled him,' Emma said. 'I think it was the same person who pretended to be you when he called to Angela Devine's house.'

'You mean Fergus Massey?'

'Yes.'

'But why? Why would Massey go to such trouble? I mean, what purpose could it serve?'

'I think Fergus Massey and Maeve Wilson might be working together to destroy Todd Wilson. I don't have all the answers yet but I can guess at some of them. I think Massey resents the fact that Todd Wilson – the person he helped climb the ladder of success – has dropped him from all his business enterprises.'

Connolly nodded, considered her assessment, and raised a questioning eyebrow. 'H'm, that would piss Massey off right enough but . . . well, it comes nowhere near explaining the murders. OK. He might want revenge; he might even want to frame Todd Wilson for murder but why would he pick on Ethel Cassidy? What did she ever do to him?'

'I think it has something to do with the death of his wife. Marina Cassidy told me about the fight Ethel and Massey's wife had on Ireland's Eye. What if Massey blamed Ethel for his wife's accident?'

'If that were the case,' Connolly said thoughtfully, 'wouldn't he also blame Maeve Wilson? She was there as well.'

'Like I said, I don't have all the answers but I think I can guess at why Matt Dempsey and Johnny Griffin met their deaths.'

'Right, I'm listening.'

'Matt Dempsey, unwittingly, smuggled drugs to this country. His contract at the time was to drive for SUCCOUR. Massey was the one to hire the truck in the first place. What better cover for smuggling drugs than a Third World aid truck. It was only when Dempsey had the misfortune to be involved in an accident and have his haul of cannabis exposed that his life became endangered. Massey, incensed at losing a huge pay out – quarter of a million I'm told – lost his cool, took his frustration out on the driver, had him killed. He knew that if questions were ever asked about the haulage company concerned, it would be shown that Todd Wilson owned the holding operation that controlled the truck business.'

'That's quite a dollop of conjecture to swallow in one dose; but let's assume, for the sake of argument, that I buy that, tell me why did he have Johnny Griffin killed?'

'On that I'm not so sure, but I have a few theories.'

'Shall I tell you what I think,' Connolly said, not wanting to be left behind in the guessing game. 'Let's just suppose for the moment that we go along with your theory that Massey is behind everything that's going down. Suppose Massey heard that Johnny Griffin was putting it about that Todd Wilson had homosexual tendencies. And suppose Massey decided to use the rumours to embarrass Wilson. He could have backed Griffin's highly publicised action.'

'Yes,' Emma conceded, 'it's possible . . . but, if that were the case, why would Massey go and kill him?'

'Because Griffin was stupid. Let's suppose he got a tidy sum of money from Massey and then, seeing how easy it had been, got greedy, looked for more, threatened Massey – blackmailed him in effect. Massey wouldn't like that. Solution: get rid of Griffin, remove the problem. And, by the same token, point the finger of suspicion in Wilson's direction.'

'It could have happened like that,' Emma said. 'So, where does that leave Todd Wilson? Are you going to let him go?'

'Dammit, I don't know, Emma. He'll probably sue me for wrongful arrest. But I'm not letting him go just yet. I'm hoping my friends in the Navan shop manage to crack the two suspects they're holding . . . the two fellows that ran Vinny off the road. We know they're the same guys who abducted Matt Dempsey from his mews. The registration number on the four-wheel drive that you saw at the derelict house in Leixlip was the same. If we can get them to talk, tie them in with Todd Wilson, it would explain why you were pushed down an escalator, why your car was run off the road. You see, Emma, Todd Wilson has a motive for wanting to keep you quiet: you've been making life difficult for him, exposing his dubious business practices in your articles. That's why I'd like to get confirmation from the guys in the Navan nick that Wilson is pulling their strings. In the meantime, I'm going to contact Maeve Wilson and Fergus Massey, ask them a few questions – take it from there.'

'Yeah,' Emma said, 'I think that would be a very good idea.'

A rare smile creased Connolly's face. 'Just tell me one thing, Emma, will you? Did you really, I mean really, think I could possibly have had anything to do with the killings?'

Emma returned his smile. 'No, no, of course not, not for a single moment,' she answered, allowing the lie to trip off the tongue with poetic intonation.

Maeve Wilson instructed her secretary to inform Detective-Inspector Connolly that she was not in today. She did not want to take the detective's call, not yet, not until she was sure what course of action to take. She had come into her office extra early this morning to sort out her thoughts on what she ought to do about her husband's continuing incarceration. She had spent the previous night tossing and turning, thinking about her present predicament but mostly thinking about her disastrous marriage to Todd Wilson. Twenty years of hell, that's what it amounted to. Only one good thing to come out of it: Jamie. And Jamie was dead. Todd had not been a good husband, she had not been a good wife, together they had not been good parents. The boy had suffered as a consequence.

But whatever about Todd's faults, unforgivable and all as they were, she knew he was not a murderer. It took little effort to convince herself that she owed him nothing but her conscience refused to let matters lie there. That same conscience, something that had never bothered her too much in the past, now told her to go public in her defence of him. Weighing up the options on how best to go about this line of action bothered her.

She had expected Fergus Massey to sleep with her the previous night but without explanation he had failed to show. This bothered her. He always found solutions to her problems. It didn't mean she had to take his advice. She often ignored it but it was good to have a sounding board. Her attempts to make contact with him had not been successful but she hoped he would pick up one of the several messages she had left on his mobile answering service.

In his absence, she decided on a course of action. She picked up her phone and asked her secretary to get Emma Boylan at the *Post* for her. While waiting for the call to come through, Maeve thought about the day she had spoken to Emma in the Shelbourne Hotel. She had liked her and felt she was someone she could trust. The same day Fergus Massey had lambasted the journalist for her investigative pieces on Todd. Most media people would have done a dance there and then on the spot and written a stinker of an article the following day. Emma Boylan had shown that she was bigger than that. She had retained her objectivity. That was why she would talk to her now, give her an exclusive interview, attempt to set the record straight in regard to her husband.

Maeve was still thinking about what she would say to the journalist when her secretary reported back that Ms Boylan was not available at the moment. 'Do you want me to leave a message?' the secretary asked.

'Yes, just let her know that I called. Try her again in fifteen minutes.'

Taking her leave of Connolly, Emma headed back to her office. She was still ten minutes away from the *Post* building when a message came through on her mobile phone. Receptionist, Moira, who worked in the newspaper's front office, informed her that Maeve Wilson had rung in twice in the last half-hour wanting to speak with her. Emma felt a surge of excitement. 'Maeve Wilson asked for me personally, mentioned me by name, is that right?'

'Yes and no.' the receptionist replied. 'It wasn't Maeve Wilson herself on the phone; but it was her secretary and, yes, it was you she wanted to talk to. I can give you her number if you want to contact her on your mobile.'

'No, don't bother. I'll drive to her office straight away. I want to talk to her face to face. I have a feeling this could be very important.' Emma hit the 'end' button on the mobile and headed in the direction of the SUCCOUR headquarters.

Maeve had never seen Fergus Massey look like this in her life. Never. The man was a mess. His clothes were rumpled, his shirt open at the neck, and his hair, something he normally took such care with, was all over the place.

'What on earth has happened to you, Fergus?' she asked. 'You look like you've been out selling the Big Issue.'

'Yes, Maeve, I know. I look and feel, godawful, which is why I want you to come with me and get the hell out of here. I've so much to tell you. I've been up all night . . . didn't get to go home, to wash, shave or eat.'

'But . . . but, what were you doing, Fergus? What could possibly have got you into the state you're in?'

'I've been sorting this whole thing out – all this bother with Todd. It's been going round and round in my head, driving me mad. I just had to get to the bottom of it. Last night I put the whole thing together. Todd never did any of the things they're accusing him of; he couldn't have.'

'Well, I know that; Jesus, we both know that. As a matter of fact I've just put a call through to Emma

Boylan to give her my side of the story – let the media know that Todd is not the monster they're making him out to be.'

'You rang Emma Boylan?'

'Yes I'm expecting to hear from her any minute.'

'That's not such a good idea, Maeve. I need to talk to you first. I want to fill you in on what I've discovered. I can give you chapter and verse on who's behind this plot to destroy Todd.'

'Well then, I'll let you talk to Emma as well.'

'No, there're some very delicate matters I need to discuss with you first, sensitive issues concerning the missing £85,000 and our truck – the one found carrying drugs.'

'OK. Talk to me.'

'Yes, I will but not here. We need to get away for a few hours – away from the media, disappear from circulation. I need time to fill in the picture for you . . . hear what you think. What we don't need are inter-ruptions.'

'So, what are you suggesting?'

'Come with me to my boat. I think best when I'm on the water . . . no distractions. Out to sea, with no one to bother us, we can sort this out. But you've got to come with me now, straight away, no time to lose.'

'Jesus, Fergus, you're frightening me . . . but OK, fine, if this'll help sort out the mess with Todd, I'll go along with you.'

'It will, I promise . . . now come on, we must hurry.'

'What about Emma Boylan?'

'Let her wait. When you hear what I have to tell you . . . then you'll really have something worthwhile to give her.'

Fifteen minutes after getting the message about Maeve Wilson's telephone call, Emma was in Marino Crescent, attempting to find a parking space behind the SUCCOUR building. On the point of giving up, she saw Maeve Wilson being driven out of the car park by Fergus Massey. 'Damn, damn, damn,' she shouted, pounding her fist on the steering wheel to emphasise each word. 'Shit, piss, scutter, fuck, I've missed her,' she told herself, watching the dark green Lexus move into the main stream of traffic. It took Emma all of two seconds to decide what she would do. She did not intend to miss an opportunity like this. In a manoeuvre that would have done Michael Schumacher proud, and her engine no good at all, she reversed her Volvo, smoking her rear tyres in the action, before shooting forward on to the busy traffic lanes.

The green Lexus was a long way ahead of her but she could still catch the odd fleeting glimpse. *Oh, please, don't let me lose them.* Hoping no speed traps were in operation, Emma drove like one possessed, trying desperately to get closer to her quarry. Horns blared, fists waved and a chorus of expletives from other road users did nothing to impede her progress. Driving along Fairview, she saw Massey jump lanes and take a left on to the Howth Road. She did likewise. Could they be going to Wilson's house, she wondered, finding it easier now to keep them in sight but staying far enough behind not to be spotted.

Through Killester, past Raheny, Emma followed as closely as she dared until they joined the Dublin Road going towards Sutton. Emma had driven this very route some days earlier when she visited Mrs Devine. Could it be, she asked herself, that Maeve Wilson and Fergus Massey were about to call to see Angela?

But the green Lexus sped past the exit into Glencarraig, where Angela lived, continuing on its way without interruption to the Hill of Howth. Emma's biggest surprise came when she saw them ignore the turn off that led to Wilson's house. *Where the hell are they going?* She tailed them all the way to Howth's West Pier where she watched them park in front of Wright's fish merchants shop. They remained in the car for two minutes before getting out. Together, they walked quickly along the pier to where boats of all shapes and sizes were tied up.

Emma parked nearby, letting neither Massey nor Maeve Wilson out of her sight for a minute, careful at the same time not to let them see her. She remained in her car and watched as Massey made his way down the steps of the pier wall, and stepped on to a pleasure boat. There was something different about him. He no longer moved with the athletic grace she remembered and his clothes looked as though he had slept in them. Even his face, so devilishly handsome, looked somehow out of sorts.

Maeve Wilson remained at the top of the steps and

appeared to be remonstrating with Massey. Emma quickly lowered her driver's window in the hope of catching what was being said but immediately realised the futility of her action. Every manner of noise imaginable contrived to blot out their conversation. Gulls screamed overhead, fishing boats putt-putt-putted in the choppy waters, a JCB pulverised a footpath beside her, and delivery trucks serviced Wright's shop.

But whatever about not hearing what Maeve and Massey were saying to each other, Emma could tell by their hands, head and arm gesticulations that something wasn't right. Maeve did eventually descend the steps and accept a helping hand from Massey to bring her onboard. Almost instantly, the boat, with Massey hunched over the wheel in the cockpit and Maeve sitting behind him, sprang to life and pulled away from the peer. Emma watched as the bow of the boat lifted and slapped against the water, sending a V-shaped wake throbbing to each side. It was obvious to Emma that the boat was heading for the nearby Ireland's Eye.

One thing was certain, she couldn't follow them across the water in her Volvo but she stubbornly refused to give up. Using her mobile phone she dialled Connolly's number. 'You're in luck,' a voice told her. 'Detective-Inspector Connolly was just about to leave the building. Hold on a second and I'll put him on to you.' Emma waited impatiently, watching Massey's boat as it neared Ireland's Eye, until Connolly's familiar sound assailed her ear.

'What's up?' he asked straight away.

Emma gave him a quick résumé of what she had witnessed before asking what action she should take.

'Stay where you are, Emma. I'll be with you in half an hour. Say midday. I'll need to organise a speedboat to get us across. Oh, Emma, here's something you'll be interested in: I've been told that the guys who ran Vinny off the road have decided to talk. They've admitted that Massey is their paymaster. I'll tell you more when I get there.'

Emma closed the line on her mobile and looked out to Ireland's Eye. Bright sun beat down on the small island, its reflection on the water's surface dazzling in its intensity, making it difficult for Emma to see exactly where Massey's boat had gone. Glad to get out of the car, she walked along the pier wall to where Massey's boat had been berthed. There wasn't a lot she could do until Connolly arrived. She found an old abandoned, up-turned rowboat on the pier, sat on its hull, filled her lungs with fresh sea-scented air and looked impatiently at her watch. The waiting was unbearable even though all indications suggested that the day would be the hottest so far this summer.

40

What little faculty remained active in Maeve Wilson's brain tried desperately to figure out whether she was alive or dead. She certainly felt dead. Her body, if it was still attached to her brain, had no physical feelings but if she were dead, really dead, how could she still have the ability to think? Part of her intellect must still be functioning. All had been dark . . . dark as death, but a sensation of sorts now made itself felt . . . pain, yes, she felt pain, a foggy far-away sort of throbbing pain, hovering above her, trying to prod her into wakefulness.

Wait a minute! She could hear a voice. That had to mean she was alive, didn't it? Someone was talking to her. But the pain, the pain had become more manifest, more focused. Her head ached. Her memory, along with her senses was taking hold. Alive. She was definitely alive – but in pain.

Other sounds? Water? Yes, she recognised the sound of swirling water echoing all around her. A man's voice, distorted, distant, disembodied but becoming clearer. Now, single words penetrated her consciousness. She recognised the speaker. It was Fergus Massey. He sounded disjointed, otherworldly. She couldn't see him because her eyes remained shut. With this realisation, she tried to open them. A blinding light hurt her eyes as soon as they blinked open. A bright, sun-filled sky hung above her, framed by a rock face funnel. Now, she remembered. Yes, she remembered what had happened to her. She tried to scream but only a hoarse sound came from her throat.

Fergus was talking to her but she wasn't listening. She needed to reconstruct the events that had led to her present predicament. Back in the caves she had been forced to look into a pool of water, to confront the dead face staring back at her. She had recognised Marina Cassidy's dead eyes and screamed. In that awful terrifying moment she realised she was at the mercy of a madman. It was then that the back of her head exploded in a cosmic flash. Blackness rushed in, a blackness that had lasted until now.

With this newborn consciousness came a slow dawning reality. Her body, she realised, could not move; it lay fixed in a horizontal position, her legs and arms immobile. Massey continued to talk, his words mere abstract sounds to her as she struggled to change position. Her wrists and ankles, she discovered, were secured by ropes. The surface beneath her was hard rock. Now, with a sickening flash of total under-standing, she knew exactly where she was and what had happened.

'Are you listening to me?' Massey asked, his words now getting through to her.

'What? What?' was all she managed to say.

'So good to hear those dulcet tones again,' Massey said casually, as though he were enjoying an after-dinner conversation. 'Tell me, Maeve, how does it feel to be the one stranded on the Body Rock? A reversal of fortunes, wouldn't you say? I waited for this moment . . . Christ, how I've lived for this day.'

'What . . . what are you talking about?' Maeve asked weakly.

'Why, Maeve darling, I'm talking about the day you all left me on the Body Rock to drown, of course. Remember? All of you, Todd, Ethel, Marina and you. You were the worst of them . . . but all of you knew I couldn't swim. I kept shouting, telling you I couldn't swim but you still left me there on the rock, the tide coming in fast. Already over the top of the rock – up to my shins. I screamed and screamed . . . begged and beseeched you not to leave me . . . begged for my life, watching the waves splashing up to my knees, listening to your laughter fade in the distance as you sailed away in Todd's boat.'

Maeve needed a few seconds to recall the incident Massey was describing. It had happened such a long time ago, an episode she had, until now, put from her mind. Todd, she remembered, had decided to play a joke on his friend Fergus at a time when neither man had yet married. On the day in question they had gone to Ireland's Eye for a picnic and a booze-up. Todd, who lived within sight of the island and knew everything there was to know about the place, inveigled them to visit the Long Hole. Tanked up on alcohol, they allowed Todd take them in his father's boat into the mouth of the Long Hole, to what he called the shrine of the Body

Rock. He encouraged them to enter the hidden caves behind the rock and told a creepy story about a murder that had once occurred there. Having drunk their fill, Todd decided to play a practical joke on Fergus. Fortified on cider, vodka and beer, she had, along with Ethel and Marina, helped Todd in his laddish prank. Between them they managed to strand Fergus on the Body Rock, then desert him. It had been a joke but the joke had almost cost Massey his life.

The last chime of the midday Angelus bell sounded as Connolly brought his Toyota Corolla to a stop beside Emma. Seeing Todd Wilson get out from the passengers side brought a gasp of undisguised dismay from Emma. Connolly, noting her concern was quick to explain. 'I've brought Mr Wilson along with me because he knows every inch of the island. He thinks he knows exactly where Massey has taken his wife.'

Wilson held out his hand in welcome to Emma. 'Good to see you again, Ms Boylan,' he said, shaking her hand firmly. 'We seem to have a habit of meeting under unusual, if not dramatic, circumstances.'

'Oh, yeah,' Emma said, remembering the episode with the hanging mannequin. 'Let's hope what's happening today turns out to be another false alarm.' As they spoke, a high-powered motor boat pulled into the space where Emma had seen Massey leave half an hour earlier. 'That's our boat,' Connolly announced, waving to an athletic middle-aged man onboard. 'This is Sergeant David Langan; he's a friend of mine and he's kindly offered to help us. Come on quickly; let's get on board. The quicker we get over to Ireland's Eye, the sooner we'll find out what the hell is going on.

The first in a series of gentle waves lapped Maeve's body, salty spray penetrating her mouth, nose and eyes. Terror like nothing she had experienced before took hold of her. 'Get me off this rock,' she yelled. 'You've made your point Fergus. OK? What we did was wrong – stupid, infantile. It should never have happened and I'm sorry; I'm really sorry.' Her last two words were lost as another wave washed over her face.

Massey looked on, half seeing what was happening to her, half lost in his own delirium of thought. 'I died that day, Maeve. Did you know that?' he continued. 'Yes, I died that day several times over. With each wave that crashed over me, each wave that threatened to knock my legs from under me. The water reached my waist before my legs finally gave way, swept me into the wash, buried me in the incoming tide, unable to breathe, lost . . . dead.'

'No, you didn't drown,' Maeve shouted, water now splashing about her face with alarming regularity. 'We came back for you, dammit; we came back. Todd dragged you to the rocks. I gave you the kiss of life. I saved your life for Christ's sake. Come on Fergus, quickly. Untie me . . . get me the hell out of here. I'll drown soon if you don't do something. You hear me, for God's sake, Fergus. Fergus!'

But Massey appeared not to hear her. He seemed

lost in his own recollections, spilling out bitterness like some overflowing cesspool. 'After I died . . . and returned, I fought the sea . . . my enemy, the sea . . . took my life away. I learned to swim, took up water sports, discovered boats. I took on the sea and beat it. You hear me; I beat the sea. But then I discovered I had gone to war with the wrong enemy. The sea didn't want to kill me. Too late, I realised that. Todd killed me. Ethel killed me. Marina killed me and you, you most of all, killed me. You represent the real enemy; you were the enemy all the time – a crafty, insidious enemy. It's taken me years to plan a counterattack and now, by God I will have my day in the sunshine. All I want, all I ever wanted was justice . . . justice . . . justice.'

Todd Wilson gripped the boat's handrail as if his life depended on it. His face had taken on a sickly pallor as the vessel, its throttle fully open, cut through the swell, dipping and rising as it slammed into the crashing waves with a vengeance. Emma winced as the bouncing craft played havoc with her ribs. Wind whipped into her face; spray spat up from the bow and soaked her. Gulls soared above the foamy wake, their raucous screams barely audible above the roar of the boat's inboard engine.

Halfway between the mainland and the island, the sole occupant of a small rowboat, tossed about in the power craft's wake, shook his fist at them in angry protest. Sergeant Langan, shouted an apology to the irate sailor, his words lost in the din, but he kept the throttle fully open.

Nearing the island, Todd nudged Langan's arm and pointed in the direction he wanted him to head for. Much to Emma's relief, the boat slowed down, tracing a course parallel to the island's coastline until Todd indicated a cleft in a rocky headland. With the engine's volume down to normal levels it was now possible to hear each other talk. 'If my guess is right,' Todd shouted, 'this is where Fergus Massey will have taken Maeve. It's called the Long Hole. It's become something of an obsession with him over the years.'

'Are you sure there's room to bring the boat in there?' Sergeant Langan asked. 'It looks a bit on the narrow side to me.'

'There's room enough,' Todd replied, 'but you must be careful. Just cut the engine and we'll paddle in on the rising tide.'

Emma, fearful of the jagged rocks on either side of them, breathed a sigh of relief when she saw a boat ahead of her. 'He's here,' she shouted, 'that's his boat; Massey and Maeve are here.'

They could see the smaller boat in an open space encircled by a towering rock face. Langan berthed beside the smaller craft and helped his passengers scramble on to the rocks. Todd, experiencing some difficulty manoeuvring his bulk on to the wet rocks, was first to see Maeve. He screamed. 'Look, she's tied to the Body Rock, the water is washing over her.'

Connolly removed his shoes and dived into the water. Emma followed suit. Both swam the few yards to the barely visible submerged rock. Maeve, they could see, was still alive. She stretched her head upwards, struggling to breathe, trying to keep her nose and mouth above the incoming swell.

'Hold on,' Connolly shouted to Maeve, trying to secure a foothold on the rock. 'We're going to get you out of here.'

Emma made it to the rock seconds later and began immediately to untie the ropes securing Maeve's legs. She and Connolly worked vigorously at untying the knots, conscious all the time of the rising water. The frantic exercise seemed to be taking forever but in reality they had her free in a matter of seconds. Spitting out water, trying to gulp down air, Maeve allowed them to bring her to the border of rocks where Todd and the sergeant waited anxiously. After a bout of retching, Maeve began to understand she was among friends. Her voice, little more than a croak, attempted to string words together, her eyes all the time fixed on her husband. 'Todd, oh, Christ Todd, I was so scared. Fergus tried to drown me. He's killed Marina Cassidy already. She's in the caves – dead. He's gone mad . . . wants to kill us because . . . because . . . She couldn't say any more, her body shaking uncontrollably.

Connolly, dripping wet from his immersion, looked around the Long Hole. 'Where's Massey?' he asked, 'I don't see him anywhere.'

Todd Wilson, who had been holding his wife's hand, stood up and looked around the enclosed space. 'He's at the back, in the caves. We're going to have to go in and get him out.' As Todd pointed to the area where the caves entrance lay hidden, Fergus Massey appeared, as if by magic, on the very spot.

'Ahoy there, Todd,' he hollered, 'making a habit of rescuing drowning people from the Body Rock, I see. Pity you weren't here last night when Marina went the way of the fish.'

'Bloody Hell, Fergus, what's got into you! You gone completely off your rocker or what? Come on, tell me for Christ's sake: what do you think you're doing?'

'Trying to get even, Todd, just trying to get even.'

'Get even? Get even for what, Fergus? What did we ever do that would warrant all this?'

Massey began moving, foothold by foothold, up a steep incline as he shouted back to Wilson. 'You should ask Maeve, your slut of a wife, what you did . . . what she did . . . what Ethel and her whore sister did.'

'No, Fergus, you tell me. Come on, tell me what the hell you're ranting on about?'

By now Massey had climbed some way up the ledge on the vertical rock face, steadily edging his way towards the rim of the hole some twenty feet above. 'You want to know? Huh? Right then, I'll tell you. Ethel Cassidy killed my child, along with her whore sister, Marina. That's right . . . they had the child aborted in Liverpool.'

Todd had by now begun to climb his own route up the steep wall. 'You're not making sense, Fergus,' Todd roared, 'Ethel wasn't pregnant by you . . . '

Fergus threw back his head in mirthless laughter.

'Huh! You thought it was yours, Todd. You thought you were the father? Well let me tell you something: you weren't. I let you think you were the father. Ethel, dumb woman, believed you were the father too. If you recall, we were both screwing her on a regular basis at the time. Only difference was: it couldn't have been you that made her pregnant. You couldn't father anything because your spunk wasn't worth a fuck. You're sterile.'

'You're a goddamned liar,' Todd roared, hauling his bulky frame higher up the rocky incline. 'That's not true and we both know it.'

'Oh yeah?' Fergus replied through another maniacal burst of laughter. 'You had yourself tested by my good friend, the gynaecologist, Dr Pinkerton. Right? He told you a cock-and-bull story about you having a low sperm count. A load of bollix, my friend, you were firing blanks – sterile as a cut cat.'

Todd reacted with fury. 'No, Fergus,' he screamed, 'you're talking through your arse. How do you suppose Jamie came into the world?'

'Jesus, Todd, even you should be able to figure that one out. I helped bring him into the world. Pinkerton used my sperm in his experiments on Maeve. Jamie was the result . . . he is . . . was my son.'

Down on the base rocks, Maeve who, along with Emma and the others, watched the two climbers approach each other from different directions, shook her head in disgust. 'It's not true,' she shouted out, loud enough for Massey to hear. 'You're a liar, Fergus Massey. You were the sterile one . . . you told me so yourself. That's why Jillian never became pregnant.'

Massey, who seemed to have temporarily forgotten about the people below him, stopped moving and looked down at them. His face had distorted into a cruel twisted mask, his eyes blazing like angry coal in a furnace. 'Yes, Maeve, I did lie about that. But the truth is: Jillian was the one with a problem. She was barren – but I was firing live rounds.'

'I don't believe you,' Maeve yelled back up at him.

Massey continued to look down at her, unaware that Todd was moving ever closer to him. 'I visited Jamie a week before his eighteenth birthday,' he shouted down. 'Told him I was his real father, gave him a signed certificate to that effect.'

Todd, now on a level with Massey, reached out to grab him. 'You bastard,' he barked, attempting to pull Massey towards him. Massey, shocked to discover Todd's close proximity, recovered quickly and let fly with a right fist. Todd, anticipating this response, blocked the blow but lost his footing in the exertion. Panic-stricken, he grabbed Massey's hand to steady his balance. But the momentum of the action was unstoppable. Todd, hanging on to Massey, fell from the ledge. The two men cartwheeled through the air as they plummeted to the water below. Todd, by far the heavier, seemed to swing Massey in an arc above him on the way down. With a huge splash, Todd plunged into the water while Massey, caught in the loop of the arc, landed on the shallow water covering the Body Rock. The onlookers screamed in horror as they witnessed

Massey's body smash on to the block of granite. His head, catching the edge of the rock, crumpled and shattered like a cracked eggshell.

As Todd emerged groggily from his ducking, he looked to where Massey's broken body lay. White foam had turned pink as the dead man's blood seeped into the wash. Connolly dived back into the water and swam out to help Todd drag Massey to the rocks by the edge of the hole. Emma stayed with Maeve and watched the two men struggle with the dead body.

A moment earlier, as Emma watched Massey connect with the rock and heard the snap of breaking bones, time itself seemed to warp and stretch out of kilter for her. It was as though the action had altered to slow motion. She saw Massey's face go through a series of expressions, all of them triumphant, and would remember his smiling eyes and gleaming teeth in that split second before his skull hit the water and fragmented on the sharp edge of rock. Seeing blood pour from his crushed body appeared to colour her world red. In a subliminal flash, she saw her baby being taken from her, saw the blood on her legs, saw her baby look at her with accusatorial eyes. The vision in red evaporated. Back in real time, she saw Todd and Connolly haul Massey's corpse on to the rocks. She wondered about the expressions on Massey's face in those milliseconds before death. Would he have realised he was about to meet his maker? Was he thinking about Jillian and how she had met her own death in not too dissimilar circumstances, on the same island? Perhaps he had wanted it to end like it did? The truth, she accepted, would never be known. Her thoughts returned to Maeve Wilson. The woman was in a state of abject shock and in need of immediate medical attention.

Emma continued to comfort her as Sergeant Langan talked into his mobile, giving details about what had happened, requesting emergency back-up from the air-ambulance service and asking that the state pathologist be informed. In the midst of all this activity, Maeve shook free of her stupor and squeezed Emma's hand. 'Emma,' she said, her voice hoarse, 'Marina Cassidy is back in the caves. She's dead. He drowned her on the Body Rock – as he tried to do to me. Thanks for showing up when you did.'

'It was your telephone call to me that did it,' Emma said. 'Most important call you ever made in your life. It just saved your life.'

Maeve nodded her agreement and began to sob.

Emma could not hold back her own tears. But her crying was for an altogether different reason.

41

In the week that followed the tragic events on Ireland's Eye, Emma saw little of Vinny or their apartment for that matter. Bob Crosby, on the other hand, was spending every waking hour by her side. She could not remember a time when he had been so excited. Circulation figures, according to him, had leaped into a new stratosphere. 'Well done, Emma! This is your best work ever,' he said with enthusiasm. 'I just hope you don't get any fancy notions about leaving us. The other papers will be sniffing around you like dogs in heat, trying to woo you after this.'

'Well, Bob,' Emma said, half joking, half in earnest, 'if the *Post* were to give me an appropriate salary hike, I'll be glad to stay on as your slave for another while.'

Emma was well aware that her reporting of the deaths of Fergus Massey and Marina Cassidy had succeeded in gripping the country's imagination. Following so closely on the heels of the earlier connected deaths, readers from all walks of life had become engrossed in the dramatic revelations. Because of her very personal involvement with all aspects of the story, the pieces she penned for the *Post* made compelling reading. The term – on the spot reporting – had never taken on a more literal meaning.

It had been a week like no other week.

Sensational revelation had been overtaken by other, even more, sensational revelations. Emma had become, much to her amazement and delight, the darling of the media. She was, Vinny warned her, in danger of becoming overexposed. It was difficult to pick up a newspaper, turn on a radio or watch a television programme without being aware of her role in the unfolding drama. Bob Crosby, did not subscribe to the 'overexposed' theory, especially when it came to his beloved newspaper. Lest even the slightest opportunity of gaining advantage over his rivals be lost, he had arranged for the *Post* to open a web site dealing exclusively with Emma's involvement in the whole affair.

But Emma's elevation to this heightened prominence represented small fry when compared to the saturation coverage afforded to Todd and Maeve Wilson. True, the Wilsons had always been newsworthy but this media feeding frenzy was an altogether new phenomenon even for them. Like specimens under a microscope, minute details of their everyday existence were probed, dissected, digested – and spat out again. Their lives were held up to scrutiny like nothing they had ever experienced before. Facts, fiction, half-truths and downright lies all got thrown into the mix, ingredients guaranteed to create overblown and distorted impressions.

In an effort to counter the outpouring of mis-information and regain the initiative, the Wilsons held separate press conferences. Even though Maeve disavowed all knowledge of Massey's wrongdoings, she still felt honour bound to resign from SUCCOUR. Emma, who attended the media briefing, could see that Maeve remained visibly shaken by what had happened. She had shed the aura of self-confidence that had, for so long, been her hallmark. When asked by Emma about the future of her Third World aid agency, she could not say whether the organisation would remain in existence or not. Emma's own feelings suggested that without Maeve at the helm, the agency would lose its energy and direction, and eventually flounder.

Todd Wilson, in contrast to his wife, lost none of his old bravado. At a well-attended press conference, he stoutly defended his reputation. He answered questions from the floor with a sureness of style that belied the stress and difficulties he had so recently experienced. He refused to contemplate resigning his seat in any of his companies. 'To do so,' he informed the gathered media, 'would imply that I had done something wrong. I want to assure you that nothing could be further from the truth.'

Emma remained quiet while a journalist from a rival paper suggested to Wilson that all his business dealings might not be strictly legitimate.

'Rubbish and rot,' he bellowed, 'malicious lies and gossip put about by my competitors and picked up by inept journalists too lazy to search for the truth.' Ignoring the journalist who had posed the question, Wilson singled out Emma from among the assembled reporters while delivering this rebuke. It didn't bother Emma. She knew he was bluffing. She knew that some of his past business deals were less than legitimate but she decided not to pursue that topic on this occasion. There would be another day for that.

Emma had only one real regret about her written account: the absence of Fergus Massey. Not having him to face the media was a bit like Hamlet without the Prince. Her readers, she knew, were genuinely intrigued by the dubious role Massey played as 'friend' to both Wilsons. As details became clearer, the full extent of his duplicity unfolded. His involvement in illegal activities began to take on awesome proportions. Emma's trawl through his business records showed that his entrepreneurial ventures in recent years had been neither prudent nor profitable. Maintaining a lifestyle of excess on an ever-dwindling income had, it appeared, become impossible for him to sustain.

He had stolen £85,000 from his own organisation, SUCCOUR and, then, sought to lay the blame elsewhere. But this sum of money represented a one-off injection to his finances, nothing like enough to provide the sort of on-going income required to sustain his palatial home, his boats, his plane, his wardrobe and his patronage of fine restaurants. Massey was not the kind of individual to contemplate any diminution to his elevated position in society.

He saw drug trafficking as an easy option to generate revenue. Using Third World misery as a front, he had come up with a way to move consignments of cocaine, ecstasy and heroin across frontiers and borders. Taking advantage of Maeve Wilson's high profile as a bona-fide aid-worker, he shamelessly exploited SUCCOUR for his own purposes. Likewise, he used Todd Wilson as a cover for the movement of paintings, paintings that had been found to contain half a kilo of heroin, with a street value in excess of £120,000.

Emma's compilation of evidence against Massey mounted steadily. Connolly, at his most cooperative, up-dated her hourly. According to him, Massey's front man in Midland Antiques, Paul Newman, was busy spilling his guts to him, providing evidence that focused all blame on his dead paymaster. The two men who had kidnapped Matt Dempsey – the same two who had run her car off the road – were doing likewise, more than willing to lay the blame for their actions at Massey's door.

Angela Devine had contacted Emma as soon as she heard the news about Massey's death. Showing none of the reticence she displayed on the night Emma met her in the airport, the teenager now freely admitted that it had been Fergus Massey who visited Jamie a few days before his eighteenth birthday. She told Emma about the photocopy enclosed in Jamie's letter to her. Delivered on the day after the suicide, the letter claimed Todd Wilson was infertile and that Fergus Massey, through in vitro fertilisation, was Jamie's biological father.

'Had Jamie any doubts about what he was hearing?'

'No, none whatsoever; he totally believed everything Massey told him. You see, even before Massey talked to him, Jamie had been going through a particularly rough patch. Ethel Cassidy, the one person he revered had been sacked. His parents were at loggerheads and spent little or no time with him. Being told that Ethel once had an abortion really upset him . . . and then, hearing all that stuff about his true parentage . . . it was more than he could take.'

Thinking back to a conversation she had had with Marina in Liverpool, Emma remembered being told about a phone call Ethel had made only days before Jamie's suicide. Ethel had told Marina that Jamie's father had gone and told the boy the truth – destroyed everything. At the time Marina had understood her twin to be referring to Todd Wilson when she used the word father but it was obvious now that Ethel had meant Massey.

Emma thought it possible that Jamie had pasted a copy of Massey's paternity affirmation on his wall collage along with the clipping about Jillian Massey's accident on Ireland's Eye. It would help to explain why Ethel Cassidy who, not wanting the world to know the ugly truth, would have removed the two pieces. Emma considered another possibility: what if Ethel did not accept what was contained on the certificate? Would it have made any difference? She knew that anyone reading the page, signed by Dr Pinkerton, would believe that Todd was sterile; they would also conclude that he could not be the father of the baby she had aborted in Liverpool. Reading the clipping about Jillian Massey's accident on Ireland's Eye, the distraught woman would have linked the two items, and realised that Massey could pose a threat to her. That might explain her words at Jamie's funeral – at least you buried Jamie under the ground. It seemed obvious to Emma now that Ethel had not been speaking exclusively to Todd and Maeve at the time; her comments were more likely directed at Fergus Massey.

It was only after Connolly had got his people to check into the affairs of Dr A. J. Pinkerton that serious doubts about Massey's paternity claims became evident. Connolly had unearthed information that showed Pinkerton's clinic in Ailesbury Road no longer existed. On top of that, Emma had discovered further facts on the doctor. Three years earlier the medical authorities had summoned the consultant obstetrician and gynaecologist to an investigative hearing. Allegations of malpractice had been brought against Pinkerton but the doctor fled the country before the enquiry could sit. Without Pinkerton, it would be impossible to discover if Massey's semen had been used in treating Maeve Wilson or whether a certificate had ever been issued to that effect. Although the original certificate was missing, presumed burned in the fire that had claimed Ethel Cassidy's life, Emma went to the one person who had a copy of the document.

Angela Devine allowed Emma and Connolly to take away the duplicate certificate Jamie had sent her. On examination, Connolly concluded that the authenticity of the document was very doubtful. It was unlikely that a gynaecologist – even one with a questionable record like Pinkerton – would ever have issued such a certificate. It was more likely, he decided, that Massey had concocted the whole thing himself. And if that were the case, it raised the question: was Massey really Jamie's father? Was it Massey's child that Ethel had aborted in Liverpool?

Emma agreed with Connolly when he maintained that Massey's document, the one pasted on Jamie's wall, had the effect of pushing the boy to his suicide and had been responsible for bringing about Ethel Cassidy's death. She did not believe that Massey was Jamie's father or that he was the father of Ethel's aborted baby. It seemed more likely to her that Massey, not Todd, was the one who really was sterile. But unwilling to accept this fact, Massey had invented a make-believe story rather than accept the truth. In the end, his delusions had for him become reality. He manufactured evidence to affirm his flawless manhood and then totally accepted it as the truth.

The more Emma discovered, the better she began to understand the psychosis that drove Fergus Massey to do what he did.

Connolly's people in the fraud squad division had discovered, after a long and torturous paper trail that led to a an off-shore account in Cayman Islands, that the bail money paid to release Matt Dempsey had originated from an account controlled by Massey.

Discussing this revelation with Emma, the detective speculated as to why Massey would have wanted Dempsey released. 'I believed Massey was afraid of the information that would be revealed when Dempsey appeared on the witness stand.'

'And disposing of him presented the best option?' Emma asked, scepticism evident in her voice

'Yes, Emma, it's a bit drastic, I agree but you have to bear in mind Massey's mental state of health at this stage. With Dempsey locked up it would have been impossible for him to do anything, so it became essential to get him out on bail.'

'And having had him killed,' Emma said, now seeing merit in the detective's argument, 'what better way to pin the blame on Todd Wilson than to dump the body in his car.'

Emma had most of the answers she needed but still no solid evidence had been found to connect Massey to the fatal crash involving Johnny Griffin. Neither had there been a breakthrough in regard to who exactly had pushed her down the escalator. Because the escalator incident, and its tragic consequences, concerned her on such a personal level, Emma had some difficulty retaining her objectivity. In this one area alone, she counted on Connolly to come up with the answers. He had no doubts whatsoever that Massey was the person behind the efforts to take her out of the picture. 'Our forensic people are examining the red wig we found at the scene,' he assured her, 'and it's only a matter of time before they establish a link with this item and one of Massey's henchmen. I believe Massey feared you were getting too close to the truth.'

No matter how often Emma thought about Massey and what he had done, one question always remained uppermost in her mind: Why? She found it hard to come up with a plausible answer but Connolly had no such hesitation in formulating a rationale. 'I believe that Massey allowed his near-drowning incident at the Body Rock to fester over the years and blight his life. It's quite possible that lack of oxygen to the brain at the time caused damage – a psychological scar that led him to undertake the bizarre actions he took. In more recent times, after his business interests failed, Massey looked around for a scapegoat, something or someone to blame for his misfortunes. Jealous of Todd Wilson's success, he harked back to the near-fatal prank his friend played on him when they were both young men. He began to see Todd Wilson, and those connected to him, as his enemies. As with a cancer, he allowed this one incident to fester and spread, to eat away at him, to cloud his judgement, diminish his faculties until, inexorably, it devoured him whole.'

Emma, punch-drunk with theories and counter-theories still found difficulty in believing that someone who looked and acted as sane as Massey could harbour such evil intent beneath that handsome exterior. But not a lot made sense any more; after a week of unrelenting activity, the deluge of ugly facts and revelations were having a numbing effect on her brain. Which is why, on the seventh day after the Body Rock deaths, Emma, with biblical reverberations, decided it was time she rested. She could take no more. She needed a break. Time to get off the merry-go-round, preserve her sanity.

Anticipating her desire to get away, Vinny had, with the collusion of George Laffin, organised a special treat for her. Vinny had been in constant contact with George since his departure to London and between them they had concocted a plan.

'You, Madame, are going to London,' Vinny informed her.

'What do you mean?' Emma asked, 'Who's going to London?'

'You are – along with myself and Ciarán. We are going to spend some time in Bloomsbury,' Vinny replied, showing her the airline tickets. 'George Laffin has invited us to stay as his guests for three or four days – or as long as we like.'

'Why would George want to do such a nice thing?'

'Because of you, Emma. He was besotted by you on his visit here, sees you as some sort of heroine. On top of that he enjoyed meeting Ciarán and wants to take him on a pub-crawl around some of his favourite watering holes in the city. He's also keen to show us where he had displayed the Harry Clarke drawing we gave him.'

'I think it's a great idea, Vinny. When do we go?'

'Now. We check in for our flight in two hours' time. Ciarán is already on his way to the airport.'

'This is mad, Vinny, but I love it. OK, great, give me

a few minutes; I need to pack a few things. We might take in a show in the West End . . . I'll need some decent clothes.'

Vinny gave his wife a most flirtatious smile. 'Not too many clothes, Emma. Think of this as a second honeymoon. George owns a beautiful Georgian house in Bedford Square. I'm hoping we can spend a goodly proportion of our time staring at the ceiling in our bedroom – from the horizontal perspective, of course – the ideal atmosphere for making babies.'

'I see,' Emma said, an enigmatic smile to rival the Mona Lisa's playing on her lips. 'So that's what you've got in mind, is it?'

'Yes it is. Can you think of a better way to get our family plans back on track? Now hurry up, grab whatever you need and let's go.'

Emma went to the bedroom, made a selection from her wardrobe, hurriedly placed them in her hand luggage clothes carrier. She took her contraceptive pill pack from the drawer of her dressing table and placed it in her handbag. Doing this, she glanced at her reflection in the mirror and nodded thoughtfully. I'm not ready to go through all that again, she said silently to the face looking back at her, no, not for another while . . . maybe never.

AUTHOR'S NOTE

Ireland's Eye, the Long Hole and the Body Rock, locations described in this book, do exist. It is also a fact that an artist, William Burke Kirwan, was tried at the Bar for the murder of his wife Maria on Ireland's Eye in the year 1852. Kirwan's sentence and subsequenet unjust imprisonment are verifiable facts. However, I have taken some artistic licence in regard to specific geographic and geological details concerning the immediate area surrounding the Body Rock.

KILLING TIME

A HIGH-TENSION THRILLER

Shocked beyond measure, she attempted to kiss the gaping wound, pressing his head with her hands so that the wound closed. Blood oozed between her fingers, on to her face; she could taste his blood on her tongue. 'Alan, Alan . . . oh sweet mother of Jesus, my Alan.'

The murder of her lover, politician Alan McCall, is the latest in a series of tragedies to befall Jacqueline Miller: There was a time when she seemed to have the world at her feet, but a horrific road accident and a broken engagement change her life forever. Her affair had offered hope of happiness; but suddenly that hope has been shattered.

The fact that the 'family man' McCall was murdered in his mistress's bed is bad news for the government too, and to avoid a scandal, an elaborate cover-up is set in motion. Meanwhile, his killer goes undetected and will strike again. Investigative journalist Emma Boylan knows that all is not as it seems and as she probes deeper and deeper, an ugly web of deceit is exposed. After a series of unexpected twists and turns and a bloody climax, Emma finally discovers the true identity of Alan McCall's murderer.

K.T. McCAFFREY

Marino

Marino Books, an imprint of Mercier Press, 16 Hume Street, Dublin 2.

Next from K. T. McCaffrey:
a sensational new thriller

The Judas Kiss

Coming soon from Marino Books

THE JUDAS KISS

Released from the dual slip-leash, the hounds bound forward. With amazing acceleration, they reach maximum speed by their third stride. Ahead of them, a hare bobs up and down, scurrying away over the uneven ground. Running for its life, the hare knows it must outwit the greyhounds if it hopes to reach the escape pen at the top end of the open field in one piece. It's an uneven contest. Moving at forty miles an hour, the hounds will catch up with the hare before it gets to the last quarter of the coursing field.

Ted Harris, dressed in full hunting livery, sits on a chestnut stallion observing the proceedings. For a man nearing his seventieth birthday, he appears to be little bothered by the chill in the February air. A lifelong devotee of the sport of coursing, it is his job to decide which greyhound will qualify for the next round. As he moves about, seldom faster than a trot, concern shows on his weather-beaten face; he is aware that it has been a bad morning for the organisers of the meeting. With only two stakes completed, each consisting of sixteen dogs, three hares have already failed to make it to the safety zone. It is the sort of situation guaranteed to enrage the large organised band of animal-rights activists who have come to protest. For the moment they remain corralled by the security stewards at the entrance to the grounds, but he knows from previous experience that they are a volatile, unpredictable lot. He tries to ignore the threat they pose, concentrating instead on the chase taking place in front of him.

Carnival Princess, a brindled bitch wearing a red collar, breaks first. Taking advantage of a better turn of speed than her rival, Little Mac, she closes in on the terrified hare. A hissing sound from the crowd urges the hare forward. Punters holding betting slips in their hands are less concerned with the smaller animal's fate; their concentration is fixed firmly on the dogs' progress. 'Come on the red collar!' they shout. 'Come on, ya good thing!' Just as Carnival Princess's teeth prepare to snap closed on the hare's hindquarters, the smaller animal swerves sharply to its left, evading the killer fangs. Unwittingly, the hare has veered into the path of the white-collared Little Mac. It must again swerve if it is to escape the other dog's sharp teeth. As the fleeing hare feels Little Mac's hot breath, the terrified animal's lightning agility allows it to escape a second time. The crowd gasps as they watch Carnival Princess shoot ahead of the pair. They think the dog has lost sight of the hare but they are soon proved wrong. Carnival Princess, experienced in the art of coursing, knows the hare will swerve into her path after its second change of direction.

This time the hare has left itself little room to manoeuvre.